The Reapers' Song

Also by Lauraine Snelling
in Large Print:

A Land to Call Home
A New Day Rising
Hawaiian Sunrise
An Untamed Land

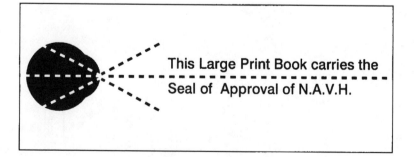

This Large Print Book carries the
Seal of Approval of N.A.V.H.

Lauraine Snelling

The Reapers' Song

Red River of the North

4

Thorndike Press • Waterville, Maine

Published in 2002 by arrangement with
Bethany House Publishers.

Thorndike Press Large Print Christian Fiction Series.

The tree indicium is a trademark of Thorndike Press.

The text of this Large Print edition is unabridged.
Other aspects of the book may vary from the original edition.

Set in 16 pt. Plantin by Al Chase.

Printed in the United States on permanent paper.

Library of Congress Cataloging-in-Publication Data
Snelling, Lauraine.
    The reapers' song / Lauraine Snelling.
      p. cm. — (Red River of the north ; 4)
   ISBN 0-7862-4025-3 (lg. print : hc : alk. paper)
    1. Red River of the North — Fiction.   2. Frontier and
pioneer life — Fiction.   3. Norwegian Americans — Fiction.
4. Dakota Territory — Fiction.   5. Large type books.
I. Title.
PS3569.N39 R43 2002
813'.54—dc21   2002019901

To
My Mom

1

Springfield, Missouri
Early Summer, 1885

"He's dead."

"But . . . I didn't come to kill him. I just wanted to know . . ." Zeb MacCallister stared at Abe Galloway, the man lying on the ground, blood pooling in the dirt by his side. Now it would only continue. The fight between the MacCallisters and the Galloways was turning into a repeat of the Hatfields and McCoys back east. To this day Zeb didn't know what had started it. Now he might never know.

"You tried to stop this thing, but 'twon't work now. You better git." The wizened man scrubbed a lined hand across the crevices of a face weathered by storms of both soul and climate. "Ah knowed no good would come a this." Jed used a dirty finger to close the dead man's eyes. "They say dead men look peaceful, but ya gotta have peace in yer soul first."

Zebulun shook his head. Peace was what he'd been seeking. He hadn't meant for this to happen. Would the sheriff believe self-defense? Not much chance. Too many men had heard Zeb's father, Zachariah Mac-Callister, order his only son to swear on the family Bible that he would seek vengeance for Zachariah's spilled-out blood. It didn't matter how many years ago that promise had been made, nor how many times Zeb had tried to restore the friendship between the neighboring families. Old Abe Galloway was as dead as he could ever be, and Zebulun MacCallister had pulled the trigger.

Zeb stared down at the rifle clenched in his hand. The desire to fling it into the oak scrub brought his arm up, poised to release the stock and send the gun spinning into eternity. Guns had been used for killing folks far too long already, and there was no end in sight. But years of having his pa's creed hammered into his head enabled him to keep the grip firm, and he brought the Winchester back to his side. He could hear the words as if Pa stood right beside him. *"Treat your rifle better'n you do any woman, for only your rifle will remain faithful to you."*

Today bore out that truth. His rifle had saved his life.

"Yer bleedin', son."

Zeb looked at the trail of red oozing down his arm. "Only a flesh wound."

" 'Twere mighty close."

"Granny says 'an inch is as good as a mile.' "

"That she do. What you want to do with the body?" Jedediah MacCallister, Zeb's nearest uncle, nudged the dead man's leg with the toe of his boot.

"You think there's any chance they'll think he's run off if we bury him?"

Old Jed shook his head. "They knowed he was comin' to meet with ya."

"Then leave him here." Zeb spun on his heel. "Maybe Ma's got breakfast ready. Come on."

"Sure ya don't want ta dump 'im in the cave?"

Zeb paused. "That might slow 'em down a mite." He turned and grasped the dead man by the ankles. "You take the head and I'll lead. We'll clean up the trail on the way back."

Grunting, the old man did as Zeb told him. In spite of the snow white hair, now hidden by his slouch hat, Jed rarely gave his opinion unless asked and had never volunteered for the job of family head, in spite of being the eldest remaining male of the direct MacCallister lineage.

I couldn't a stood lookin' at his face, Zeb thought as they lugged their burden through the thickets and down into a shallow valley. Behind a moss-covered boulder, the mouth of a limestone cave welcomed them with a damp, cool breeze. Some said the Ozark Mountains were so riddled with caves that an earthquake would collapse the southern half of Missouri and most of Kentucky. Zeb didn't much care about the rest of the country. Right now he was only concerned about his own hide.

Why did Abe go for his gun? He knew we was only comin' to the clearing. The thoughts crowded his head while he stumbled farther into the cave, looking for the pool of water that collected there every year. If they weighted the body, the discovering of it might take even longer.

He knew the cave well. He and his sisters had played there often on hot, muggy August days, as the cave was always cool. A shiver ran up his back. Never had he tried to hide a dead body there, though. The temperature changed, as he knew it would, telling him the pool lay right ahead. He stopped and listened. Only the drip of water off the shelf to the back of the pool broke the stillness.

"Fill his boots with sand, and I'll add some rocks to his britches and pockets." Zeb went about his business even as he spoke. Within minutes they rolled the body forward and heard the water welcome its treasure with a gentle splash. "Wish I could say 'rest in peace, Abe,' but there ain't no peace where you are, I'm sure."

Together they turned and left the coolness of the cave, brushing their footprints away with a branch. Back in the clearing they made sure the bloody forest duff and leaves were hidden, knowing full well that if the Galloways brought their hounds, the dogs would find the trail no matter how well they tried to hide it. When they got back to the horses, they swung into the saddle and headed for home, no longer trying to hide their trail. Speed made more sense now.

The MacCallister hounds set up their own ruckus before the men even reached the home farm. Zeb could hear old Blue leading the chorus, singing a song of welcome, since the dogs already recognized who was coming. The tone would indeed be different for an approaching stranger.

Something caught in Zeb's throat, and he coughed several times trying to clear it. He sniffed and hawked, but that lump in his throat wouldn't be spit out.

He would have to leave home.

Mary Martha, four years older than he and more mother than his ma had ever been

11

in his younger years, jumped down from the weathered porch. Her curls billowing behind her, she darted across the grass and ran down the lane to meet them. When he was young, his ma held the farm together while waiting for his father to come back from the war. After Zachariah returned — minus an arm and a foot — and withdrew into bitter silence, she still kept the farm running.

Today she was cooking his birthday breakfast and, unbeknownst to her, his last meal at home.

"I heard shots." Mary Martha plowed to a stop before them, her skirts swirling around her legs, a furrow separating her china blue eyes. "There's blood on your arm."

"Just a flesh wound." Zeb slid his foot from the stirrup and leaned forward to give her a hand up.

With a grace born of long practice, Mary Martha swung up behind him and settled her skirts over her knees. Immediately she began to inspect the wound. "What about Abe?"

"He weren't interested in talkin'."

The *clip-clop* of the horses' hooves sounded loud in the silence.

He shook his head when she started to say something. "Don't ask. What you don't know can't hurt you."

Jed held up two rabbits in his left hand. "Shame it took two shots to bag these. If'n anybody should happen to ask, I got the hides to prove it."

Mary Martha laid her forehead against her brother's back. "Yer leavin' then?" Her tone said she wasn't really asking a question.

Zeb nodded. "Soon's I can get some things together."

"Ma has breakfast ready."

"Good thing." He stopped the horse at the side of the barn. "I'll be up in a minute."

"You go on," Jed said. "I'll git yer horse ready. You want to take two?"

Zeb swung to the ground, his left arm burning as though someone had laid a fiery branding iron against it. "No sense in it. You need the horses here for fieldwork. Buster and me, we'll make out just fine."

Zeb walked toward the house, studying it as if he could commit to memory every leaf shadow, every grayed board and shingle to draw on in the days ahead. He inhaled, adding to his mental storehouse the smell of bacon frying and corn bread fresh from the oven, oak trees and bridal wreath, woodsmoke and new hay in the field. The dogs whined, their tails rattling the fence. A rooster crowed and a half-tailed cat chirped and wound itself around his ankles.

Mary Martha met him at the door with a basin of warm water, lye soap, and rags. "Set." She pointed at the rocker.

Zeb sat. He studied the sagging porch step and the splintered section in the porch rail. He'd been meaning to fix them, but fieldwork came first, and there were never enough hours in his day to even begin all he wanted to do, let alone finish. And now with the eldest, Eva Jane, married and in a home of her own, the burden fell back on Mary Martha and their mother. How would they manage without him?

His ma wasn't as young as she used to be and older than she should be. The war had been harder on the women than the men. Carrying on was tougher than dying.

How he knew all these things, Zeb couldn't say. He just knew it was so.

"There, you keep that clean, and healing should be no problem." Mary Martha got to her feet and, swishing the now pink water around in the basin, dumped it onto the bridal wreath bush that sprawled to the right of the steps. As children, they'd made crowns of the white blossoms.

The memory stabbed him like a thorn from the red roses that arched over the entry. Once they'd tried weaving the two together. Only once.

"You go set now."

"And you?"

"I'll be gettin' your things together."

"It all has to fit in the bedroll and saddlebags. Buster can't carry much extra weight, not if we're to make some time."

"I know." She refused to look in his face but spun on her toes and headed for the dusky interior of the house.

Zeb paused in the doorway. The kitchen and living room shared the front of the house, since the family could no longer afford to hire help to cook out in the summer kitchen. An oval braided rug kept bare feet off the cold floorboards in the winter. The dogtrot between the house and the summer kitchen had become the storage shed for keeping wood dry in the winter.

"Set." His mother, hair dappled gray like the horse he rode and twisted into a knot at the base of her skull, pointed to the chair. She used words like pepper — only enough to season. Likewise her smile. But when it shone forth like now, the whole world felt the blessing.

As Zeb did. That lump returned to his throat.

She asked no questions but set the full

15

plate before him and laid a hand on his shoulder.

Zeb bowed his head. *Lord God, bless . . .* Even his thoughts could go no further, let alone his words.

"Bless this food to my son's body and keep him in your grace."

"Amen." He choked on the simple word.

So many things he wanted to say. So many he needed to hear. Like why the Galloways hated the MacCallisters to the point of murder.

He cleaned his plate, using the last of the corn bread to sop up the egg yolks.

Mary Martha picked up his bedroll, wrapped in a piece of canvas, and set it down on the chair beside him. His mother handed him a Bible, the leather cover worn from hands searching for truth and comfort.

"But, Ma, this is your own —"

She stopped him with a look.

"Thank you, Ma. It will never leave my side."

"Nor will the good Lord." She handed him his hat off the rack by the door. "Go with God." Her hand found his and clenched it once, then again.

The last he saw of her, she and Mary Martha were standing on the top step between the porch posts, the red rambler rose vine arching over them, as if promising to keep them safe. He lifted his hand in farewell and kicked his horse into a lope. They had miles to cover, and only God himself knew what lay ahead.

2

Dakota Territory
Spring 1886

"All I want to do is go home," Zeb MacCallister muttered as he sat on his horse and stared at the raging Missouri River.

Buster snorted and pawed at the muddy bank.

"You don't really want to swim this floodin' beast, do you, fella?"

His mount shook his head, setting the bit to jangling. A tree floated by, pointing its black and gnarled roots toward the lowering sky.

"Didn't think so." Zeb looked back over his shoulder. Nothing to see but prairie grass sprouting fast enough to watch it grow. The last man he'd talked with spoke a guttural combination of languages, most of which he'd found unintelligible. He'd gotten the drift, though, and shaken his head. No, he didn't have any firewater to sell or trade. And he didn't want the skins the Indian showed him either.

Home. He closed his eyes and could see his sister Mary Martha running across the field to meet him. His mother would be standing on the porch, waving her apron. The smell of something good cooking would waft out on the breeze and add its welcome home. Old Blue would be barking fit to kill, and Uncle Jed would hustle out of the barn to see what was causing all the commotion. For nearly a year now he'd been on the run, working for a while here and there until some inner sense warned him it was time to move on. Had the Galloways called in the law? Or, as he most suspected, were the two younger sons trailing him? Nightmares haunted him, where he saw himself turning around just in time to see a gun flash.

He looked skyward. "Your Book speaks of vindication, God. I think you done hid your face this time." Even the lowering clouds seemed to indicate God's displeasure. What was the sense of it all? He thought of riding right into that flooding river and letting it carry him on to the next life.

Buster shook his head. Zeb patted his shoulder. No sense wasting a good horse that way.

"I got a bargain for you, God. You leave me alone and I won't pester you neither."

The wind whipped up the brown river, sending wavelets to wash his horse's hooves.

He let the reins loosen so the animal could drink. A bloated cow drifted by, turning with the current. Somewhere up this god-forsaken river, some farmer had lost part of his stock in the flood. At least he knew there were other people in the area. Cows like that didn't run loose on the prairie.

"So you s'pose that farm is on this side of the river or t'other?"

His horse raised its head and, ears pricked, looked toward the west. Thunder-heads mounded on the horizon like mountains blotting out the sky.

Zeb followed the direction his horse pointed. Was that someone coming toward him? He studied the growing shape, knowing that even this far from Missouri, he didn't dare trust that the Galloways hadn't found him. Strange, all the way he'd traveled and still he was bound by the word "Missouri." More like "misery" out here. Not many trees to hide in. Most of them were trunk-deep in floodwater.

He waited.

The rider drew closer, skirts billowing about her legs as she sat astride her horse.

Zeb let out the breath he hadn't realized he held.

"Hey, mister, you seen an old red cow around here?" she called as she drew close enough to be heard.

"I saw one floating by about midway out there." He pointed to the river.

"Oh horsefeathers!" She slapped her thigh in frustration. The horse swerved and she pulled him to a jolting stop, just far enough away so she could see Zeb's face and he hers. She crossed her hands over the reins on her horse's withers and studied the stranger.

"You sure it was a red one?"

"Yep. But I'm not sure it was your red one. I couldn't tell its age."

The girl looked to be about twelve. A faded brown fedora, well ventilated in the crown, was pulled low on her forehead and shaded her eyes. Straw-colored hair poked out of two of the holes, strands pulled loose from the braid he'd seen bounce when she stopped. A man's black coat flopped wide open, showing a skirt and top that hadn't seen wash water any more recently than her face.

"You said floating. You sure it weren't swimming?"

"Not on its side like that." He hated to give her more bad news. It looked like she'd had too much of that already in her short life.

"Oh." She slumped and after a deep sigh

looked up again. "Look like any chance if'n I snagged it, we could butcher it out?"

Zeb thought a moment, then shook his head. "Not bloated like that."

She appeared to be studying the mane in front of her hands, but when her shoulders began to twitch, Zeb knew she was crying. Now what to do? He couldn't go off and leave her like this. And yet — he let out a sigh, much like the one she'd given. No way did he want to get mixed up with . . . with what? A family in trouble? As if he wasn't in enough trouble of his own. But his mother had taught him well. "Do thou unto others as thou would have them do unto thee." She'd burned the golden rule into his mind and heart from the time he could lisp his first verse.

"Look, miss."

"I ain't 'miss.' And I don't need no one's pity. So the old cow was stupid enough to go drink in a flooding river. I was tired of milking her anyway for the little she gave. Thankee." She jerked her horse into a spin and drummed her heels on his sides. One hand clapping the hat in place and the other working the reins, she headed back the way she came.

"Well, that settles that." Zeb glanced up as a gust of wind tried jerking his jacket off his back. The thunderheads seemed to be racing each other eastward, with him directly in their path. He turned his horse and loped downriver in the hopes that he'd find a friendly settler before the storm found him.

He hadn't gone twenty paces when he stopped and looked heavenward. "Din't you hear my bargain?" He chewed the edge of his mustache. "You know this ain't my idea, don't you?" He shook his head and reined his horse around again. "What if I can't find her farm?" But the feeling didn't let up. It was as if God had him lassoed and was dragging him west after that youngster who hadn't even a nodding acquaintance with soap and water. And who'd been much too proud to let him see her cry. The quaking shoulders had done it in spite of her.

Drops the size of teacups were soaking him by the time he heard a dog bark, which was the only thing that kept him from riding on by the soddy that lay half buried in the side of a small hill. Since it faced south, the hillock had about hid it from sight, until he followed the sound of the barking dog and nearly rode right over the roof. He swung off on a curve and rode into what might have been called a yard at one time. A corral, or what was left of it, stuck out on both sides of the sod wall that housed a door with one window beside it. Zeb had seen other dugouts like this in the Sand Hills of Nebraska. People used whatever they could to create a shelter from the harsh climate. Right now, he and his horse could use some shelter all right. But there was no barn in sight, and the door to the soddy never opened in welcome. Was this the right place?

"Halloo the house?" He waited. A horse whinnied and Buster answered. Was the horse inside the dugout? Zeb debated for about a second more, then swung off his mount, his slicker dumping a river of icy rainwater down his neck. He grumbled to himself as he led Buster through the missing fence section and up to the door. He hated to tie his horse out in a downpour like this, but what other choice did he have?

He pounded on the door with a gloved fist. "Anyone home?"

The dog slunk out from wherever he'd disappeared to when Zeb rode up. "Some watchdog you are." The dog whined, his ears and tail perking only a mite at the sound of the man's voice.

Zeb knocked again. Nothing. The law of the prairie said a man was welcome to an empty home if he needed shelter. Lightning slashed and thunder crashed. He reached for the latchstring, only to realize there wasn't one, or it had been pulled in.

The door creaked open just enough to show part of a face and a hand clutching a rifle. "Whatcha want?"

Along with the lack of soap and water went a lack of manners. Where he came from, the two were gospel. "If I could get out of the rain?"

"Don't allow strangers in here. Pa said."

"Well, tell your pa I ain't no stranger. I helped you find your cow." He knew that was stretching the truth, but he'd at least saved her further looking.

"Cain't."

"Look, my name is Zebulun Mac-Callister. I just want a place out of the rain, and since your house is the only one around. I had hoped to shelter here. Land sakes, young lady . . ."

She waved the gun at him as though she might actually use it.

"Is your pa here?" he quickly asked.

"No. Gone to get supplies. That's why I cain't open the door to strangers."

"How about sick folk?" He sneezed once and then again.

The door cracked open a bit more. The dog slunk in, leaving Zeb wishing he could do the same. He knew he could push the door open. The thought had already crossed his mind more than once. "Well, then, miss . . ." He waited, hoping she would give a name. "Thank you for nothing. Tell your pa you did indeed abide by his wishes." He turned and, flipping his reins around his horse's neck, reached for the saddle horn. The seat ran water. He shoulda just stayed in it and headed east like he wanted. Must not have been hearing right, thinking the Lord wanted him to come here. One more strike against the Almighty.

"You can come on in. No room for your horse, though."

"Pardon me?" He turned back to the doorway.

"I said come in, but you'll have to tie your horse to the fence. Only got room for one in here."

"May I bring in my saddle?"

"If'n you want."

He did want. Jerking a rope out of the saddlebags, he tied it around his horse's neck and then to the one fence post that looked as if it might last out the storm. He slid the bridle off and looped it over his shoulder, but his gloves were so wet, he could barely unthread the cinch. After several attempts, he pulled one glove off with his teeth and jerked the latigo loose. Swinging the saddle over his shoulder, he headed for the house.

Once inside the door, he breathed in the smell of damp dirt, horse manure, and flickering smoke from the stub of a candle melting on the tabletop. The light reached not much farther than the table on which the candle sat. Zeb let his eyes grow accustomed to the dimness and set his saddle on the dirt floor by the door. A horse snorted back in the darkness.

"Manda?" A voice so frail he wasn't sure if it came from a child or an adult broke the silence.

"Hush now." Her voice curt, the girl faced Zeb from across the table, her gun at the ready.

"Look." Zeb spread his hands in front of him.

"Don't you go movin' any." She raised the barrel of the rifle. "Yer outa the rain and that's what ya wanted."

"Thank God for small favors." He hoped to lighten the mood, but the frown she wore informed him it hadn't worked. "Look, Miss Manda."

"Don't call me that."

"Why not? Where I come from, Miss Manda is the polite form of address. My mother taught me that, along with verses from the Good Book and even some poetry. Now, you wouldn't want to cause my mother any distress in thinking that her son might be disrespectful, would you?"

He watched the inner argument chase its way across her face. The gun barrel wobbled. Swift as the water moccasins he'd caught in the swamps back home, he grabbed the rifle, making sure it pointed upward, and jerked it out of her hands. Setting the stock on the dirt floor, he kept the rifle beside his leg.

"What you go doing that for?" She came at him, tipping the flimsy table in her surge for the rifle. The candle died at the same time as she hit him in the solar plexus with the top of her head. The force of it drove him back a couple of paces. He tripped over his saddle, and the two of them crashed to the floor.

It was all he could do to keep hold of the rifle with one hand and try to fend her off with the other. She sat on his chest, pounding her fists into whatever part of his flesh she could connect with.

"Ow. Stop that! I wasn't going to hurt you or take anything, and you darn well know it. Stop that now." His cheek stung. His nose ran wet, and still he couldn't get a good hold on her.

"You gimme that rifle and I'll let you up!"

"Let me up?" He gave a mighty heave and, tipping her to the side, wrapped one leg around her torso and pinned her to the ground. Never in his entire life had he treated a female like this. His ears burned at the thought of what his mother would say. Or did they burn because the girl lambasted him on the way over?

He finally managed to clamp hold of one of her wrists and twisted it until she yelped. Now his ears burned from the stream of invectives she hurled at him.

"If you'd quit trying to break my head, I'd let you up."

"Gimme my rifle, you . . . !"

He tried to ignore the remainder of her sentence.

"I will *not* give you the rifle until you calm down. You might accidentally set the thing off, and —"

"I don't never *accidentally* fire that rifle." The sneer in the word, in spite of her bound condition, nearly made him laugh. Spitfire didn't begin to describe the courage of the girl he held. When she elbowed him below the belt, he left off laughing and roared instead.

"Now you done it." Ignoring the pain, he shoved the rifle off toward the wall and used both hands to clamp her arms tight against her sides. He used her as a brace to get his feet under him and surged to his feet, pulling her up with him.

She drummed her heels against his shins, her breath now coming in gulps.

A sobbing whimper from the back of the dugout froze them both.

"Who's there?"

"I said 'hush.' "

They both spoke at the same time.

He set her on the floor, keeping a strong arm about her waist and her arms locked against her sides. "Now, if you can promise to behave yourself, I am going to —"

She stomped on his foot, her heel catching him right across the toes.

Zeb gritted his teeth. He hoisted her under one arm, opened the door, and shoved her outside. "You can come back in when you've cooled off enough to talk some sense." He leaned against the door, taking a deep breath. She hammered the door with her fists, calling him every name he'd ever heard and then some.

"Mother, please forgive me. I couldn't think of anything else to do." He wiped one finger under his nose and off on his pant leg. Sure as shooting, she'd given him a nosebleed.

The silence from outside made him uneasy. What was she up to now?

"M-m-manda?" Surely it was the voice of a child.

"Manda will be back in a minute. Soon's she can learn to be a bit more welcoming to a stranger."

"M-m-man-d-da." Sobs floated through the stillness, sobs so weak they near to broke his heart.

"Who are you, child?"

No answer, only sobs and sniffles. The creak of a rope-strung bed told of the child's movements.

"Where's your ma?"

Hiccups.

"Your pa?"

Silence. A sniff. Nothing from outside.

What to do? Zeb realized he'd rather stir up a nest of rattlers than open the door to see what Manda had in store for him. He felt around for a board to bar the door. Locating it off to the side, he slid the bar in place. He was safe on this side at least.

The storm had passed, letting more light in the small window. He made out the outline of the fallen table and righted it. He could now make out the rope-slung bed in a corner of the small dugout. Then the daylight went out. He turned to see Manda at the window, or at least the outline of her that was visible through the greased paper covering the small square.

"Don't worry, Miss Manda, I'm not ruining the place, just putting it to rights. You can come back in if you can behave." He kept his voice conversational, hoping the tone, if nothing else, would soothe both her and the whimpering child. It worked with horses anyway.

Manda pounded on the door with something more than her fists. "I'm a'gonna let your horse loose."

"Be my guest, if that will make you happy." Zeb knew he could summon Buster with a whistle. He'd taught him to come that way before the animal was weaned.

He stopped at the side of the bed and looked down on a body so slight it didn't even raise the covers. Peeling back the tattered quilt, he flinched at the sour smell that assaulted his nostrils. "Oh, dear God." He sank down on his knees and laid a gentle hand on the small head. "You poor baby." While he couldn't see the child's eyes in the dimness, he could feel the body shrink away from his touch.

"Now, I'm not going to hurt you, but I know I can help. You think we can get Manda to calm down so I can let her back in the house?"

"N-no."

"I didn't think so, either. What is your name? I don't want to keep calling you 'child.' You do have a name, don't you?"

"Uh huh."

Zeb waited. The smell nearly gagged him. The horse shifted restlessly, jangling the bit. Manda hadn't even had time to remove that.

"I-I-I'm Deborah."

He almost missed the name, it came so softly.

"Deborah. That's a lovely name. Right from the Bible." His mind sped through all he could remember of the Deborahs in the Scriptures. "Deborah was a strong woman, but once she was a little girl like you. How old might you be?"

No answer.

"How long since you had anything to eat?" The thought of these children starving out here on the plains made him choke worse than the stench.

"M-Manda shot a rabbit. We ate that."

She talked too well for a baby, but the size of her body . . . He'd seen skeletons with more flesh on them than she had.

"Look, I'm going outside to see if I can talk sense with Manda. You stay right here, all right?"

"Yes."

His knees cracked as he stood. At least up here the air was a bit better. While there wasn't a whole lot in his saddlebags, he'd bet that rifle he had more food than these two did. Or had had for a long time. Where were their folks?

"Miss Manda, I'm coming out. You going to talk to me civil-like?"

No answer.

What was the matter with that girl? Couldn't she figure out by now that he didn't plan to hurt them? If anyone had been hurt, it was him. He fingered a swollen lower lip. His nose felt puffy too. At least it had quit bleeding.

"Lord above, you're going to have to help out here. I sure as fired don't know what to do." He waited, hoping for some sign, but knowing that hope was in vain. God didn't seem to send burning bushes or talking donkeys these days. "You must figure we got enough sense now to figure some things out for ourselves." Shoot. He reminded himself he didn't aim to converse with the Almighty anymore. Got to get out of the habit.

But what to do about this mess? He shook his head. *Sure wish I'd rode the other way.*

"Prayin' don't work." The weak voice spoke from the bed.

He knelt back down to be able to see at

least the outline of the child's face. "Why do you say that?" Even though he now agreed with her, he wasn't about to tell the child that.

"Manda prayed and our ma died anyway."

"I'm sorry to hear that." Deborah was surely older than the three or four he'd figured. "What about your pa?"

She shook her head. "Manda said not to tell anyone."

"Oh." If he were a betting man, he'd win this one hands down. Their pa had gone on to his reward too. "How long since you saw your pa?"

No answer.

"I have some cornmeal in my saddlebags, beans too. You think you and Manda might know what to do with it if I made us up some vittles?"

"What's that . . . v-vittles?"

"Supper."

He could feel the little one quiver. "How long since you ate?"

No answer.

He stood again. How was it that a kid like Manda could flimflam him to the point he couldn't do what he knew was best — for him anyway. Pride, that's all it was.

"Well, the Book says pride goeth before a

fall, and Miss Manda, you are about to fall."
He muttered but kept it quiet and quick
enough so that Deborah wouldn't catch his
drift. Between the two of them they had
enough pride to start a war. Or sheer guts
and backbone. He thought of his sisters
back home. What would Mary Martha do in
a fix like this? He shook his head again. *She*
wouldn't be in this fix because *she* would
have sweet-talked that wild one out there
into scrubbing her face, sitting down at the
table, and saying "please" and "thank you,"
nice as pie.

Manda *had* said thank you when she rode
off after he gave her the news about the cow.

What to do?

He heard a rustling behind him, and then
the horse nudged him in the back. Without
further thought, he took the hint and led the
animal toward the door. Careful as he
could, he lifted the bar and set it aside.
Then, with a jerk he pulled the door open
and slapped the horse on the rump. Out the
door it leaped. Manda shrieked, dropped
whatever she'd had in her hands — to
clobber him with no doubt — and leaped for
the animal.

Zeb followed right behind the critter in
time to see Manda swing aboard, in spite of
her skirts, by only grasping a hank of mane.

She stopped the horse by some unseen means and turned back to the soddy.

Zeb stood in the doorway, the rifle held across his chest. "Now let's get one thing straight here. I am not going to do you or your sister any harm. My ma would skin me alive for not helping out when I can."

"We don't need no help."

"Yes, you do. We all need help at some point or another. Now I got some beans and cornmeal in my saddlebags, and I'm willing to bet either you or I could bag another rabbit or some such without too much trouble. Prairie chicken would taste mighty good, don't you think?"

She stared at him, no sign of her thoughts crossing her face.

"So . . . you want to start the fire? You want to go hunting, or should I? The beans need to cook awhile anyways. A'course, we could eat the dog."

That got a rise out of her. "I ain't eatin' the dog."

"Or your horse."

"That neither." She swung down and marched up to stand in front of him, her fists planted on her hips. "If'n you're such a hot shot, you go hunt. And you can take your own rifle and gimme mine back."

"Not until I know you're not going to

shoot me and throw me in the stewpot."

The look she gave him would have fried a rabbit had he already bagged one.

When he returned some time later with a brace of prairie chickens tied to his belt, he could see the smoke rising from a chimney that blended into the hillside so well he'd missed it before. The dog set up a ruckus again, but this time its tail wagged and the whine low in the throat welcomed Zeb back.

"If that young lady in there was as smart as you, we coulda eaten long time ago." He lopped the heads off the birds and threw them to the skinny cur. They were gone before he could blink. He skinned and gutted the birds, tossing the entrails to the dog, who waited with chops quivering. "At least one of us has a full belly."

He knocked at the door, glancing to the side to see that more of the corral had been chopped away. At least they'd had something to burn to keep them warm. "Don't go get all fired up. I brought some supper." He pushed the door open with the toe of his boot, waited, then entered.

A fire crackled in the cast-iron stove, and a pot bubbled, sending the welcome fragrance of cooking beans that helped cover the stench of the dugout. The two chairs had been righted and a candle found. Manda sat on the edge of the bed, spooning gruel into Deborah's mouth.

"She couldn't wait."

"No, I don't s'pose she could. You got a skillet? We can fry two of these and boil the other with the beans. Fryin's faster."

"Don't got no grease."

"Then we'll use a bit of water till their own fat melts."

Manda left off with feeding her sister and dug an iron skillet off a shelf that had once held stores. Several empty cans and a couple of flat sacks attested to that. She pushed the bean pot to the back of the stovetop and set the frying pan on the hottest part.

"Did you find the salt?"

"Yes."

Talkative, she wasn't.

Zeb cut the birds in smaller pieces and laid them in the skillet, dipping them in the bean water first. The sizzling meat added a fragrance of its own, making the putrid place seem almost homelike. Heat and cooking food had a tendency to do that.

Zeb thought of his mother's house — the braided rugs, curtains at the windows, tables and chairs, a pantry full of preserved food, and both a root cellar and a smokehouse that held more of their larder. She always put up more than they could use, but she often said it hadn't been like that during the war. She never wanted to see her children go hungry again. Nor anyone else. If only he could send these two packing back to his mother. Between her and Mary Martha, they'd drive that hunted look out of Miss Manda's eyes right fast.

But they weren't here. He was.

God help him, he was. And he didn't dare stay.

3

"We ain't goin' with you and that's that."

Zeb could tell that his patience, the patience he'd been gripping with both hands and his teeth, was about to snap. He sucked in a deep breath and tried again. "I don't see any way the two of you can remain on your homestead by yourselves like this."

"Pa's comin' back."

"Who you tryin' to convince — me or yourself?"

Her glare could have struck sparks if he were flint.

"Look, Miss Manda —"

"I said more times 'en I care to count, don't call me that."

"Okay, don't get all riled up again. Let's just talk, sensible-like. Your ma is gone on to heaven, and your pa is either with her or run off."

"Or hurt and cain't get back till he's better."

"That too. Either way, with Deborah as sick as she is and no supplies, you're going to starve to death with her, but first you'll have to bury her out there by your ma. She won't last as long as you." Zeb knew he was being cruel, but he couldn't see any other way. Manda wasn't about to budge.

"If'n we don't stay, how will our pa find us?"

"We can leave him a letter."

"Where would we go?"

That was the question all right. Leave it to her to zero right in on the heart of the matter. Zeb propped his chin on his hands and his elbows on the table. "Surely there is someone in the nearest town who would help out two orph—"

"We ain't orphans and don't you go sayin' so." She slammed her palms on the table, her rush to her feet nearly overturning the wobbly thing again.

"All right." He raised both hands, palms out. "Your pa is coming back when he can."

She nodded and settled back in her chair.

"And if'n we left and he was gone too long, some rotten claim jumper might come and take up in our absence. We could lose our homestead thata way."

"True." Zeb stared around the room. Between them they'd heated water and washed the blankets so a clean Deborah now slept in a clean bed. She looked to have a bit more color in her sunken cheeks, and now it wasn't from the fever. Even Manda's face looked a bit less haggard. Of course scrubbing off the dirt had helped with that. After he'd threatened to scrub her himself, she'd washed behind the curtain, and he'd scrubbed her clothes. That had set up another storm of invectives. But now, as long as she kept her mouth closed, he couldn't imagine that this respectable-looking child in front of him was the same dirty hoyden he'd met at the river. No mistake, though, when she yelled at him, which she did with regularity. Especially whenever he suggested they leave with him.

"You could stay here."

He blinked. Had she said what he thought she said?

"Huh?"

"Nothin'! I din't say nothing."

"You did. And I thought about that. But I got to get on to Canada before —" He clamped his lips closed.

"A'fore what?" She cocked her head and studied him out of mistrusting eyes.

"I just got to do it, that's all." With the ease of train travel now, the Galloway brothers could be anywhere. While he had grown a mustache — a beard had itched too bad — someone could put two and two together. No matter how hard he tried, he couldn't let go of the way he talked. Up here his Missouri accent stood out like a black sheep in a flock of white. Maybe he should have headed south to Mexico.

"Then you just git on yer goin'. Deborah and me, we'll be fine, and our pa will come home any day now. Don't you worry none."

"I wish." While he muttered it under his breath, the look she shot him reminded him she had good ears. He sat up straighter. What he wouldn't give for a cup of coffee right about now. Or something stronger. He tried again. Reasoning with her was like trying to talk a polecat out of the hen house. If it doused you or ate the chickens and eggs, you lost either way.

"That deer I brought in won't last forever. The beans are about gone, and we cleaned up the cornmeal this morning. Lessen you got something stored in the back you ain't tellin' me . . ." He let the sentence drift off. He knew there was nothing more than what he'd brought in. Even worse, she was down to three bullets for the rifle. The best shot in the world couldn't live long on that. If he knew more about the edibles in this godforsaken land, he'd have gone out digging for tubers and such. Like his ma did to survive the war. She'd taught him well. But until

44

something sprouted, he didn't know where to look. Just digging anywhere was a mighty big waste of time and muscle. He hadn't yet suggested snares for rabbit, but if he couldn't get her to go with him, short of throwing them both over his saddle, he'd show her how to set some.

Manda leaned against the chair back, her arms clamped across her skinny chest like a whalebone corset strapped tight. While she tried to hide it, the war within showed on her face.

Zeb could feel his tightly strung patience taking a breather. At least she was considering what he'd had to say.

"Manda?" Deborah's voice was stronger now.

"Coming." Like a child released from school on a summer day, Manda sprang from the chair and dropped to the floor beside her sister's bed. The hand that had tried to beat him senseless only three days earlier now stroked the child's head with the gentleness of a mother's touch.

She needed a mother's touch herself, not to *be* the mother. And father and . . . Zeb shook his head. If the defeated men in the South had half the gumption of this young girl . . . He didn't let that thought go any further. Visions of his own bitter father who'd never regained his heart and health hurt too bad.

"We'll go with you in the morning" was all she said.

They reached Pierre just as night fell. He shifted the child sleeping in his arms. His left arm had gone to sleep hours earlier. Too well he knew the scarcity of the money in his pockets. No way could they stop at the hotel. And he didn't dare go by the local sheriff's.

Light, laughter, and a tinkling piano tune spilled out the door of the saloon. They rode to the end of what appeared to be the main street. All the other businesses wore dark windows and shuttered doors.

Should he try at the livery? Perhaps the owner would let them sleep in his barn. They'd stopped earlier and eaten the last of the cooked beans and part of the cooked venison. If only he'd had time to smoke some.

Carting two kids along sure did slow him down. By himself he'd just roll his blanket out in someone's barn or ask if he could exchange work for a meal and a place to bed down. Many a night he'd spent under the stars. But this night the stars hid behind roiling clouds. He could feel the coming rain in the wind on his face. Rain-laden clouds just smelled different somehow.

A gust brought the first of the raindrops.

"You could tell 'em yer our pa." Manda spoke from off to his left.

"I ain't old enough to be your pa."

"Big brother then."

On the second spattering gust, he made up his mind. Livery it was.

But when he returned from talking with the hired hand at the livery stable, he could feel the anger burning under his collar. The weasel said no. They had a perfectly good hotel in town, and he could ask there.

Deborah coughed as he took her back from Manda. She weighed less than a sack of flour, and if he didn't get her out of the cold and wet . . .

"Come on." He kicked his horse into a lope.

"We could check with the sheriff." Manda caught up with him, then pointing, said, "That's the store where my pa done business."

"Yeah, and he probably owes a list as long as your arm." Zeb regretted the unkind words as soon as they were out of his mouth.

"Where we goin' then?"

"The church." He hadn't known that, but the building appeared out of the mist like an angel dressed in white.

When he knocked on the door of what must have been the parsonage alongside the church, no one answered. Pulling his hat lower on his head, he waved Manda to stay where she was while he checked out the church. "Thank you, God," he breathed when the door of the building swung open at the turning of the latch. Surely the good folks of Pierre wouldn't mind if three strangers took cover there. He knew for certain God wouldn't mind.

He tied his horse in the three-sided shed and crossed the yard to the house where Manda's horse stood by the closed gate. "Come on." He reached up and took the quilt-wrapped child from Manda's arms. "We'll sleep in the church. Maybe there's even wood for a fire."

But without a light of any kind, Zeb gave up that hope. And after seeing that the girls were wrapped warmly in their quilts, he rolled his own around him and fell asleep with a "Please, God" on his heart and mind.

He woke to the feeling of something nudging his side. *That* was a boot toe that belonged to a man whose belly refused to obey the confines of his belt. A six-shooter that usually resided in the empty holster at the man's side now pointed directly at Zeb's head.

If this was the preacher, Zeb figured God was scraping the bottom of the barrel for help. But a star that had long lost its glitter announced the man's occupation.

"Well, Sheriff, what can I do for you this fine morning?" Zeb strove to sound as northern as a native. But when he tried to sit up, the gun drew closer. He glanced over to see that the girls were still sleeping. Or at least, he hoped so.

"What are you doing in this here church?"

Sleeping, you ninny, what does it look like? But Zeb refrained from the obvious reply and kept his voice respectful. "It was raining, and since I didn't have money for the hotel, and the livery denied us a roof, we came here. We haven't damaged anything, as you can see."

"Oh." The gun wavered and then clicked into the holster. "You shoulda asked."

"Who?" With the gun out of sight, Zeb rolled back his quilt and sat up. "No one answered at the parsonage and the — my little one's been sick. We needed shelter right bad." He hoped and prayed Manda was still sleeping, but a twitch of a shoulder let him know she wasn't. *God forgive my white lie here, please.* It had slipped out so natural-like. No one would suspect he was Zeb MacCallister, wanted for a killing, while he traveled as a man with two children. So he was a mighty young-looking thirty, and no, he hadn't fathered Manda when he was thirteen.

When he rose to his feet, he looked down on the other man's chest and read "Deputy" on the dull star. The man hadn't corrected Zeb when he'd called him "Sheriff." Short, paunchy, and power hungry. Zeb had met men like that on his travels, and he gave them as wide a berth as a hornet's nest. They could be twice as stingy and ten times louder.

"Well, the pastor, he done died in the flu. Kilt himself takin' care of all the folks around here. Doc died not long after. Been a hard winter." The deputy relaxed his stance somewhat. "Soon's your children wake up, you clear on outa here, ya hear?"

"Yes, sir, I surely do. Thank you for treating us so fair." Zeb doubted the man could hear the sting behind the words. Calling him "sir" and licking his boots a little would hide a mile of sarcasm.

"See that you do, now." The man hesitated as if he were going to wait until they cleared out, but when Zeb smiled again and extended his hand, the deputy spun on his heel and left.

And if the rest of the town is as accommodating as you, we'll just shake the dust from our feet and keep on going. He leaned down to pick up his quilt and heard what he thought to be a snicker from the other bedroll.

"Anytime you can be ready, girls, we'll be rolling on."

Manda and Deborah both sat up, the smaller girl rubbing her eyes. She smiled up at Zeb and the angel brightness dimmed his eyes. Manda, however, gave him a look that said he would pay for this later. She might not be sure how, but she had a long memory.

Zeb understood that look. His oldest sister, Eva Jane, had one that matched. And she always collected. He hoped her husband had learned how to handle her, or —

He shut off the thoughts of home. They still hurt, in spite of the length and distance he'd traveled.

"There's a privy out back and the sun is shining. What more could we ask for?" He rolled his extra shirt and pants in the quilt and the slicker around it all. Glancing up, he saw the girls hadn't moved.

"Breakfast," the two said together.

51

"I'm getting to that." With his roll under his arm, he paused. "I'm going to saddle up. We'll water the horses at the livery and get a bit of grain for them."

"What about us?" With both hands, Deborah brushed wispy white hair back from her cheeks.

"I said I'm getting to that." Their concentrated stares made him want to shift from one foot to another. He kept still. "We'll stop by the general store and get something." *If only I could find someone to work for, someone who could pay in cash, not just room and board.*

Manda watched the horses eat while he walked back to the store. He'd parked Deborah up against the barn wall on his bedroll and warned her not to move. Maybe the sun would warm a little strength into her frail body.

A bell jingled overhead when he entered the narrow false front building. Mingled fragrances of pickles in a barrel, spices on the shelves, leather from boots and saddles, flour, cornmeal, and molasses blended together to spell "store."

"Good morning, stranger. How can I help you?" The aproned woman behind the counter turned from weighing and bagging dried beans. The smile on her face made him sure the remainder of the town wasn't cast in the deputy's mold.

"I need some supplies and a little information, if you have it." Zeb removed his hat and brushed his hair back with one hand.

"The supplies? I have about anything you can think of." She swept her hand wide to indicate the wealth of stores. "But as to the information? You ask and I'll help you if I can."

"How about a couple pounds each of beans, cornmeal, and hard tack. A bit of salt, some sugar, and . . ." He inhaled and caught the perfume of fresh-baked bread. "Do you have bread for sale?"

She nodded. "Just came outa the oven not ten minutes ago."

"Good. I'll take a loaf. And cheese? You have any cheese?"

She indicated the wheel set under glass. "This much?" She spread her finger and thumb about two inches apart. "Or more?"

Zeb could feel his mouth water at the thought of coffee. How he wanted to buy coffee. "That'll be fine." He eyed a jar full of peppermint sticks. Surely a peppermint stick would bring the smile to Deborah's face that nigh unto broke his heart. But he knew the state of his wallet. "You got any milk?"

She shook her head. "But the Stoltzfusses up the road, they might."

He nodded. While she measured and wrapped, he stalked the aisles. Should he ask?

He returned to the counter. Lie number two was about to be born. "I have a cousin by name of Elmer Norton, and I heard he homesteaded somewhere to the west of here. You know anything about him?"

"We surely do. Man's had a hard time. Why, he was by here . . ." She squinted her eyes to think. "Here, I can check when." She opened a leather-bound ledger book and ran her finger down the column of names. "About what I thought. He was in just before that big snowstorm in early spring. Bought seed, wheat, some flour, and things like that. He apologized for running his bill up. Proud man but paid when he could. I sent two peppermint sticks home with him for his little girls. Poor things — their mother died clear last fall."

Zeb felt a weight crushing down on his shoulders. Mr. Norton had never made it home. And he hadn't run out either.

"You go straight west of town, about a day's ride, I guess. Not too many folks out there. Them bare hills don't grow much. Tell him Mrs. Abrahamson said hello, and I sure am glad he made it home. The storm that night was a killer."

Zeb dug in his pocket and withdrew the soft leather pouch that held the last of his cash. He paid the bill. "Thanks for the information. I surely will pass your greeting on to Elmer." He picked up his packet and turned to leave.

"Here, wait." Mrs. Abrahamson unscrewed the lid of the candy jar and took out two peppermint sticks. "You give these to those two girls of his. They're the light of his life, they are."

"Thank you again." Zeb clapped his hat on his head as soon as he stepped out the door. Was another lie in the offing? He who never told a lie after the last whupping from his ma was getting right into the habit of it. And the one to the deputy would now haunt him.

Within half an hour they were trotting east. Maybe the Stoltzfusses could use a hand for a while. At least Deborah would have fresh milk to drink.

4

"Uff da."

Ingeborg Bjorklund straightened from picking beans and pushed the basket ahead with her foot. Only about five feet to go and she would have the row finished.

Sixteen months old and with a voice that carried clear across the Red River, Astrid scrunched her face and cried again, louder this time. "M-m-a." She used her hands to boost herself back to her feet and, arms in the air for balance, toddled over the rough garden clods of Dakota dirt toward her mother. Wearing a yellow gingham dress as dirt-stained as her face, the child ignored the green bean her mother held out and reached instead for the front of her dress.

"Astrid, see? Look to the end of the row. You can wait that long, can't you?" Ingeborg pointed to the post at the end, then swiped a lock of hair back from her forehead with the back of her hand while glancing at the sun. "Not even midmorning yet." She drew in a deep breath, the fragrance of string beans, both leaves and pods, heightened by the shimmering heat of the August sun.

Astrid shook her head and pulled again at her mother's dress.

"Ja, and it feels more like midafternoon." Goodie Peterson stood upright and kneaded the middle of her back with her fists. "Why don't you and Astrid sit in the shade and snap these while I go punch down the bread? The men will be heading in before we can finish the picking."

Ingeborg nodded, pushing her faded sunbonnet back so she could tuck the stubborn strand of hair under the golden-hued braids she always wore wrapped around the crown of her head. Tall at five foot seven and strong of both chin and frame, she wore her dark skirt and white blouse with an air that commanded respect. Except from her young daughter.

Baby Astrid raised the volume on her demands.

Ingeborg bent to finish picking the row, feeling the seepage from her milk-laden bosom. Often she felt like one of the milk cows, but they let their milk down only twice a day, while she did every time she heard a baby cry. "Uff da," she muttered again. Now she would have to change

57

before dinner. "Little one, if you could have waited only a while longer."

"You mark my words, that one will never willingly wait for anything."

"She is impatient, isn't she?" Ingeborg sent a smile to the other woman working across the bean rows. "So soon she'll be racing after her brothers. They grow up so fast."

Astrid plunked herself back down in the row and buried her face in her skirts, the cries enough to break a hardened heart, let alone her mother's.

"This Dakota country, it grows everything fast." Goodie Peterson set her basket of beans on the bench in the shade of the sod house, which had become home for her and her two children after the Bjorklunds had built the frame house that spring. Up till then, they'd all shared the soddy. Goodie had come to live with the Bjorklunds after her husband died the winter before. "You want we should dry these instead of canning them? My mother used to hang pairs of bean pods, hooked together by their stems, over a string above the stove. Called them leather britches and cooked them along with bacon or salt pork." She held up two connected pods as an example. "You dry them before the beans inside get very big.

Tastes a whole lot different than dried shelled beans."

Ingeborg looked at the bucket and basket, both full of slender bean pods. "I didn't pick mine with the stems on." While she talked, she picked up Astrid and carried her to the bench beside the soddy. Sitting down, she loosened her shirt and set the baby to her breast with one arm encircling the child, leaving her hands free. Ingeborg adjusted her pose to make Astrid more comfortable and reached for a handful of beans. "We can dry yours and snap mine. Leather britches, hmm."

"You want a drink of water?" Goodie shaded her eyes at a squeal from the barn. "Those two are playing in the haymow again."

"Yes, to the water, and can't hurt about the children." Ingeborg loosened the ties of the sunbonnet she'd finally consented to wear and let it fall behind her. Her wide-brimmed man's felt hat shaded better than the calico bonnet, but the bonnet kept her hair cleaner. She'd finally succumbed to the pressure from the other women, and from Haakan too, to put away her man's attire. A breeze tickled the damp hair on either side of her face. She sighed and leaned against the soddy wall.

Just past four and large for his age, her younger son, Andrew, had assumed full charge of Goodie's nearly four-year-old daughter, Ellie. The two were now responsible for feeding the chickens, and Andrew was teaching Ellie which were weeds and which were vegetables in the burgeoning garden. Between the two, they kept the sweet corn and potatoes weed free and collected potato bugs in cans of kerosene. Whenever loosed from chores, they headed straight for the hay-filled barn, sliding down the side near the trapdoor to the lower level. Goodie feared they might forget to close the trap, shoot right down to the rock-hard dirt floor below, and break an arm or leg in the landing.

Ingeborg snapped beans, dropping the broken pieces into her skirt basket and listening to the contented guzzling of her baby. Astrid nursed as she did everything — with gusto.

"Here." Goodie handed Ingeborg the dipper of water, cold from their well, and set another basket on the bench. At a halloo from the road to their town of Blessing and the railroad siding at the southwestern corner of Bjorklund land, she shaded her eyes again. The heat of the golden sunlight shimmered around a man wearing a hat, wider brimmed than most men wore in this area, and carrying something tall and stick-looking on his right shoulder. He waved again.

"It's Olaf."

Ingeborg looked over the rim of the dipper to see Goodie's face about to break with the smile so wide. "Fancy that." Ingeborg took another long draught of water, chuckling inside at the red that swept from Goodie's neck clear to her cheekbones and up to the hairline. "Maybe he brought mail. Why don't you go see?"

Goodie didn't need a second invitation. She shot Ingeborg a grateful smile and headed out. "Uff da," she muttered for Ingeborg's ears alone. "You'd think I was a young maid again."

Ingeborg set the dipper down on the bench and smiled to herself. She hadn't felt so different not that long ago, and like Goodie, she had been married before and widowed too. Thoughts of Haakan striding across the plain with his axe on his shoulder made her smile again. He'd come to Dakota Territory in answer to his mother's plea for him to help his distant relatives, and he never returned to the north woods of Minnesota to log the giant pines. Instead he'd set up his own logging outfit here on the

61

banks of the Red River and, together with Ingeborg, farmed the rich alluvial soil of the valley.

She glanced down at the child on her lap. Astrid reached up and patted her mother's face, milk trickling out the side of her mouth. She belched, giggled at the sound, and slid to the ground.

Ingeborg grabbed the fleeing one's arm and wiped her mouth. "You needn't waste that milk, you little piglet you."

"See Andoo." Astrid pulled away, giggling all the while. Her laughter rippled out over the garden much like the song of the larks in the early morning.

"God dag," Olaf called. "She sounds happy, that one."

"God dag to you too. Come sit. I see you brought your own chair." Ingeborg peered around the corner of the house, letting them know she was decent again. "I'm sure Goodie will fill this dipper for you. Sweet well water on a hot day like this is always welcome."

Olaf set down the chair he'd been carrying on his shoulder and sat himself on it. "Ja, I knew the soddy needed another chair." He drew a handkerchief from his back pocket and lifted his hat with one hand, mopping his sweaty brow and back over his thinning hair with the cloth. " 'Tis a warm one, that is for sure." He took the dipper Goodie offered and drank deeply. "Mange takk. This cold drink is welcome all right, and now I have something for you." He withdrew a packet of mail from the breast pocket of his white shirt. "Here. This one from Bridget must tell us when she is coming." He dug in another pocket. "Penny sent these for you. Said they came in on the morning train." He put the packet of sewing needles with the letters.

As she took the letters Ingeborg noted that he wore a clean white shirt and winked at him. "You look ready for church, and here it is only the middle of the week. Any special reason?" She ducked her head to hide the smile caused by his reddening neck. Those two blushed so easily it was impossible to keep from teasing them. Not that she or anyone else tried terribly hard — to refrain, that is.

"And how are you today, Miss Astrid?" Olaf leaned forward, arms extended for the child to come to him.

She threw her mother a laughing glance over her shoulder and, talking in her own language as if they all should understand her, toddled over to stand within the circle of his arm and the haven of his knees.

Olaf took the baby hands in his and patted them together. "Pat-a-cake, pat-a-cake, baker's man . . ."

While he played with the child, Ingeborg carefully lifted the flap of the envelope. With paper so precious, they would reuse the inside of the envelope. Her eldest child, Thorliff, coveted every bit of paper for the stories he wrote. Drawing the thin sheet from the envelope, she started to read aloud.

Dear Ingeborg and all of our Amerika family,
We are well here, as I hope and pray all of you are too.

A soft grunting from the child captured Ingeborg's attention at the same time as a ripe odor floated upward. "Uff da. Astrid, could you not wait even a few minutes longer?" She glanced over to see the concentrated gaze of the child filling her pants.

"Here, let me take her." Goodie lifted the little girl and wrinkled her nose at the same time. "Pew! Let's get you presentable for your admiring onkel." She paused. "Or would you rather keep her as she is now?"

Olaf shook his head. "I'll wait."

The leaves of the cottonwood tree

Ingeborg had planted when the soddy was built rustled in the breeze as she continued reading the letter aloud.

> We have our tickets to leave Oslo on the first of August, so if God wills that all go well, we should see you before the end of the month.

Ingeborg laid her hands in her lap. "They won't be here for the wedding after all."

Olaf moved his chair into the shade. "There will be plenty of folks there anyhow. With harvest so near, we are cutting things close, but if we do not get married now, there will be no time for the next two months."

"Or more. I've never seen the wheat so thick and heavy. This is to be a bumper year for certain."

"Ja, and the price fell again."

Ingeborg groaned. "How are we to get ahead when they keep dropping the wheat prices?" While she knew Olaf had no answer, she still voiced the complaint of all the farmers. The prices per bushel had dropped for the last two years. Rumor had it that the grain buyers for the Minneapolis flour mills had joined together to make sure they made a huge profit, at the expense of the farmers. And the railroads were charging more to ship the grain too.

She shook her head and returned to the letter.

I am bringing Katja with me, as there are no young men here who catch her eye, and you said single men are the majority in the west. I want her to marry a God-fearing man, and if he owns his own farm, it would be like the frosting on the egge kake.

Ingeborg chuckled at that. Bridget was renowned for her egg cake, and her frosting recipe had been handed down from her mother. "Hard to believe that little Katja is ready to think of marriage. They grow up so fast." Her gaze returned to the paper. "Oh, dear."

"What is it?" Olaf had removed his pipe from his pocket and was scraping the bowl with the small blade on his knife.

"She is bringing Onkel Hamre's grandson with her." She returned to reading aloud.

Hamre is now twelve, and since his mother died of the chest congestion, he has been living with me to help us out with the chores. Johann wants him to stay here so there is someone in the family to help him with the home farm, but Hamre is determined to go to Amerika. He says he wants the new life too. Such a strong mind for such a young boy.

Ingeborg looked up again, her forehead wrinkled in thought. "This should work out well, then. We will let them have this soddy, since Goodie and her two will be with you in your new house when it's built."

"Mayhap we could put a wood floor in it for them before winter." Olaf tamped his tobacco down with his thumb.

"Ja, and a new coat of whitewash." She smiled at the man now heading into the soddy to get a light from the stove for his pipe. When he returned, he nodded. "I heard tell these old soddies are warmer in the winter than wooden frame houses any day. As used to dark winters as those Norskys from the old country are, this shouldn't be such a burden."

"Humph." Ingeborg shook her head. Nothing pleased her more than the many windows Haakan had insisted on for their new house. She stared across the short space to the two-story frame house with a porch facing the west. The look of it still thrilled her deep into her soul. This year perhaps the howling winds wouldn't bring on the inner darkness that seemed to attack her most in the winter. The long winters in Norway had never caused the darkness of her soul that the winters in the soddy had brought upon her after her first husband, Roald, died. Sometimes now, even with Haakan and the children, she felt herself being sucked back down into the pit.

She shook the specter away and returned to the letter.

I hope this will not be an extra burden for you, but Sarah Neswig desires to come also. She is the daughter of my second cousin and a good worker. When her parents heard we were leaving, they made a special trip clear from Oslo to ask if she might go along. How could we say no? Her fiancé was drowned in the same storm that took Hamre's far to his watery grave. Onkel Hamre still blames himself, believing that if he had been along, the boat would not have gone down.

"There's a mite too much snow on his mountain for him to be fishing the north seas any longer, isn't there?" Olaf shook his head, the smoke from his pipe circling around them.

"Ja, that is why his son Jacob had taken over. He, too, is — was a fine fisherman. Young Hamre will miss the sea here."

"He could pretend that wheat is the sea. Bending in the breeze like that, it looks like gentle sea swells, although a mite gold in color."

Ingeborg smiled at his sally. Olaf had never been addicted to the sea like Onkel Hamre. Fishing was all the old man could talk about or wanted to talk about.

Goodie returned with a now sweet-smelling child. "You want her back, or shall I put her down on the quilt?"

Ingeborg nodded toward the quilt they had spread in the shaded and fenced plot. They had put up the fence so Astrid could not crawl away. Now that she was walking, the fence was even more important. Goodie set the child down and handed her a hunk of bacon skin to chew on. Two days earlier a second lower tooth had cut through, and the nub beside it would soon sparkle white. With her four sparkling teeth, Andrew dubbed her "rabbit."

Ingeborg finished reading the letter and returned it to its envelope to be read again at the dinner table. "So, we will have four new lives here with us."

"Good thing these you already got are moving on." Goodie stood beside Olaf, close but not touching. She glanced up at the two laughing children emerging from the cow barn. "But those two will be lost without each other."

Andrew slammed the door shut and yelled, "Race you to the well."

Even from the distance, the adults could tell that he hung back and let Ellie win.

"That Andrew, he will be a fine man someday, the way he cares for others, both human and animal." Olaf puffed on his pipe, nodding as the smoke wreathed his head.

Ingeborg sniffed in appreciation. "You use the same tobacco as my far did. I always liked the smell of pipe smoke."

"How about cigars? I saw a new box of them over at the store. Penny says they are selling good." He chuckled at Ingeborg's wrinkled nose.

"Ishda to both that and those awful cigarettes some of the men are rolling. Mark my words, those are dangerous in this dry weather."

"You must be carrying water to your garden. Some others are looking pretty wilted by now."

"Thank God for the good well we have. At church on Sunday some were saying their wells are going dry." Her hands busy with the snapping beans and her eyes on the child jabbering to the rag doll on the quilt, Ingeborg enjoyed the conversation.

"Ja. I been coopering barrels for hauling water," Olaf said.

Goodie glanced from the chair to his face. "Besides making me a new chair? Olaf, do you never sleep?"

"Sure, and I will be sleeping better soon."

At his sly comment, Goodie's face flamed again. "Ach," she muttered under her breath, her hands furiously snapping beans.

Ingeborg hid her smile. These two were so good for each other. When Goodie and her children arrived, nearly starved and the boy sick unto death, there hadn't been much laughter for a long time. When spring finally thawed the frozen ground, Goodie had been able to put her Elmer under the sod, freeing her from a heavy burden of grief. Now Ingeborg knew she would mightily miss working and visiting every day with her friend when she left. They'd become part of the family. The good Lord surely had been merciful to them all.

Andrew and Ellie skidded to a stop in

front of her. "Ma, can we go find Thorliff and the sheep?"

"I thought maybe you would like to take a water jug out to your pa and ride the horses in when they come for dinner. Tante Kaaren will be ringing the dinner bell before too long."

Andrew, blue eyes sparkling above rosy cheeks, turned to his playmate. "You want to come?"

Ellie, her hair bleached pure white by the sun, nodded, setting her pigtails to flopping. "I can carry the jug for Onkel Lars."

"There's some buttermilk in the springhouse. Why don't you take that too? Nothing like buttermilk to quench their thirst."

As the two scampered off to their errand, Goodie shook the snapped beans into her basket from Ingeborg's skirt. "I better be gettin' over to help Kaaren with the dinner. We got enough here for that and more. You going back to picking?"

Ingeborg nodded. "We should have a boilerful soon." With the three stoves going, they could cook the meals at one place, can at another, and have the diapers boiling at the last. Four in diapers meant plenty to wash, about every other day. Kaaren's twin girls, Grace and Sophie, were running around, Sophie caring for her deaf sister. Grace had been born without hearing, a severe trial for the younger couple, although more so for Lars. He still struggled sometimes against ignoring the silent twin, favoring her chattering sister.

"The big boys will be helping with the picking this afternoon, ja?"

"We'll let Baptiste run the fish trap so Metiz has plenty of fish to keep drying, and he can check the trapline too." Ingeborg knew she was getting spoiled with the extra help, but there still were never enough hands to do all that needed doing. Thanks to the boys' hunting and the leftovers from last year's smoking, they hadn't had to butcher anything but chickens.

She heard the shriek of a hawk flying above and automatically checked the chicken yard. The hens had heard the same cry and were flapping their way into the hen house to safety. They didn't realize Haakan had stretched chicken wire over the top of the pen, preventing marauding hawks from helping themselves.

"You want I should help you pick the beans?" Olaf tamped the remains of his smoke from the pipe and ground the ashes into the dirt with his heel. "Or does anyone need more wood chopped?"

"Olaf, you are such a kindhearted man. I know you'd rather be with Goodie, so you two go on. Kaaren has plenty needing to be done over there." Ingeborg brushed the black flies away from her now slumbering daughter. Astrid looked as if sleep had caught her midrock. Her bottom stuck up and tiny fists pillowed her right cheek. Golden curls lay against her damp scalp. If the flies weren't so fierce, she'd be tempted to let her sleep as she was. Instead, Ingeborg picked up the sheet on the fence and fluttered it down over the sleeping child, face and all. While she'd get warmer that way, she'd be protected from the flies and the sun by the cotton material.

Ingeborg took her now empty basket and headed for the bean rows. Sitting still never got the work done. The letter crinkled in her apron pocket. She would read it to the others over the dinner table.

When the triangle clanged for dinner, she kept on picking, knowing it would take some time for the men to make it in from the fields and for the boys to come from grazing the flock of sheep. Today Hans, Goodie's ten-year-old son, would stay out with the sheep. The three boys took turns when they could.

Ingeborg thought longingly of taking the

gun and setting up along the deer trail about twilight. They hadn't had venison in a while. Baptiste said he saw an entire herd of deer tripping down to the river a day or so ago. The fawns would be weaned soon, but she wouldn't take a doe anyway, not with the bucks available. Bringing in a deer or an elk close to home wasn't as easy as it had been in the early years. What with all the settlers around them, game had been getting scarce.

She could hear the jangling of harnesses and the thudding of approaching hooves. A cow bellered, echoed by another, both greeting the returning horses. One of the horses whinnied back. The men would take different teams out for the afternoon of sod-breaking. Most likely Lars would choose the oxen. In this lull before harvest began, they were trying to finish breaking the last forty acres of the original homesteads. Some land they kept fenced for pasture for the horses and cows, but the rest was either hayfields or under cultivation. Not that they hadn't already hayed those forty acres in June.

Ingeborg wiped away the sweat dripping off the end of her nose. They sure could use some rain and cooler weather. While the thunderheads frequently piled dark promises on the horizon, the rain never made it to their property. She grasped the handles on each side of her full willow basket and headed back down the row. She and Thorliff would finish the picking while Goodie and Kaaren snapped the already picked beans. Drying more for leather britches sounded more appealing by the handful.

She stopped at the carrot row, set down the basket, and sorted through the feathery carrot tops until she found one that looked large enough to eat. She wiggled it loose from the dry dirt that did its best to keep the carrot growing and wiped the dirt away on her apron. Munching the crisp orange root, she closed her eyes to better appreciate the flavor. This was the way carrots should be eaten, not cooked nor dried nor limp from long storage in the root cellar.

"Forgive me, Lord," she murmured around the carrot's crunch. "I am grateful for the supplies that lasted us through the winter, but peas and carrots are best just like this, right from your good soil." With the sun hot on her shoulders and the beans sharing their own particular perfume, she waited. God felt so near; surely He would answer her. She strained her ears. Was that Him in the chuckle of the cottonwood leaves? In the lilt of the lark? In the laughter of the men unharnessing the horses? She shook her head at her own fancy. God was indeed in everything around and within her.

Like David of olden times, dancing for joy before the Lord seemed about the right thing to do. So much to be grateful for. Words just didn't seem enough.

She sent another thank-you winging skyward as she picked up the basket and carried it to the bench, setting it in the shade next to Goodie's. Then gathering up the sleeping baby, Ingeborg strode toward the soddy on the other side of the center pasture. "Blessed be the name of the Lord," Ingeborg declared to the glorious world around her. Astrid whimpered at the skip her mother threw in for good measure.

"Hey, wife, you look good in that sunbonnet." Haakan turned from the wash bench and dried his hands and face on the towel hanging from a peg in the wall.

"Thank you, sir," Ingeborg said. She knew what he was about with that compliment, but it felt good anyway. Haakan tolerated her donning of men's hats and pants but much preferred her in skirts and sunbonnets.

"Thank you again." She smiled up into eyes that always recalled the blue of Norwegian fjords on a summer day. Bjorklund blue, so many called it now, as if it were a color all its own. A shock of wheaten hair flopped forward, breaking the line of tan and white that bisected his and every other farmer's forehead. A fedora hat brim didn't do much to shade a man's lower face, but it did save his eyes.

As usual, her heart beat faster at the sight of his broad shoulders, square jaw, and the smile that sent warmth flooding through her body. While Haakan smiled and laughed easily, this smile he saved for her alone. Perhaps tonight they would come together and the life of their son would begin. He nodded, just a dip of his chin that said he understood and wanted the same thing. A son for Haakan, a son of his own, since both Thorliff and Andrew were Roald's sons. Close kin but not the same. While he said nothing could make him happier than his daughter, Astrid, she knew he wanted a son, many sons. All men did.

The men and boys sat down at the well-set table, and the women stood behind them while Haakan bowed his head, followed by the others. "Father God, we thank thee for this food thou hast given us this day. We ask thee to continue thy protection over and around us and fill us with thy peace. Amen."

The others chimed in with the "amen," and Baptiste reached for the mashed potatoes before the n finished sounding. Ingeborg cleared her throat, and he shot her a questioning look before dropping his hand. At her nod, he reached again, as did the others. The bowls of food emptied swiftly and Kaaren filled them again from pots on the stove.

"We have a letter from home . . . er . . . Nordland." Ingeborg caught her error. So hard it was to always remember that the prairie, not the mountains of her fatherland, was now home forever. "I can read it while you eat."

Haakan looked up from cutting his baked ham. "From Bridget?"

Ingeborg nodded and slipped the letter from the envelope.

"Can I have the envelope when you are done?" Thorliff spoke around a mouthful of potatoes and gravy.

Ingeborg gave him one of her son-you-know-better-than-that looks. A glance that covered a multitude of meanings.

He ducked his head and finished swallowing. "Sorry. But can I?"

"May I." Kaaren, ever the schoolteacher, laid a hand on his shoulder as she set another platter of meat in the center of the table.

Thorliff sighed and tried again, his eyes rolling in the look of persecuted children, no matter their age. "May I have the envelope when you are finished?"

"Of course you may." Ingeborg and Kaaren kept their exchanged look hidden from the three boys at the table. Teaching manners and proper English was a never-ending task. Ingeborg unfolded the flimsy sheet of paper and began reading, enjoying the second time almost more than the first with the added comments from her family.

She glanced at Andrew, wondering why he was so quiet. Usually he had sixty-five things to bring to everyone's attention. Did his face look more flushed than usual? Continuing to read, she walked around the table and laid the back of her hand along his bright red cheek. Sure enough, the child was hot with fever. Could it just be from playing so hard in the hot haymow? But inside she knew. Something was wrong.

5

"Achoo!" The sneeze nearly knocked her off the ladder.

Penny Bjorklund swiped the last bucket rim with her feather duster and scrambled down the ladder she'd used to reach the top row of merchandise just under the high ceiling of the Blessing General Store. Another sneeze caught her by surprise and then a third that doubled her right over.

"God bless you." A deep voice from the doorway sent the telltale blush whooshing from her neck clear to her forehead. Would she never outgrow that silly habit? Feeling twelve years old again, she quickly wiped her nose on the side of her apron and turned to face her customer.

"Thank you. Mercy, the dust coats those saddles and things faster than I can keep them dusted. Should take them down and give them a good cleaning with saddle soap. You don't by any chance need a well-padded, deeply carved western saddle, do you? The horn is built especially sturdy for roping cattle."

The man removed his wide-brimmed hat and held it over his heart. "No, but if I did, I surely would buy it from one as comely as you."

There went the blush again. Penny ignored it and gave him a smile fit to warm anyone's heart. "How then can I help you?"

"Well . . . ah . . . is your father here, miss? I could use some help in choosing new boots." He glanced down at boots that looked to have seen more gravel than grass. "You do carry boots, don't you?"

"I sure do. Right this way." She led the man down to the third aisle toward the smithy. "But my father won't be able to help you. He died years ago." Penny hid the grin that her comment brought to her lips. Whatever made her answer like that? She knew she should have put her hair up. Wearing the curly mass of gold down her back did nothing to make her look matronly. And the pink ribbon she'd tied in a bow at the collar of her gingham dress didn't exactly help either. Maybe if she could keep from smiling so much or take the bounce out of her step. . . .

"Oh, I . . . I'm sorry. I just thought . . . ah . . . is your . . . ah . . ."

Penny took pity on the gentleman. "Look, mister, my name is Penny Bjorklund — Mrs. Hjelmer Bjorklund — and this is my store. My husband has the blacksmith shop right next door. Now, if it's boots you're wanting, I know a whole lot more than he does about the line of boots I carry here, since I did the ordering."

Now it was the man's turn to suffer the pangs of discomfort. "I beg your pardon, ma'am. You look hardly old enough to be out of the schoolroom, and . . ."

She could see the awareness of what he was saying dawn in his eyes.

He clapped his hat back on his head and turned toward the door. "Do you mind if I go out and come back in? We can start this conversation all over again, and maybe I'll be able to keep from chewing on these beat-up old boots of mine. They don't fit too good in my mouth, you see."

"I'm sure they don't taste too good either." Penny smiled and gestured toward the straight-backed chair she'd set in the aisle just for this purpose. "If you'll sit down and tell me what size you wear, I'll bring you a pair to try on."

"I don't rightly know." He raised his foot in the air. "What do you think?"

"I think I'll bring several, and we can put

them against yours till we get close." She studied the boot a moment longer. Thinking size ten to twelve, she lifted several pairs down and returned with an armful.

"My pa made these boots before I left home." He looked up, studying her face in the sunbeam that streamed through the sparkling clean windows. "You know, you look mighty familiar. You got any family living in Ohio?"

Penny stopped opening the boot in her hand. She gazed at him intently. "I used to. We were from near Lima, but after my pa and ma died, I went to live with my aunt and uncle. We came out here."

"You know where your pa come from before that?"

Penny wrinkled her forehead, trying to remember. "Maybe somewhere around Cincinnati? I'm just not sure."

"Well, I'll be. Was your name by any chance Sjorenson?"

Penny nodded. *Please, God, let this be true. Does this man really know my family?*

"And your pa was Able Sjorenson?"

Penny nodded again. She couldn't force any words past the lump in her throat.

"Well, I'll be a gallopin' gopher." The man stood and extended his hand. "My name is Ephraim Nelson. My ma is your

84

pa's older sister. You look just like her — my ma, I mean."

He took off his hat again, revealing a receding hairline above the hat mark on his forehead. With the crinkles at his eyes and creases in his cheeks, he wasn't as young as she'd thought originally.

"My ma was a lot older than him, her being the eldest and him the last of ten children, you know."

"No, I didn't know." Penny studied the box in her hands. When she looked back up, a sheen of moisture made her blink. "Ma and Pa didn't say much about their families. I got the feeling there was something that happened."

Ephraim nodded. "There was a falling out." He reached for the boot box and sat back down in the chair. "To think I'm buying boots from my own cousin, clear out here in Dakota Territory. If that don't beat all."

Questions fluttered in Penny's mind like moth wings against a lamp chimney. Did he know anything of her brothers and sisters? If he was her cousin, did he know others? Would she really have a family again, after all?

"Looks a mite small." He looked up again from checking the new boot length against his own. "That there a bigger pair?"

Penny jerked back to pay attention. "Why, yes, it is." She handed him the boots. "Excuse me, I need to go call my husband." Without waiting for an answer, she clutched the third pair to her bosom and dashed out the back door. "Hjelmer! Hjelmer, where are you?" She checked in the blacksmith shop, but all was quiet. Not even the cat was in the barn. She spun back. The sack house. She knew Olaf was cleaning it out to get it ready for the new wheat deliveries when harvest started. Had he gone to talk with Olaf? She heard the bell tinkle over the door to the store. Gracious! Was Mr. Nelson — Ephraim — leaving without paying?

She darted back in the shop to see her stranger still working with the boots. She let out a sigh of relief. Hjelmer had given her a lecture just the other day about watching people more carefully so nothing was stolen. With all the strangers coming through town on the railroad, a thief could be riding the rails as easily as an honest man. While Penny had agreed with him in principle, she hated the thought of someone stealing from them. If they needed a thing that bad, they could just ask, and likely as not, she'd give it to them.

Hjelmer also said she was a sucker for a sad story.

"Excuse me." She handed Ephraim the other boot and went in search of her latest customer. "Why, Mrs. Valders, how are you today?"

"Fine, fine, Penny, and you?" Hildegunn Valders patted Penny's arm. "I just need a few things. Anner says he needs to take the wagon into Grafton for a wheel fitting later this week, so he will pick up the staples."

"Hjelmer could tighten the rims, you know." Penny forced herself to stand still when she really wanted to take three steps back.

The woman in front of her shook her head. "You know that and I know that. And Anner does too, but he is so stubborn. He wanted to buy that land from Mr. Booth, you know."

How long, O Lord, will we pay for Hjelmer's land-buying deals? "Yes. Well, it is better to let bygones be bygones." Now she sounded just like her aunt Matilda.

"You know that, I know that, the Good Book says that, but men, sometimes they have a hard time forgetting."

Penny sighed. Men could be so stubborn. "What can I get for you, then?"

"You have some of Ingeborg's cheese?"

Penny nodded. "I just got in a shipment of needles too."

"Oh good, I'll take a packet." Mrs. Valders fingered the yellow-and-white checked gingham. "This would make such a lovely dress for my niece, don't you think?"

All Penny could think of was the man over by the boots. "Yes, yes, of course." *Where is Hjelmer?*

The bell tinkled again. "Excuse me. Why don't you think about the gingham, and I'll see what this person wants."

"Good afternoon, Penny. You have any mail for me?" Reverend John Solberg tipped his hat and smiled his sunny smile. Seeing him and his cheerful ways could make anyone feel good.

"I most surely do." Penny stepped behind the counter to the rows of cubbyholes with names above them. Besides owning and running the store, she'd been appointed postmistress by the Dakota Territory once the train started tossing off a mailbag when it stopped for water. While the pay wasn't much, many people purchased things they needed when they came for the mail. Anything to increase business.

She handed him a letter and a flat package. "Here you go."

"Ah, wonderful. My book has arrived."

Reverend Solberg put the letter in his pocket and began untying the string. "I ordered this from St. Olaf College, you know."

Penny handed him a pair of scissors. *How is Ephraim doing with the boots?* She kept the thoughts and the impatience off her face. "Can I get you anything else? Ingeborg just brought in cheese and eggs this morning. Oh, and butter."

Mrs. Valders laid the bolt of material on the counter. "Well, Reverend Solberg, are you ready for the baptizing on Sunday?"

"Oh yes. It's not often a pastor gets so many to baptize at once. We should have done it last spring. You ladies will be meeting for quilting Saturday, won't you?"

"Wouldn't miss it. Probably will be the last time until after harvest, not that we're not busy harvesting our gardens. I have extra beans if you would like some."

Penny shifted from one foot to the other. What was the man doing back there by himself?

"I'll take four yards of this gingham and a packet of the needles," Hildegunn said before turning back to visit with the pastor.

Penny measured out the crisp material and folded it carefully. "I have some lace over there that would look real good around the neckline and sleeves. You want to see it?"

Mrs. Valders nodded. "Have you called on that new family south of town, Pastor? They come from Wisconsin, I think."

"Yes, I have. They plan on bringing their baby to the baptism on Sunday too."

Penny set a roll of two-inch lace on the counter and a roll of one-inch, along with a spool of yellow thread for Mrs. Valders. Then she turned to Reverend Solberg. "Can I get you anything else, Pastor?"

"I'll take some of that cheese, a dozen eggs, and a pound of butter. There must be something special the Bjorklunds feed their cows. They make such good butter and cheese."

Penny turned to the wheel of cheese she had sitting on the side counter. She moved the knife around the circle until he said to stop and cut a wedge.

"You might as well cut mine at the same time. Make it about double that," Mrs. Valders said. "I'm thinking this winter I might lay by a whole wheel if Ingeborg has it. She still taking things out to the Bonanza farm too?"

Penny lifted the chunk off the scale and wrote down the weight. "Far as I know. I think St. Andrew Mercantile isn't getting much anymore, though. I've kind of taken their place."

"Never hurts to be family." Pastor Solberg drew out his wallet. "How much do I owe you, young lady?"

Penny added up the figures. "That'll be fifty-two cents."

He handed her the change. "Are you thinking of carrying bread too, by any chance? I never have been good at baking bread."

"I hadn't thought of that, but it's a good idea. You know of anyone who might like to bake for me?"

"No, but I'll study on it. Along with my new book." He picked up his parcels. "Thank you, my dear, and God bless."

Mrs. Valders leaned across the counter but spoke loud enough for the departing pastor to hear her. "We just need to work harder at finding him a good wife."

"Maybe we should put a sign in the window." Penny wanted to take back her words as soon as they came out, but Hildegunn went on as if she never heard.

"Shame there aren't more marriageable women around here. There sure are plenty of single men."

Penny wished she could check on Ephraim, but for some reason she didn't want Mrs. Valders knowing he was back there. At least not until she'd told Hjelmer the good news. Once Hildegunn Valders caught on to something, the entire Red River Valley knew it within the hour.

"You sure there's no mail for me?" Mrs. Valders peered at the box with her name. "Oh, I see there's some for Odells. I'll drop theirs off on my way home."

Penny handed her the mail and finished wrapping the cheese. "That lace would look real nice."

Mrs. Valders laid it across the bolt, then wrapped some around her wrist. "You're right. Give me a yard and a half of the narrow — no, make it three. I'll stitch it in along the placket. What do you think? And a collar maybe. Round." She nodded. "Thank you. It surely is nice to be able to buy these things right here in Blessing."

Yes. Now if only your husband would bring his horses here for shoeing and the wagon wheels for refitting, Hjelmer needs the work too. "I'll make sure I have plenty of sugar and coffee and such for when the weather starts to change, Mrs. Valders. Then you won't have to go to Grand Forks or Grafton for your supplies this winter."

Penny totaled the purchases, but before she could say the amount, Mrs. Valders leaned closer. "Could you put that in the book, please?" she whispered. "I hate to ask that, but until harvest . . ."

"I know." Penny withdrew the ledger from under the counter and penciled the amount in a column under the Valders' name.

"Thank you." The woman gathered her bundle together. "We'll see you on Saturday at the quilting, won't we?"

"If Hjelmer can take time to look after the store." Penny came around the counter. "Here, let me help you out with that." She took the cheese and package of notions and material and led the way out the door. The horse tied to the hitching rail shook its head and shifted so that the buggy creaked. Mrs. Valders climbed up in the buggy seat and took the packages from Penny.

"Thank you again." She unwrapped the reins from the whipstock and clucked to her horse, pulling back on the reins at the same time. "Bye now."

Penny waved and hurried back into the store, trying to look as if she wasn't hurrying a bit. What if Ephraim had left?

But when she turned the corner into the aisle, she stopped instantly. Her guest was still in his chair, one boot on, one off, chin on his chest, eyes closed.

She studied him from the distance. He looked worn, and not just his boots. The frayed cuffs, the hat faded light in some places, the dark stains around the sweatband, and the pants patched on one knee by someone not accustomed to using a needle and thread. His face, slack in sleep, had once been good-looking but now seemed ground down by the heels of life. She guessed his age to be forty or so, but sun and wind had a way of aging human skin.

Yet it was a good face, void of the lines of bitterness worn by so many who passed through on their way to a new life out west.

An idea lighted her mind like the flare of a newly lit lamp before the chimney is set in place. Maybe he would like to stay on and work for some of the folks in the area. Haakan and Ingeborg were always in need of another hand, and once harvest started, the need would be even greater.

Besides, now that she finally had a member of her family within touching room, she wasn't about to let him go. She had plenty of questions to ask. In the stillness, she heard his stomach rumble.

Her intake of breath woke him.

"Ah . . . I . . . ah . . . sorry." He straightened, instinctively searching for his hat. "Guess I was tired."

"I guess so, if you could sleep with all that's been going on around here. I have dinner about ready. Would you like to join us?" Us, if she could ever find Hjelmer. Where could he have gone? And without telling her. What if someone had come needing a blacksmith immediately?

"I don't want to put you out none."

"You won't be. How did the boots fit?"

"Right fine, this pair." He held those up by his side. "How much are they?"

Penny caught her bottom lip between her teeth. He didn't look as if he had two nickels to rub together. She named the price she paid for them.

He nodded. "Figured as much. Maybe I can find someone with a boot last and can mend these of mine again."

"My sister-in-law, Ingeborg, has one. But if you need those . . ." She glanced at the boots he had pulled back on. One side was cracked out, the soles on both looked thinner than the gingham Mrs. Valders had taken home with her, and she could see his toes on the left one. She thought quickly. How to save his pride and yet get him into some decent foot coverings?

"I have a pile of wood that needs splitting out back. My husband hasn't had time to get to it, and —"

"Thankee, ma'am, but I ain't one to take charity." He got to his feet.

"It isn't charity when one member of a family helps out another. And I got a lot of catching up to do on family." Penny gentled her voice. "Please." Men could be so stubborn. "You'd be doing me a favor."

"Well, if I can work 'em off somehow . . ."

"Good. You will." Penny snatched up the others he'd tied together again by their laces. "You can wash up for dinner out back. Man can't chop wood on an empty stomach." She turned as the bell rang again. "You go through that door over there. Washbasin is on the bench — water in the reservoir of the cookstove. I'll be back soon as I take care of this customer." Then she sang out in a cheery voice, "Coming."

But her voice and smile hid the thoughts crowding her mind. *Could something have happened to Hjelmer?* Immediately she banished that idea to the woodshed where it belonged. Why, he'd been out in his shop not over an hour ago. Or was it longer? Seems she'd spent half her life waiting for that man.

"Morning, Miz Bjorklund. You got any chewing tobacco?" asked one of the workmen that was checking the track.

She shook her head. "Sorry, but I told

your friend that yesterday."

"How come there ain't no rooming house here in Blessing?"

"No one's thought to build one yet. Guess we didn't know there was a need." Penny stepped behind her counter. "I've got some fine cheese here, though. Better for you than tobacco, anyhow."

"Any bread?"

Penny started to shake her head. She could feel her brain gearing up with a new idea. "How many men on your crew?"

"Three. Why?"

"Did you bring dinner with you?"

"No. Where would we get that? The place in Grafton don't provide meals, just beds. And not so good a ones at that. Charge a quarter too." The man shook his head. "Highway robbery, if'n you ask me."

Penny could barely wait for him to quit griping. When he paused for breath, she leaped in. "If the three of you want to wash up, I'll set the table. I'm serving beef stew with new carrots and potatoes, fresh baked bread, and custard pie for dessert for . . ." She paused. Swallowed. "For two bits apiece."

"All you can eat?"

Please, Lord, let there be enough. She swallowed again and nodded. "All you can eat."

Her voice squeaked on the "eat."

"I'll go ask the men."

"You do that, then come around that side of the building." She pointed to the left.

As he went out the door, she sliced off a hunk of cheese and dug some dill pickles out of the barrel. By the time she had finished, he stuck his head back in the doorway.

"They're comin'."

She flipped the sign on the door to closed and hurried back to her kitchen. A red-and-white checked oilcloth already covered the table. She could hear Ephraim out back sloshing water and humming. She dipped more hot water into a bucket and set it on the bench. "Could you draw me another bucket from the well? We got more company for dinner."

"Why, sure." He hung the towel back up by the mirror. "There somewhere special you want this water tossed?"

"On the roses there." She pointed to a pair of plants under the kitchen window. Hjelmer had given her those for her birthday not long after they were married. One red and one white. She stepped out and, taking her shears out of her apron pocket, snipped two blossoms of each.

Setting them in a jar on the table, she

quickly set four places. If and when Hjelmer came home, he'd have to wait. Somehow the thought didn't aggravate her a bit, though it might him. But then . . . She cut off the thoughts and sliced the loaf of bread she'd made the day before. After putting that full plate on the table, she dished the stew into a serving bowl. My, but it smelled good.

"Where you want this?" Ephraim asked, hefting the bucket.

"Pour as much as you can into the reservoir. Oh, and please fill the teakettle." She whirled from slicing the cheese. "Oh, Mr. Nelson, please forgive me. Here you are a guest, and I'm treating you just like family."

"You said I *was* family, remember? And I told you I wanted to earn my meal, so this be just fine." He did as she'd asked, finishing just as the now washed railroad men rapped at the back door.

"Come right on in and set yourselves." Penny pointed to the four places at the table. "This is Mr. Nelson, if the three of you would be so kind as to introduce yourselves."

Hats in their hands, the three shifted from one foot to the other, their noses going like bloodhounds in full cry. "Ma'am, this here kitchen smells like a little bit of heaven."

The three hooked their hats over the backs of their chairs and sat down, beginning to pass the plates immediately. By the time Penny had poured the coffee, the stew bowl was empty and the leader of the three was looking up, ready for more.

There was one piece of pie left when they finished. Hjelmer would have to have a cheese sandwich. As they went out the door, they each gave her their twenty-five cents, and the foreman put in an extra dime.

"Can I pass the word about eating at the store in Blessing?" he asked.

Penny nodded. "You surely can. Will it be every day or . . ."

"We'll try to let you know in advance, but that's not always possible. Depends on where we're working. If you'd get a telegraph receiver in here, that would make it easy."

Better not give me any more ideas this morning, Penny thought. *Wait till the news of this gets out.*

"Name's Joe Porter." The foreman stopped before leaving. "Any chance you might get some chewing tobacco in stock? You'd sell a lot of it."

Penny avoided shaking her head. "I'll see what I can do." She kept the smile on her face till the door closed, then turned to the table where Ephraim sat nibbling on the last slice of dill pickle.

"You don't like chawin' t'baccy?"

"Not at all. It smells terrible, and I'm not having gobs of spit all over my floors." She shuddered.

"How long you had this here place?"

"The store?"

He nodded.

"We opened for business the first day of June. So two months it is. Not too long after our wedding." She crossed to the table and sat down. "Never thought I'd be serving meals for travelers too."

"They weren't travelers. Just hard-working men who appreciated a good meal. Like this one here did. Now, I better get busy to earn out my boots, let alone the dinner." He glanced at her out of the side of his eye. "Looked to me like you already got a good stack of wood out there."

Penny nodded, then slapped her hands on the oilcloth table cover. "But it won't last long if I get to cooking and baking for people like those men. Makes me think of cooking for a threshin' crew, and I know plenty about that. Who'd ever thought my working at the hotel in Fargo would be of use in Blessing?" She cocked her head to one side. "But then whoever would have thought there'd be such a place as Blessing?"

Ephraim got to his feet. "Well, as that old hymn says, 'God do work in mysterious ways, His wonders to perform.' "

Penny eyed him as he talked. "You ever done any cooking?"

He shook his head. "Not that anyone would want to eat unless they be starving."

"Worked in a store?"

Again the headshake. "No, I've tilled fields, milked cows, made hay, and butchered when the time was right. I can fix most anything that's broke, and I ain't afraid of hard work. That's why I'm thinking of homesteading out west. Planned to go as far as the train would take me and then look over the land."

"It'll take you all the way to the Pacific Ocean now, but not this little line that goes up here. You got to go back to Grand Forks or Fargo for that."

"I know, but I didn't want to go to the Pacific Ocean. I like Dakota Territory, and once it becomes a state, this is going to be an even better place to live."

"How so?"

"Just a feeling I have. Now, I gotta get to that woodpile." He reached for his hat. "Thank you for a mighty fine meal."

He got as far as the door before she stopped him. "You any good with sums?"

"I can add, subtract, multiply, and divide, if that's what you mean."

"Read?"

"And write."

"Good." Penny thought she'd better talk it over with Hjelmer before offering the man a job. She pushed her chair back and began clearing the table. The coins jingled in her apron pocket when she reached for the dirty plates. The clock in the sitting room chimed one o'clock.

"Where is that man of mine?" she asked the steaming teakettle. She cut a piece of bread and laid the last two slices of cheese on it. After setting the sandwich aside for Hjelmer, she finished clearing the table, putting the dishes in the pan waiting on the cool end of the stove. She poured hot water over them, crumbled in a bit of the soft soap she kept for that purpose, and wiped off the table.

Just as she dried her hands on her apron before taking it off to go look for Hjelmer, a yoo-hoo came from the front of the store.

"Coming." If only she could call Hjelmer as easily. *Can't they read the closed sign?*

6

"Have you slept at all?" Lars Knutson raised his head from the pillow.

Kaaren, his wife, sitting in the rocking chair with a whimpering girl in one arm and a nursing one in the other, shook her head. "Their throats hurt so they can hardly nurse. And they'll have nothing to do with gruel and honey. Mumps are miserable for ones so little."

"And for their mother." He threw back the sheet and climbed from the rope-slung bed. "I'll walk one while you nurse the other, but I thought you had them about weaned."

"They were until they took sick." She handed him Sophie, who was rubbing her eyes with her fists.

Lars settled his daughter against his shoulder and began humming in her ear as he paced the floor. Three long strides and he'd covered it, detouring so as not to knock his shin on the rocker. He jiggled Sophie while he walked back to the bed, turned, and circled the oilcloth-covered table this time.

Kaaren leaned her head against the back of the chair. Her eyes felt as if they held half the grit of the Dakota plains. And with all she had to do in the morning. Not that morning wasn't already here. She rocked the chair gently and gazed down at her daughter. Grace sucked a moment, then whimpered. She never really cried, but her fist beating against her mother's breast spoke well of her misery. Her cheeks were swollen to twice their normal size, and while her temperature had dropped, she was still plenty warm. Even though the twins were nearly two, being ill made them demand to nurse, then fuss while doing so.

Kaaren stroked the soft hair back from where it lay plastered on the baby's forehead. At the stroking, Grace opened her eyes, one half-swollen shut, and stared at her mother. "Oh, to be knowing what you would say, little one," Kaaren whispered. Whispering, shouting, neither did any good. Grace was born the second twin and had never heard a sound.

Kaaren shifted the child to the center of her chest, with Grace's cheek against her mother's throat. She always seemed to settle best in that position, and Kaaren resumed her humming. She kept the chair moving and let her eyes fall shut. As always, when Grace cuddled like this, Kaaren picked up where she had left off before Lars woke up. *Heavenly Father, how do I help this little one thou hast given me? Thou art all-knowing, all-loving, my Father. Teach me about the world she lives in. How will she join in with other children? How do I keep her safe?*

Surely as if He stood right behind her — or was speaking heart to heart — she knew the words: *You just love her and I will keep her safe.*

Kaaren felt the burn of tears behind her eyes and at the back of her nose. Both began to run. *Father, I love her so much, and at the same time, I can't leave anyone else out.* She waited, peace stealing around her shoulders like love from a warm hand.

Be not afraid. You are mine. Be not afraid.

Kaaren wanted to fall on her knees. She wanted to sing and dance in a meadow of light. She wanted to praise her Lord.

"Why are you crying?" Lars and Sophie stopped beside the rocker. Sophie lay against her father's shoulder, a thumb barely held between slack lips. She sucked once and slept on.

Kaaren shook her head, unable to speak.

Lars wiped her tears with the edge of the

sheet she had thrown over her shoulder. "I think we can put them back to bed, don't you?"

She nodded and sniffed. Was it really God who had spoken? She'd heard people say "God told me" this or that but never really believed she would hear Him, or feel Him, or whatever it was that had just happened. *Be not afraid,* He'd said. Had she been afraid?

Lars laid Sophie in the bed first and then took Grace from her mother's arms and laid her next to her sister. Before he had time to draw up the sheet, Sophie had put an arm across her twin, as she'd been doing since they were only weeks old. Kaaren stood beside Lars, marveling at the picture the two made. One dark, one fair, both with swollen cheeks and a bright flush on their round faces.

Lars put his arm around Kaaren's waist and drew her close to him. "I believe God has something special in mind for these two," he whispered in his wife's ear.

"How do you come to know that?" Kaaren thought back to the early months when Lars couldn't bear to hold Grace or even touch her.

"I know this is strange, but it seemed a few minutes ago that God was walking right beside me. It was like I could hear Him or feel Him, and He said not to be afraid." Lars spoke with a voice of wonder. "You think I am going crazy in these middle hours of the night?"

Kaaren pulled a hanky out from her nightgown sleeve and blew her nose. The tears had slowed but still one followed another. "No, my husband, I believe we have been given a miracle, for I knew the same thing. That is why I cry." She looked up to see tears in his eyes also. "We are so blessed. Two beautiful daughters and a fine healthy son. Maybe Trygve won't catch the mumps." But Kaaren knew that the way Grace and Sophie patted and kissed their nine-month-old brother, this was highly unlikely.

Lars wrapped his arms around her, and she leaned into his chest. Was God standing with His arms around them? She surely felt it was so. All she could think was *Thank you, Father, thank you* over and over until, back in bed, she fell asleep, safe in the crook of her husband's arm.

When she woke, she lay alone in the bed. She knew Lars was over milking cows in the big barn next to Ingeborg's house. He had let her sleep. She looked around the room, wondering what had awakened her. The babies weren't fussing. All was quiet in the soddy. She slipped from under the sheet and went to stand at the screen door.

Outside, the hush before the sun broke the horizon lay gentle on her ears. Off across the pasture she could hear one of the men whistle for Thorliff's dog, Paws. A cow mooed and another answered. A rooster crowed, and with the sound, the birds left off their twittering in the eaves and broke into their morning chorus, welcoming the sun and another day. Inhaling deeply of honeysuckle, roses, and morning dew made her sniff again.

She reveled in the coolness of the hard-packed earth floor on her bare feet. After the heat of the last days, this morning's freshness felt like a gift. While the soddy remained cooler than the frame house during the hot days, there were no windows to open for the cross breezes.

The men promised to build her a house this fall. But the dark interior of the soddy didn't bother Kaaren as it did Ingeborg. Once they had whitewashed the walls and sealed off the leaks in the roof, besides adding the lean-to, she loved her home.

She dipped still-warm water from the reservoir into a pan, washed, and as soon as she'd dressed, wound her waist-length hair that Lars called liquid gold into the bun she wore at the base of her head. Sometimes she thought of trying a new hair style, but this way was so simple. A bun during the day, a long braid at night, except when Lars unbraided her hair and ran his fingers through the richness of it.

The thought of what followed brought a warmth pooling in her belly. She looked at the face reflected in the small mirror Lars had brought one day from St. Andrew. The warmth had spread to her cheeks too. She smiled at the pinkness. They'd been married three years this month. And look at all the richness God had bestowed upon them. With her apron firmly tied about her waist, slim again after being stretched to far beyond what she'd thought skin could stretch, she went over to check on her three still-sleeping babies.

As she looked down upon the twins, she couldn't believe her eyes. The swelling was gone. They both lay on their sides, nestled together spoon fashion, and both tiny ears lay smooth against their heads, not lost in the mumps that had reminded her of chipmunks hoarding their seeds for the winter. Did mumps usually go away this quickly? Trygve lay in his usual position, rump in the air, knees bent underneath him as if ready to scoot out the door.

She took the gift of extra moments, picked up her Bible, and went outside to sit on the bench beside the door. She turned to the Psalms, beginning with the first and reading it aloud to contribute her part to the swelling morning symphony. Praise the Lord, indeed. She could do no other. And when she closed her eyes in prayer, she promised, "God, I will store this night and day away in my heart, like thy Word says Mary did. I know it was so she could take it out and look at it again later when she needed the blessing."

Kaaren prayed for the sick children at Ingeborg's — Andrew had shared his mumps with the others — and for Metiz who had not been feeling well. By the time she had prayed for the men and their work for the day, the family in Norway as Bridget prepared to leave home and come to the new country, her friends, the family all around them, she knew she'd better hurry to get breakfast on the table. Any day now harvest could begin and these few wondrous minutes would seem even more precious. She threw in a prayer for the quilting meeting on Saturday. It now looked as though she maybe could go. If the mumps really were gone.

When Lars came home with a partial bucket of milk for their use, he set it on the counter along the wall and kissed her neck as she stood turning bacon at the stove.

"Did last night really happen, or did I dream it all?" The breath of his soft words tickled her neck.

"Go see." She pointed to the babies' bed.

He returned, shaking his head. "Do children always get well this fast?"

Kaaren shook her head and smiled up at him. "Just another of God's miracles."

"And to think before I married you, I not only didn't believe in miracles, but God seemed to be just a mighty person in a long story." He sneaked a slice of crisp bacon off the warming shelf. "You want I should toast the bread?"

Kaaren nodded. "That would be nice. There's cream for the plum sauce, and the eggs will be ready in a minute."

She heard the first squeak from the twins. "And just in time too."

7

"Penny?"

She heard his voice but felt more like yelling or hiding than answering. Where in all that was necessary had he been? She glanced at the clock above the sink. Four o'clock. He'd been gone for more than six hours without mentioning at all that he might be gone.

It seemed to Penny she had spent half her life waiting for Hjelmer Bjorklund. And all that in the two years she'd known him.

Just then she heard the tinkle of the bell above the shop door. Instead of answering Hjelmer's call, she pushed through the curtain hanging over the doorway that separated the store from the house. "Coming," she called.

Seeing no one in the store, Penny raised her voice. "Hello?"

"Me here."

"Metiz!" Penny knew the voice. She hurried to the counter, checking each aisle as she went. "Where are you? This is the first time you've come to my store." She found the woman studying the display of knives. With her black hair gone gray and her snapping dark eyes, she so often reminded Penny of a gray squirrel. The variety of knives were perfectly arranged in a circle on a square piece of wood, all the points meeting in the center. Penny extended her hand. "How have you been?"

Metiz clasped Penny's hand in both of hers. While gnarled and dark like walnut stain, the hands sent messages of both strength and comfort. The old woman looked deep into Penny's eyes, then smiled, her eyes nearly disappearing within the folds and creases of skin.

"No baby yet, but will come." She patted Penny's cheek. "No worry."

Penny started to say something, then stopped. She'd heard Metiz make statements like this before and found them to always come true. Had she been thinking about a baby? Not that she was aware of. After all, she and Hjelmer had only been married a couple of months.

"What brings you to my store?"

"Knife for Baptiste. Good knife."

"Does Baptiste know you are buying him a knife?"

Metiz shook her head. "Surprise."

"Good. I had a surprise today." Penny lifted the knife board down.

"What?" Metiz stroked the handles of the knives with a reverent finger. "Fine."

"Thank you. I met a cousin today, a real honest-to-goodness member of my family. He came in looking for boots. Can you believe that? In *my* store."

"Cousin?" Metiz tipped her head just the slightest.

"Cousin. He is the son of my father's older sister." With great effort Penny kept her feet from dancing out a tune on the wood floor.

"He out back cutting wood?"

Leave it to Metiz — she never missed a thing.

"Yes, he is."

"Big heap."

Penny grinned. "He doesn't seem to mind hard work." She dropped her voice. "I don't remember my relatives, and I haven't heard from anyone, brothers or sisters either, since my father and mother died and all the children were sent to different homes. I always thought I would find them one day." She stared at the carved horn handle of one of the knives, then to Metiz. "Maybe the someday is beginning now."

"Family good. Friends good." Metiz

pointed to the skinning knife set in a carved bone handle. "That one good for boy."

Oh, that's the most expensive knife I have. Now what to do? She knew Metiz wouldn't have enough money to pay for it. She turned the board over and untied the thong that held the knife in the display.

"How much?"

"A lot. One of the other knives will cost less."

"No." The old woman swung the pack from her shoulder to the floor. Bending over, she pulled out three rabbit-skin vests, two pairs of beaded moccasins from deer hide, and four knife sheaths, also from deer-skin. "You need more?"

Penny shook her head. "This is plenty." She put the knife in one of the sheaths. "Here, this is yours now."

"Good." Metiz tucked the knife and sheath back in her pack. "You sell. I make more."

"I'd be proud to trade with you." Penny fingered the soft rabbit fur on the vests. "These are beautiful." She set them on the shelf. "Come, I must write this all down."

"I walk around store, all right?" Metiz made a circular motion with her hand.

"Of course." Penny turned at the tinkle of the bell again. But when she looked up, she saw a most familiar tall man removing his hat and searching the store. Her heart recognized him almost before her eyes. His eyes were a dead giveaway that he was born a Bjorklund.

"What does one have to do to get waited on here?" He turned at the tapping of her heels on the floorboards. "Penny, guess what?"

"I've been guessing for six hours." She stopped several feet away from her husband, hands on her hips, willing herself to stay stern. She stared at his top shirt button, knowing if she looked at his smiling mouth she'd be forced to smile back.

"I didn't have time to let you know I was leaving."

"Really?" Her tone said anything but.

"Ja, a man leaned out one of the train windows at the water stop and asked if I knew Hjelmer Bjorklund." In his enthusiasm, Hjelmer's Norwegian accent became more pronounced, even though he'd worked hard to lose it when he lived and worked in St. Paul. "When I said I was him, he invited me to ride along to Grafton with him. He sells farm machinery and asked if I might be interested in handling a line of machinery here at the blacksmith shop."

"And you said?"

"After listening to all he had to say and looking at pictures of some of the new reapers and binders, I said yes. Especially now with harvest about to begin. All the farmers will be coming soon to deliver their wheat to the sack house. They've even come up with a steam tractor. Wait until you see that. Hiram — that's the fellow's name — says the tractor will take the place of horses for pulling machinery in the future. I'll have some pieces right out where the local farmers can look them over while they wait for their wagons to be weighed and unloaded."

"And they can have a piece of pie and a cup of coffee while they wait too." In her eagerness to tell him of her own adventure for the day, she'd forgotten all about how angry she'd been.

Hjelmer asked, "So that's who's chopped all the wood and is now stacking it?"

Penny nodded and leaned closer to whisper, "I knew he couldn't afford the boots, but he sure needed them. I invited him to stay because he's the only family I have out here."

"You have plenty of family, just not blood relatives. Agnes and Joseph been your family far longer than your real one."

"True. But I still want to know about my

brothers and sisters. Someday I want to see them again, know how they are, send letters back and forth. Maybe some of them would like to come west and homestead or buy land."

"There's not much of either available right around here."

"I know that, but I was thinking. Maybe Ephraim would like to help in the store. That way I can cook and bake and offer dinner to travelers and workingmen."

He nodded. "That's a good idea. And if he doesn't want to help in the store, he could probably help me refit wheels once harvest starts. Also, I know Haakan and Lars could use another hand. There's plenty of work around here for anyone who wants to work."

"You suppose Ephraim can stay with Olaf over at the sack house? We're going to have to make this house larger pretty soon."

"Don't know why not. The wedding isn't for a couple of weeks." He reached for her hand. "You're not trying to tell me something, are you?"

Penny stared at him, feeling about as blank as she knew her face looked. "Telling you something? About what?"

"About needing a bigger house. Are you in the family way already?"

"Sorry, no. But that's the second time today someone mentioned it." She told him of her strange conversation with Metiz and about the beautiful things they'd traded.

Later that evening, with Ephraim settled on a pallet at the sack house, Penny and Hjelmer both sat at their kitchen table, she with her record books for the store, he with a farm equipment catalog.

When he looked up to see her chewing the end of her pencil, he said, "All right, what is going on in that golden head of yours? I can hear ideas popping like popcorn."

"If I could find someone to bring in fresh-baked bread every day and if along with the cheese we had some kind of meat, people off the train could stop and buy their dinners right here and not have to go on to Grafton. Reverend Solberg said today he would love to buy bread here if we had it."

"So, ask Agnes if she would like to bake for you. Seems to me she's been down in the dumps lately." He turned another page. "See, here's a picture of that tractor I told you about." He turned the catalog so she could see.

"It looks gigantic."

"It is kind of unwieldy right now, but Hiram said that will change."

"This Hiram, he made a big impression

on you." She looked up from studying the picture of the tractor. The man steering it looked like a dwarf, the thing was such a monster. "This tractor looks like it could eat a team of horses and not even burp."

Hjelmer chuckled. "Steam is the power of the future. You watch."

Silence fell for a time. Penny finished adding her columns and put the record book off to the side. "Hjelmer, I've been thinking."

Hjelmer groaned. "How come every time you've been thinking, I have more to do?"

"That's not true." She stopped. "Well, not always anyway."

"You got any coffee made?"

"Now, don't change the subject. About this machinery thing." She paused, chewing on her bottom lip.

"Out with it. You have that look about you."

"Well, Mrs. Valders was in today for a few things. She only comes when Anner is off to Grafton or Grand Forks or some such. He doesn't want her to trade here, just like he won't ask you to shoe his horses or sharpen his plowshares and such."

"I know. All because he says I cheated him out of that land. I bought that piece fair and square. In fact, I paid Booth more than the going rate."

"Anner is holding a grudge."

"Ja, and Pastor Solberg preached on that last Sunday. Sometimes I think that the people who need to hear the lesson the most ignore it the easiest." He shut the catalog. "Why, now I wouldn't sell him that land if he were the last man on —" He stopped his ranting enough to catch Penny's raised eyebrow. "Well, I won't. Besides, Anner can't afford it."

"How do you know?"

"Word gets around."

Penny laid her pencil down. "You could lease him the land." She kept her voice soft and gentle.

"Johnson is farming it just fine. If he says he don't want it anymore, then I'll make other arrangements."

"I just thought if . . ."

"If what?"

"If he was farming that land, then he'd, well, he'd feel obligated to —"

"I don't want no one coming to me because of obligation." Hjelmer got to his feet and paced the room. "If he wants me to fix his wagons and such, fine, I'll do that, but if he wants to drive clear to Grafton, that's his problem." He turned and strode back to the window. "Besides, he's only hurting himself. No skin off my nose."

Penny watched the red rise on Hjelmer's neck. While he talked as if this didn't matter, his body screamed otherwise. Was there more to this than she thought? Hjelmer hadn't done anything illegal when he'd bought Mr. Booth's land and sold part of it again to the railroad. She had talked with Haakan and been reassured about that. But it had been a mite sneaky. In the "gray area," as her aunt Agnes called it.

And Hjelmer had made a good profit. That's what stuck in the craw of some of the farmers. Besides, he still had the extra land the railroad hadn't bought up.

She'd heard her husband referred to as "the gambler." He had promised her he wouldn't play poker anymore, at least not for money. But if the men got together to play cards, she didn't mind if he went.

She nibbled on her bottom lip. Was it all a matter of jealousy?

What would it cost them in the long run?

8

"You're sure you don't mind?"

"No. I told you I'd take care of the store." Hjelmer slipped the neck loop of the canvas apron over his head and knotted the ties behind his back. "If someone needs a blacksmith, I'll put up a 'see me out back' sign. Besides, all the women will be at the church anyway."

"Ephraim said he would help." Penny checked her bag to make sure she had plenty of quilt pieces. Since she started selling fabric in her store, she kept the leftovers from each bolt for the quilting bees.

"You want me to train him in the bookkeeping and wrapping of packages?"

"No. I will do that this week." She glanced around the kitchen one more time, sure that she was forgetting something. "You can always send Ephraim over to get me if you need me. It's not like the church is miles away or anything."

"Penny." His tone of voice and the look in his eyes brought a smile to her lips and chased away the frown between her eyes.

She laughed. "I'm acting like a brand-new mother hen trying to keep track of her one and only chick, aren't I?"

"That's a fair description." He fluttered his hands like he was trying to shoo chickens into the coop, or out of it, as was the case in this instance. "You'll be late."

"And I live the closest." As Penny gathered her bags, the bell tinkled over the shop's door. "Don't take any wooden nickels."

Hjelmer raised his right eyebrow.

Penny slipped out the back door as he parted the curtains to the store. If she was like this about the store, what would she be like with a new baby? she wondered. The thought brought on another smile. What a glorious Saturday morning! Today they were hoping to finish tying off the quilt the ladies had made as a wedding present for Goodie and Olaf. Usually they quilted the pieced wedding-ring pattern in even stitches, but there hadn't been time to get another one finished since she and Hjelmer had married in the spring. As Agnes had said, they'd better get more quilters the way the weddings were popping up.

Ingeborg had promised to make sure Goodie stayed home with something special to do, and since the twins were doing poorly with the mumps, along with Andrew and Ellie, this was perfect. Penny sneaked a little skip into her fast walk across the four acres to the church. Now that the Bjorklunds had plotted Blessing out in acre parcels ready for sale, she thought of the people who might buy there.

Olaf Wold managed the sack house, where the community's wheat was stored, and had broken sod to build a home on the acre he'd bought right next to it. That was another thing the community would be doing before harvest — raise a house for the newlyweds.

Would there be more businesses? Like what? With the blink of an eye, Penny could see her store expand to include an eating establishment, much larger than the two tables she'd been thinking of. What if they had a hotel? Or at least a rooming house. She'd heard tell of someone who wanted to open a saloon.

"I know that's one thing I'm going to bring up for discussion today," she promised the crow that flew overhead, his raucous cry a bass note in the singing of the prairie grasses. While Haakan and Lars had hayed this entire area, the grass had sprouted again, thanks to the spring rains.

Now the stalks stood golden like wheat, only riper and bending to harmonize with the always present wind.

"You surely do seem happy this morning," Agnes Baard called from her wagon seat.

"Oh, Tante Agnes, on a day like today, who wouldn't be?" Penny said with a grin as big as the sun.

"Anji for one."

"How come she's not with you?" Agnes's daughter usually came along to take care of the smallest children while their mothers were busy quilting.

"Her neck is still puffy from the mumps. My land, that epidemic sure ran through the families. I think every child in the area had chipmunk jaws, some sicker than others. Ingeborg told me even the twins had them, but Kaaren said that the night before last a miracle happened at their house."

"A miracle?" Penny tied Agnes's horse to the hitching post and removed the bridle. Then while her aunt climbed down, Penny unhitched the horse and tied him again to one of the wagon wheels on a long line so he could graze. Together they carried in their baskets of food and quilting supplies. Back before they had a church and the group was smaller, they met in homes and the hostess made a pot of soup or stew, and the others brought the rest of the meal. Now they all brought sandwiches and a dessert of some kind.

"So, tell me about the miracle."

"I'll let Kaaren do that. After all, it's her story."

"Then why'd you bring it up? You know how much I hate waiting," Penny said.

"Seems you'd be over that by now. The good Lord put you in the waiting room for training, I think."

"Waiting for Hjelmer was different. And you have to admit, it paid off." Penny began laying out the pieces of material she'd brought.

"Waiting is waiting."

"Speaking of waiting, how's Petar?"

"He's not waiting, he's pining. That little chit running off like that near to broke his heart."

"I never did like Clara Johnson much, anyhow. She always thought she could get any boy if she shook her blond curls and twitched her —"

"Penny!"

"Nose." The younger woman raised her eyebrows. "Why, Tante Agnes, what did you think I was going to say?" Her chuckle carried a bit of impishness in it. "Besides, I heard that things weren't going quite so well for Miss Johnson. Like she's still a 'Miss,' not a 'Mrs.' As you always said, she made her bed, now she has to lie in it."

"That might be what I said, but I ain't too sure that's proper talk for church, and besides, that's gossip." Agnes sat down with a sigh.

Penny studied her aunt. Agnes used to be a full-figured woman, with a laugh that shook not only her bosom but a body as strong as a man's. Now her feet seemed permanently swollen, as though the rest of her had seeped downward and pooled between her toes and her knees. While Agnes's smile still came regular-like, Penny realized she hadn't heard her aunt really laugh in a long while. Ever since her last baby was stillborn. And that was some time ago.

"Tante Agnes?" Penny knelt at her aunt's knees. "Are you all right? Truly?"

"Why, a'course, child. What could be wrong? As you said, this is a day for everyone to be happy."

Penny took her aunt's gnarled hands in her own. "You would tell me . . . if . . . if something were indeed wrong? Wouldn't you?"

"Ah, Penny, my eldest 'daughter,' you know I couldn't love you more if you'd come from within me."

Penny nodded. She saw Ingeborg standing in the doorway but didn't let on when Ingeborg raised a finger to her lips. She looked up at her aunt.

Agnes had a faraway look in her eyes, as if she could see something the others didn't.

The jingle of harness and other voices let Penny know they didn't have much time. "That's not what I asked you."

"I know." Agnes came back. "There's something, but I ain't sure what. I been asking of the Lord, but He ain't seen fit to answer yet."

"Do you hurt anywhere?"

"No more'n usual. I get tired more easily." Agnes cupped her hands around Penny's jaw. "The good Lord is just giving me a chance to thank Him for all things, even when I'm not too sure what they are. Or where they're leading. You might just think once in a while to say an extra prayer for me."

"I will." Penny got to her feet as a group of women came chattering through the door. As soon as she had a chance, she cornered Ingeborg.

"Do you have any idea what's wrong with Tante Agnes?" she asked without preamble.

Ingeborg shook her head. "Not for certain, but she's never been the same since the stillborn baby. I was there with her. She took it mighty hard in her heart, and it seems like her body never got over it either."

"Was it a hard birth?" Penny kept her voice low and tried to look unconcerned, as if they were having any normal kind of visit.

Ingeborg thought a moment. "Not so terrible hard, but the baby had been dead some time. I think she knew that long before the pains came." Ingeborg leaned a bit closer. "Your tante Agnes sets great store by babies, you know. She don't feel right if'n she don't have one hanging on her skirts or in her arms."

"I know."

"Guess it's about your turn to have the babies and let her love 'em as much as possible."

"Guess we'll have to leave that in the good Lord's hands, as someone we know would say."

"Would say what?" Kaaren, with the pieced quilt-top over her arm, stopped beside them.

"I'll tell you later." Ingeborg raised her voice. "We better get at it, if we're going to get this done. Goodie suspects something is going on, since she helped make two others."

Laughter rippled through the gathering group. While two women set up the wooden frame, several others laid out the sheeting, then the wool batting made from the poorer-grade fleece from around the legs and necks of the sheep. Since Ingeborg had the largest flock, she donated many of the battings. Finally the top was laid in place and the three layers pinned and fastened into the frame.

"You think maybe we should tie this one, what with everyone being so busy with getting in the garden and such?" Mrs. Dyrfinna Odell asked.

"I thought we already decided to tie it," Penny said.

"Well, you know, Miz Peterson would think then we don't care about her as much as the others. Once you start a tradition, you got to make sure no one feels slighted," Mrs. Hildegunn Valders said, surveying the quilt on the frame. She shook her head. "This one don't have so many nice colors as the one we made for Solveig."

"I brought extra materials," Penny said. "But that's for the next top, isn't it?"

"You want we should take some of those squares out and add in others?" The timid voice of Mrs. Brynja Magron could hardly be heard above the children laughing outside.

"No. We have not the time for that. It will just have to be as it is," said Hildegunn. Certain that no one would argue with her, she took a seat at the frame. "Brynja, you sit there and, Dyrfinna, you there." She pointed to the seats on either side of her. "Penny, do you want to take the other side? Or Kaaren?"

"Why don't we put two to a side, and we can get finished faster?" Ingeborg suggested.

"Then who will lay out the next one?"

"And cut the pieces?"

Brynja and Dyrfinna spoke nearly at the same time.

"I wish Kaaren would read to us while we sew," Brynja went on. "Remember when she read the Psalms? That was one of my favorite meetings."

Kaaren and Penny exchanged looks, their thoughts obvious. Brynja Magron with two opinions at one meeting? Would wonders never cease?

"Well, I'm sure if Kaaren is willing . . . that does leave us with one less to stitch, you know."

By this time everyone had taken their places, some around one table choosing pieces as soon as they were cut and stitching the squares together for the wedding-ring pattern. The others sat around the sides of the quilt frame.

"Before we begin with the reading, I have something I wish we could talk about." Penny raised her voice so all could hear her.

"Why, whatever would that be?" Mrs. Odell asked.

"That will wait until we have been edified by our readings," Mrs. Valders said with a nod of her head. The bit of lace she wore on her upswept hair bobbed as if it, too, thought other ideas frivolous.

Penny bit her lip to keep from saying what she was thinking, but a wink from Ingeborg and a secret smile from Kaaren helped her settle back. A nod and a smile from Agnes beside her made Penny feel like one of them, not like the young-woman-who-should-listen-to-her-elders feeling she got from Mrs. Valders.

Kaaren began with Psalm 118. " 'This is the day that the Lord hath made, let us rejoice and be glad in it.' "

"Amen" came from several places.

As she continued moving from one Scripture verse to another and reading some that were requested, even the shouts and laughter from the children outside seemed to fade away at the beauty of the words and the power of the promises. "Fear not . . ."

While Kaaren was searching for another psalm just requested, one of the women confessed, "It is easy to say not to be afraid in the summer like this when we are all together, but sometimes in the winter when the wind and the wolves are howling at my door, I'm so frightened my teeth chatter. I will hold this day in my mind to comfort me when winter comes again."

"That wind makes me think of Satan prowling around. It is him, not the wolves howling, I feel sure," Ingeborg added with a shudder.

"Nevertheless, God says He will gather us under His wing as a hen does her chicks. That picture comes to me when I begin to be afraid," Kaaren said softly. "And again, He says He will hold us in the palm of His hand."

"And against His bosom."

"He says He is always with us." Mrs. Odell turned to Agnes. "Can you beat that?"

"Now, now, ladies, let us remember to be reverent. These aren't words to be taken lightly," Mrs. Valders scolded.

Penny felt her aunt nudge her knee. She ducked her chin so the smile that tickled the corners of her lips wouldn't seem like sacrilege. Did God really expect them to go around with long faces all the time?

Kaaren must have read her mind, for next she read, " 'Praise the Lord. Let them praise his name in the dance; let them sing praises unto him with timbrel and harp.' "

After Kaaren finished reading Psalm 149, Mrs. Valders pushed her chair back. "We need to switch places now. Thank you, Kaaren, for your beautiful reading."

"I think a prayer would be in order now." Mrs. Magron brought on more surprised looks.

"Oh, well, I . . ." Mrs. Valders huffed before looking again to Kaaren. "If Kaaren is willing to lead us, I suppose we can take the time."

Kaaren nodded gravely, but Penny saw the twinkle in her eyes before they all bowed their heads.

"I have an idea," Kaaren said, her voice as gentle as the dawn. "I will begin the prayer, and then if any of you have something to add, speak up, and afterward, I will begin the Doxology and we can close with that."

"Well, I never . . ." Mrs. Valders muttered under her breath.

"Father in heaven, we come before thee with hearts full of praise for all the gifts thou hast bestowed upon us. Thou art our God and we are thy people, the sheep of thy pasture. We thank thee for this day and for the time we have together." With that, Kaaren paused and a sigh slipped around the room. Silence reigned.

Mrs. Odell whispered into her clasped hands, "I . . . I thank thee for my family and my friends who help make living here on the prairie less of a burden."

Penny bit her lip. Why was praying out loud with others present so difficult? She nearly sighed in relief when another voice began.

"Father, I thank thee for the new baby that will be coming to our house. I ask that thou keep thy hand upon me and the babe to keep us safe. Frank wants a son again, and if it be thy will, I will rejoice with another boy."

Penny knew Mrs. Veiglun wanted a daughter. Her first had died in infancy. Why did men think boys were so much more important than girls? She corralled her wayward thoughts, knowing she needed to pray aloud to overcome the fear, if for no other reason.

"Father God, I . . ." Her mind acted like a blackboard wiped clean. She worried her lip again. The silence stretched. She could hear Agnes breathing beside her. "I pray for my tante Agnes that thy hand may bring strength and renewed health to her, that she will again go about with singing. Father, I miss her laughter." Penny fought the tears rising in her throat. "I thank thee in advance for hearing my prayers." She wanted to say more, so many things needed praying for, but the words wouldn't — couldn't pass the pocket of tears. So she prayed them silently: for her newfound cousin, for her store, and for Hjelmer, that he would find a way to mend the fences his land-buying had brought down.

Others prayed; some sniffling could be heard. The silences between the words no longer seemed to stretch and plead for someone to say something. Now the silences were part of the prayers and were filled with peace. When Kaaren began to sing the Doxology, she hadn't sung more than two notes before the others joined in.

"Praise God from whom all blessings flow. . . ."

Penny glanced upward, sure their music could be seen rising like smoke from an ancient altar, drifting heavenward and directly into the Father's ear. She swiped at the tears that dripped onto her hands before the final amen sang out in full harmony.

"My," said Mrs. Odell as the last note hung on the air before fading away. "That sounded like angels singing. I know it did."

She blew her nose and wiped her eyes with her handkerchief.

"Guess we better get to stitching." Agnes tucked her handkerchief away in her pocket. She shot Kaaren a look of gratitude. "Mange takk, my friend. You surprise me over and over at the way God uses you in our lives. Like the apostle Paul said, 'I thank my God for every remembrance of you.'"

"I say you have to tell us about your miracle." Penny leaned toward Kaaren. "What happened?"

Kaaren smiled gently and told about the sensation both she and Lars had felt of Jesus being right with them, and the next morning the twins were healthy.

"God be praised," Brynja whispered.

"Amen to that," Agnes added.

As the chatter about houses and gardens resumed, Penny finally got up the nerve to broach the subject she'd been wanting to bring to the women. "Did any of the rest of you hear about the man who wants to open a saloon in Blessing?"

Talk about a dead silence. The room shut down with a gasp.

"A saloon?" Mrs. Odell squeaked. "Surely not in our town."

"No one has come to us about buying one of the parcels of land and building such a thing." Ingeborg looked at Kaaren, who also shook her head.

"What about the property to the south? Who owns that now?" Mrs. Veiglun asked.

"Why, I guess Hjelmer does. But he wouldn't . . ." Penny trailed off at the look she received from Mrs. Valders and her two cohorts.

"Hjelmer will do anything to make a dollar." Hildegunn Valders said the words as if God himself had spoken.

Penny leaped to her feet, the pieced squares in her lap flying in all directions. "That's not true!"

Hildegunn straightened her spine and threw back her shoulders. Fire shot from her eyes, and her lips cut off each sound like the sharpest of shears. "Are you calling me a liar?"

"No, of course she ain't." Agnes put a hand on Penny's arm, drawing her back into her seat while at the same time placating Mrs. Valders with her other. "Now, we got something serious here to discuss and getting all het up won't help us a bit. We must let bygones be bygones. Ain't that what forgiveness is all about?"

"Humph."

The rude sound raised Penny's hackles another notch, but the hand on her arm never faltered. The old witch was acting like Hjelmer stole something from her personally instead of being a smart businessman.

"The question is" — Kaaren spoke in a firm but quiet voice — "what are we going to do about this?"

"What *can* we do?" someone else asked.

"We can let it be known that we do not want such a business in our town," Ingeborg said.

"As if the men would listen to us."

"Oh, I'm sure that we all have means of making our men listen." The smile and raised eyebrow combined to give Kaaren's lovely face the hint of mischief that brought snickers from around the room.

"We could talk with Reverend Solberg too."

"Ja, and . . ." The talk flowed with noddings and more than a few chuckles.

Penny looked over at Mrs. Valders. A sigh came up from her toes. Now she'd have to ask forgiveness for the way she felt about the bossy woman. How come she hadn't foreseen the rumpus her question would cause? All she wanted was to enlist the aid of the other women.

"You are not to worry your head about this," Ingeborg leaned close to whisper in Penny's ear. "You did right."

"Thank you," Penny whispered back. How lucky . . . she amended the word — *blessed* she was to have friends like Ingeborg and Kaaren. Back when the twins were born, she'd lived all those months at their house helping Kaaren with the tiny babies who had come so early. With all the time spent together, she felt as close to the two women as if they were her own sisters.

When the time came to break for dinner, they called in the children. Everyone sang grace and fell to their meal. With the desserts lined up on one of the tables and the coffee hot, the meal passed quickly. When they finished, the youngest children were laid on quilts to nap while the older ones went back outside to play.

As the quilting resumed, Ingeborg said, "You know, there is something that has been bothering me, and I thought maybe some of the rest of you mighta thought the same."

All eyes were trained on the speaker.

She waited a moment before continuing.

"I know we all want Blessing to grow and become a real town." She looked around the room, seeing nods of approval. "I been thinking that a bank might be a good thing to have here. Why should we have to take the train or the riverboat to Grand Forks or

Grafton to do our banking and . . . and then depend on the whim of someone who doesn't even know us to decide how our money can be used?"

"Why . . . why you have to be rich to start a bank," Mrs. Valders said, but while the words sounded like her normal know-it-all way, the question came through in her hesitant tone. It was as if she had shouted, "Don't you?"

Ingeborg nodded. "In a way, I suppose. Usually that might be the case, but what if we all pooled our money — you know, like the men are talking about a cooperative for our grain so that all the small farmers won't be at the mercy of the big mills setting the prices for wheat anymore. Look at us. We get together to sew quilts and build houses and harvest. We all work together and for each other."

The silence fell again as each woman looked around at her neighbors and thought her own thoughts. "I think a bank in Blessing is a fine idea," Mrs. Magron spoke up.

All the women looked at her as one. The mouse had spoken. For the third time that day.

"So . . . who knows anything about starting a bank?" Mrs. Valders looked to Ingeborg.

"I guess we'll just have to find out how to do it," Ingeborg said with a firm dip of her chin.

But Penny noticed that she clenched her hands together under the quilting frame. Could it be that Ingeborg wasn't as confident about starting a bank as she sounded? Or was something else bothering her?

9

"What do I know about starting a bank?" Ingeborg slapped the reins to signal the horse to speed up. Since Goodie had remained at home to take care of her daughter, Ellie, she also kept Kaaren's and Ingeborg's children with her, leaving Kaaren and Ingeborg time together. They'd taken advantage of the situation by letting the horse plod its way home.

"You know as much as any of us," Kaaren answered.

"That won't churn butter, let alone start a bank. We've all been on the other side of the desk. I suppose Mr. Brockhurst would tell me if I ask him."

"Why wouldn't you ask him?" Kaaren turned slightly on the hard wagon seat.

"If we begin a bank here in Blessing — we, meaning others besides us Bjorklunds . . ." She paused at Kaaren's slight sniff. "I know you are a Knutson, but you are still a Bjorklund too, and . . ." Ingeborg paused again. "Well, the truth of the matter is that we will be removing a sizable amount of money from Mr. Brockhurst's bank and starting up competition. He might not appreciate that, you know."

"I guess I hadn't thought about that."

Paws, Thorliff's caramel-and-white dog, welcomed them with staccato yips, jumping beside the wagon and racing around it, his tail spinning circles in his joy at their return.

"Good dog, Paws. Now, don't go running under the horse's hooves."

"You could write to Mr. Gould, couldn't you? Surely he knows plenty about starting a bank, or he could find out."

Ingeborg nodded. "Ja, I'm sure he does." She slowed the horse to a walk again. "There's just one little problem with writing to him." As the barns and houses drew nearer, Kaaren finally prompted her. "And what is that?"

"I think Haakan is just a bit jealous of my New York angel."

"What makes you think that?"

"He gets that tightening of the jawline when a letter comes. You have to look quick to see it, but . . ."

"But it is there, and you don't want to make him angry?"

"Yes. But you see, he has nothing to be angry or jealous about. Gould has been a good friend to all of us. From the moment he rescued me in New York until even looking for Hjelmer for us last year, why, whatever I would ask for, if he could bring it about, he would. Isn't that what friends do for one another? I only regret I have been able to do nothing for him in return."

"Maybe that is what is bothering Haakan."

"What, that I can do nothing in return?"

"No, more that maybe Mr. Gould can do more for you than Haakan can."

"That is tullebukk of him."

"Be that as it may . . ."

"So what do I do? Write the letter and not tell Haakan? Deal with Mr. Brockhurst myself and hope the man doesn't get upset?" She thought a moment. "Or maybe he'll give us the wrong information because he doesn't want another bank in the area. Uff da, why do things have to get so complicated?"

"Asking God for direction might be a good place to start." Kaaren's voice wore a smile.

"Ja, there is that too. But what if I don't like what He says?"

"Mor, Mor, Andrew . . . !" Thorliff's shouts interrupted the conversation, and the women turned their heads to see the boy running across the field, waving his arms and shouting.

"Now what?" Ingeborg slapped the reins again. Here she'd been dawdling and now there was a problem. "What is it?"

"Andrew fell out of the haymow, and now he won't wake up."

"Giddup!" She slapped the reins hard, startling the horse to break into a gallop. "Oh, dear God, please take care of my son. He's yours, but I want to keep him for a long time. Please, please." She lapsed into Norwegian, her English being too slow and stilted for the agony of her heart.

She pulled the horse to a stop and threw the reins to Kaaren just before Thorliff leaped up the back stoop of the frame house. Even so, Ingeborg hit the ground almost before the wagon finished rocking. "Take care of the horse, Thorliff," she ordered over her shoulder, her feet pounding up the four steps as she gathered her skirts in her fists so she wouldn't trip on the way.

Her heart hammered against her ribs as if she'd run clear home from the church.

"In here," Goodie called when Ingeborg burst through the door.

Andrew lay on the bed, eyes closed, a purple knot raising the damp cloth on the right side of his forehead. His face looked whiter than a snowbank.

Ingeborg sank to her knees beside the bed. "How long has he been like this?"

"Not long. It only just happened. Ellie came screaming to the house, and I went out and carried him in." While she spoke, Goodie took the cloth and, dipping it in a pan of cool water, wrung it out and laid it on the boy's forehead again.

"Has anyone told Haakan or gone for Metiz?"

Goodie shook her head and at the same time said, "Baptiste has gone for Metiz. Haakan is working over on the piece he bought from Polinski. Hans is caring for the twins. Baptiste took Trygve home along with Astrid."

Ingeborg stroked the curve of Andrew's cheek with gentle fingertips. "Oh, my son, please hear me. You must wake up now. I know you will have a headache, but you are strong and as hardheaded as the rest of the Bjorklunds." She paid no attention to her words but kept up the soothing murmur of mothers everywhere with sick children.

"How is he?" Kaaren entered the room and stopped beside Goodie.

"He don't even blink." Goodie clenched her hands until the knuckles turned white. "I shoulda been watching them two more closely. How many times have I said, 'Don't go playing near the trapdoor'? I tried to keep them out of the haymow and now look." She raised eyes filled with anguish. "Little Andrew might die cause I warn't careful enough."

Ellie, who'd been hiding at the foot of the bed, burst into loud sobs. "I wanted to play in the haymow." Tears ran between her tiny fingers as she hid her face in her hands.

Kaaren scooped Goodie's little daughter up in her arms. "There now. You mustn't carry on so. Andrew wouldn't want you to cry like this." She rocked the little girl and patted her back as she sobbed into Kaaren's shoulder.

"It could have happened if I was here too," Ingeborg said without looking up from her son's face. "You know I've told them they could play in the barn. Accidents happen. That is all." But while her words sounded so sensible, her heart cried out, *If only I had been here.* She felt a gentle hand on her shoulder.

She turned. "Metiz! Thank God you are here."

"You call. I come."

"Thank you." Ingeborg saw Thorliff and Baptiste huddling just inside the bedroom door. "You boys go on and start the chores. I'll call you if there is anything you can do.

Who is watching the little ones?"

"Hans. He said for us to come here. Andrew isn't going to die, is he?" Thorliff asked.

Ingeborg shook her head. "No, but sometimes when you get a bad bump on the head, sleep is the best thing for you. You watch, Andrew will be up and running around again soon. A bump on the head can't keep a Bjorklund like him down." If only she believed the words herself.

The very stillness of his body frightened her beyond belief. Andrew was normally moving from the time he got up until he collapsed in bed at night. Since the day he'd been born, he had given new meaning to the word motion. It seemed like years ago that he'd outgrown the need for a nap.

Right now, everything seemed like years ago. Ingeborg found herself breathing with her son. She held his hand while Metiz lifted the child's eyelids and laid her ear against his chest, gently probing the wound and the area around it.

"No break. Just a hard bump. We wait." She settled herself on the floor with her back against the wall.

"Is there nothing in your simples that can help him?"

Metiz shook her head. "Sleep best thing.

We sing to Great Spirit. He will hear."

But he's not just sleeping. If he were sleeping, he would wake when I call his name. Oh, Andrew, my son, my son. How long, O Lord, how long? Her attention journeyed back to the room at the sound of Metiz chanting her native tongue with a haunting refrain. The sound soothed her anxiety, and she found herself humming "Deilig er Jorden," a hymn she learned at her mother's knee. *Mor, what would you do now?* Her thoughts of panic couldn't exist in her mind at the same time as the hymn, so she forced herself to keep singing.

She could feel peace tiptoe into the room, shy as a fawn. As long as she hummed, it drew closer and wrapped her in its arms. It stole across the little boy, circled the old woman, and wrapped the others, too, in its warmth. Ingeborg knew with all her heart that if she turned quickly enough, she would see Jesus himself, or one of His angels, standing right behind her shoulder.

Her song shifted to "Blessed assurance, Jesus is mine . . ." The whispered words brought tears to her eyes. In that room, right that minute, she felt that "foretaste of glory divine." Though Andrew slept on, the fear had fled.

"This Jesus you sing of. Who he?" Metiz asked softly.

"The Son of the Great Spirit. We call the Great Spirit God and Jesus is His Son."

"His spirit here."

Ingeborg nodded. "Yes, He is."

"Bad spirit gone."

"I know."

"You talk to Andrew. He better soon."

"Goodie is starting supper, and I'm going home to care for the other children." Kaaren spoke after another time of singing softly. "Can I bring you anything?"

Ingeborg shook her head. "All I need is here."

"You want a drink of water?" Ellie pushed strands of sun-bleached hair from her wet cheeks as she crept close to Ingeborg.

Ingeborg reached out and gathered the little girl into her side. "Ja, I would like that. And when you come back, you can help me talk to Andrew."

"Will that wake him up?"

"Oh, I hope so."

When Ellie returned, Ingeborg drank the cool water and passed the dipper on to Metiz. The little girl crept back into the circle of Ingeborg's arm.

"What do I say to him?" Ellie asked.

"You could tell him about the chickens."

Ellie looked up, reproach in her light blue eyes. "He knows that."

Ingeborg made a smile come, although she didn't feel like smiling. "Don't matter. Just tell him."

Ellie climbed up on the bed and sat cross-legged on the sheet. "Andrew, it is almost time to feed the chickens, and you know I can't carry the bucket of feed by myself. You got to come help me. And if you aren't there, that big rooster is going to chase me again. I don't like him one bit, and he knows it." She went on reminding the sleeping boy of each of their favorite hens and the nest they found in the barn with a broody hen on it. She'd gotten out of the chicken yard and hidden herself away.

With only half an ear, Ingeborg listened to the child prattle on. Her throat had dried out with the singing, so she repeated Bible verses that she had memorized while riding on the plow. With the new machinery, the fieldwork no longer took every ounce of concentration, and so the few times the men allowed her in the field, she'd put the time to good use.

Dusk was purpling the fields when she heard the jingle of harness and Paws yelping his welcome home. Ellie lay curled beside Andrew, sound asleep, her breath coming in tiny puffs. Metiz sat with her back still against the wall and her chin on her chest. The heat and the quiet of the room had captured Ingeborg also. She had caught herself nodding off from time to time, but the sounds of the men returning from the fields brought her instantly alert.

The evening breeze lifted the yellow-and-white gingham curtains at the window and blew refreshing coolness across her cheek and neck.

"I watch. You go."

"Bless you, Metiz." Ingeborg rose to her feet, her knees cracking loud in the stillness. She rotated her shoulders and pressed her fists against the small of her back, arching over them. "How can you sit like that? I'm stiff and I sat on a chair."

Metiz only smiled at her and began her low humming chant again.

As Ingeborg entered the kitchen, Goodie turned from the stove, where she'd been stirring something that made Ingeborg's stomach set up a chatter of its own. "Any change?"

Ingeborg shook her head. "I'll go tell Haakan."

"I been prayin'."

"Mange takk." No matter how much Ingeborg tried to speak only English, in times like this, her mother tongue brought comfort.

Haakan finished swinging the heavy harness off the back of the horse and carried it to hang across the pegs on the barn wall before turning to her with a smile. The smile died at the look on her face. "What is it?"

Ingeborg kept the words gentle as she told him what had happened.

"He will be all right." There was no question in his tone, only absolute certainty.

"By the grace of God." She stepped into the shelter he offered by spreading his arms wide. Wrapped in his strong embrace, she settled her ear against his chest, the thudding of his heart steady and sure.

The dark horse that still wore its harness stamped a front foot and snorted.

"Ja, I am coming." After a kiss dropped on her forehead, Haakan released his wife and turned to finish the work at hand. "Where are the older boys?"

"They started chores early. Needed to be busy."

Haakan lifted the second harness off and set it on the pegs with the other. "I'll go help with the milking now, if you'll take these two out for a short drink and then to the pasture."

"You don't want them brushed down first?"

"That can wait for one of the boys. Who's with Andrew now?"

"Metiz." Ingeborg clutched her elbows with her palms. How much stronger she had felt when in the circle of Haakan's arms. "Don't you want to see him first? Andrew, I mean."

"I'll stop at the house before I go to the barn. Kaaren knows?"

Ingeborg nodded, then realizing he wasn't looking at her, added, "Ja." She fought against the words she wanted to say, to plead *Please hold me. I feel safer in your arms.* She won the battle over her fears, and as Haakan headed for the house, she led the horses to the trough by the well. They weren't at all pleased when she jerked them away after only a few deep draughts, pulling against the lead rope and dripping water on her arm.

"Come on, you get more later. You know you don't drink a bellyful when you are still sweaty." Slobbering on her seemed their revenge, as after deep sighs they followed her to the pasture gate. The first thing they did when released was trot over to the wallow and roll in the dust, grunting and kicking their hooves in the air.

"Oh, Andrew, how you would laugh at the picture they make. Please, God, let me

157

hear his belly laugh again soon."

Hans came from the hen house with a loaded basket as Ingeborg headed back to the house. "I done Andrew's chores," he said, the sadness in his eyes matching the droop of his mouth. "He's gonna be all right, ain't he?" One side of his tanned face still bore the traces of the mumps.

"Pray God he will."

"I been saying my prayers for him ever since I heard he got hurt. I heard people sometimes sleep a long time, weeks and months even. You think that could be Andrew?" The boy shifted from one bare foot to the other.

Ingeborg forced a smile to her mouth. At least she hoped it was a smile. "Metiz doesn't think he will sleep long. She said he will wake up soon."

His shoulders dropped in relief. "Metiz is smart. She knows lots of good things." He looked up again at Ingeborg. "It weren't Ellie's fault, you know. They both liked to play in the hay."

Ingeborg laid a hand on his shoulder. "Don't you even think such a thing. There's no fault for anyone. If this is the worst bump Andrew gets growing up, he'll be lucky. Remember how sick you were when you came to us?" At his nod, she continued. "You got well and Andrew will too, all by the grace of God."

She met Haakan coming down the steps from the back door.

"Don't you worry," he said with a smile that lighted his eyes and therefore hers. "It takes more than a bump on the forehead to keep a Bjorklund down for long."

The adults took turns sitting with the unconscious child through the evening. While the older boys came and went, whispering in the room as if afraid to disturb Andrew, Ellie remained by his side. Metiz only left the room for her supper and afterward resumed her place on the floor against the wall.

"Come, Ellie," Goodie said after the dishes were done and the kitchen cleaned up again. "It is time for you to go to bed."

The little girl shook her head, setting her pigtails to slap her cheeks from the force. "Andrew needs me."

"You can come see him first thing in the morning."

Another headshake, this one even more determined. When her mother picked her up to carry her to their soddy, Ellie let out a scream that made even Metiz wince.

"Andrew needs me here!" She flailed her arms, grabbing for anything to slow their progress.

Goodie gave her daughter a shake. "Now, behave yourself, or we will have to stop out by the woodpile."

"No, no!" The scream turned to the most pitiful of cries. "Please, Ma, let me stay."

Ingeborg shrugged. "There is no harm for her to stay. She can sleep on the floor by Andrew's bed. I'll fetch a quilt."

The cries turned to whimpers and ceased altogether. Ellie put her arms around her mother's neck. "Thank you, Ma."

Goodie kissed her daughter's cheek. "Now, you be good and don't cause no more problems."

"I'm good." As soon as her mother put her down, the little girl ran straight to Andrew's room and climbed right back up on the bed. She refused to sleep on the floor, curling up instead at the foot of the bed, with one hand on Andrew's leg.

Ingeborg hadn't the heart to force her to do anything else. Before morning she lay right beside Andrew and fell into a light sleep, knowing she would hear instantly if Andrew awakened.

But he slept on. Through the night and even while they changed his bed in the morning.

As each hour passed, Ingeborg fought her personal demons, the black hole of despair trying to suck her into its depths. Each time the pit yawned before her, she repeated another of her Bible verses, claiming peace and strength, hope and grace. Tears flowed when she repeated the Twenty-third Psalm, making her stumble over the verse about walking through the shadow of death. Surely God wasn't taking Andrew home; He wasn't going to let the boy sleep his life away.

Kaaren came in the afternoon and sat with her Bible on her lap, reading the passages she felt contained the most hope.

Andrew slept on.

The jingling of the horses' harnesses again brought Ingeborg from the sick room. One look at her husband, though, and she felt another weight settle on her shoulders. "Haakan, are you feeling all right?"

He looked at her through pain-glazed eyes. "I will be all right."

"But your face, your neck, they are swollen."

"I will be all right!" But when he raised his arms to lift the harness off the backs of the team, he fell in a heap on the ground.

10

"You have the mumps."

"How can you tell?"

"You look just like the children did — fat cheeks and neck. You're hot as the kitchen stove, and . . ."

"And I've got to get out to the barn." Haakan raised up on his elbows and tried to swing his legs over the edge of the bed. He fell back with a groan.

The roosters crowed in a duet that reminded Ingeborg how much time was passing. Haakan had passed out after they got him to the bed the night before and slept the night away.

Sweat broke out on Haakan's forehead as he gripped the edge of the bed frame with one trembling hand to pull himself up. "Help me, please."

"Haakan, you are too sick to milk cows or do anything else. I've heard tell that when adults get the sicknesses of childhood, they get terribly sick."

"Ja, well, I do not have time to be sick.

Once I'm on my feet, I'll be all right." He peered up at her standing at the bedside. "Why are you wiggling so?"

Ingeborg shook her head. "I am standing perfectly still. And if you need help to sit up, how can you walk to the barn, how can you even pull on your pants?"

"Would a dipper of water be too much to ask?" Haakan groaned when he tried again to roll to his side.

"No, I'll get it, but only if you promise you won't try to get up while I'm gone."

He muttered something under his breath.

Ingeborg took it to be agreement and headed for the bucket of water in the kitchen that she'd already fetched from the well. She'd just filled the dipper when she heard a thump that sounded like —

She dropped the dipper back in the bucket and flew to the bedroom. She wanted to be with Andrew in case he woke, yet Haakan needed her too.

Haakan lay sprawled on the floor by the bed, his silence frightening her as much as Andrew's did.

She knelt at his side and laid a hand against his cheek. Hot. Burning hot. She smoothed the swelling in his neck and sighed in relief when he groaned.

"Got . . . to . . . get . . . to . . . the . . . barn."

Each word took its toll, she could see by the white lines deepening around his eyes and bracketing his mouth.

"No, and now we have to get you back in bed. Can you help me?" She could hear Goodie come in the back door.

Haakan only groaned. "Water?"

Ingeborg shook her head. "If you had stayed in bed like I asked, you'd have had your drink by now. I dropped it when I heard you fall."

She felt a presence beside her and looked over her shoulder to find Metiz staring at the fallen man.

"Him bad."

"That is for sure. Would you please go ask Lars to come help me get him back in bed?"

"We do it."

"Is something wrong?" Goodie asked from the doorway but knelt at Haakan's side without waiting for an answer. "Oh, land, the mumps. He has them too." She shook her head. "Why couldn't he get 'em as a boy like the rest of them?"

Ingeborg nodded but without answering, knowing Goodie didn't expect an answer. "We've got to get him back in the bed."

"You want I should call the boys?"

Haakan groaned. "No, I don't want them to . . ."

"I know, man's pride." Goodie shook her head. She rocked back on her heels. "Way I see it, I take one arm, you t'other, and Metiz brace him from behind. Your legs got any strength a'tall?"

"They will." He spoke from gritted teeth.

The three women took their places.

"Now, on three?" Ingeborg looked each of them in the eye. "One, two, three." With that they got their shoulders under his arms and hoisted him to a sitting position.

He bit off a cry, his teeth clenched so tightly they could hear them grinding. His jaw whitened. Sweat broke out on his forehead.

"Haakan, can you push with your legs?"

"D-don't . . . kn-know."

Ingeborg looked at Metiz, asking the question silently that she couldn't ask aloud. *Why is he in such pain? Where is it coming from?*

Metiz shrugged. "Lift now."

Like beaching a wounded sea lion, they half rolled, half lifted him onto the bed.

As if they had a mind of their own, his hands went to cover his private parts.

Metiz and Goodie stepped back, offering him some privacy.

"Haakan." Ingeborg leaned close to his ear. "Is that where the pain is?"

165

He nodded. She wiped the sweat from his forehead, using the brief moment to try to understand. She knew he had the mumps. His swollen face and neck attested to that. But this other?

Goodie beckoned her from the doorway.

"I'll get you that water now," Ingeborg said as she turned to follow the other woman.

Once in the kitchen, Goodie spoke in a low voice. "I seen this before. When a grown man gets the mumps, it seems to settle in their privates. 'Tis terrible painful. Swelling like a . . . a . . ." She shook her head. "Terrible. They can't hardly pass water either. Your man is in for a bad time."

Ingeborg rubbed her forehead. How to help Haakan? "And Andrew, how is he?"

"Same." Metiz joined them. "Ellie still asleep at foot of bed."

Ingeborg could hear the cows bellering as they made their way to the barn. Either Lars or the boys had gone to get them. She glanced out the kitchen window. The lightening sky outlined the treetops that formed their eastern horizon along the river. By now the milking should be half finished, breakfast nearly ready, and the bread set for rising.

None of it was started, let alone done.

"Goodie, would you please go tell Lars

what is happening? Metiz, if you would take the dipper of water to Haakan?" At their nods, she turned for the stairs. "I have to see how Andrew is."

As the others went about their assigned tasks, she climbed the stairs with a heart so heavy she could barely lift her feet. The old thought *What am I being punished for now?* made her stumble on the top step. She knew if she turned, she would find the black pit yawning in the stairwell behind her. How she'd prayed during the long vigil at Andrew's side that the morning would bring a flutter of eyelids to her son's still face and his usual first words of the day, "I'm hungry, Mor." Andrew — always hungry, always moving — lay so still now. She forced herself to move close to the bed so she could see his chest rise.

"God, I felt so sure this would be the morning," she whispered.

The day's not over yet. She wasn't sure if she'd heard a voice, or if it was just a strong impression in her mind. She could have sworn she heard the black pit snap shut, as if angry at being overcome again.

Kneeling on the floor at Andrew's side, she laid her forehead on her clasped hands. "*. . . but with the trial will provide a way of escape that you might not fall into despair.*"

That verse and others rolled through her mind like a warm rain washing the dust from the air and leaves.

"Mange takk, heavenly Father," she whispered. No other words could slip past the tears rising in her throat and burning at the back of her eyes. But in her mind, she shot praises heavenward, basking in the peace that saturated the room and her soul.

In spite of the sadness of seeing her son so still, Andrew's room became a haven from the turmoil of caring for Haakan and trying to do her other chores at the same time. The cheese she'd planned to start that day still sat in the milk pans waiting. She could have watched the beans grow had she had time to go near the garden.

Thank God for Goodie, who made and baked the bread, cooked the meals, and made sure Andrew's chores were taken over by Hans.

"We really should start harvesting those wheat fields closest to the house," Lars said after supper. "Maybe I better talk to Baard and get going on it."

"I thought you planned to wait until after the house-raising?" Ingeborg and Lars were sitting on the back stoop, where they could catch a bit of the evening breeze.

"We did, but it's been so dry the wheat is

ripening faster than I thought it would. We could get a hailstorm any day and knock it all down, you know."

"I do know. But . . ." She fell silent, watching the sun paint a silver lining around the tops of the dark clouds on the horizon.

"It could be some time before Haakan is on his feet again." Lars stared at his hands, loosely clasped between his knees.

"I know." *What if those clouds dump hail on us tonight?* "Every day is so precious. You could start with the cutting in the morning. You think Thorliff or Baptiste could drive the horses while you keep the binder running?"

Lars nodded thoughtfully. "Could be. Baptiste, he is better with the horses. He don't go off in a daydream somewhere."

"Thorliff will have to run the trotlines then, besides taking the sheep out to graze."

"They were a big help in the barn this morning, not that they always aren't, but both Baptiste and Thorliff milk almost as good as a man now."

"I could take the team up to backset that last sod cutting." The words came before she had time to think.

"Now, Inge, you agreed to no more working the fields, remember? It just ain't seemly no more."

"Not that it ever was — seemly, that is.

169

Just necessary." Her mind skipped back to the hours of soul-crushing labor, breaking the sod with a walking plow behind the oxen. "With the new riding plow it is much easier."

"Ja. And between you and Kaaren, you already do the work of three women."

"Add Goodie and we make five."

"Pert near." He turned his head enough to smile at her over his shoulder. "I know Haakan will get out of that bed no matter what if you put on britches again and go back in the fields."

"Ja, well . . ."

"I got to git on home. I'll go tell Haakan what I — we decided."

"If he's awake."

"Ja, that too." Lars stood and stretched his arms over his head. "You planning on a trip to the Bonanza farm anytime soon?"

"I was, but now?" She shrugged. "Those chickens will just have to get bigger. Leastways they won't spoil. Penny is selling a lot of our cheese, so I don't have much of that to take."

She turned her head at the sounds of pounding feet in the house.

"Mrs. Bjorklund, come quick. You know, Andrew . . ."

Ingeborg leaped to her feet. *Dear Lord, now what?*

11

Ingeborg almost ran Goodie down in her haste to climb the stairs. She could hear Ellie babbling, but the words failed to penetrate the wall of her mind. "Please, God, please," she pleaded with each step.

She burst through the curtained doorway.

Ellie danced beside the bed. "See. I told you."

Ingeborg stopped as if she'd hit an ice wall.

Andrew blinked and smiled a sleepy smile. "Mor, I'm hungry."

With tears streaming down her face, Ingeborg fell on her knees beside the bed and she cupped a hand around his cheek.

"Why are you crying?" Andrew turned to look at her. "You sad?"

She shook her head, taking his hand in hers and kissing his palm. "No, Andrew, I am not sad at all. I am just so happy."

He gave her that look that said you-don't-make-sense-but-I-guess-it's-all-right. He'd learned it from his father, as did all boys.

Metiz and Goodie pushed aside the curtain and entered the room.

"See, Ma, I wasn't telling a story. Andrew's awake." Ellie turned to her mother.

"Hush, I can see." Goodie took the few steps to lay a hand on Ingeborg's shoulder. "I should think our boy wants something to eat. I can warm up the leftovers from supper." She looked over at Andrew. "Or would you rather have bread and cheese with a glass of milk?"

"Ja."

"Both?"

Andrew nodded. "I am *really* hungry." He started to sit up but blinked in surprise when his body didn't do what his mind said. He blinked a couple of times and then fell back. "My head hurts."

"You fell on it, out of the haymow." Ellie climbed up on the bed to be nearer her friend. "You been asleep for . . ." She scrunched up her eyes trying to figure out how long, then shook her head. "Long time. Too long." She held out an arm that sported a red scratch. "See, that rooster got me when I tried to pick the eggs. You gonna bash him for me?"

Andrew nodded. "But I gotta eat first."

Goodie laughed. "Ain't that just like our boy?" She turned and headed down the stairs, chuckling to herself.

"Oh, I must tell Haakan." Ingeborg braced her hands on the mattress to rise.

"I go." Metiz melted out of the room, the swish of the swinging curtain the only sound.

"I tole 'em you was gonna get better." Ellie sat cross-legged on the bed beside Andrew, her elbows propped on her knees, chin on hands. "Why'd you sleep so long?"

"Did I?" Andrew looked from his mother's face to Ellie's.

They both nodded.

"My ma says you was lucky you didn't break your fool neck." The girl shook her head. "She whupped me for playing in the haymow."

A frown wrinkled Andrew's pale brow. "But why? We always play in the haymow. That's our best place."

Another headshake. "She says she hopes we learned our lesson. You gonna play in the haymow again?"

Andrew yawned and blinked his eyes. "I'm still sleepy." He reached for Ellie's hand. "I'll talk to your ma about the haymow after I eat."

When Goodie pushed open the curtain, Andrew lay sound asleep again.

"He okay?" She set the tray down on the

173

chair beside the bed.

"He's sleeping regular now, not like before." Ingeborg motioned for Ellie to come sit in her lap. "You took good care of our boy, child. You're the kind of friend the Bible talks about. 'A friend loveth at all times,' it says."

"Andrew's my bestest friend in the whole world." She turned to study Ingeborg's eyes. "He coulda died, huh?" At Ingeborg's brief nod, the little girl looked back at Andrew. "My fault."

"Oh no, Ellie, it wasn't your fault." Ingeborg hugged the stalk-thin body closer. "You didn't *push* Andrew out of the haymow, did you?" When the little girl shook her head, near-white hair as fine as corn silk tickled Ingeborg's chin. "It was an accident," she assured the child, "and accidents just happen sometimes."

" 'Twouldn't a happened if you hadn't been playing in the haymow," Goodie said with a sigh. "Young'uns just seem to have to climb and slide and play in high places. Me'n my brother loved to climb trees. Back in Ohio there were trees to climb in everybody's yard. He fell out of one and broke his arm. Hurt something awful. I never climbed those trees again, let me tell you. And I couldn't sit down for a week from the lickin'

I got from my ma. She'd warned us, just like I warned you."

Ellie nestled closer to Ingeborg, as if seeking shelter, and sighed. "Sliding down the hay and swinging from the ropes is the bestest fun."

Andrew's eyes fluttered open again.

"Your supper is here." Ellie slid off of Ingeborg's lap and clambered back onto the bed. "You want I should help you eat?"

"Why?"

"Here." Goodie leaned over and propped another pillow behind him, then hoisted him by the shoulders so he sat against the pillows. She set the tray across his lap and motioned the wriggling girl to sit still. "You're gonna make him spill."

Andrew ate the sandwich of cheese and sliced meat, but when he tried to pick up the cup to drink his buttermilk, his hand began to shake. As the liquid sloshed to the brim, Ingeborg took the cup from his hands and held it to his lips.

"Tomorrow you'll be lots stronger, you'll see."

A bit later, she left the two friends talking, or rather, Ellie talking and Andrew listening. Strange to see her son so still. "Thank you, Father," she whispered as she descended the stairs. "You brought him back to us, and he looks to be okay. Now please lay thy healing hands on Haakan. He wants so to help with the house-raising on Saturday. And harvest is ready to start. How will we ever get it all done before the frost comes if he is laid up?"

She heard Lars talking with Haakan when she neared the sickroom. "Can I bring you both a cup of coffee?"

"Just water." Haakan lay drenched with sweat again, the sheet clinging to his body from the moisture. Even from the doorway she could see the swelling. Metiz stopped her with a hand on her arm. She handed Ingeborg a willow twig.

"Make him chew on this. Helps with pain."

Ingeborg nodded. Now, why hadn't she thought of that? Steeped willow bark helped with pain and fevers. Why not chew the stalk and get the medicine straight?

Haakan took it without even a grumble. He wrinkled his nose at the bitter taste but chewed anyway.

"That surely is wonderful news about Andrew," Lars said, glancing up at Ingeborg from his chair at the bedside. "You want to sit here?"

Ingeborg shook her head. "I'll get the coffee."

"You could put some of that whiskey in mine," Haakan said.

"I could add a few drops of laudanum."

He nodded. "Anything."

When Lars left the sickroom some time later, he stopped to talk with Ingeborg. "One of the men said you could ah . . ." He studied the hat he clutched between his big hands. "You could make a . . ."

Ingeborg waited. What on earth could be causing his cheeks to flush like that? Was he coming down with something too?

Lars took in a deep breath.

"I could make a . . ." Ingeborg waited for him to finish her — or rather *his* thought.

Lars shifted from one foot to the other. He shook his head. "I'll get Kaaren."

"Lars, don't be silly. What is it?"

He started again. "A sling."

Ingeborg waited. The look on his face almost made her laugh. If only she could figure him out. "A sling . . ."

"You know . . . for his . . ." A brief sketch with his hands finished the sentence.

"For the swelling in his —" She stopped suddenly at the horrified look on his face. She nodded, keeping her smile locked carefully away. "So, should this sling —"

"Truss."

She almost missed the word. "Ah, truss,

be loose or tight or . . . ?"

"Firm." He clapped his hat on his head. "I gotta go check the binder. We'll start cutting first thing in the morning." The heat from his face left the room somewhat warmer than when she'd entered it.

"How's Pa?" Thorliff asked when he dragged himself into the house sometime later.

"You can go on in and talk with him. He'd like to hear how the hunting went." Ingeborg turned to look at her son. "What happened to you?"

"Ah, I just slipped and fell in the river."

"Fell in the river?" While the boys frequently swam in the muddy Red River, they usually did so without clothes. Thorliff looked as if he'd been rolling in the mud. Black river gumbo soaked his clothes and spiked his hair. His Bjorklund blue eyes seemed even bluer peering out of a black face. A streak on his right cheek showed where he'd wiped some away.

"You know how Metiz says mud keeps the mosquitoes off you?" He winked at her.

Ingeborg nodded.

"It works." He held out his arms. No welts. Sometimes when the boys returned from evening hunting, their arms were swelled twice their size from mosquito bites.

The vicious things even bit through clothing, so long-sleeved shirts, tightly buttoned, only helped a little.

"There's a washtub outside. The water's still warm in the reservoir."

"I know." At nearly eleven years old, Thorliff now looked her in the eye, even across. No matter how much food he inhaled, it never stuck to his bones, leaving him nearly as skinny as little Ellie. But the man's work he did made for muscles that belied their stringiness. If he continued the way he was going, he would most likely top his father, Roald, in height, though he was built more like his onkel Carl, both of whom had died the second winter the family had been in the new country.

"You all right, Ma?" Thorliff studied her face.

Now it was her turn to nod. She clapped her hands to her cheeks. "Thorliff, I forgot to tell you. Such wonderful news." Her mouth opened and shut like a fish caught on the end of a line.

"What?" He leaned forward, question marks warring with the mud on his face.

"Andrew! Andrew woke up!"

She hadn't finished the words before Thorliff was halfway up the stairs, taking the steps three at a time. She could hear

Ellie squeal and the sound of something hitting the floorboards. Ingeborg too raced up the stairs, but when she parted the curtain, she knew what had made the thuds. Thorliff was on his knees by the bed, his little brother clasped close to his chest while Ellie danced on the sheets.

Tears had streaked gullies through the mud on the older boy's face, and when Thorliff released his bear-trap grip, Andrew looked like he, too, had been wallowing with the pigs in their mudhole. Ingeborg let the curtains swish closed. Tomorrow would be plenty soon enough to wash the bedding and the boy.

A bit later she heard Thorliff's boots thud back down the stairs and into Haakan's room. She finished sewing the strips of muslin together, frequently holding the unusual garment up to see if she could make rhyme or reason out of it. With tails on both ends to tie around his waist, the thing looked like nothing more than a hodge-podge. But all that mattered was for it to help him. If only she had some ice or snow to pack around him.

She wiped her forehead with the back of her wrist. While they all were dripping wet in the humidity, only water from the deep well was cool enough to help. Maybe she should move a pallet out to the springhouse for him. For once, the evening breeze had failed them, leaving the heat of the day smothering the house and its occupants. Even the song of the crickets sounded raspy, as though they needed a drink.

Bugs hit the screen like peppering shot, attracted by the light. She slapped at a mosquito on her arm. The things seemed to ride in on anyone who opened the door, hovering there in wait.

"Pa's not any better." Thorliff sank down beside her, looping his arms around his upraised knees.

"No." If anything, he was worse.

"How long?" He looked up at her. "I mean, ah . . . how bad . . . ah . . ."

He sounded like Lars now.

"You mean the swelling?"

Thorliff nodded. A flush shone through the streaks where the mud had been wiped away.

"I don't know." Ingeborg clasped her hands in her lap. "I've never seen anything like this."

"Metiz?"

"She hasn't either."

"We could take him to the doctor in Grafton or Grand Forks."

"We can hardly roll him over without him

passing out from the pain." Ingeborg thought of the Scripture she'd read just that morning. "Trust in the Lord with all thine heart." While she'd agreed that was a good principle, the doing of it — when her husband writhed in pain then froze because the slightest movement caused it to worsen — was taxing her reasoning. "You keep praying with us, son. I sure could use a good dose of God's wisdom right about now."

"What about using the telegraph?"

"What?" She leaned forward as if she hadn't heard him right.

"You know, send a message to the doctor or the hospital and ask them what we can do."

"Thorliff Bjorklund, you are a genius." She tweaked his ear. "Now why didn't I think of that?" *Because you aren't used to all this newfangled equipment,* the other side of her mind answered.

"I could ride into Grafton and do that. One of these days we'll have a telegraph office right here in Blessing."

Ingeborg rose to her feet, the truss falling to the floor in her rush. "I'll get paper and pencil, and we'll write it out."

Thorliff picked up the material and held it up. "What are you making?"

Now it was Ingeborg's turn to feel her

neck go from warm to hot in one breath. Discussing such things with a woman was not the easiest thing. With Lars it had been difficult, but now with her son? Impossible.

"You get the paper, and I'll tell you what to write."

12

Thorliff opened the paper and reread the message they'd written. "Is Pa really this sick?" His blue eyes reflected the gray of a storm-tossed sea.

Ingeborg nodded. "Metiz and me — Kaaren too — we don't know what else to do." Ingeborg wiped her hands on her apron. She stopped when she realized her hands weren't wet. More and more often lately she'd caught herself drying dry hands. Was she losing her mind with all this? "Just you hurry. Take Jack. He needs a good run."

"You want me to run him all the way?" Thorliff's open mouth and wide eyes showed his surprise.

"No, no. Right now I'd give anything if we had someone trained to take and send messages here at the Blessing stop."

"Onkel Olaf could do that."

"Ja, Onkel Olaf can do about anything, but there just ain't enough hours in the day as it is. Go on now, hurry."

"Mor?" Andrew's voice floated down the stairway, punctuated by the thunder of Ellie's feet.

Ingeborg looked upward. "I'm coming."

A groan from the bedroom where Haakan lay sent Thorliff hustling out the door. He hit the ground at a dead run, leaping from the top of the three-stepped stoop. Ingeborg glanced out the window to see him flying toward the corral. Should she have sent Lars? Was Thorliff at ten old enough for a job like this one?

She shook her head at her worrisome thoughts. Thorliff had been doing men's work since he'd started school or before. As soon as his hands were big enough to squeeze the teats, he'd been milking cows.

"Andrew's hungry," Ellie announced, as if delivering a message from the president himself.

Another groan came from the bedroom.

Ingeborg turned and nearly ran over Baptiste. She clapped a hand to her bosom. "Heavens, boy, you nearly scared me out of my wits. How about telling me when you come in?"

Baptiste smiled his slow smile, his black eyes twinkling. "I come like Grandmere."

"I know. She does the same thing to me." Ingeborg laid a hand on his shoulder. He was as tall as she now, with Thorliff not far behind. "You boys are growing so fast."

"That is good, yes?" His smile, once so elusive and now always at the ready with those he called family, made her smile in return.

"Ja, that is good."

"The milking is done and the pans set for skimming. Tante Kaaren says she is going to churn butter today. Lars said we would go to the Baards' as soon as chores were done."

"Breakfast will be ready in just a few minutes. You go wash."

Harvesting would begin today, and Haakan lay trapped in bed. Ingeborg sent a prayer heavenward. Perhaps he was too sick to care.

But as soon as she entered the sickroom again, she knew that was not the case. He squinted from eyes sunken from the fever. "Are they gone?" he croaked, the fever drinking up all the liquids she tried to pour into him and rasping his throat.

"Soon." She held his head while he drank from the cup, his hands shaking so the cup clattered against his teeth. "You want more pillows?"

"No. Flat is best."

"You need a wash? Cool water would feel good."

"Not if I have to move."

She laid a hand on his forehead. "Uff da." She studied him for a moment. "How about if I soak towels and just lay them across you?" What she would give for ice right now. "If we could move you to the springhouse . . ."

He shook his head. Goodie stopped in the doorway. "Any better this morning?"

"Ma, Andrew is hungry." Ellie pulled on her mother's apron.

"You know, child, if you took as good a care of those chickens as you do Andrew . . ."

"I'll feed them later."

"The food is all ready if you would just put things on the table. Thorliff took a telegram to Grafton to the doctor. He's to wait for a reply." Between her two sick ones, Ingeborg felt like the rope in a tug of war.

"I'd be willing to bet the doctor is going to say 'Keep the man comfortable until the body heals itself.' " She turned to look at Haakan. "Best thing for you might be that rotgut whiskey over to Anner's. You drink enough of that, and I can guarantee you'll be singing a different song."

"I hate even having the stuff in the house," Ingeborg said. Memories of long Norwegian winter nights and a father who figured vodka was the best antidote to dispel the gloom pulled Ingeborg's mouth down at the corners. More than once he'd been passed out on the floor when she and the other children came down in the morning. No one was surprised when he wound up frozen in a snowbank one night. But surprised or not, the hurt never did leave.

"Don't matter. If'n it could help him through this. . . ."

Ingeborg nodded. "Anything that would help."

"I'll send Hans on over, then."

Ingeborg could hear the others in the kitchen as she dipped cloths in cool water and laid them across Haakan's body. By the time she reached his feet, those on his face were already dry.

"If only we could let you float in the cow's water tank."

Haakan barely moved his head, but the nod said he agreed.

When Thorliff returned just before noon, he carried two messages. The one from the doctor said do anything to keep the man comfortable and let the disease run its course. A firm truss was helpful and cold, wet cloths.

Ingeborg just shrugged her shoulders at Goodie's I-told-you-so look.

The other message was the one that caused a stir. "Tomorrow!" Ingeborg looked up, her mouth open. "Bridget and the others are arriving tomorrow. I forgot all about them." She looked again at the telegram in her hand. "She says she has four others. I thought she was bringing Onkel Hamre's grandson and Katja, the youngest daughter. Oh, and Sarah Neswig. Who is the fourth?"

"You'll know tomorrow. Not to worry about room for everyone. They can have the beds in the main room of the soddy. Me and mine and the boy will sleep in the lean-to. I'll turn the beds all out next. Them beans can wait an hour or two." A bushel basket of beans ready to snap sat upon the countertop.

"No, Andrew and Ellie can snap the beans," Goodie continued. "That ought to keep him quiet for a while. Thank God children recover so quickly."

"He'll probably eat half of what he snaps. I never saw a child that can eat like he can. Even right after he woke up from sleeping for two days after landing on his head." Ingeborg shook her head, but the light in her eyes showed her pride in the youngster.

Ingeborg glanced around her kitchen. She had planned on a thorough housecleaning before Bridget came, and now that was impossible. Beans to can, a very sick man needing plenty of attention, harvest starting, and Andrew . . . thank God for Andrew's coming out of the sleep. If she thought on that, maybe she wouldn't worry so much about the other things.

"Why don't you go on over to Kaaren's with the telegram and let me put the beans we got done to cooking? Once I get the beds put back together, the soddy is ready. Baptiste can beat the blankets and rug for me. I'll turn the ticking. Couple more days and we coulda put in fresh straw. Now that woulda been fine."

Ingeborg let the words roll over her. Goodie was a talker, that was for certain. But the heart that beat within her breast was as big as the Dakota skies and twice as generous. Ingeborg would miss her and her two children when they moved to their new home after her marriage to Olaf. And this Saturday was the house-raising too.

"Ja, I think I will do that." She peeked in the door of the sickroom. Haakan lay on his back, eyes closed, and breathing in the regular way of real sleep. Might be that the laudanum she'd mixed with his cooled dinner coffee was doing its work. "If he calls, or Astrid wakes up, send one of the boys to get me."

"We'll see."

While it had been hot in the house, the direct sun beating down brought sweat to her brow immediately. She fanned herself with her handkerchief, thinking how nice a grove of shade trees would be between the two houses. Stacks of lumber from last winter's cutting lay drying in the sun in preparation for building a frame house for Kaaren and Lars. They would put it up after harvest.

Before harvest, after harvest, there was never time enough for all that needed doing. Winter would be on them far before they were ready for it. She shook her head at the crazy way her thoughts skittered around. Here she was dripping sweat on an August afternoon and thinking about winter being right around the corner.

"Heavenly Father, you must think us such silly creatures, always worrying about tomorrow and letting today slip by." She stopped to admire a black-eyed Susan blooming along the fence of the pasture that separated the two houses. If the cows or horses had been pastured there recently, they'd have leaned through the fence to gobble the flower. No matter that they had plenty of grass inside the fence. "We people aren't too different from the cows, are we? Never content with what we have, always leaning through the fence in search of more. And, Father, right now my more is for you to please bring healing to Haakan's poor body. He is so sick, and I ask that you help him to endure this trial. He and *sick* don't get on well, as you know. Thanks for listening."

She shaded her eyes with her hand to see the two binders cutting and bundling the wheat over at the Baards'. She should have been over there helping Agnes cook for the crew or at least should have sent Goodie over. Since Trygve had been running a fever and coughing, Kaaren hadn't gone either.

Tomorrow she'd have to take the team and wagon into town to meet the train. That thought put wings to her feet. Kaaren didn't even know her first mother-in-law would be arriving that soon. Some sister-in-law she was. Or were they still sisters-in-law since the husbands that were brothers were gone?

She tapped softly on the frame of the screen door to the northern soddy. This was naptime for the children, and Sophie woke so easily. Going full tilt until sleep side-whacked her, Sophie only slowed down to take care of her sister, Grace. And to tell her, in the twins' own indecipherable way of communicating, what someone had said.

"Come in, come in. What are you waiting for?" Kaaren whispered as she opened the screen door.

"Why don't you come out here and we can sit in the shade? We may be able to catch a breeze there."

Kaaren nodded and slipped out the door. "I just got Trygve and the girls to sleep, so we should have an hour or so of peace." She wiped her forehead with the corner of her apron. "Three in diapers keeps that boiler going all the time it seems. Between the washing and the canning . . ." She shook her head. "I'm not complaining, you understand?"

"I know, and I should have sent Goodie over." The two moved the washbasins from the bench and sank down in the relative coolness.

"It's not like you have nothing to do. How is Haakan? Lars said he'd rather have had us cut off his foot than go through what is happening to Haakan."

"Ja, but at the time he wouldn't have thought so." The two shared a smile. Saving Lars's foot that had become infected after frostbite had been one of God's many miracles, and they all believed that to the depths of their marrow.

"I guess it takes a man to appreciate how Haakan feels."

"Humph. We do the birthing, remember?"

"Ja, but then we have something wonderful to look forward to. I'd go through anything to hold a new baby in my arms." Kaaren fanned herself with her apron.

"Trygve don't cuddle well, does he?" Ingeborg smiled at the thought of her busy young nephew. He and Astrid were definitely cut from the same cloth.

"He wants to walk so bad he sits on the floor and screams when the girls leave him."

"Sounds like men everywhere."

"Ingeborg Bjorklund, what has got into you today?" Kaaren gave her friend a dig in the ribs with her elbow.

"What has got into me is this telegram." She held it out for Kaaren to read.

Kaaren reached for the folded paper, then drew back her hand. "It's not bad news, is it?"

"Not unless you think having Bridget and her brood arrive tomorrow is bad news."

"How wonderful!" Kaaren paused. "Isn't it?"

"Ja. They must have got an earlier ship. Last time we heard, it was for next week." Ingeborg clucked her tongue. "It's just with Haakan so sick . . ."

"So Bridget is a good nurse. And I'll have no trouble putting Katja to work. But you mark my words, she'll be the belle of the ball around here. If she's turned out as pretty as I always thought she'd be, the men will be around her like bees on a blossom."

"Besides Katja and Sarah, they've brought someone else too, but no mention of her name. Young Hamre will fit right in with Thorliff and the boys. You know, I been thinking, maybe Sarah could go on over and help George and Solveig."

"What a great idea! I can't wait to hear all the news. Letters are wonderful, but they just don't say enough. I want to know how Far and Mor really are. Wouldn't it be wonderful if they came too?" Kaaren wore the dreamy look that told Ingeborg this wasn't just a passing fancy. Kaaren had been wanting to see her mother and father again, just like so many of the young people who came over.

"Someday maybe they will."

A cloud darkened Kaaren's sky blue eyes. "I don't think so. All of the rest of the family is still there." She slapped her hands on her knees. "No time for wishful thinking, not when we have so much to be thankful for right now. Bridget will take over the hearts of the little ones before we've seen two milkings."

"And have three pairs of socks, a sweater, and both mittens and gloves knit by night-fall."

"Inge!" The two looked at each other and laughed. "She is rather capable, isn't she?" Kaaren chuckled again.

"A paragon. She puts the woman of Proverbs 31 to shame." Ingeborg shook her head. *That wasn't nice,* she could hear her own mother's voice say in her ear. "I just wish I got as much done in a day as she does. Is my face turning green?"

"No. You're not that jealous. You think she's learned any English?"

"I wouldn't be surprised." Ingeborg got to her feet. She blinked as her world tipped a bit and put a hand against the sod wall to steady herself.

"Are you all right?"

Ingeborg nodded. "Just confirms what I've been suspecting. I felt like throwing up this morning. Frying the bacon did it."

"You just sit yourself down there and rest for another moment or two. Take ten if you need them. I'll get a dipper of water." Kaaren took Ingeborg firmly by the shoulders and sat her back down. "How wonderful. Now you can give Haakan that son you been hankering after."

Ingeborg let herself be fussed over. How

good it felt, even for the moment, to let someone else take charge. She watched a prairie hawk drifting on the air above them. His wild screeching cry brought a thrill to her heart. How free he was. How beautiful with the sun parting his wing feathers with gold. The cry came again.

If she were free like that, she'd go hunting. It had been so long since she donned men's britches, taken the rifle, and headed for the game trails. Or she would take the team out, hitched to the plow, and go busting sod. In her mind she could taste the rich aroma of a newly turned furrow. The black earth of the Red River Valley had a fragrance all its own, one that promised riches if one were willing to work hard and long enough to harvest. And rich they were.

"Here." Kaaren thrust the dipper of cold water into her hands. "What were you thinking of with that smile on your face?"

Ingeborg shrugged. "Nothing much." Kaaren still disapproved of Ingeborg's wearing men's britches and of her hunting, in spite of the fact that Ingeborg had kept them alive and the land together with the use of them. Riding the plow was so much easier than fighting to keep the blade of the walking plow running straight and digging just deep enough to cut the sod and roll it over.

She drained the dipper and handed it back. "Mange takk."

A child's whimper came from within the soddy.

"Oh, Sophie, couldn't you sleep just a bit longer?" Shaking her head, Kaaren turned back to the house. "You sit here and rest. I'll see if I can get her out of there before she wakes the others."

Ingeborg let her thoughts wander back to the fields again. With all the men tied up in the harvest, no one would be breaking sod or backsetting it either. Once the men were on the road with the threshing machine, she could go out a few times. Haakan need not know. At least not until he saw the turned sod. The thought made her heart leap. With Bridget caring for the children, surely no one would mind.

She sat up straighter and glanced up at the hawk. She caught sight of him, wings pinned to his side as he dove for the earth. Within seconds he flapped his mighty wings again and rose, a gopher dangling from his talons.

If the hawk could do as he pleased, so could she. Both of them were doing their best to provide for themselves and their families.

Sophie rode her mother's hip, her cheek,

pink from sleep, rested against her mother's encircling arm. "Tante Inge." She smiled and reached out her arms. "Andoo come?"

"Sorry." Ingeborg took the child and settled her on her lap. "But Andrew is better."

"Andoo owie?"

"Ja, but Jesus made him better."

"Good Jesus." Sophie's ringlets bounced as she nodded her head for emphasis.

"Truer words . . ." Ingeborg hugged the little girl and kissed her on the tip of her turned-up nose. "You are one smart cookie."

"Cookie?"

"Now you've done it." Kaaren rolled her eyes.

"How about if I take her home with me? She can play with Astrid if she's awake and the others can sleep."

"If you don't mind."

"Not at all. Come on, turnip nose." Ingeborg tweaked the little nose. Sophie giggled.

"More."

Ingeborg tweaked the bit of a nose again and set the child down. "Come on, let's go see Astrid."

"Andoo."

"Ja, him too." She shook her head. "Stubborn Norwegians. Can't change their minds even when they're barely able to walk. Mange takk for the drink and the visit. Don't say anything about the . . . the you know. I'd like to tell Haakan myself." She glanced down at the child studying her with wide blue eyes and back up at Kaaren.

"I won't." Kaaren knelt by her daughter. "You be good now for Tante Ingeborg."

Sophie nodded. "Good. See Andoo."

"Bye." Kaaren waved as the two started off. "No sticks, leaves, flowers, or bugs, Inge, you hear?"

Ingeborg waved back and reminded Sophie to wave too. Since the twins weren't ready to be weaned after Trygve was born, she had nursed them. Now, both of the girls treated her like a second mother. And while Grace had been the one needing it longer, Sophie seemed to have developed a special kinship with her aunt.

Setting Ellie and Andrew to playing with Sophie in the fenced plot in the shade of the house, Ingeborg pumped water into a basin and took it into the sickroom. Two long days now her husband had been like this. How else could she help him?

Haakan blinked and tried to smile, but the swelling made even that simple task an effort. "I hear you brought company?" The sound made her throat hurt in sympathy.

200

"Ja, and some good news also." She took the telegram out of her apron pocket and read it to him.

Haakan groaned. "Some way to greet company." He sighed. "What a mess."

Ingeborg debated. Maybe some further good news would help cheer him. "How about some cool water here, and while I do that, I have something wonderful to tell you." She dipped the cloths and, wringing them only partially, laid them across his body.

"So?"

"So you are going to be a father — again."

"Ahh." This time the smile almost looked like one. "That is good."

"Good?" She planted her hands on her hips. "Is that all you can say about something this important?" She chuckled and sank down on her knees beside the bed. Taking his hot hand in her own cool ones, she kissed his knuckles. "I think Metiz already figured it out. She gave me one of those looks of hers yesterday." At his sort-of smile again, she continued. "You could be thinking of names while you lie here."

"Wasting time?"

"I'd say getting better isn't really a waste of time. I could prop the Bible on a pillow so you could read that. Maybe you'd find a good name in there."

"We'll name her after your mother."

"You better think of a boy's name this time around." Ingeborg returned to cooling the cloths. "Let's see, August, July, three months back, we should have another April baby."

"Give Astrid a birthday present?"

Ingeborg smiled into his face. "Ja, and you too."

"Did Thorliff bring a newspaper?"

She nodded. "Perhaps someone will read it to you later. You want the Bible?"

He shook his head. "My eyes don't focus right."

"Can you sleep?"

"Get me a few swallows of that rotgut and I will."

After dosing him with willow-bark tea and a chaser of Anner's homemade whiskey, she left him dozing just in time to hear Astrid stirring. She checked on the three playing in the shade. Andrew and Ellie were telling Sophie a story using sticks and bits of cotton to make people. After changing Astrid, Ingeborg settled into her rocker and put the baby to her breast. She could hear Goodie in the kitchen. A fly buzzed against the window, trying to bang its way back out. The rocker sang its own song, playing the bass line for the guzzling baby.

Ingeborg let her head rest against the chair back. She could be reading to Haakan while the baby nursed, but she was so tired her bones seemed to melt into the chair. How easily one forgot the harder things of bearing children, tired inside out, swollen feet, aching back. She looked down at the silken-haired infant in her arms.

"You're worth every bit of it, you know."

Astrid drew back her head and smiled up at her mother, a bit of mother's milk dribbling from the side of her mouth. Then she sucked again in earnest, her blue eyes fast on her mother's face.

"I pray to God you are always healthy like this," Ingeborg whispered. "And that our new baby will be just like you. Fat and sassy and the best baby ever."

Astrid gurgled and waved her fist.

"Please, God." A shadow drifted across the sunlight streaming in the window.

13

"That Anner! I swear he is going to break his neck looking the other way when he sees me." Hjelmer shook his head. "You'd think I robbed him or something. He could have done the same as I did if he'd been paying attention."

Penny looked up from her account books spread across the kitchen table. "He's jealous, that's all."

"Short of giving him the Booth property, I don't know what else to do." Hjelmer stared out the window.

"He'd never take that."

"I know. He says he'll never take or buy anything from me again."

"How do you know that?"

"Oh, someone told me." Hjelmer glanced back over his shoulder. "You think he is hurting your store too?"

Penny tapped her front teeth with the end of her pen. "Not so's I'd notice. Some come in spite of him. They don't want to take sides, but they don't want to go all the way to Grafton either. You watch, he'll come around."

"You know Mor and the others are coming in tomorrow. I wish we had room for them with us." Hjelmer changed the subject.

"We can always add on."

"You say that like adding on is easy as . . . as baking a pie."

"Speaking of which . . ." Penny got to her feet and crossed to the stove. Taking up potholders, she opened the oven door and stood back a moment to let the rush of heat out.

"Umm, that smells like heaven itself."

"I didn't know heaven would smell like apple pie." She removed the three pies and set them on the counter to cool. "Now, take the blossoms on those red roses at Ingeborg's — that's what heaven will smell like."

Hjelmer inhaled again. "You set those on the windowsill where the folks from the train can catch a whiff, and you'll be baking pies twenty-four hours a day."

Penny spun around, sending her skirts above her ankles. The sight brought an appreciative grin to her husband's face. "Yes, pies would do it."

"Do what?"

"Bring more people into my — our store."

He waited for her to continue.

"If we had a sign out front, 'fresh pies' . . ." She shook her head. "No, that wouldn't work. Everyone around here bakes their own pies."

"The men on the train don't. Like your bread, they buy a whole loaf at a time, you know?"

Penny nodded. "Well, we'll be plenty busy soon as harvest starts."

"They started cutting at Baards'. Haakan is laid up, you know."

"What? No, I didn't know. What happened to him?"

"Caught the mumps. All the kids had it."

"So?"

"So when a grown man gets the mumps, the swelling travels to other parts of his body."

Penny raised her eyebrows. "So?"

He stared at her without saying a word, only one eyebrow cocking in that way he had.

What is he talking about? So the swelling went to . . . "Oh no."

"Ja, he can hardly move. Think I'll go ask if they need some help. You could send someone out to get me if need be."

She knew he meant if someone needed some blacksmithing done immediately.

"You could take Ephraim with you."

Hjelmer nodded. "He's got enough wood split to size every wheel for a five-mile radius. I figure I can do that while they wait in line to empty their wagons there at the sack house. We'll go on out in the morning, and I'll be back in time for the train. Then I can take Mor out to Ingeborg's. She'll find plenty to do taking care of Haakan and Astrid."

"Saturday we have the house-raising for Olaf and Goodie."

"I know. He's got enough sod cut for the lower walls, and we'll frame the rest. Haakan said he's donating the lumber."

"Well, I have curtains sewn for two kitchen windows. And the quilt will be done in time for the wedding. You'd think they could have waited until after harvest to get married."

"Like we could have waited longer?" There went that eyebrow again.

"We didn't dare wait. You might have taken off again, and then where would we have been?"

"Pretty sad, at least on my side." He sat down in his big stuffed chair. "Come here, wife, and I'll show you why we didn't wait."

"Now, Hjelmer."

He crooked his finger and patted his lap. "You scared?"

"Scared? Me?" Penny flounced to her feet and, crossing the room, plopped herself in his lap. "What if someone comes in?"

"Like who?"

"Oh, Cousin Ephraim."

"He's sound asleep over in the sack house. He believes wholeheartedly in working from dawn to dusk. Up with the roosters and to bed with the hens."

"Hjelmer!" She thumped him on the shoulder at the leer on his face.

"Chicks, hens . . ." He nuzzled her neck with gently biting kisses. "I was scared, you know. Half out of my wits."

"Why?" She turned and leaned her forehead against his.

"I kept hearing about some Donald fellow, and it sounded like you were pretty serious about him."

"I was, until I realized I had to settle things with you first."

"So." He kissed her, butterfly kisses on her nose and eyelids. "Are we settled?"

"More or less." The warmth his kisses always brought was traveling from her middle out to her fingers and toes.

"More?" He settled his lips on hers.

"More what?" She whispered back after a time of silence.

"I love you more each day, Mrs.

Bjorklund, and I can't wait to introduce you to my mother. She still can't believe someone actually got her youngest son to settle down." He set her off his lap, rose, and took her hand. "I think it's bedtime. This rooster is getting mighty droopy eyed. And he needs his hen."

The two of them blew out the lamps and, giggling, made their way to the bedroom. Later, with Hjelmer snoring gently beside her, Penny lay still, watching the wind flutter the white curtains. She had heard so many things about Bridget, all of them good, but all of them leaving her wondering if she'd measure up. *If I was carrying a babe by now, then* . . . She quickly shut off that line of thinking. She'd prayed for a baby, and as Ingeborg had reminded her, "The good Lord sends babies when He decides the time is right." *But please, God, let your time be soon. I want a baby so I can have a real family of my own.* She thought of the brothers and sisters she'd never seen after they were split up among the relatives. Five children, with her the oldest. But at least Ephraim had given her news about those who were alive. How exciting to hear that she still had brothers and sisters. Were any of them wanting to find their family as she did?

★ ★ ★

The next afternoon the train whistled its arrival.

The wooden platform was buried under Bjorklunds. Hjelmer stood off to one side with Penny glued to his side. Her cousin was minding the store, but anyone who had come to town had come to the wood-planked stretch from the sack house to the tracks to see what the ruckus was about. Once their questions had been answered, they stayed. Happy occasions like this didn't occur every day.

Kaaren and Ingeborg tried to keep track of their children and keep them clean long enough to greet this new and much heard about group of relatives. Andrew, bouncing back from his head injury with the speed of children, tried to keep Sophie in hand. Between him and Ellie, the giggling twin only fell down twice.

Andrew brushed her off and hissed, "Stand still."

"Andoo, run." Sophie tried to slip by him, but Ellie headed her off.

"Sophie!"

The little girl came to a skidding halt. She knew better than to keep going when her mother's words wore *that* tone.

Grace clutched her mother's skirts with

both hands. Her eyes took up her entire face.

Trygve waved his arms and crowed as Andrew ran by.

"He wants down." Ingeborg rocked Astrid on her hip, calming the child against all the noise.

Thorliff and Baptiste corralled all the young ones, threatening them with bodily harm if they didn't stop the running around.

"Do you think she'll recognize me?" Thorliff asked his mother. Ingeborg nodded.

"All she has to do is look for a young Roald-and-Carl combination. You look more like them every day."

"Both of them?"

"Well, parts of each."

He smiled at her, nearly on eye level with her now. He'd spurted up these last months, and he wouldn't be eleven until November. He swung Sophie up into his arms, much to her delight, and motioned Andrew to stand beside their mother.

Lars joined Kaaren and bent down, picking Grace up and settling her on his hip. The love shining in her eyes when she patted his cheeks and looked him straight on brought a catch to Ingeborg's throat. It took so little to make that one happy. Gentle Grace was already living up to her name.

As the train hissed to a stop and the conductor stepped down, Hjelmer drew close beside him. Setting the stool down for the last step, the uniformed man turned to the crowd. "Well, now, isn't it nice you all came to see me like this?"

Those who had heard him over the hissing of the train laughed.

One man, obviously a traveling salesman by his two cases, stepped down and headed toward the store.

The conductor waited, watching the doorway. The group waited too.

What if she missed a connection somewhere? Ingeborg kept up her juggle-the-small-child rhythm. If only Haakan could be here. So much he was missing. She watched Hjelmer. Why did he seem so nervous? Fidgeting like that certainly wasn't like him. But then, how would she be if this were *her* mother? A lot calmer, she decided, swallowing again. Greeting her own mother would be much easier than greeting the mother of the father of her two sons. All these years of letters back and forth. Had they become friends in the process?

"Katja!" Hjelmer stepped forward and lifted the lovely young girl down from the last step. She wrapped her arms around his neck and hugged him like she would never let go.

"Oh, Hjelmer, we thought never to see you again." She thumped him on the shoulder. "Now, put me down, you big oaf. Mor should take a strap to your backside for not ever writing." She grinned up at him. "And in Amerika I am to be called Katy. Much more fitting, don't you think?"

"Still a tongue on you. I thought you might outgrow that Katy, huh?" He set her on the ground and reached for the hand of the white-haired woman descending the steps. "Mor."

Bridget Bjorklund stumbled a bit as she fell into her son's arms. Of four sons, this her youngest, was the one who always made her laugh. "Oh, Hjelmer, Katja — I mean Katy — is right. You should be thumped, but I am so glad to see you." She stepped back, the better to look at him. "You've grown into a man."

"I should hope so." He kept her hand in his and drew her over to where Penny waited.

Thorliff looked up at his mother. "Don't they speak English?"

"I don't know."

To Ingeborg the pure Norwegian language sounded like angel songs. Here in the new country, they had changed so many words, made up some from both Norwegian

213

and American, and spoke mostly English now, so it had been some time since true Norwegian was spoken. Andrew had been speaking English from the beginning, and while Norwegian was Thorliff's first language, he now used English all the time too.

After Bridget came a sturdy boy with a black porkpie hat pulled low on his forehead. Thorliff and Baptiste stepped forward. "Hamre?"

"Ja." The boy held on to his valise as if they might take it from him.

"I am Thorliff Bjorklund, and this is my friend Baptiste. Welcome to Amerika." He spoke perfect Norwegian, and Baptiste bobbed his head, a smile lighting his black eyes.

Hamre ducked his head and moved off to stand behind Bridget.

Thorliff looked at Baptiste and shrugged.

"And you are Thorliff, are you not?" Bridget put her hands on his shoulders. "You look so like your far and onkel I would recognize you anywhere. So much you have grown."

Thorliff nodded. "I remember you." He cocked his head. "But you are different too."

"Ja, I am older. More snow on the mountain." She touched her hair nearly hidden under a black hat with a black feather.

Thorliff shook his head. "No, that is not it. You were so big, tall I mean."

Bridget and Katy laughed together, their cheeks rosy in the heat. "You were little then. Five years old and trying so hard to be a man already." She patted his shoulder. "Your far would be very proud of you this day."

"And every day," Ingeborg added from her place behind Thorliff.

While Bridget turned at a question from Hjelmer, Ingeborg smiled at the young woman loaded with two valises and looking more than a bit lost. "You must be Bridget's niece Sarah. Welcome to Amerika."

"Ja, mange takk." She set her cases down and wiped her brow. "I did not know it would be so warm here." Then even more color came into her face. "I did not mean to complain. I mean . . ."

Ingeborg smiled and took her arm. "You leave those heavy cases for the men and come over here with us."

Bridget turned then from her greeting of all the others and motioned a half-grown girl to join them. "This is Ilse Gustafson. Her mor and far died on the boat, along with many others. Dysentery ran through those in steerage, knocking people down like a terrible windstorm. Too many of them never got up again. I told Ilse that since she had no more family, she could come with us. That you would have plenty of room for another Norwegian emigrant."

Ingeborg stepped forward. "Of course we do. Thorliff, why don't you and Baptiste take those boxes and go load them in our wagon?" She reached out a hand to the girl who had yet to smile. "Welcome to Blessing, and I hope being with us will indeed be a blessing for you."

The "mange takk" was nearly buried in the girl's chest as she nodded in return.

Poor child, losing her family like that. Ingeborg resolved right then to do all she could to help out this poor girl. Surely there would be a place for her somewhere, if not at the Bjorklunds.

"I knew you would say that." Bridget turned to Ingeborg with another hug. "I never thought to see any of you again, and here I am. God is so good. He has allowed me to cross that ocean and this huge, huge land and come here to meet my grandchildren." She patted Andrew's cheek. "I would have no trouble telling that you are a Bjorklund through and through. He looks so much like Carl when he was a baby that this is like stepping back in time."

Ingeborg put her hand on Andrew's

shoulder. He did not like being called a baby.

"Astrid is the baby." He looked his bestemor in the eye as he said it.

"Ja, that she is." Bridget glanced from Ingeborg to Andrew, a twinkle in her eye. "Spoken like a true Bjorklund."

Ingeborg was so proud of her young son, she could have popped her seams right there. He even spoke in Norwegian, which she wasn't sure he would do, or could do without prompting. While Bridget went to talk with Kaaren and fuss over her three little ones, Ingeborg helped shepherd all the group together. When all the baggage was unloaded, including the mail, which the men handed to Penny, the train whistled again, the conductor shouted "all aboard," and set his stool back up on the car bed. Wheels screeching, steam hissing, the train began to move, and gathering momentum, took off down the track.

Lars and Hjelmer, along with the bigger boys, loaded the boxes and trunks in the wagons and then rounded up the people.

"Come on. Goodie and Agnes have coffee ready and everyone can visit then." Hjelmer turned to his mother. "Mor, why don't you ride with Ingeborg? That way you can hold Astrid or Trygve, since I am sure you are not about to let the babies go."

Bridget laughed. "I feel younger already. It must be this Dakota air."

"Well, it sure ain't the altitude or the mountains." Hjelmer helped her over the wheel.

Bridget fanned herself with a hankie. "I surely can understand why the women here don't wear wool skirts in the summer." She smoothed her skirt down and tucked her sweater in beside her. "I will have to get some material and make us clothes like the rest of you wear." She turned to smile at Katy, who sat in the back with the children, all of them asking her questions about Norway.

Ilse Gustafson sat by herself in the corner, her arms wrapped around her knees. So far she hadn't said a word.

Andrew stood and leaned close to his mother. "Ma, why don't she say something?"

"Maybe she is shy."

"What is shy?"

"Shy is when you are afraid to say something. You feel like no one wants to talk with you. You're just plain scared of new people."

Andrew turned to look at the newcomer. He looked back at his mother. "She looks mad."

"Or maybe sad?"

Andrew studied the girl. He nodded. "Maybe Paws can make her happy?"

"Maybe. Maybe you and Ellie can too."

"Can she say English?"

Ingeborg shrugged. "I don't know. Why don't you ask her?"

With the wagons loaded, Ingeborg flapped the reins with a hup and a jolt as they headed east to the Bjorklund houses.

In Norwegian, Andrew asked Ilse if she spoke English.

Ilse shook her head. She scowled at Andrew and shook her head again, then buried her face in her knees.

Andrew tried standing again to talk with his mother, but she ordered him to sit down before he fell down. He did so, right beside Ellie.

"She don't like us," Ellie whispered.

Andrew shrugged. "Come on." He led the way, crawling over and around things until they got to the back of the wagon where Katy had Thorliff and Baptiste laughing. Like Ilse, Hamre and Sarah Neswig sat off to the side, not taking part in the fun.

Andrew and Ellie swapped looks and shook their heads.

Katy tried to include her cousin, but he

turned the other way when she asked him a question. "Come on, Hamre. Tell them about your bestefar's fishing boat. I know they haven't seen anything like that out here."

"I remember a long trip on a ship when we came to America." Thorliff hung his feet over the wagon tailboard. "I thought we were going to live on that ship forever, but my far kept telling me about all the animals we would have. He didn't know how many there would really be. He said one or two sheep, and we have about a hundred. He said one cow, and now we milk twenty-five twice a day."

Baptiste gave him an elbow in the ribs. Thorliff elbowed him back, and Katy laughed along with them.

"Good thing we know how to milk cows," Sarah said with a smile brightening her oval face. Like Katy she wore her hair in a bun, trying to look older than sixteen.

Ellie and Andrew perched on a box right behind her.

"So, do you two come as a pair, or . . ."

Ellie looked at Andrew and shrugged. "What'd she say?"

"Are we a pair?" Andrew thought before translating. He looked at Katy. "I don't know." He leaned closer. "Ellie is my bestest friend."

"Andrew just got over a knock on the head. He fell out of the haymow." Thorliff turned and gave his brother a light punch on the arm. "But nothing can keep our Andrew down."

"They say Bjorklunds have hard heads."

"Ja, and blue eyes." Thorliff looked at Katy. "You and me and Andrew and our pa, we match." He turned to look at Andrew. "Huh, Andrew?"

"Ja, but Katy is pretty and Sarah too."

Katy turned around and tousled his near-white hair. "And you, my dear Andrew, I think you got all the family charm, and that's a real gift to have."

Andrew looked at her, cocked his head to one side, and asked, "What is charm?"

"You make people laugh." Thorliff spun around so his feet were in the wagon and leaned over to tickle Andrew.

Andrew giggled, then broke out in his belly laugh that soon had everyone laughing. Everyone but Hamre and Ilse.

Ingeborg looked back over her shoulder. "Don't you let him fall out of the wagon now. One bump on the head is enough."

That set them laughing again.

Driving into the yard, Ingeborg said, "That soddy is where you will be staying, but we'll drop your things off later. Goodie is at the door. She is so excited to meet you all."

Astrid took that moment to let out a wail. Bridget tried to distract the toddler with a game of peekaboo.

"Astrid's hungry, Mor," Andrew sang out.

"I think he is a mind reader," Ingeborg said, digging in her bag for a piece of dried bread. She gave it to Astrid, who first eyed it with a scowl, then put it in her mouth. "He can tell us what any of the little ones want, even Grace. Between Sophie and Andrew, they'll figure out a way to get Grace what she needs and wants. I think they have their own language already."

Astrid whimpered around the bread.

"I know, son, I'll feed her as soon as we get in the door. Thorliff, will you take care of the horses?" She pulled the team to a halt by the back stoop. Hjelmer met them at the wheel and handed his mother down. Then Ingeborg handed Astrid to Bridget and climbed over the wheel herself. "Haakan says that one of these days we are going to have a buggy, but we sure couldn't haul a load like this in a buggy." She whisked her skirts into place and took the now-teary Astrid back in her own arms. "I think when her teeth start to hurt, she thinks nursing is the only answer. Such a child."

"She's a lusty one." Bridget took her son's arm. "If that is coffee I smell, lead me to it. We haven't had a decent cup of coffee since we left home."

"Uff da!" Bridget said later, when she saw the misery Haakan was in. "Guess I got my job cut out for me. I saw a man with a case like this once. At least in Norway, we had ice to help the swelling. Near as I can tell, time is what helps best, so we'll just keep you comfortable." She turned to Ingeborg. "He won't mind a stranger helping out, will he?"

Ingeborg didn't dare look at her husband's face as Bridget took over the sickroom, for she knew she would break out laughing. Haakan was, or had been before he got the mumps, a private man when it came to his own body.

"I feel like I'm on display," he whispered when Ingeborg had settled herself and her toddler in the rocker.

"Ja, well, Bridget will have you up and about in no time, or will know the reason why."

"I hope so," Haakan muttered. "I truly hope so."

They could hear the laughter and chatter from the rest of the house, so the bedroom

223

seemed an island of peace. Ingeborg adjusted her child so both of them were more comfortable. "We got two young folk that don't appear too happy to be here," she told her husband, describing to him how the greeting had gone. "And to think that tomorrow is the house-raising. 'Uff da' is right."

14

"No, you go on to the house-raising," Haakan insisted. "That's a great chance for you to get to know all the people around here. Besides, they've all been looking forward to meeting you. Ingeborg said she and Metiz would take turns being here."

"Well, if you are sure . . ." Bridget cupped her hands at her waist, the only time they were ever still. Usually they held a ball of yarn and knitting needles if nothing else. Since all the babies had already adopted her as their own, one or more usually perched on her arm or clung to her skirt.

"The wagon is all packed." Ingeborg stopped in the doorway. "Thorliff will drive." She shifted from foot to foot rocking Astrid on her hip. She looked from her husband to Bridget. "Is there something wrong?"

"I can stay here." Bridget gestured toward the man in the bed.

"No, you go on. Goodie will introduce you around, and you already met Agnes

Baard." She stepped closer to Bridget so Goodie wouldn't overhear. "They really need every needlewoman they can get. The wedding-ring quilt for Goodie and Olaf isn't finished, so as many of the women as can are going to stay out in the church and try to finish it. I'll be along in a while."

"What needs to be done?"

"Just the tying of it. Last time I saw, it was about half finished."

"And bind the edges?"

"Ja, that too."

"Katy is a wonder with a needle. I'm not sure about Sarah."

"If Ilse would help watch the younger children, that would be good."

Bridget shook her head. "Poor child, to watch both her mor and her far die like that. She tried so hard to save them. We had to restrain her to keep her from throwing herself into the ocean after them — at the burial, you know."

Ingeborg closed her eyes. *Oh, Lord, such pain and agony for one so young. Help us to be her family.*

"Come on, Bestemor." Thorliff stuck his head in the door. "We might miss out."

"I'm sure there will be plenty to do." Ingeborg smiled at her mother-in-law. "You go on now and have a good time. I saw

Kaaren and Lars go by a few minutes ago. Besides, you've never seen sod cutting and building like we do here. You'll learn of many new things."

Bridget nodded. "I'll get my sewing supplies and a fresh apron. Maybe I can buy some cotton for summer dresses for Katy, Sarah, and me. Dakota is warmer than I thought." She fanned herself with her apron. "And not even midmorning yet."

When the house stood quiet again, Ingeborg looked out across the fields. So many things had to be done before winter — harvesting, canning and pickling, fall butchering and smoking the meat. And no one was even busting sod. Haakan's acreage hadn't been touched since last fall, and they still had fifty acres to break on the last half-section they'd bought. She sat down beside Haakan's bed to nurse Astrid.

"I cannot believe I am so sick I can't even move." He rolled his head from side to side. "Four days now and still I'm no better. Worse, for that matter." He looked at Ingeborg. "How can such a simple thing as mumps cause such . . . such . . ." He sighed. "I don't know which is worse, the liquor or the laudanum. My head feels like it's ready to burst."

"You want I should read to you?" She

cupped one hand around the nursing Astrid and leaned forward to retrieve the Bible from the stand by the bed.

"No, you go on."

"I can't drive and nurse Astrid at the same time, so I may as well read." She opened the book in what lap she had left and began reading Psalm 91. " 'He who abides in the shelter of the most high . . .' "

"No, not there. Try Job, the part where his friends are forsaking him."

Ingeborg turned to the requested passage, keeping the smile his request brought tucked safely away. This was one of the last sections she would ever choose to read. But if Haakan was feeling like Job right about now, with swelling or running sores, neither were borne easily. She looked up to see that he'd drifted off to sleep, as had his daughter.

Ingeborg put the Bible away, adjusted her clothing and, carefully rising with the sleeping bundle in her arms, left the room. Astrid was getting too big to be carried around like this. Perhaps with the new baby on the way, she should think about weaning Astrid. She put the thought away to bring out later. She sighed. Babies grew up so fast.

Metiz sat on the back stoop weaving a willow basket. The new shoots that she worked with bent easily in her fingers, now crooked with swollen joints. "You go. I will stay."

Ingeborg sat down on the steps with her friend. "I will, but in the meantime, is there anything else we can do for Haakan to make him more comfortable?"

Metiz motioned to a basket she was filling with the willow bark she stripped off the limbs. "Drink more tea."

"Is there any kind of poultice that would draw out the swelling?"

"Don't know. Ask Great Spirit."

"I have been." Ingeborg propped her chin on her hands and her elbows on her knees. "I should go hunting instead of to the house-raising. With all these extra mouths to feed, a deer would sure help."

"Send Baptiste."

Ingeborg nodded. "Yes, I will tomorrow, but I miss the woods, the hunt. It's so different than here at the house — quiet and cooler under the trees."

Metiz slapped a mosquito buzzing around her ear. "Bugs too."

Ingeborg smiled. "You're right. There's always a fly in the ointment."

Metiz looked her a question.

"Just a saying." Ingeborg got to her feet. "Dinner is in the oven." She watched Metiz' flying fingers. "You ought to sell your baskets in Penny's store."

"This is for Goodie. Wedding gift." She squinted up at Ingeborg. "I ask Penny."

When Ingeborg finally arrived at the house-raising with Astrid, everyone was hard at work. She'd just stepped out over the wheel rim of the wagon when Thorliff ran up. "I'll take care of your horse." He wiped his forehead with his sleeve. "Think I'll go dump a bucket of water over me when I get the horses a drink."

"Would you please bring the baskets from the wagon when you come?" Ingeborg slung Astrid onto her hip and lifted one of the baskets out with her other hand. "Thanks, son. You are always such a big help."

"Hi, Inge. Can you use some help?" Penny met her and reached for Astrid, who waved her arms and jabbered a welcome all her own. "She's going to be talking before you know it."

"Ja, and now that she can walk, she'll soon be running after those brothers of hers."

"When did that happen?" Penny tickled Astrid and made her giggle. "So you're a big girl, walking now."

Astrid reached for the ground with both arms.

"Ja, but she gets in a hurry and it is back down on the knees. It's hard to crawl on the dirt with a dress, but she manages. Hard on the dresses, though."

"You should put her in pants." Penny whirled around to make Astrid laugh again.

"Penny Bjorklund, what an idea." Ingeborg laughed along with the other two.

"Well, if her ma can wear pants . . ."

"Shush." A finger to her mouth did nothing to stop the dancing in her eyes.

"I'd wear britches in a minute if Hjelmer wouldn't have an absolute conniption." Penny kept her voice low. "Especially when I ride."

The sound of hammers and saws, laughter and shouts told of everyone having a good time in spite of the hard work. Ingeborg looked around. "Where's Hjelmer?"

"Oh, a man came needing the tongue repaired on his wagon. Hjelmer is teaching Ephraim to help in the blacksmith shop, so they'll be along later once they get it fixed." She twirled Astrid around again. "Well, I suppose I better get on over to the church. Looks like they put Katy to carrying the water bucket today." She grinned over at Ingeborg. "That's one way to get her introduced around."

"Ja, if some of those men don't fall off the roof asking for a drink."

"How's Haakan?"

Ingeborg shook her head. "Not too good. I probably should have stayed home, but Metiz is there. She'll keep pouring her teas down him, even though he says they taste so vile he's going to get better just to get away from them."

Penny waved back at a greeting shouted from one of the men on the house framing. "I should have just brought the mail with me. Guess I'll open the store later so people can get their mail and whatever else they need before they head home."

Carrying their baskets, they made their way to the already laden tables set up in the shade of the sack house. After setting her burdens down, Ingeborg gave in to Astrid's demands to be let down.

"I'll watch her." Braids bobbing as she ran, Anji Baard skidded to a stop beside her. "Ma said to come on over to the church soon as you got here. We've got the little ones playing in the sack house."

"Mange takk." Ingeborg relinquished her daughter. "Is Mrs. Bjorklund over there and Sarah too?"

"You mean Grandma Bjorklund?"

Ingeborg nodded. At that same instant

she heard a voice raised, this time in anger, not glee. She turned to where the older boys were splitting shingles.

As big as the oldest one there, Hamre stood so fast that the wooden butt he was sitting on toppled sideways. He threw down his tools and stalked off.

"What is that all about?" Ingeborg started toward the shingle splitters.

Lars came up behind her. "Let me handle this."

Ingeborg looked at Thorliff just in time to catch him snitching a roll from a covered basket. She shook her head and nodded toward the other boys. Thorliff shrugged, stuffed the roll in his mouth, and dogtrotted to catch up with Lars.

When Lars came back a few minutes later, Ingeborg asked him a question with her eyebrows.

"I have no idea." Lars shrugged in return. "Something or someone got under Hamre's skin, but no one is talking. I got me a feeling that boy has a bad temper with a mighty short fuse on it."

"So where is he going?"

"To walk this off. He'll be back." Lars pushed his hat back to wipe the sweat from under his hat band. "You think it's the heat?"

"Penny, where's Hjelmer?" one of the men called.

"Over home on a hurry-up wagon repair."

"Ja, he's too busy making money to help out like the rest of us." Anner Valders spoke just loudly enough for Penny to hear.

When Penny started forward, Ingeborg put a hand on her arm. "Just let it go."

"Good thing someone's making money," someone else said and brought a laugh from those around him.

But Ingeborg caught the look on Anner's face and knew *he* wasn't teasing. *Oh, Lord, how long will that man carry this grudge? Instead of getting better, I think it's getting worse. Please do something to bring him to his senses.*

"Come on, let's go work on that quilt."

"Anner Valders makes it real easy for me to hate him."

"Oh, Penny, please don't go that far. That's what's wrong with him, and you don't want to be like that. You know what God says about letting a root of bitterness grow. It can destroy a person."

"Sometimes I wish it would destroy Anner."

"Penny Sjorenson Bjorklund! For shame!"

15

"Mark my words, he's smitten."

"Agnes Baard, whoever are you talking about?" Ingeborg gazed at her friend, letting her eyebrows continue the question.

"Reverend Solberg, that's who. He took one look at your Katy, and —"

"In the first place, she isn't *my* Katy and —"

"In the second place, when he met her, he looked like someone had hit him on the head with a beam. He's been needing a wife. This will sure put a stop to some match-making mamas."

"Ja, well, she is pretty enough to steal any man's heart, but she's still a child and —"

"Oh, she'll grow up soon enough when she has little ones to look after." Agnes eased her swollen feet up on a box that now held empty kettles to take home again. "Uff da."

"You need to take better care of your-self." Ingeborg motioned to the painful-looking feet.

"Look who's talking. And don't change the subject."

"What subject?" Penny sat down on the blanket beside Ingeborg. She leaned over and tickled Astrid's tummy. "How's the best little girl in all the world?"

Astrid smiled at her, reaching up with both arms.

"Babies like you," Ingeborg said with a smile. "Of course, everyone likes you, so that is not surprising."

"Not everyone." She glared over to where Anner Valders was sawing boards for the siding on the new house. Different men had different tasks in this house-raising, and Anner usually ended up with a saw in hand because he measured and cut so precisely.

"It's not you he has a problem with." Agnes fanned herself with her apron. "Uff da! It is hot today. Even here in the shade."

The sack house cast a shady spot for little ones taking naps and for adults taking breathers. Several younger children lay sprawled on the quilts, and Agnes had volunteered to watch the sleepers while most of the women had disappeared back to the church to stitch on the quilt.

"His problem might not be with me, but anyone gets mean about my husband, and I'm like a she-wolf protecting her cubs."

Penny picked up Astrid and held her in the air above her head. She jiggled the child, and Astrid grinned, her round face lighting up as if reflecting the sun. She waved her arms and pumped her legs as though she couldn't wait to get going. "You know, child, you're just about too big for me to lift like this." Penny lowered Astrid to her lap.

"If you're like that with your husband, what will you be like with children?"

A cloud passed over Penny's bright smile, but after a sigh, she said, "Anyone bothers my children, they better watch out. If I ever get to have any, that is."

"Penny Bjorklund, you've been married only . . . let's see." Agnes closed her eyes to count the months. "End of May to June, July, August. Only three months and you are already fussing about no baby on the way?"

Penny laid Astrid back on the quilt and tickled the child's bare feet. "Sorry, Tante Agnes, I know how you —"

"No, child, you don't know how I feel. And I hope to God you never do. Losing a baby early on is real hard, but to have one stillborn, that's even harder. She was so perfect, like a rose that never fully opened. And if that weren't enough, I guess the good Lord thinks I'm too old for raising more of His children."

Penny rocked back and clasped her

skirted knees with her hands. "You're not old. You're just not all better yet."

Ingeborg listened to the two. Agnes had never regained her robust health, and she tired easily. Before this last baby, she'd have been the last one sitting here minding the youngsters. Her needle would have been flashing as fast as her tongue over there in the church, hustling everyone to hurry and finish the stitching. She'd have kept them laughing at the same time.

Not like this pensive woman beside her, with swollen feet and eyes that no longer twinkled with laughter at the slightest provocation.

Ingeborg kept her own joyful news to herself, although Metiz had already figured it out and Goodie wore that knowing look when Ingeborg returned from rush trips to the outhouse, so that the others wouldn't know yet.

"But, near as I can tell, He's sending one to Ingeborg here. You told Haakan yet?"

"What?" Ingeborg jerked herself back to the conversation. "Agnes, you old . . . how did you know?"

"You have that breeding look about you. Not hard to recognize if'n you know what to look for. I was waiting for you to say something."

Ingeborg turned a heavy-eyed Astrid on her tummy. "I know how sad you've been, and I didn't want to make you feel sadder."

"Ah, Ingeborg, friends share both the joys and sorrows, as you well know. Your good news would never make me sad, just glad for you and ready to pray a healthy baby into this world of ours."

"Mange takk, as always. I should have known you would feel that way." Ingeborg reached over and patted Agnes's hand. "Thank you, I've already been praying for this little soul. I want a son for Haakan's sake."

"I got me a feeling that you are more concerned about a son than Haakan. 'Pears to me he figures Thorliff and Andrew are his every bit as much as that little angel there. Bjorklund blue eyes is Bjorklund blue eyes, no matter who the pa. I bet you that if you put all the Bjorklund cousins together, even the family couldn't tell who belonged to who, let alone strangers."

"Now wouldn't that be something, a gathering of Bjorklunds."

"Well, look at Hamre. He could be a big brother to Thorliff and Andrew, and no one would know the difference."

"Ja, other than that scowl on his face. I thought he wanted to come to the new country."

"You asked Bridget yet?"

Ingeborg shook her head. "She's so busy over there with the ladies, I can't get a question in edgewise. Besides, we stayed up talking last night till near time for the roosters to crow and didn't begin to get caught up on all the news of home."

"Kaaren too?"

Ingeborg nodded again. "Katy fell asleep in her chair. Left us old ladies to talk the night away."

"Katy's too young to appreciate a good gossip. That only comes with nights pacing the floor with a sick one or washing clothes for two days straight or lasting out these blizzards with a sane mind."

"Or any mind." Ingeborg smiled at Penny. "See what you have to look forward to?"

"I wouldn't mind waiting if I had a family of my own nearby."

"Lord, child, what do you mean? If we aren't family —"

"No, Tante Agnes." Penny raised her hand. "You and Onkel Joseph, you *are* my family. But somewhere I have brothers and sisters of my own, and I'd like to find them so I can write to them and maybe they'd come out here to see us. Or we could at least send letters. Cousin Ephraim coming like he did makes me want to see them all the more. If they are still alive."

"I guess I always knew you missed them, but after we moved out here, you never said much." Agnes shook her head. "We should have taken all of you, like I wanted."

Penny looked up at her aunt. "Like you wanted?"

Agnes nodded. "Me'n Joseph, we said we'd take all five, but your other relatives said that was too much and the children should be split up." Agnes now shook her head. "I should've done what I thought best and just taken over."

Penny moved close to Agnes's side and leaned her head against her aunt's thigh. "Bless you for caring so much. I sure do wish it had happened that way. But getting all of those kids into a wagon coming west, now that would have been some sight."

Agnes stroked Penny's hair. The mass curled down her back when allowed to hang free as it did today. "You know I couldn't love you more if'n you were bone of my bone."

"I know that. When I think of mother, yours is the face I see."

Agnes laid her cheek on the top of Penny's head. "We'll all pray that God sees fit to bring you a baby soon. And that somehow He'll help us find the rest of your family too."

"Thank you." Penny squeezed her aunt's hand and got to her feet. "I better go get Katy. She can help me carry the water bucket around again. Those men look more than ready for a cup of cool water. Maybe some on the outside would be just as welcome." She stopped. "On second thought, let Sarah help her."

"The sight of two such lovely faces won't hurt 'em neither."

"You think *Mister* Valders needs water? Or maybe he'd rather wait until his wife brings it out to him."

"Long wait that'll be," muttered Agnes.

"Agnes Baard, and to think you were just telling Penny that forgiveness goes both ways."

"When did I say that? Not today anyway, even though I do recollect saying some such to a certain friend of mine who shall remain nameless." The two friends shared a smile, the kind of smile that comes with having gone through the valleys and cliffs of life and having held each other up along the way.

The two women watched the builders for a time, sharing the comfort of not having to talk but just being together. The three-bedroom house had gone up quickly with so many willing hands. House- and barn-raisings were such common events by now that everybody knew who did what best and let them do it. The young boys had moved their tools to the shade of the store, their froes and mallets flying as they raced to see who could split the most shingles.

Hamre had returned to the work but set his tools apart from the others. Ingeborg looked around again, searching this time for a sorrowful face that reminded her so much of Solveig, Kaaren's sister, when she came to them after the train accident. But Ilse was younger and had lost much more than a happy face. Without parents and relatives in this country, she could be sent to an orphanage.

"Who are you looking for?"

"Ilse. Have you seen her?"

"She might be with Mrs. Bjorklund over at the church. I thought she'd stay with Katy."

"Think I'll go see." Ingeborg got to her feet, sighing in the process.

"She could always come live with us. You know I have room for another at any time."

"Thank you, and maybe that is a good idea. She could help you with the younger ones and earn her keep. Not that there isn't plenty to do around our house. And Kaaren can always use help with her three."

"You are going to miss Goodie."

"I know. But Bridget will do as much as three, even though she's a grandmother. And Katy . . ."

"Katy will be the next one to be married around here."

"Agnes Baard, you could hire out as a matchmaker. You have marriage on your mind all the time."

"Ja, well, did you notice Petar?" Agnes shook her head and smiled at the same time. "He's wearing that same dumb-struck look as Reverend Solberg. That girl will have to fend suitors off with a stick."

Ingeborg laughed and headed for the church. Leave it to Agnes. She waved at Reverend Solberg, who was nailing rafters to a beam. Usually Haakan was right along the rooftop, directing anyone who needed extra help. These men could all do so many different things and had learned to work together like a team of twelve-up or more.

The thought of that many horses needed at once reminded her of the steam engine. They would need twelve-up to pull that monster and four more to pull the thresher. Where would they get all the horses? And if they took them all on the road, what would they use at home to break more sod? Good thing the Bjorklunds still had two span of oxen. They might be slower than horses, but speed wasn't all that counted. Of course, they might take the oxen to pull the thresher.

It all came back to the fact that they needed more horses trained for heavy pulling. While the new machinery saved many hours, it also took more horses to move from place to place.

She could hear the women chattering and laughing before she got to the church doors. With all the windows open to catch any stray breeze, the voices could be heard easily. She stopped in the doorway to watch.

The wedding-ring quilt was stretched out in all its glory, the colors of the small squares that formed the rings glowing where the sun touched them. Needles of the eight women who occupied the chairs around the frame flew as fast as their tongues. Norwegian and English blended together, well punctuated with laughter as the women teased and told stories on one another, mostly for Bridget's benefit.

Children too old for naps or already awake were blocked in a corner by chairs lying on their sides, so they could play without being underfoot. The child watching them was the serious-faced Ilse. At least she wasn't scowling. Sophie crawled over to the girl and pulled herself up on the chair.

"Me, up?" she asked in English. She raised her arms and fell backward, smack on her plump little bottom.

Ilse didn't move.

Sophie pulled herself up again, raised her arms, wobbled, and caught herself with one hand on the chair. "Up!" This time there was no asking. Sophie already knew the value of an attack on an unsuspecting victim.

Ilse shook her head. "You play there." Her Norwegian flowed quickly, abruptly.

As if she had a window into the little girl's head, Ingeborg could see Sophie's mind working. Sophie switched to Norwegian and a winsome smile. "Me, up?" She rattled the angled chair back with both hands. At the clatter, her eyes lit up and she shook it again.

Ilse sighed and, shaking her head, stepped over the barricade and knelt on the floor.

Sophie's grin as she turned and dropped to her knees made Ingeborg smile. Who could resist such charm? Certainly not that very sad child that had come to live with them. Perhaps sending her to be with Kaaren and the twins would be the best thing for her. When Sophie set out to charm, the victim hadn't a snowball's chance in July of ignoring her.

Sophie crawled right up in Ilse's lap and, wiggling around like a little puppy trying to make a nest, parked her bottom on the girl's knees. She looked up at the older girl, babbling out her own story and taking over. It made no difference to Sophie if she was understood or not. But something got through, because a smile glimmered on Ilse's pale face. Though lasting only for a moment, that glimmer was a break in the sorrow.

Sophie was better than a puppy for bringing out a smile any day.

Ingeborg looked over at Kaaren, who nodded to say she had seen the same thing. Bridget smiled at both her daughters-in-law and kept on stitching.

When the time came to shift positions, Ingeborg took one of the chairs at the quilting frame, sitting between Hildegunn Valders and the silent Sarah.

"So what have you heard from Mr. Gould?" Hildegunn stopped stitching to ask.

"Nothing yet. I just mailed the letter to him and Mr. Brockhurst in Grand Forks last week." She turned to the rest of the group. "I wrote to get information on how to start our own bank here in Blessing."

At their murmurs, Ingeborg just smiled. More and more she was convinced that a bank was just what they needed. Now to learn how to set one up.

"Why can't Grace hear?"

Ingeborg turned from her concentration on the trotting team to look over her shoulder in shock. Ilse stood right behind her shoulder. These were the first words she'd heard out of the child's mouth.

"We don't know. She was born deaf."

Ilse clutched the back of the bench seat when the turning wagon wheel dropped in a rut. The jingle of the harness and the clumping of horses' feet that spurted miniature clouds of dust sounded loud in the late afternoon stillness. While some of the families remained to put the finishing touches on the new house, Ingeborg had taken her wagon and headed home. The big boys had run on ahead of them, leaving Andrew and Ellie dozing in the wagon bed.

"Will she ever hear?"

"We don't know. That's up to God."

The girl snorted. "God don't listen too good."

Ingeborg wished she could wrap her arms around the child and hold her close, but one glance at the stiff shoulders, and she knew that even if she clamped the reins between her knees to free her hands, Ilse wouldn't allow the touch.

Instead she nodded. "Ja, I thought that way too at one time."

"I hate God."

"I did too."

"He made Far and Mor die."

"Seems that way." *Oh, child. He loves you so. Father, please give me the right words, the wisdom to help Ilse.* But no words came, so she remained silent.

"He did too."

Ingeborg turned enough so she could see the young girl. Teeth clenched, fists tight at her side, tears frozen behind eyelids that ached from fighting the onslaught, this one was already learning how to be tough so as not to shatter under the sorrow.

"Your far and mor are in heaven and watching out for you, even though they couldn't stay here."

Braids slapped her cheeks at the violence of her headshake. "They put them in the ocean."

"Where we are buried doesn't matter. Our heavenly Father catches us up to himself in heaven."

"I hate God."

"Ja, but He loves you anyway. Here. You want to drive the horses?" She lifted the reins just in time to keep Ilse from climbing over the wagon side.

"Really?"

"Why sure. You climb up here with me, and we'll hold the reins together until you get used to the feel. You ever driven a team before?"

When Ilse settled herself on the seat, Ingeborg wrapped one arm around her and, while hugging the board-stiff body to her side, handed the reins over to the small hands and then cupped her own over them. While her heart beseeched the Father for help, her hands and arms melted the ice within until the girl leaned against her side.

"This is nice." Ilse looked up and a ghost of a smile touched her dark blue eyes.

"Ja, driving horses always makes me feel better too. You were good with Sophie at the church."

"Mange takk."

Paws ran out to greet them, pink tongue lolling out the side of his mouth. He yipped and danced beside the wheels, first on one side, then the other.

"I had a dog at home." Ilse handed the reins back, stiffening up again at the same time. "I want to go back to Nordland.

Bestemor and Bestefar must miss me. They don't know about . . ." She couldn't finish her sentence.

A glance to the side showed Ingeborg that the child was fighting with all she had to keep the tears inside.

"Mrs. Bjorklund wrote to them, and the steamship company would have notified them too."

"Oh."

Ingeborg tightened the reins so the horses stopped by the back stoop. "Do you know how to milk a cow?"

The look she got in return said plenty. As if any ten-year-old girl didn't know how to milk cows, and what a stupid question to ask.

"Good, then you can help Thorliff and Baptiste with the milking. The pails are in the springhouse right over there. I see they already have the cows all in the barn."

"Mor, we're hungry."

"Yes, Andrew, I'm sure you are, but we have chores to do first."

Ingeborg swung over the wheel and to the ground. "You and Ellie can feed the chickens while the rest of us milk. I'm going to check on your pa first." She scooped the sleeping Astrid up in her arms and mounted the steps. "You show Ilse where things are.

251

Have her start with Bess." She named the gentlest cow in the herd.

A stew bubbled on the back of the stove, greeting them with the rich fragrance. Metiz came out of the sickroom.

"Him sleeping."

Metiz carried a half-finished basket on her arm, this one a different shape, so Ingeborg knew the other one was finished.

"Rain tonight."

"Then it is a good thing the men stayed to nail down the roof. That house went up so fast, Metiz, you would be amazed."

"Tepee faster." Metiz' black eyes sparkled.

"Ja, tepees go up faster, come down faster, and let you freeze in the winter faster." Ingeborg knew her friend was teasing. More than once, Metiz had commented on Ingeborg's "fine" house. She loved the light coming in the windows about as much as Ingeborg did.

Later that night when all the others were tucked in bed, Ingeborg sat beside Haakan and, while changing the cloths again, told him about the talk with Ilse on the way home.

"I'm surprised she talked with you at all. Bridget said she hadn't heard a word from the child since the ship's men restrained her."

"I know. I was so shocked I about dropped the reins." She partially wrung out a cloth of cool water and laid it across his belly. He flinched but smiled up at her.

"I think you like making me flinch like that."

"No, but if you can smile at me, you must be feeling better."

"I think so. As long as I don't move my legs or anything." He laid his head first one side, then the other. "See, at least this end of me works."

"Good. Reverend Solberg asked if he could come see you tomorrow after church."

"And you said . . . ?"

She looked at him, astonishment widening her eyes. "I said of course. He's coming for dinner." She leaned closer. "I have a feeling he isn't coming just to see you, though, or he would have been over here before."

Haakan quirked an eyebrow.

"Katy."

"Ah. Then he probably won't mind that I can't get up and greet him."

"Most likely not. Although he did say that anything that could fell Haakan Bjorklund had to be pretty bad."

"I wouldn't wish this on my worst

enemy." He groaned when he tried to roll over. "Never thought I'd be hankering to walk to the outhouse."

She handed him the thunder mug. "The things we take for granted when we are well."

What other things had she been taking for granted? Ingeborg pondered that as she nursed Astrid for the last time that night. God forbid anything else bad would happen.

The sound of the rain tapping on the windows reminded her that no one would skip church tomorrow to harvest. The grain would have to dry again before it could be cut. *Please, God, protect the wheat.* A hailstorm now would be the end of harvest for sure.

They were discussing the rainstorm both before and after church the next morning.

"Flattened fields south and west of here," one man said.

"Thanks be to God He spared the fields around here," someone else added.

Ingeborg couldn't help but silently add "for now." Nothing was certain until the grain was bagged and shipped, and the uncertainty of falling wheat prices kept the farmers on the edge of worry.

16

"Haakan Howard Bjorklund, you just get right back in that bed!"

The thud when his body hit the floor brought all of them running. The women piled through the doorway with Ingeborg in the lead. Her heart started beating again when she recognized the stubborn-mule look on her husband's face.

"I . . . have . . . to . . . run . . . the . . . steam . . . engine." He spoke from between teeth clamped so hard together his jaw glistened white. Sweat ran in rivulets from the effort he'd made.

"You think you didn't give Lars good training? He's run the steam engine before, and he will do so again." Ingeborg signaled to Goodie, who took Haakan's other arm. "On three now. One, two, three." With them hoisting, he straightened his legs enough to lift him back to the edge of the bed. Even the effort of sitting up kept the sweat pouring down his face and chest.

"Ingeborg, I have been sick for over a

week. The fields are cut and shocked. We need to get the separator going."

"Ja, that is true, but the *we* will not include you yet." She stood in front of him, arms akimbo and a jaw nearly as tight as his. "If you conk yourself on the head, you'll be laid up that much longer. Besides, you need all your strength for getting better, not for getting out of bed. If you want to sit in that chair while Goodie and I change your bed, that'll be a help."

Bridget appeared in the doorway. "Can I do anything?"

"You can try to talk some sense into this man here."

Bridget shook her head. "Not a Bjorklund man when he has his mind made up. Like a bear trap, they are." She turned and said over her shoulder, "I'll go kill chickens for dinner. That's much easier."

"Spoken like a truly wise woman." Goodie helped settle Haakan in the chair and handed him a damp towel to wipe his face. "You just behave yourself, Haakan Bjorklund. You know you are supposed to stand up with Olaf at our wedding this Sunday. Asking for help would go a long way to getting your strength back sooner."

Haakan wiped his face and neck. "At least I can feel the bone and muscle in my neck again. That's something to be thankful for."

"You have plenty to be thankful for." Goodie stopped stuffing the goose-down pillow into the pillowcase. "Two sons, a daughter, another baby on the way, a wife who stands by you, and a farm the riches of which I bet you never dreamed."

"You're right, Goodie. It's just hard to remember those things when I'm supposed to be out in the fields providing for all that I have." Haakan leaned against the back of the chair, a white line around his mouth, evidence of the strain the effort cost.

"Perhaps the good Lord gave you this time of quiet to help you remember."

Between the two of them, the women turned the mattress, fluffing the sweet hay stuffing at the same time. With dry sheets spread and tucked in, they helped Haakan back to bed again.

"Now you rest, and in a while we'll come back and help you walk, if you can stand the pain. Perhaps moving about more will ease the swelling some."

Haakan gave Ingeborg a look that said what he thought about Goodie's bossing him about like he was still in short pants. Ingeborg quirked the side of her mouth in what passed for a smile that Goodie wouldn't see but let Haakan know she understood his frustrations.

"Perhaps we can tighten the truss somehow to give you more support. It's worth a try." She whispered the words as she held a cup of cool water for him to drink. "You've lost so much weight. . . ." She just shook her head and didn't bother to finish the sentence.

That night Lars, Joseph, Petar, and the boys all crowded into the sickroom.

"We got to start." Joseph Baard took the floor. "And you know it, well as we do, that if we wait any longer, someone's liable to lose their crop to a hailstorm or some such." He scratched his scraggly beard. "Now, near as I see it, we haul the steam engine and separator to that same spot we did last year when we hired that outside crew. Four to five families can bring their wheat shocks there. They can pick up their straw later."

Haakan nodded. "I know. I been thinking the same thing. You going to haul wood to burn for the engine or use straw?"

"What do you think?"

"Pa says wood don't burn too fast, makes the heat more even." Thorliff spoke up as if he was one of the men.

Lars, Haakan, and Joseph all grinned at one another.

"We cut more if needed," Baptiste offered.

"Ja, we will burn wood while we have it. I heard of a boiler that exploded with straw fire."

"Two men killed." Joseph shook his head. "We got to be real careful. Some of these men get in such a hurry."

"I checked all the belts before . . ." Haakan sighed. "Just be careful, you hear?"

After more discussion, the men filed out, leaving Haakan to force himself to count his blessings rather than curse his own body for betraying him this way.

In the morning he heard the crack of the whip, the horses' hooves digging in, the shouting, and finally the moving of the steam engine. When silence finally fell again, he stared at the ceiling. Had he told them everything they needed to know? How could he lie there and let others do his work for him? But when he tried to turn over, he knew why. He couldn't get his pants on even if he could stand up.

But with the aid of the women, each day he walked a little farther, from wall to wall in the bedroom, then out to the kitchen, the parlor, and finally he could sit in a chair on the front porch. He stared at his hand, shaking as if with palsy just from the effort of walking out the door. Every night Lars reported how the day had gone. By Saturday, Haakan could get his pants on. On the third Sunday morning in August, at the wedding service following church, he stood beside Olaf, and Ingeborg stood up for Goodie as Reverend Solberg united the two in holy matrimony.

"Mor?" Andrew tugged at his mother's skirt when the wedding party joined the rest of the congregation at the tables groaning with hams, fried chicken, beans, mashed potatoes, vegetables of all kinds, both cooked and pickled, rolls, salads, and lemonade. Off to one side, the desserts decorated a table of their own.

"Ja?" Ingeborg finally turned from the person she was talking with and answered her son.

"Mor, Thorliff said Hans and Ellie are going to live at Onkel Olaf's new house."

Ingeborg nodded. "Sure they are. Olaf is now their pa. You saw them get married."

"But" — he shook his head — "Ellie lives at our soddy."

"Not anymore. I told you." Thorliff came up beside his brother.

"Go away." Andrew turned on his brother and pushed him with all his might.

"Andrew, whatever has come over you?"

Ingeborg took her younger son by the shoulder. "Come with me."

She walked him over by the wagons that sat in the shade of the church with the teams tethered to the wheels. "Now, what is this all about?"

Andrew looked up at her, his eyes swimming in tears. "But Ellie can't move away. She's my bestest friend."

"It isn't like she's moving to Grand Forks or something. You'll still get to see her at church, and they'll come to our house to visit and we'll go to theirs."

Andrew shook his head until his curls bounced. "Please, Mor, keep Ellie at our house."

Ingeborg sank to her knees and pulled her little son to her, wrapping him in her arms. "Ah, Andrew, we can't always make people do what we want. Children live with their parents, and things change. Pretty soon Sophie will be big enough to play with you, and . . ."

"Can I go live with Ellie?"

"No, but she will come stay with us tonight yet." Ingeborg stood, keeping his hand in hers. "Come now, let us go eat and show your pa what a big boy you are."

Andrew rubbed his eyes with the back of his hand and sniffed again. "When Ellie and me gets married up, she can stay with us, huh, Mor?"

"Let's just get through this wedding before we begin planning that one, all right?"

Andrew sniffed the air like a dog on a scent. "I want a drumstick. No two. One for me and one for Ellie."

Ingeborg shook her head. "Oh, Andrew, the things you come up with."

Later, when she told Haakan the story, he chuckled. "That boy of ours! You got to admit he's smarter than many kids lots older than him. I wouldn't be a bit surprised if he does what he says."

"Haakan, he's just a baby."

"That's what you think."

Before the sun rose the next morning, Haakan and Hamre backed the loaded wagon out of the barn where they'd stored it overnight to keep the dew off the bundled wheat. Along with another wagon that Lars drove, they headed off across the fields to where the steam engine and separator were set up at the junction of four properties. Wagons full of bundled grain were already lining up by the time he and Lars got the steam engine burning hot enough to begin building steam in the boiler. While they waited for the gauge to reach the needed pressure, Lars oiled all the moving parts, and Haakan showed Hamre how to reset and check the long belt for the proper tension.

"Why is it crossed like that?" Hamre pointed to the X made in the middle of the wide belt that joined the separator to the steam engine.

"Keeps the belt on the pulleys that way. If that belt flies off or breaks, it could mean the end of a man's life."

"Like the winches on the fishing boat?"

"That's right. It's dangerous to be around machinery if'n you don't know what you are doing." Haakan studied every inch of the belt, pointing out the places where he'd restitched it. "Better to fix it before it busts." He turned to the boy at his side. "You want to be in charge of the oil can? When Lars or I holler, you climb up and pour oil into whatever hole we tell you."

Hamre nodded. "Ja, I can do that."

"Come on then, I'll show you where all the places are." Haakan and Hamre climbed all over the separator and the steam engine, being careful to keep from getting burned as they neared the firebox. "You can help keep the fire up too. Between the three of us, we should be able to keep this contraption going." He gave the steam engine a slap on the side.

"She-e's ready," Lars shouted. When he threw the lever, the pulleys began to turn. The *kerplunks* of the engine joined the screech of metal against metal, and in a few moments the rig settled into the rhythm for the day. At Lars's nod, Haakan threw the long-handled lever on the separator, and the belt engaged. With more screeching and grinding, the separator bed began to bring the bundled grain closer to the maw of the monster.

The men on the first wagon forked the bundles onto the moving canvas, and within a few moments chaff flew out of the stack, and golden grain poured into the sacking bin. Lars finished hooking the gunnysack over the square frame at the side of the machine, and with the twist of another handle, kernels of wheat began rounding the bottom of the sack.

When the first sack was full, he spun the handle to shut off the golden stream and, grabbing the sack by the two sides of the open mouth, hoisted the entire thing off to the side and between the knees of one of the older men, whose job it was to stitch the mouth closed. His big needle, threaded with hemp, flashed in and out as he whipped the sack closed. Swen, at almost fourteen the oldest of the Baard children, hefted the sack and tossed it into the waiting wagon. As the day progressed, the men changed jobs but the rhythm remained the same.

As did the wheat chaff that worked its way into shirts and pants and made everyone itch. The sun rose higher in the sky, raising sweat to pour over the rash from the chaff. When Knute Baard brought the water bucket and dipper around, he had instant friends.

"Noisy, huh?" He shouted to be heard. When Hamre ignored him, Knute set the bucket down and clapped his hands over his ears. "I said noisy, huh?"

Hamre wasted no motion with his nod. He took the dipper, drank, and handed it back. Knute took it and poured some over his own head, then motioned for the other boy to do the same. Hamre shook his head, his eyebrows meeting to finish the frown.

Knute shrugged and went on his way. When he got to Haakan, he looked over his shoulder at the newcomer.

"Just give him time," Haakan said, clapping a hand on Knute's shoulder. "I sure do thank you for both the drink and the shower." He used two dippers full like most of the men had. One to drink and one to pour.

"He's some mad, ain't he?" Knute looked over at Hamre again.

"Don't worry. It wasn't nothing you did." Haakan waved to catch Hamre's attention, then pointed to a place on the steam engine that needed oil. "You just go on about your water carrying. Far as I can see, you're the most popular man on the crew."

Knute touched a finger to the brim of his flat hat and, picking up the now empty bucket, headed to the water wagon for a refill.

With Bridget, Katy, Kaaren, and Sarah doing the cooking for the threshing crew and Ilse watching the younger children, Ingeborg drove the wagon for Thorliff and Baptiste to load with bundled wheat. Only by convincing Andrew that Ilse needed his help was she able to get out the door without him. She could still hear his pleading "M-o-o-r." He woke up crying during the night, asking for Ellie. Ingeborg sighed. They really didn't need another young one underfoot, not with all the cooking to be done. Once they finished with dinner, they had to start right away on supper. She left the full wagon and team, waved at Haakan, and slapped the reins over the backs of the waiting horses. Halfway home, she met Ephraim on his way out to the Bjorklund farms.

"I come to help." He swung up onto the wagon seat beside her.

"Well, we sure do appreciate every spare pair of hands we can get." She swung the empty wagon out onto the field. Just ahead of her plodded a team of oxen, pulling a nearly full wagon. The boys jabbed three-tined forks into the bundles and lifted them into the wagon, trying to keep them straight and balanced so the wagon would hold more and the unloading would go easier.

When Ephraim looked around, Ingeborg tipped her broad-brimmed hat back and smiled. "The men are over running the steam engine and the separator. We're the team here."

"Oh." The one word carried a multitude of meanings. Ephraim stepped over the wagon wheel and to the ground. "I'll help them load then."

At midmorning Katy brought out a jug of water. "I can come help if you want. We got things nearly done up at the house."

"Won't turn down any offers." Ingeborg jumped to the ground and waved Katy up on the seat. "You have driven before, haven't you?" Katy nodded. "Good, and by the way, that bonnet looks good on you."

"It should. It's yours."

"I know. But I like this one better."
Ingeborg touched the wide brim of her felt
hat, a last relic of Roald's.

Katy nodded, setting her sunbonnet to
bobbing. "With this sun, you sure got to
have something on your head. I can handle
a pitchfork too, you know. Back home we all
had to help with the haying, even though we
never had fields the size of these."

Ingeborg thought back to Norway to the
hay draped over wooden fence rails to dry
and the wheat they cut and bound by hand,
then shocked and flailed in the winter. No,
things surely were different here. She caught
herself nodding. She knew for certain she
had no desire to return to the old farming
ways of Norway. She looked toward the west
where they could see the smoke rising from
the steam engine furnace and hear the *chunk-
a-chunk* clear across the fields.

Haakan said that one day there would be
steam engines doing most of the work of
horses. While she found it hard to believe,
that belching, brawling machine they were
using over west was certainly increasing
their wheat yield.

They switched teams and she left Katy
driving the empty wagon while she headed
back to the threshing. Next trip they'd bring
the dinner.

Later, after helping serve the two wagonloads of food they brought out, she drove a load of filled wheat sacks to the sack house. When her turn came to unload, Olaf weighed the wagon, counted the sacks, and wrote the tally down on his board.

"Aren't you going to check the sacks like you do the others?" Ingeborg asked.

"If I thought a Bjorklund would put rocks in a sack of grain or bring in moldy wheat, I'd hang up my shingle right now and take up rocking."

Ingeborg shook her head and laughed at the same time. "No time for rocking with the family you got now."

"No, but I'll never doubt a family member either."

"I'll be back."

"I'll be here. And knowing Goodie, she will too. Right now she's up to her elbows in bread dough."

"Hey, Mrs. Bjorklund!" Hans leaped off the unloading platform and, arms flying, raced up to the wagon.

"Hey yourself." Ingeborg tugged on the reins.

"You think you could use another hand out there?" He looked up at her, eyes pleading his case.

"What would your ma say?"

"I can ask. Onkel Olaf — er, Pa said I could if you said so."

"You go on and get her permission while I get a drink from Penny." Ingeborg stepped down from the wagon, stifling a groan as she straightened. That wagon seat got harder as the day grew longer.

"Penny, you there?" She rapped on the frame of the back door.

"Come in and sit down! I'll be right there," Penny called from the store.

"I'll come in," Ingeborg muttered, "but that sitting down can be better left for another day." While she waited, she poured herself a basin of water and sloshed it on her face and arms, deliberately getting enough on her dress to make her feel cooler instantly. Once she started drinking, she feared she may not stop.

"I have some lemonade left from dinner," Penny said when she brushed aside the curtain hanging over the doorway.

"That might just be a small piece of heaven on earth." Ingeborg hooked the dipper back over the edge of the enameled water bucket.

"Did Ephraim find you?" Penny poured a glassful of lemonade and handed it to Ingeborg, who took a sip and closed her eyes in delight before answering.

"He's helping the boys load another wagon right now. Sure do appreciate your sending him on."

"Figured you needed him worse than me." Just then the bell over the front door of her store tinkled to announce another customer. "Take your time." She raised her voice. "Coming." The curtain swirled behind her.

Ingeborg finished her drink and met Hans at the back step.

"I can come."

"What about Ellie?"

"She's taking a nap. Ma said she was too grouchy to live with so sent her to bed."

Ingeborg swung up to the wagon seat, picked up the reins, and clucked the horses forward. "She sick?"

"If'n you call missing Andrew sick, she sure is."

"We'll take her home with us later then." Ingeborg turned the wagon toward home.

"Ma said you could bring Andrew into our house for a few days until you get harvest done. She's been baking for Penny's store too, she said to tell you. Otherwise she'd come help."

Ingeborg smiled at Hans. She'd never heard him talk this much. Maybe that was because she'd never been alone with him before. Hans, Baptiste, and Thorliff had

271

been like one person ever since Hans came to their house so sick they feared he would die.

"That will make him one happy fellow."

Four days later, the steam engine and separator moved on. Ingeborg hugged Haakan one last time and dabbed her eyes with the corner of her apron.

"It's not like I'm going to the north woods or some such." Haakan tipped her chin up with one callused finger.

"I know." Ingeborg straightened her shoulders. "Guess we're all just a mite tired, is all."

"Ja, and that little one growing inside you is taking his own too." Haakan laid a hand on her belly. "I'd say take it a bit easy, but knowing you, it would be a wasted breath." His words could have stung but for the grin that lighted his eyes. She looked up at him, feeling as if she was drowning in pools of blue. That old familiar warmth rose all the way from her belly to her cheekbones.

"Go with God." She forced the words past the lump in her throat.

"I always do and pray His blessing on all of you here at home. See you in a month or so."

She nodded and forced a smile to her trembling lips. "See you." She stepped back and looked down at the tug on her skirts. Astrid raised her arms.

"Up."

"You should be in bed." She swung the little one to her hip.

Astrid leaned toward her father. "Up."

Haakan chucked her under the chin. "You be good for your ma, now, you hear?"

"Up, Pa." She reached again, her smile designed to get her way.

Haakan took her in his arms, hugged her close, and handed her back to her mother. "You be a good girl." He stressed the word "good."

"Wave good-bye," Ingeborg said in a gentle voice. *God, Father of us all, keep them safe and bring him home soon, having done his work as we will do ours.*

Haakan waved once again and climbed into the wagon that now wore the white canvases to make a traveling house. He, Lars, and Hamre would sleep in the wagon and cook if they needed to.

"Bye, Pa," Astrid whispered, then sighed. She pulled at her mother's dress. "Mo."

"You and Andrew." Ingeborg turned back to the house. Morning chores, including feeding children, waited for no one.

Haakan hadn't been gone two days before Ingeborg stared longingly at the untilled fields. Beyond them lay the land yet to be broken by the plow. While the women and boys slaved from dawn to dark, the fall work was not getting done.

Yes, the men needed to be off with the threshing machines. Yes, the extra grain would bring in extra money. Yes, they needed the money. She knew all the answers. She and Haakan, Kaaren and Lars had discussed them often enough.

When she found herself wanting to swat a whiny Astrid, Ingeborg knew she had to get out of the house. As soon as the little girl was down and asleep in her bed, Ingeborg pulled her dress over her head and donned the britches she had folded away in a box under the bed. She buttoned the shirt to her throat, pulled on her boots and strode into the kitchen.

"Ingeborg!" Bridget's eyes matched her open mouth — big *O*'s.

"We need some venison." Ingeborg took the rifle off the pegs above the door. "If I'm not back by dark, send Thorliff looking for me. He knows where the game trails are."

"Can't Baptiste go?" Bridget clamped her hands together under her apron.

"He's doing something for Metiz. She asks for his help so seldom, I don't want to disturb them." She took her hat from the peg by the door and clapped it on her head. "Don't hold supper for me. The deer come down to drink at dusk."

Once out in the freedom of the woods, Ingeborg felt like throwing herself on the ground and rolling as the horses did when let loose after a hard day's work. She looked up to see the sun gilding the edges of the cottonwood leaves above her. The leaves whispered secrets to the breeze, and a crow announced her arrival.

She strode off down the trail, feeling her cares drop off one by one until she could have been running with no more effort, or flying, she felt so light. "Thank you, God!" she called, raising her face to the shaft of light that split the green canopy. She paused. Surely He had said, "You're welcome." She shook her head at her foolishness. "Velbekomme."

After a long walk watching for deer signs and ignoring the grouse she scared up, she settled in next to a giant elm tree with a clear view of the trail the deer followed to drink at the river. Mosquitoes took up a hum as if announcing to the world that dinner was served. She pulled her hat down low and her shirt collar up high.

She'd forgotten how pesky the things were.

A squirrel chattered overhead. Two grouse pecked their way down the trail, searching for seeds and any careless bugs. Ingeborg could feel her eyelids growing heavy.

A mosquito buzzed her nose. She took her hand off her rifle to brush the thing away when she saw them. Three deer, tiptoeing their way down the dirt track, ears and noses scanning the world around them.

Ingeborg waited. She could tell that the doe was still nursing her half-grown fawn, so she sighted on the buck. One shot and he dropped. The other two were gone before she could blink.

She waited a moment, letting the peace settle back on the riverbank before going to the fallen animal to cut its throat and begin the dressing out. She should have brought lacings for a travois to haul it on.

That night, the welts on her neck and arms burned like fire. Yet in spite of that, she fell asleep with a smile on her face. Freedom, even for only a few hours, had tasted mighty good. And the fried liver made the mosquito bites worthwhile too.

She spent the next days curing the meat,

readying it for smoking, and showing Bridget how they salted a hide down to make the hair come off when it was ready to tan.

Bridget fingered a piece of hide Metiz had given her. "And yours will feel like this?" While she asked a simple question, the look on her face shouted her doubt.

Ingeborg nodded. "We can make it soft or leave it hard for shoe tops. But we generally use cowhide for boots. It is thicker and wears better. Elk is good too."

"We used to cut the meat in thin strips and smoke it on racks over an open fire. Metiz taught us that. Did the same with fish. We owe her more than I can ever tell. Thanks to her we fared better than many of the settlers back in the beginning."

She looked up at the sound of a galloping horse. Paws ran barking and yipping toward the charging animal.

"It's Haakan." Ingeborg turned to look at Bridget. "Something is wrong. Something is terribly wrong."

17

"Come quick. Anner's arm got mangled in the separator!" Haakan leaped from the horse and bounded up the steps.

Dear God above, help that poor man! Ingeborg prayed all the while her hands flew, gathering the things she needed from the medicine store.

"Go get Metiz."

"Right!" Haakan barged through the door on his way out.

"Can I help?" Bridget asked.

"Ja, by taking care of things here. No telling how long I'll be gone." She shook her head over the shortage of rolled strips of cloth for bandage.

"The wagon's ready," Haakan announced, coming in the door. "Metiz is waiting. She brought her simples too."

Ingeborg looked in her cupboard one more time, picked up her full basket, and followed Haakan out the door. She stopped at the clothesline.

"Why — what?" Haakan turned around

when he realized she wasn't right behind him.

"I need bandages," she explained as she jerked half a dozen diapers off the line. She laid the sweet-smelling white squares on top of her other supplies. Then rushing over to the wagon, she handed up her basket and climbed aboard. "How did it happen?"

"There's precious little to tell," Haakan said after hupping the horse into action. "One minute things were going along like usual and the next he was screaming and blood flowed everywhere. We tied a tourniquet right below his shoulder, and Lars took him home. I came for you."

A short time later one look at the horrible wound said it all.

"We've got to take it off." Ingeborg leaned against the porch railing of the Valders' home.

"You cannot do that." Hildegunn Valders shook her head. She could hardly speak through her clenched teeth. "It will destroy him."

Metiz spoke from the outside of the circle. "He die then."

Hildegunn whirled around, advancing on the old woman as if she might rip her limb from limb. "You — you dirty Indian!

What do you know?"

Ingeborg grabbed the avenger around the waist and hauled her backward before she could reach Metiz. "She has come to help! Hildegunn Valders, you know how Metiz has helped so many." But when Ingeborg looked up, Metiz was gone. "Now you've done it!" She stepped back and clenched her fists on her hips so they wouldn't reach out and shake the woman. *God, help me, I am losing control here.* She took in a deep breath and began again. "You know at this time we need all the help we can get."

"I won't have no dirty Indian touching my Anner." Hildegunn slumped for a moment against the porch post, her head hanging forward. One strand of hair escaped the severe bun at her neck and hung down the side of her face. "Ingeborg, he might die."

The cry stabbed Ingeborg's heart and melted the anger like sun on a winter icicle. "Ah, Hildegunn, we will do all that we can. But I agree with the men. The arm must come off. There is no way we can cleanse that poor shredded . . ." She closed her eyes at the memory of mangled flesh and gleaming white bone protruding in all directions in more places than she had counted. "It might save his life."

She crossed the few steps to Hildegunn's

side and laid a hand on the woman's shoulder.

With a sob that near to broke Ingeborg's heart, the woman turned and buried her face in Ingeborg's apron bib. She wrapped her arms around the heaving shoulders and patted her back, soothing her as she did her own children. Maybe if the Valderses had been blessed with children, this tragedy would have been easier to bear. But Anner and Hildegunn only had each other. And that might not be for long.

"Hush now. You must be strong for Anner's sake." Ingeborg crooned the words, well knowing that the tone was all Hildegunn could hear. "Hush. All will be well. God is in His heaven, and all will be well."

"How can you say that?" Hildegunn stepped back and, taking a cloth from her apron pocket, mopped her eyes. "Nothing will ever be the same again."

"No, but God knows what is going on, and He has said He is here."

"I don't feel Him here. I . . . I . . ." She stared into Ingeborg's eyes, as if answers to the questions ripping her apart might lodge there.

"Trust me. He is here and right now. He is trying to give you the strength to be strong

281

and make the right decisions for Anner."

The grieving woman shook her head, looking as if the weight of it might sink her into the porch. "I cannot." She cupped her elbows in her shaking hands. "I cannot. If I say cut off the arm, he will hate me forever."

"No, he won't. Once he gets his health back, he will be glad to be alive, and . . ."

Hildegunn slowly shook her head again. "You might think so, but you don't know Anner." She turned toward the doorway, then stopped and looked over her shoulder. "And, Ingeborg, please tell Metiz I am sorry I screamed at her so."

Haakan held open the door for the woman who looked as if she'd been beaten with a two-by-four. His eyebrows asked the question.

Ingeborg shook her head.

"But it has to come off. He won't live otherwise."

"I know." Ingeborg turned into the haven of her husband's arms. "She is so afraid."

Haakan wrapped his arms around her and rested his chin on the top of her head. "He threatened to kill any of us who would cut off his arm."

"Uff da."

"I figured that was the pain talking. You say about anything when it hurts like that must. I poured both the whiskey and the laudanum into him, so he is sleeping now."

"The bleeding?"

"Stopped it with the tourniquet." He rubbed his chin on her hair. "After I been in that room, you sure do smell good. Like roses and sunshine." He cupped her chin with two callused hands. "Promise me that if something like this ever happens to me, you'll take no mind of a pain-crazed man's ranting and raving, but just go ahead and do what needs to be done."

Ingeborg looked deep into his eyes, searching his soul. Finally she nodded. "Ja, I will do that."

When they entered the sickroom, Hildegunn looked up from where she sat, back straight as if someone had stuck a steel rod up her spine. "Just do it now," she said.

An hour later the arm lay in a bucket, and Haakan laid a red-hot poker against the stump.

Ingeborg raced outside at the stench of burning flesh. After throwing up in the flower bed, she returned to the room.

"You all right?" Haakan and Lars, both still dripping sweat from holding Anner down, looked at her from their tableside positions.

"Ja, I will be." She stitched the gaping

wound closed and, after wrapping it in whiskey-soaked cloths, stepped back. "Now we can only pray."

"You think we ain't been already?" Lars wiped the sweat from his forehead with the back of his arm. "I hope I never have to do anything like this again."

Olaf nodded. "Nothing more I can do here. I better get back to the sack house. Where's the missus?"

Ingeborg looked around. "I don't know. She was boiling water last I saw." She kneaded her fists in the middle of her back. Looking down, she made a face at the blood-stained apron. "He has lost so much blood."

Olaf patted her shoulder. "You done the best you could. We all did. Now we have to leave it and him in the Almighty's sure hands." He headed for the door. "I'll send Goodie right back. She's champing at the bit, wondering how she can help."

"Someone needs to be with him all the time." Ingeborg looked around the kitchen. "So much yet to do here."

"We'll let someone else do the cleaning up. I think it is time I take you home." Haakan looked up at Lars. "Let's move him to the bed. He's likely to start thrashing and fall right off this table."

The four of them each took a corner of the long oak table and carried it to the bedroom door.

"Too wide," Olaf said as they set the table back down. "Let's roll a blanket under him and use that to carry him."

"Where's Hildegunn?" Ingeborg asked, pushing past the table and going to the bed. She started to pick up the quilt folded across the footboard and stopped. No sense getting that all bloody unless they had to. Looking around, she spied several sheets folded and stacked on the shelf above the clothing pegs along one wall. Taking down two, she unfolded them, matched the corners, and put them together. *Why isn't Hildegunn here doing these things? Where in the world has she got to?*

They rolled the snoring man onto the sheets, and with each again grasping a corner, they carried him to the bed.

Ingeborg stared down at Anner. "If we can just keep the infection out . . ."

"That is God's job now. We done all we can." Olaf headed again for the door. "Goodie will be back soon's she can be."

Ingeborg and Haakan exchanged looks.

"You better go find Hildegunn," he said in a low voice. "I'll stay here for now."

The man in the bed groaned.

Ingeborg rested the tip of her index finger against her bottom lip. "You get the whisky. The longer we can keep him out, the better off he'll be."

"If he starts to puke, there'll be a heap of trouble."

Ingeborg wanted nothing more than to go home, wash, and put on clean clothes. She laid a hand on her belly. Now that the tension had lessened, she could feel the roiling that presaged a possible eruption of her own. "I'm going outside."

The crickets were tuning up for the evening concert when she stopped on the top step of the porch. A breeze cooled her forehead now that the sun had gone to bed, leaving clouds tinted in every shade of red imaginable and then some. It seemed as if they had been there for days instead of hours.

"Hildegunn." She waited and called again. "Hildegunn." *Now, where can she be?* She'd checked the parlor on her way out. The rocker sat empty. She walked behind the house to the garden but found no Hildegunn. *Was this too much for her? Did her mind snap?* "The barn, of course," she said aloud.

The barn cats were already cleaning their whiskers, the flat bowl in front of them empty again. A bucketful of milk sat on the closed grain bin, and Hildegunn had her head firmly nestled in the flank of the middle cow of the three in the stanchions. The song of milk flowing into a bucket, cows munching, and chickens squabbling about roosting places made the mess in the house seem the unreality. Peace reigned here.

"I've one to go," Hildegunn said when Ingeborg stopped in the hard-packed dirt aisle.

"You want Haakan to finish?"

"No." Twin streams of milk kept the rhythm of pull and release.

"You have other chores?"

"I already fed the pigs. The horses are still over to the threshing." Her hands stopped.

The cow swished her tail at the flies. The *plop, plop* of manure released from the adjacent cow made Ingeborg step back.

"How . . . how is he?"

"Sleeping."

"You took it off, din't you?"

"Ja. We had no choice."

"Anner . . ." Hildegunn sighed deeply enough to rock the three-legged stool under her. "He's going to be terrible mad." She sniffed. "Terrible."

Ingeborg thought to argue with the

287

grieving woman but stopped. Hildegunn knew her husband better than anyone else did. And Anner had ordered that they not remove his arm. Had they done the right thing? "He would have died otherwise."

"Ingeborg, he still might die. Men have died from far less injuries than a mangled arm. And we both know he has lost a tremendous amount of blood."

The milk swished into the bucket.

"And now . . ." Silence but for the milk and a purring cat. Hildegunn shook her head slowly, grinding her forehead into the cow's flank. "He won't want to live."

"Surely you can't mean . . ." Ingeborg let the words trail off. The desolate tone of the woman's words echoed in her mind. There had been times after Roald died when she had wondered if she wanted to live, if death wasn't preferable to the killing grind of salvaging the land.

But Anner had his land. He'd proved his homestead and built a fine home. He and his wife were leaders in this small community of Blessing. Of course farming with one arm would be difficult, but so much so that he'd rather die?

"Goodie will be here any minute. Haakan will finish milking for you so you can be with Anner."

Again Hildegunn shook her head. She stripped the last of the milk from the cow's udder and, setting the bucket out of the way, got to her feet. "You've done enough. I will finish here, and then Goodie can go on back home. We will manage."

Ingeborg studied the woman's face in the dimness of the barn. While they weren't the closest of friends, still they'd known and helped each other through both tragedies and triumphs.

"We'll come back tomorrow to check on you."

"No need. Haakan has threshing to do, and I know you got more'n enough to keep you busy. We will manage." She set her stool by the last cow, clamped the bucket between her knees, and began the squeeze and pull of milking again.

Ingeborg cast around in her mind for something else to say, but everything sounded banal in the face of the stoic acceptance before her. "It's God's will," some would say. She remembered wanting to slam the words back down their throats. *I know how you feel.* So what? *You must be brave.* Hildegunn was nothing if not brave, but courage sometimes could only stretch so far.

"God will always be with you, knowing

both you and Anner and not letting you go." She whispered the words, hoping the woman could believe them now and in believing could gain strength from the only one able to give it. She waited a moment longer, hoping for a response, but a sniff, not the kind in pride but one soaked with unshed tears, was all she heard.

Ingeborg turned and left the barn, pounding and beseeching the gates of heaven for solace and healing for the Valderses, both of them. She just shook her head when Haakan made a move to go to the barn.

"Goodie is here. She asked if the children could come to our house for the next couple of days, and I told her we would pick them up on the way home." Haakan took Ingeborg by the arm and led her to the wagon. "I thought to stop by and ask Reverend Solberg if he would come."

"Ja, maybe he can get through to Anner once he wakes up."

But over the next days, in spite of their careful nursing, infection set in, and Anner sank deeper into the fever.

"I wish they had let you help." Ingeborg and Metiz sat on the stoop, relishing the evening breeze.

"Only go where wanted."

"I know." Ingeborg gingerly rubbed the back of her neck. She'd gotten sunburned again while picking beans in the garden. When would she remember to wear the sunbonnet Kaaren had made for her?

"Bad time ahead for them."

"I'm afraid so. I should go over there and see if I can help."

"Don't want help."

Ingeborg closed her eyes. She remembered times like that. "So stubborn we can be." Had she thought that or said it aloud?

"Yes." Metiz turned to her with a chuckle lighting her obsidian eyes. "But men worse."

Ingeborg couldn't resist laughing.

Paws' barking drew her gaze to the horse and rider coming up the lane. She shaded her eyes against the bright glory of the setting sun.

"Company, Mor." Andrew strolled from around the house, shadowed by Ellie.

"Thank you, son, I never would have guessed."

He leaned against her knee and smiled up at her, twin curves of dirt bracketing his mouth.

"You've been eating carrots."

"How'd you know?"

"A little dirt told me." She touched his

cheek. "You ever thought of washing them before you eat them?"

"I did." He showed her the grubby streaks on his bloomers. "Ellie too."

"I know. You two are a matched pair."

The rider stopped at the hitching post by the well. "How are you, Mrs. Bjorklund?" Reverend Solberg tipped the brim of his hat with one finger.

"Good. The coffee can be hot in a couple of minutes." She nudged Andrew. "You and Ellie go draw some water for his horse."

"That sounds just right. Metiz, you look well." His gaze flitted to the back door and returned to Ingeborg.

"Katy is over to Kaaren's." Ingeborg got to her feet. "Why, Reverend Solberg, I do believe you are blushing."

"I . . . ah . . ." He removed his handkerchief and wiped his forehead. "Warm for this late in the afternoon, wouldn't you say?"

"For September? No, not really."

He put the handkerchief back and shook his head. "Can't get much around you, can I? Yes, I would like to see Miss Bjorklund, but I really came to tell you that they took Anner to the hospital in Grand Forks. Left on the afternoon train."

Ingeborg raised a hand to her cheek.

"Ah, poor Hildegunn."

"Only through the grace of God will he make it."

"Did she go with?"

"Yes. Goodie said she will take care of their livestock."

"Either that or we could bring them all over here. Or," she stopped. "Bridget and Katy could go over there."

"Let's leave it as it is for right now."

"Your horse is watered." Andrew and Ellie joined the adults.

"Thank you, young man." Solberg patted Andrew on the head.

"Cookies, Mor?"

"Ja, come on in, all of you. We'll eat dessert first. Can you stay for supper, Reverend? Bridget will have it ready in a short time. The boys are nearly done with chores." She threw a last tidbit over her shoulder. "Andrew, after a cookie, will you please go fetch Tante Katy?"

With the garden pretty well harvested, the itch to get out in the field irritated Ingeborg even more. Bridget was spending more time knitting, teaching Andrew and Ellie how to card the wool that she had washed and dyed and was now ready for the spinning wheel. Thorliff and Baptiste spent all their spare time hunting and splitting wood to keep the smokehouse in business.

But with Lars and Haakan out with the threshing machine, the fall work had come to a standstill.

"What are you doing?" Bridget asked, shock rounding her eyes and mouth.

Ingeborg glanced down at the men's britches she had altered to fit her a long time before. "Pants make plowing much easier."

"P-plowing?" Bridget visibly straightened her spine. "Inge, does Haakan know about this?"

Ingeborg met her stare for stare. "He knows I used to do the fieldwork."

"And he approves?"

"He knows that getting the fall work done is necessary."

Bridget clasped her hands together on the waist of her apron. "Couldn't Thorliff and Baptiste do that for you?"

Ingeborg had the grace to nod. "They could, but they've never done so without Haakan. Besides, they can pick the field corn faster than I can. Both things need to be done."

"Then Haakan should be home and . . ." Bridget clamped her lips, cutting off the rest she'd been about to say.

"He don't trust anyone else with the steam engine and the thresher, especially after what happened to Anner." Ingeborg clapped Roald's hat on her head and tucked the string tie under her chin. "Andrew and Ellie are over to Kaaren's. We'll all be eating over there."

"Kaaren knows?"

"Ja, and she's no happier about this than you." Ingeborg strode out of the room, already sorry she'd been so abrupt with her mother-in-law. But ever since she'd seen the darkness in Anner's eyes, she'd felt it peering over her shoulder. Working in the fields, she could feel she was keeping it at bay. If something ever happened to Haakan, she needed to remember how she could keep the land, keep the crops coming in, and keep her sanity.

Besides, riding the plow was so much easier than walking behind it. She would hardly be working at all.

By noon, she knew she'd been lying to herself. Her arms and shoulders ached from holding the reins, and her right leg was sore from raising and lowering the double-bottomed plow blades.

While the children chattered at the dinner table, the women were noticeably silent.

By evening, she ached all over.

Bridget's look screamed "I told you so" when Ingeborg tripped on the top step because her legs were so tired. And by the time they'd finished milking all twenty-five cows, Ingeborg could hardly rise from the milk stool.

But in the morning, she headed out again. The days fell easily into a rhythm. Milk the cows, eat breakfast that Kaaren prepared, plow until noon, eat, plow until the sun began to set, milk, eat, and fall into bed until she forced her eyes open at the first cock crow.

Some days Andrew came with her and rode one of the horses for a while. He lasted longer when Ellie rode the other. Then the two of them would trot back across the fields, waving their thanks.

"School is going to start next week," Kaaren said one noon meal. "Reverend Solberg dropped by to tell everyone." She glanced at Katy, who winked back. "Of course I believe that wasn't his *only* purpose in calling."

"What has he heard about Anner?" Ingeborg looked up from sopping gravy with her bread.

"Still alive. The doctors are giving some hope now. They had to remove the remainder of the arm, clear to the shoulder.

Even taking the joint."

"Ah." The single exhalation said so much.

"I'll be in early," Ingeborg said as she went out the door. "I need to take the plowshares in to Hjelmer for sharpening."

"Mor, can I go with you?" Thorliff asked as he helped harness the horses.

"Why?"

"I don't know. Yes, I do. I could do some of the plowing, and then you won't have to."

Ingeborg came around the team and tapped the boy's porkpie hat, tipping it off his head. "Mange takk, son, but I won't be doing this much longer. The men will be back soon. Besides, Monday you start school."

"I could start late." Thorliff looked at her, serious eyes never flinching.

More and more he looks like his father, Ingeborg thought. *And sounds like him.* "Thank you for the offer, Thorliff, but I know how much you love school. I don't want you to miss a moment of it."

She hooked the final snap to the ring on the leather pad high on the horse's rump and gathered the reins. "Why don't you and Baptiste go fishing for a change? Fresh fish would taste mighty good for supper."

Thorliff's eyes lit up, the blue as intense as the sky overhead. "I'll go get him." He raced off, one hand clapped on top of his head holding his hat in place. Finally he snatched it off and ran faster.

Ingeborg hupped the horses and, still smiling, followed them out to the plow she'd left standing in the field.

Several hours and many furrows later, she measured the remaining distance with an avid eye. *Two more times around and this field is finished.* The thought brought a smile to her heart. While she still hadn't gotten to breaking sod, at least these acres were ready for winter, the wheat stalks plowed under to rot and enrich the soil. She glanced up at the screech of a hawk that floated on the air currents above.

One of the horses snorted and then the other. A strange buzzing sound reached her ears, growing louder than the stomp of the hooves.

"Whoa, Bob, Belle." But it did no good. The bees swarmed around the animals' heads. The horses whinnied. One kicked.

The yellow jackets, roused from their subterranean home, attacked with vengeance.

In spite of her pulling on the reins, the horses bolted.

The plow bounced over the furrows.

Ingeborg flew through the air like a rag doll tossed in play and crumpled on the clod-rough ground.

18

Pain, shattering pain, jerked her back to reality.

Ingeborg lay on the Dakota earth she had fought so hard to break, then save. The rich smell of it filled her nostrils. Part of it, rock hard, felt like a sharpened boulder in her back. Dare she move?

Breathing deep to clear her head sent it spinning instead and set her chest on fire.

"Mor!" The call came as from a great distance.

Answering took more life than she had at that moment. She took shallow breaths, learning from that one effort. She flexed her fingers, moved her feet. They all seemed to work, none causing any more pain than that which already coursed through her body. The bee stings had left their marks in painful welts on her arms and face.

"Ingeborg!"

How to answer. A crow cawed from the air above her. *You tell them. You obviously have more to say than I at the moment.*

When the world stopped spinning, she cautiously raised her head. The pain in her chest lessened as the air returned. So she'd had the wind knocked out of her. No one died from that.

The horses! *Oh, God, please let the horses — and the plow — be all right. Oh and me too, if you please.* She moved her arms, cautiously at first and then to pat and prod her ribs and shoulders. All seemed to be in working order. But she felt as if she was on fire.

She rolled to one side and, propping an elbow underneath herself, pushed up to a sitting position.

"Ingeborg!" Closer now came Katy's voice.

"I . . . I'm here. I'll be all right."

"Ingeborg." Katy dropped to the dirt beside her, chest heaving from the run. "The team came home without you. We . . ."

"Bob and Belle are all right then?" Ingeborg lifted her head to look at Katy.

"Bob and Belle? Oh, the horses. They are stung and have some cuts, I think, but you, it is you we . . ."

Bridget joined them, Andrew right behind her. "You are alive, oh, thank the good Lord. You are even sitting up." Bridget clasped her hands under her chin and raised her face to the heavens. "Thank you, heavenly Father." Her face darkened and her tone changed. "Now, let us look at you. You never should have —" She cut off her words at a signal from her daughter. "How are your legs, your back? Do you think you can stand?"

Ingeborg leaned into the comforting embrace of Katy. She wiped a strand of hair from her eyes and came away with a bloody finger. "It is nothing," Ingeborg said. "A small cut is all."

Katy checked the back of Ingeborg's head. "Another one here." She pressed a spot. "And here. But they are already done bleeding."

"Ugh." Ingeborg grunted when she shifted. "Please help me up, and — oh!" As she stood, a cramp low in her belly bent her in two. "O God above, no!"

Her wail set Andrew to crying. He grabbed her pants leg and sobbed as if his heart would break.

Katy knelt and gathered him to her side.

"Mor . . . Mor." He reached for her, and now that the pain had passed, Ingeborg hugged him close.

"It's all right, son. Your ma just took a tumble, is all. We'll go on back to the house and see to Bob and Belle. You want to run ahead and tie them up?"

"He's too little to lead those huge beasts. Besides, they might still be wild scared." Bridget motioned to Katy. "You go with him, and I'll come with Ingeborg."

Ingeborg let herself be fussed over and didn't resist the arm Bridget put around her waist.

"Lean on me."

Halfway home the lower pain sliced through her again.

She lost the baby just before sunrise.

Metiz kneaded Ingeborg's belly after Bridget, tears streaming from her eyes, carried the tiny form away. "Bring hot tea from stove," she told Katy, who had sat holding Ingeborg's hands through the long night. White crescents remained on her palms from Ingeborg's fingernails.

"It's over, isn't it?" Ingeborg whispered after a heavy sigh.

"Umm."

"I wanted this baby so bad. Haakan's own child." Her voice weakened. "How will I tell him?" A tear trickled from her closed eyelid. "I killed his son."

"Hush, now, that is no way to talk. Accidents happen and mayhap the good Lord wanted this baby home right away." Bridget laid a cool cloth on Ingeborg's forehead and wiped her face and hands with a warm cloth. "We'll get you into a clean, dry nightgown, and after a good sleep, you will feel better."

"Here." Katy handed Metiz the tea. "This smells awful."

"But help stop bleeding." Metiz held the cup.

Ingeborg took a couple of swallows before pushing the cup away with hands too weak to make much difference.

"No. Drink all."

Ingeborg held up a hand. "In a minute." *Why don't they just leave me alone? Maybe then I could die too, before having to tell Haakan what I've done. How will he ever forgive me? How . . . how will I forgive myself?*

She drank the remainder of the liquid and turned her head away. Eyes closed, she waited while the rustling from the others ceased as they left the room.

O God, how could I do such a thing? Two babies now that I killed because of my stubbornness. Father, take me home before I cause any more disasters. Not long after they had settled on their homestead, she had been hunting and had taken a bad fall, losing her first baby.

She woke to Metiz kneading her belly

again. *Let me be,* she wanted to cry out but knew the futility of that. Metiz would go right on doing what she knew to be best.

By midmorning Ingeborg's body felt better. Andrew cuddled beside her on the bed.

"Astrid is crying, Mor."

"I hear her."

"Tante Kaaren is feeding her."

"Oh, I can do it." Ingeborg laid a hand on her breast. "Andrew, go get Bestemor."

While he was gone, she pushed herself into a sitting position. How long had she been lying in bed? The milk dripping from her breasts and running down her chest was doing Astrid no good. She winced. Between smacking the earth and birthing a . . . a . . . She bit her lip to keep the tears from flowing like her milk.

With Astrid settled in for a good meal, Ingeborg looked up to see Metiz standing at the foot of the bed. "You startled me."

Metiz nodded. "You better."

"Ja, I have a strong constitution. Weak in the head but strong in the body." Remembering her cries to God to take her home, she asked, "What about Anner?"

"He home."

"Any word from Haakan?"

Metiz shrugged. "Not know. Boys want to see you."

Ingeborg nodded and adjusted the sheet thrown over the suckling child. "Tell them to come in."

Thorliff and Baptiste tiptoed into the room as if they were afraid of waking her. They stopped at the foot of the bed.

"How are Bob and Belle?" Ingeborg asked before they could open their mouths.

"I put some of Metiz' salve on Belle's hocks where the plow banged her. Broke the plow tongue and bent a wheel. They both had lots of stings. Bumps all over." He stopped. "You all right, Mor?"

She nodded. She could sympathize with the horses. Her stings still itched.

"You're not going to die?"

"Whatever gave you that idea?" She reached for his hand. "Your ma is tough. A tumble from a plow couldn't kill her." *It just killed your baby.* The voice in her mind made her blink. Each time she heard it, the knife sliced away another piece of her heart.

Thorliff changed so his hand was now clasping hers, letting her grip his fingers until the thought faded away. "You want I should go for Pa? I could, you know."

"I know. But it might be better to let him finish the harvest without worrying about me — us. There'll be plenty of time to tell him when he gets home."

In the next days, she both longed for and dreaded the day of Haakan's return. He had said one month, but it could be longer, depending on how many farmers wanted their grain threshed. The nights were the worst, when the dreams came and the "if only's" attacked. During the days, the four women handled all the chores now that the older children were back in school. But as Bridget often said, "Many hands make light work." And while none of the work on the farms was light, the visits by Reverend Solberg and Petar Baard did help, because when they came, Katy put them to work.

"Uff da, child," said her mother one day. "They come calling as suitors, you know, not farmhands."

"Well, I'm not about to sit in the parlor with either one of them, not with all that has to be done around here. Petar should have just stayed with the threshing crew. I told him that in the beginning."

"So, you are more interested in Reverend Solberg then?" Ingeborg joined the conversation.

Katy shrugged. "He is a good man."

"And handsome too," Bridget added.

Katy shrugged again. "I guess." She turned to Ingeborg. "I saw you out eyeing that plow today now that Hjelmer brought it back all fixed up again. You thinking of going back in the field?"

Ingeborg nodded, keeping her gaze on the quilt pieces in her lap. With the rain falling outside, the women had gathered in the parlor to sew together while the little children played upstairs. Bridget sat at the spinning wheel, her pumping foot keeping the wheel singing its own song as the yarn skin thickened.

Kaaren sat in the rocking chair, her foot tapping in time to the creak of it. "That's what you're planning, isn't it?"

Ingeborg could feel her stare clear down to her toes. She could also feel the censure radiating from Bridget like heat from a stove. "I . . . I have to."

"You have to? Did I hear right? You have to?" Kaaren leaned forward. "Ingeborg Bjorklund, that is the most . . . most . . ." She stopped for lack of words.

"Bullheaded, stupid thing you've ever heard of." Ingeborg finished the statement for her. Eyes flashing, she laid her stitching down. "I *have* to. Because . . ." She too paused, but it wasn't for lack of words. "I can't let myself be afraid of the horses or the plow." She whispered the thought, knowing in her heart for the first time how true it was. "You know, when you fall from a horse, you

308

got to get right back on?" She looked up until Kaaren nodded. "Well, this getting back on is what I have to do. Or . . . or the fear will . . ." Stricken eyes pleaded first with Kaaren, then Bridget, and finally Katy for understanding.

Kaaren nodded. The rocker creaked. The wheel sang. "Or the pit?"

Now Ingeborg nodded. "At night I see it creeping closer, waiting to suck me in."

"Uff da." Bridget accidentally snapped the yarn on the spinning wheel. Now she'd have to rethread it.

A giggle came from the top of the stairs, then small feet thundered down. "Cookie, Mor?" Andrew led the pack.

"Ja, there are cookies for all good children and their elders too." With a sigh of relief at the interruption, Ingeborg got up and headed for the kitchen. "Coffee will be ready soon."

"I don't believe God wants you back out there," Kaaren said later as she gathered the children and their things together.

"Ja, well, then, if God doesn't want me out there, He better send us a man to take my place. And I won't call for Haakan or Lars."

"What about Penny's cousin?"

Ingeborg nodded. "I've thought of him.

He's busy in the store, but . . ." She nodded and smiled at Kaaren. "You think we can keep him away from our Katy?"

Kaaren left chuckling. "I'll be going to the store tomorrow. I'll ask him and Penny."

But in the morning, Ingeborg harnessed the two horses while they stood in their stalls munching the oats she dumped in their grain boxes. She checked the harness over carefully to make sure it hadn't been damaged. Bob and Belle placidly took the bits she put in each mouth, and Belle nuzzled her, begging for a good ear scratching.

Ingeborg obliged, wondering if she was taking her time because she really was afraid of climbing on that plow again. "Please, God," she muttered as she led the horses outside. No clouds to promise rain, so no excuse there.

"You don't have to do this, you know." The horses' ears twitched back and forth, and Bob stamped a front foot. "Oh, but I do." Saying the thoughts aloud seemed to make the inner struggle more real. She *had* to get back on the plow or live the rest of her life knowing she'd been afraid and had given in to her fears.

"Let not thy heart be troubled, neither let it be afraid." The words came softly as if carried on butterfly wings. *Let.* Yes, that was the

word. But how? Fear could paralyze one, bring life to a stop. Take Anner, for instance. Fear and anger — the two went hand in hand.

"Fear not," the angel had said.

Ingeborg leaned her forehead against Belle's strong neck. "I know that fear is of the devil, old girl, and I know that Jesus said He came to overcome the world. Then why do I feel so overcome right now when He is right here beside me?"

Belle snorted and turned her head, brushing Ingeborg's shoulder with her nose. Paws pushed against her knee. Ingeborg squeezed her eyes shut. "Jesus." A tear squeezed from under one eyelid. "Jesus. Jesus." Others followed the leader. "Jesus, Son of God, my Savior." She wiped them away with the horse's mane. Taking a deep breath, she turned and walked to the rear, checked the traces and, gathering the reins, climbed onto the plow. All the while her mind sang the litany. *Jesus. Jesus. Jesus.* And with each utterance of His name, the yawning black pit shrank farther and farther away.

When they got to the field, she set the blade and clucked the horses forward, looking back over her shoulder to see the black soil curling up and over to form a smooth furrow. The cry of the geese in a V form flying high overhead brought up her face to be bathed by the sun. "All is well. All is well. Thank you, Father God. All is well."

She made one round of the field, the furrow dark with rich dampness framing the wheat stubble in the middle. Belle whinnied. A horse answered.

Ingeborg looked toward the south to where the team's ears pointed. Two horses trotted side by side across the stubble. A man rode one with a small child in front of him, and a young girl rode the other.

"Good morning," Ingeborg called when they grew near enough to hear.

"Good morning." The greeting came back in a rich baritone voice.

Ingeborg twitched the reins to stop the team and sat waiting on her plow. The little hairs on the back of Ingeborg's neck came to attention. No, this couldn't be. God wouldn't. . . . He didn't . . . but she knew Kaaren had been praying. And she'd so much as thrown down the gauntlet.

"God, I hear you laughing," she muttered low enough that only the horses heard her.

"Mornin', ma'am. I'm Zebulun Mac-Callister," The man tipped his hat and brought his horse to a stop.

Ingeborg cocked her head. He talked like

no one she'd ever heard before. Sort of soft and slow, as if he had all the time in the world to say what he had to say.

"Good day, again. You are riding on Bjorklund land, and you are welcome here for sure." She waited, her gaze shifting to the girl on the other horse.

"I'm Manda Norton and that's my sister, Deborah." Manda nodded to the child peeking out of the light cotton wrap around her. "She's been sick." As she said the words, she sent the man a frown and raised her chin just a bit.

With the look, the tone, and the chin raising, Ingeborg knew immediately there was something going on here. Besides, their last names didn't match. *That child has a chip the size of Norway perched on her shoulder.*

Zeb MacCallister shifted the child in front of him so she was more comfortable. "Another Miz Bjorklund, at the store in town" — he nodded back toward Blessing — "she said y'all might be in need of some help for a while. My mama raised her children to do about anything on the farm, and I'm not afraid of hard work."

His soft "ahm's" and the "y'all" enchanted Ingeborg. She wanted to keep him talking just to hear the sounds. So different

313

from Norwegian and the accented English they spoke, all with the harsh sounds of northern Europe.

"You go on up to the house, and Mrs. Bjorklund will serve coffee and whatever else she has ready. Dinner will be in" — she glanced up at the sun — "a couple of hours. You are welcome to water and feed your horses too."

"Thank you, ma'am." The "ma'am" stretched to three syllables. He tipped his hat again. "We're right grateful for your hospitality." He clucked his horse ahead. "Comin', Manda?"

Ingeborg hupped the team forward. One thing for certain sure, there wasn't any lack of good-looking men visiting the Bjorklund farm. She'd felt like telling the man he was an answer to prayer, but that hardly seemed appropriate at the time. Where would they put them up? Bridget and her brood had the soddy. At least the children could stay there, and perhaps Mr. MacCallister wouldn't mind the barn until they got the new house up for Kaaren's family. Then that soddy would be available.

"Oh, Lord, look at me weaving your story so far in advance. You sure were right when you said to let the day's own trouble be sufficient for the day." She caught herself chuckling several more times as she and her team rounded the corners and laid straight the furrows. What would Haakan say about her hiring another hand?

"You know, you two horses better start answering my questions or anyone hears me talking to myself will think I've gone loony for sure." That made her laugh again. So she sang her way around the field, going from hymn to hymn and back to the songs she'd learned as a child.

"If'n you don't look like the cat that caught the bird," Katy said as she came out to the barn to help Ingeborg unharness the horses.

"Ja, well, you got to be in high spirits when you see our heavenly Father just dumping blessing on top of blessing on you." Ingeborg grunted as she lifted the heavy harness off Bob. The big horse shook, sending dust flying everywhere. "You could have waited till you got to the field." Ingeborg slung the harness over its pegs on the barn wall and went back for the other. "You want to bring the oxen up and give them some oats before dinner? We'll see how Mr. MacCallister does with them."

"Is he really going to stay?" Katy led the horses toward the well, where she'd already dumped buckets of water into the trough.

"Ja, he says so. Don't let them have too much, then they can go roll in the field."

Ingeborg stopped by the well house on her way to the washbasin. Sure enough, there was plenty of milk to set for cheese. And the latest batch of chickens was ready for butchering. Another couple of days and she could take a wagonload to the Bonanza farm. Or maybe she should let Kaaren go so she could visit with Solveig. The two sisters hadn't seen each other since July. Had it really been that long since they'd taken over a load of produce?

"You ever driven oxen?" she asked Zeb over the meal a bit later.

"No, ma'am, only horses and mules. But I learn fast."

"More coffee?" Bridget bustled around the table, making sure everyone had plenty of the mashed potatoes, venison roast, late squash, and fresh-baked bread.

"Thank you, ma'am." Zeb held up his cup. "You have no idea how much we appreciate a meal like this. Been a long time since the last one." He looked over to catch Manda glaring at him.

Ingeborg watched the exchange, her curiosity growing by the minute. "Manda, there's plenty more where that came from.

You help yourself." She turned to the child next to her. "You aren't eating. Is something wrong?"

The little girl shook her head. "Too much."

"Ah."

"She's been sick," Manda said, with her lower lip stuck out. "She runs out of strength before she can eat enough. I usually feed her."

"Oh, I think we can remedy this." Ingeborg scooped Deborah up and sat her on her lap. "Now, we better hurry before Astrid thinks someone is taking her place."

"Who's Astrid?" The pale little face looked up to Ingeborg.

"My baby. We try to get her to sleep through dinner so we can all eat in peace." While she talked, Ingeborg spooned food into the mouth that opened and closed obediently.

Manda cleaned her plate and refilled it. "Can I please have more bread?" she asked when the plate was empty.

"Ja, of course." Bridget hurried to cut more.

Manda thanked her and buttered the thick slice. Then after glancing around as if hoping no one was looking, she sprinkled sugar over it, folded the bread, and

317

put it in her pocket.

Ingeborg and Bridget shared a glance of astonishment. Was the child that starved? Or was it for later?

Ingeborg rested her cheek on the silky hair of the child in her lap. The little one surely was older than her body weight suggested. "We're going to have to fatten you up," she whispered.

"I been bad sick." Deborah looked up into Ingeborg's face. "Are you going to be my mama?"

Questions chased each other through Ingeborg's mind like children playing tag.

"She's *my* mor." Andrew left his chair and came to stand at his mother's side. His lower lip protruded and his usual sunny smile hid out.

"Andrew!" Ingeborg put her other arm around his sturdy little body. "I'm sure there is enough of me for everyone. Besides, don't you want Deborah and Manda to feel welcome in our home?"

He nodded. "Ja, but . . ."

Manda interrupted. "It don't matter none. Just cause our mama died, we ain't looking for another. We do just fine by ourselves."

"Manda." Zeb spoke softly but firmly.

"It don't matter. We can work here, but

we ain't stayin' forever."

"Would anyone like some eggekake?" Bridget interrupted the discussion.

"Don't know what it is." Manda sat back in her chair. "She don't talk the way we do, and I can't get a word she says."

"Manda!" This time the order cut the air.

The girl slumped back in her chair, sending Zeb a look that should have melted his bones. But she ate every bite of her cake and accepted a second helping, muttering a "thank you" at the end.

"I'll help you get started with the oxen, then," Ingeborg said to Zeb when they'd finished the meal.

"That'll be right fine. Is there something you can find for Manda to do? She likes to earn her own way."

"You know how to butcher chickens, girl?" Bridget asked Manda.

Ingeborg translated for Bridget and Manda nodded.

"I can shoot too if'n you need some huntin' done." Manda got up from her chair.

"Thank you, Manda, but that won't be necessary today. And tomorrow, I think you should join Thorliff — he is my older son — and the others in school. How old are you, twelve or so?"

Manda nodded. "But I ain't goin' to school."

Ingeborg rubbed her lips together. "We shall see. Are you ready, Mr. Mac-Callister?" She glanced up just in time to catch a look passing between Katy and Zeb MacCallister. Katy appeared to have been struck by lightning or some such. *So that is the way of it.* Ingeborg tucked the thought away to share with Haakan when he came home. If he would still be talking to her, that is.

19

"Pa is coming! Pa is coming!" Thorliff hit the screen door at a dead run.

"Oh, thanks be to God." Ingeborg dried her hands and, untying her apron with one hand, reached for a clean one with the other. "How do I look?"

Sarah studied her. "While that cut is healed, the bruise around it still shows. Other than that, beautiful."

"That isn't the only bruise that still shows," Ingeborg muttered while she tried to stuff some loose strands of hair back in her braid coronet. *Haakan is home. Haakan is home.* While her mind chanted with joy, her stomach clenched and her hands shook.

After the third failed attempt to make the last stubborn strand stay put, she stuck her tongue out at the face in the mirror and headed out the door. She almost made it when she realized that the face she'd observed had a smudge of flour on the tip of the nose. She dashed to the water bucket, dipped a finger wet and rubbed her nose, drying it on her apron as she fled out the door. Should she go back and get Astrid? She paused. No! Leaping off the front step to the ground just like her son did, she ran up the lane. She caught up with Andrew, grabbed his hand so he could run faster, and kept on going.

Thorliff was already aboard the horse-drawn steam engine by the time Ingeborg and Andrew made it. She laughed up at her husband, the blond giant with eyes of the summer skies. He laughed with her and swung Andrew aboard with one hand, keeping the reins in his other.

The twelve horses it took to pull the machine plodded on with Ingeborg running beside them until Haakan had Andrew settled. Then he leaned down and gave her a hand. Safe on the platform beside him, within the circle of his arm, Ingeborg knew with all certainty she was home. She hadn't realized what a hole his being gone had created in her heart until just now when he filled it back up again. Six weeks was such a long time.

She looked up at him, tears blurring her eyes.

"Why are you crying?" Even the sound of his voice made her heart sing.

"I'm so happy." She reached up and

planted a kiss on the corner of his mouth. He turned just enough and kissed her back. Her heart settled into its accustomed place, and she took in a deep breath. "Welcome home, husband mine. We have indeed missed you. More than you will ever know."

"Oh, I know how much. Never did I dream I would miss you and the children and this farm so." He looked into her eyes. "You, most of all."

She swiped away the moisture blurring her gaze. She didn't want to miss any bit of him. "You are thinner."

"Not only was this hard work, but not everyone cooks as good as you. I think next year, if we do this again, we will take a cook wagon and make sure we have a good cook. You interested in the job?" He studied her face and touched the bruise with one gentle finger. "What happened here?"

Ingeborg couldn't look him in the eye. She stared straight ahead, out over the backs of the six teams of sweaty horses. "I will tell you all about it later."

"Pa, look at me!" Andrew crowed from the front of the smokestack.

"Okay, son, come on down from there. Thorliff, hang on to him so he doesn't fall."

Haakan handed the reins to Ingeborg, turned, and reached with both hands to retrieve Andrew, who wrapped both arms around his father's neck and threw back his head, laughing and giggling. Haakan hugged his son close, then set him on a shelf directly behind the fenced platform on which he and Ingeborg stood.

"Let me drive, Pa." Andrew reached for the reins.

"Who's that plowing over there?" Haakan set Andrew on the railing and let him hold on to the reins under the cover of his father's hands.

"Zeb MacCallister. Penny sent him over two days ago, since he needed work. Has two little girls with him, but I haven't gotten much more than 'please's' and 'thank-you's' out of any of them. He's a hard worker and good with the animals."

"He sure got a lot of plowing done for two days' work."

Ingeborg pretended she didn't hear his comment, listening to something Andrew said instead.

"Anner came home a few days ago. Reverend Solberg said he looks like a walking skeleton. Won't hardly talk at all."

"Is Reverend Solberg becoming a regular visitor?" Haakan's eyes twinkled.

Ingeborg nodded. "Ja, and Petar too. But I have a hunch —"

"You have a hunch?"

"Katy always manages to be at the barn to help unharness the team at noon. And I noticed Zeb's plate is always full of the choicest meat."

"Ahhh." Haakan turned and grinned at her. "Love in the air, huh?"

Ingeborg could feel her brow wrinkle in the frown that came every time she thought of Katy and Zeb. "I just wish I knew more about him, that's all. Wait until you hear his accent. I'm sure that's what Katy fell in love with first. It's just like warm syrup on pancakes, so smooth and drawly."

"Drawly? What kind of word is that?"

"You'll see."

"Pa." Thorliff clambered down and stood beside Haakan. "Can I drive now?"

"Sure enough." Haakan handed Andrew to his mother and the lines to Thorliff. He tucked his hands in his back pockets and said, "See how it feels? Six teams is a lot of horse power, and right now, they are tired beasts. But you never take your attention away from them. Horses can spook at some of the strangest things."

"Onkel Lars lets me drive sometimes." Thorliff looked up at his father.

"I know. You got to start off slow and easylike. Two is sure different than twelve, isn't it?"

Ingeborg leaned out to the side to look back on the train of farm machinery following them. Behind them came Lars with the separator machine that separated the grain from the straw. Behind him came Joseph with one wagon, Petar driving a remuda of horses, and another wagon following at the end.

"Bet you caused a stir when you went by the farms and towns on the way."

"You can't begin to think how much. In western Dakota the only thing bigger is the land and a train engine. Little boys like Andrew here" — he poked Andrew in the belly to hear his laugh — "their eyes near to popped out of their heads. Thorliff, take the steam engine right on down to the sawmill. No sense having to harness this bunch up again. And it's not like we have this many horses anyhow. Tomorrow we'll get them all back to their rightful owners."

He turned to Ingeborg. "That's one thing we need. More horses. I hate to borrow from our neighbors. Had one horse break a leg, and we had to shoot him. Thank goodness it belonged to Joseph." He shouted over the squeaks and squeals of the rumbling rig. "Not that Joseph could afford to lose one either."

Ingeborg leaned into the curve of his arm. How would she tell him?

"Draw it up right beside the pile of sawdust, Thorliff. We'll have to skid it back in the shelter once the ground freezes." With the horses still, Haakan leaped to the ground and started the unhitching process, wheel team first. The other men joined him, and within minutes the horses were unharnessed and ready to turn loose in the pasture.

Haakan tossed Andrew and Thorliff aboard the team he led, and with Ingeborg beside him, they walked back to the barn. "Everything looks real good," he said. "Guess maybe I'm not as valuable around here as I thought."

She poked him in the ribs with her elbow. "Just shows what women can accomplish when they work together."

"M-o-o-r," Thorliff said.

"Oh, and big strong boys. We couldn't have kept up without them. Thorliff and Baptiste did most of the milking until school started."

"Wait till you see the set of horns on the elk that Baptiste brought down." Thorliff leaped to the ground and took the reins from his father. "I'll put them out."

"You better fill the water trough later."

"I will."

"I'm sure Bridget has coffee ready. Joseph, you want some before you start home?" Ingeborg called to the scarecrow man loosening a couple of teams.

"Never was one to turn down coffee," Joseph called back. "Let me get my teams in the corral first."

"Lars?"

"No thanks. I'm sure Kaaren has some waiting. She waved when we drove in so she knows we're back."

"As if anyone couldn't know, the noise that thing makes."

Katy met them at the door, jiggling Astrid on her hip.

Haakan leaned forward and took the little girl in his arms, but she would have none of him.

"She's hungry."

"Astrid's always hungry," Andrew said.

Chuckling, they entered the kitchen, and Ingeborg kept on going till she reached the rocker in the parlor. With the windows open, it was cooler in there. Supper cooking on the kitchen stove added to the already warm room. With Astrid settled, she leaned her head against the chair back. She knew her husband. He wouldn't let the unanswered question lie. He'd soon demand an answer. How does one say — "I lost our baby"? "I killed our baby. . . . The baby died. . . . I'm no longer carrying . . ." None of the words said it all. How about, "We'll have another" or "We're young yet. Life goes on."

She sniffed back the tears that thoughts of the baby always brought. All because of her stubbornness. As Bridget said, it could have happened anyway, but —

That's where she always stopped. On the "but."

If she hadn't been plowing, if the yellow jackets hadn't attacked the horses, if she'd stayed home like she was supposed to. Guilt burdened her beyond belief. As she already knew, guilt weighed heavier than anything on earth.

Haakan brought his coffee cup into the parlor and sat down in the other rocker. "Ah, so good this feels." He looked around the room. "I forgot how nice you have made our house. So good it is to be home."

Ingeborg tensed. Here it came.

"So now, what happened that you got beat up?"

Ingeborg took in a deep breath. "I was plowing the wheat fields."

"And?"

"And an underground nest of yellow jackets flew up and stung the horses. Belle and Bob bolted, and I fell off the plow." The words came in a rush.

"There is more?"

How did he know that? Ingeborg shifted Astrid to the other breast. When she was nursing again, she looked up at her husband. "The fall made me lose the baby."

He closed his eyes for a moment, then said, "Were you hurt otherwise?"

"No, only small cuts and bad bruises."

"Thank the good Lord for that."

"Haakan, how can you be so calm? I killed our baby."

"No, you didn't kill it." He leaned his head against the rocker back. "Accidents happen. We will have more babies, but there is only one of you."

Tears welled and spilled over, running down her cheeks. She couldn't tell if they were of joy or relief or a combination of both and other things as well. "You don't hate me, then?"

"Ah, my Inge. How could I hate you? I know you. You've been tearing yourself apart because you went out and did the plowing even after I've asked you not to. I will not add to that."

"God is punishing me for disobeying."

"I don't think God works that way and neither do you."

"Didn't you want the baby?"

He stared at her, a frown beginning. "Of course I wanted the baby. Why are you worrying about this like two dogs with a bone? Nothing I say is right."

Ingeborg bit her lower lip. He had a point. Did she need him to yell at her so she could get angry back? Would a fight make her feel better? "I'm sorry." And with that the dam burst, and the tears she'd been fighting spilled forth, raining down her cheeks and splashing onto the sheet that covered Astrid. She cried for the baby lost, for the guilt, for the fears she might never have another baby. Tears flowed for Haakan and his disappointment, for the way she'd been acting, and for the load she'd been carrying around all alone.

Haakan knelt beside the rocker, then putting both arms around her, he laid his cheek against hers. "Hush now. It is over. I'm here and I love you no matter what. You are my wife, and I love you. Hush. Shh-shh-shh."

Eventually the flood retreated and Ingeborg wiped her eyes with the corner of the sheet. "Some way to greet a man coming home after so long. Uff da."

Astrid smiled at her father and patted his cheek with her hands. When he blew on her hand, she chortled and reached for him to do so again. What if this were her last baby? She gulped and swallowed the sob that threatened to choke her. No more of that!

But that night when Haakan lay sound asleep before she could even crawl under the sheet, she wondered again. Did he really forgive her? Was he so tired that he . . . he . . . She had missed his loving, and now she missed it even more. He hadn't told her how bad he felt, how much he wanted a son just to keep the peace, had he?

When she finally did sleep, nightmares raced rampant through her mind.

20

"Now that Anner is home, I think we should send Ephraim out to help them."

Hjelmer looked up from his newspaper. "Can you spare him from the store? I got too much work myself to help inside."

"If I have to." Penny turned from rolling out pie crust, her evening ritual since she began offering pies for sale and serving dinners. "Might be that Bridget or Katy could come help me. Maybe even Goodie if Ellie goes out to the farm to visit Andrew."

"You have flour on your nose." Hjelmer smiled at her and went back to his paper.

Penny glanced over at her husband, the light from the kerosene lamp creating a halo around him. She dipped her finger back in the flour bin, tiptoed across the room, and with a swoop, dabbed it on his nose. "Now, Mr. Bjorklund, you have flour on *your* nose."

Hjelmer grabbed her round the waist and pulled her down onto his lap.

"You're going to have flour in more places than on your nose," she warned him, trying to keep her hands free. She giggled when he rubbed his nose in her neck.

"You smell like cinnamon."

"It's my new perfume. Drives my customers crazy." She wrinkled her nose at him. "Let me up, please. I need to get those pies in the oven."

"You drive me crazy." He kissed her soundly before setting her on her feet. "Look what you did to my paper."

"Me?" She feigned a look of astonishment.

"Yes, you. Speaking of pies, is there any from supper?"

She shook her head. "Sorry. Ephraim ate the last piece."

The thump and bump of the rolling pin sounded loud in the stillness until the paper rustled.

"Tell me what's going on in the world," she said. "I never have time to read the paper."

"You better start. We'll be a state before long. Right now some want one state of Dakota and others want two."

"Which do you want?"

"I think two would be best. Those hotheads down in the south — I don't want to be mixed up with them."

"What does the paper say about women

being allowed to vote?"

He looked at her over the top of the paper. "Nothing. Why should it?"

"Why not?"

"Because it's not proper, that's why."

"Says who?" Penny turned from crimping the pie crust.

"It's just not. That's what you ladies got husbands for."

"To vote for us? What if we don't agree with our *husbands* as to who is best for the office?"

"Then you talk it over with him, and —"

"And he'll do what he thinks best."

"That's right. God put men in charge for a very good reason."

"I don't recall any place in the Bible saying women should not vote." She let the oven door bang open, thrust the pies inside, and slammed it shut. "You men voted for Wagg and look what a thief he is."

Hjelmer remained silent.

Penny slammed the dishpan on the stove and filled it with hot water from the reservoir. The water sloshing over the side danced and sizzled on the hot stove. Steam rose and Penny's temper with it.

"So you do not want your wife to vote. Is that it?"

"Well, if all women were smart as you and

running their own business like you do, then I guess I'd rethink my position."

"You think Ingeborg is too stupid to vote?"

"I didn't say anyone was stupid." He folded the paper and thrust it into the rack by his chair. "It's just that most women don't have no interest in politics. They are more concerned about raising their children and keeping their homes and such."

"And that's not important?" Her eyebrows flew upward so far they nearly disappeared into her hairline. She stared at her husband. Were all men this dense, or did she get an especially stubborn one?

"I didn't say that. Will you quit twisting my words?"

Penny finished washing the baking utensils and strode to the door to toss the dishwater out on her roses. Besides not wasting water, the soap in it kept the aphids at bay. Right now she felt like dumping it on her husband instead. His silly ideas were worse than aphids any day.

"Well, Hjelmer Bjorklund, I plan to do all I can to help women get the vote and make a few other changes in the way things are done in this world too. Or at least in this country."

Hjelmer groaned. "Isn't running the best

store in the Red River Valley enough?"

It might be if I had a baby, Penny thought, *but since I don't — no, it isn't.*

"I don't want to stay here. I want to go home." Manda buried her fists on her skinny hips.

Zeb shook his head. "I can't help that. I got work here. We all have food enough, a bed to sleep in, and people who care. What more can you ask for?"

"My pa might be home by now."

Zeb just stared at the floor. What could he do? If it weren't for the two girls, he could have gone on to Canada by now. Katy flashed like a shooting star through his mind. Bright-eyed, laughing Katy. He could hardly stand to be in the same room with her, she attracted him so. When he closed his eyes, he could hear her laugh, see her play with the twins, encourage Deborah to eat more, bring him cool water in the hot afternoon.

But he was a hunted man. A haunted man.

Could he make a life here? There was no sheriff in Blessing, and while soon there would be a telegraph office there, he'd not heard of his name and crime flashed along the wire. Was there safety for him and the girls here with the Bjorklunds?

"Why don't you want to stay here?" he asked.

"I hate school. Thorliff and Baptiste treat me like a girl." The final word carried all the disgust she could give it.

He ignored the girl word and concentrated on school instead. "Why do you hate school? I thought sure you'd be happy there."

She studied a new button that Katy had sewn on her dress as if she'd never before seen such a precious object.

"Manda?"

"I . . . I cain't read so good."

"Ah. So that is the problem. How much schoolin' you had?"

"Enough."

Zeb nodded. "But not enough to read well. Arithmetic?"

She shook her head. "Pa didn't hold much with book learning for girls. Said I was smart enough anyway."

"Can you write?"

"I kin write my name. My numbers and the ABC's."

"I see."

"No, you don't see. If'n I ain't to home, someone is going to come and jump our claim. Then there won't be no place for Pa to come home to — when he can. Nor for me'n Deborah." She stared him in the face, willing him to understand. "My ma gived her life for that stretch of no-account land."

And your pa too. Zeb sighed. *Lord in heaven, why me? Why did you send this my way? Didn't I have enough troubles of my own?*

He could leave the girls, just ride off in the middle of the night.

"You ain't gonna leave us, are you?" She'd nearly twisted the button off.

What? Is she a mind reader too? "No, I ain't goin' to leave you."

And to Zeb MacCallister, his word was his bond.

"If I'm to stay here with y'all, you have to go to school and do your very best. Hear me?"

"Yes, sir."

"And right now, you can go sew that button back on. You don't want to hurt Katy's feelings, do you?" *Back to Katy again. If only she and I could talk together. I know she's learning English as fast as she can, but . . .* Another voice, sounding much like his mother, intruded. *So go help her learn the language, you dolt.*

Sunday morning getting ready for church threw the entire household into a frenzy. By the time they all loaded into the wagon, Zeb could only dream of riding north — by himself. Thank God for Bridget, who'd taken to washing and mending the meager clothes Manda and Deborah owned, so that took away one of Manda's excuses.

"Don't want to go to no church," she muttered.

"Too bad. We're goin'."

"Won't understand a word they say. Why can't they all talk English?"

"You know why. What if you moved to a strange country?" *I'm not cut out to be a father.* "Now, get your clothes together. Katy is helping Deborah. And wash your face." Third time he'd said that. "What you got against soap and water anyway?"

"You just want to go so you can sit by Katy."

She had him there. "Get in the wagon," he told her as he mounted his horse.

In spite of the looks from Katy's mor, Zeb did manage to sit next to Katy in church. And the hymns were familiar. He sang the English words along with some of the congregation, and the others sang Norwegian. He didn't understand the sermon, but then, it gave him free time to think about the young woman beside him. Did she have any idea he was thinking about her?

Manda gave him an elbow in the ribs.

He brought his gaze forward. Had he really been studying Katy's hands? He was going to have to do something about that girl. Manda, not Katy. Did she think she was his keeper or what?

He followed the family down the aisle and out to shake the preacher's hand, Katy right in front of him.

"Good to see you, Miss Bjorklund." Reverend Solberg spoke in Norwegian, but any dolt would recognize the delight on his face and the extra time he held her hand.

Zeb felt like pushing forward and . . .

"Good morning," his angel said in English. "I . . . I am pleased to see you." Her eyes lit up at her triumph.

Reverend Solberg laughed with her. "You are coming along just fine. We're going to be having a class in speaking English at the school starting on Tuesday night. You are welcome to come."

Zeb couldn't understand a word he said, other than Tuesday and English. *Is he ever going to let go of her hand?*

He rode on home ahead of the wagonful of laughing and teasing people. The Bjorklunds made everyone feel a part of their family. Yet he didn't dare join in. One of these days Haakan was going to ask some penetrating questions. He could see it coming, and he couldn't give any answers. Better to be silent than tell a lie.

That night as Ingeborg sat brushing her hair in preparation for bed, she turned to Haakan. "What do you think of Zeb?"

"Mmm." Haakan squinted his eyes to think better. "He seems a good young man. He knew the hymns today and knew his way around the Bible. You can tell he's had a godly upbringing."

Ingeborg waited, her arm automatically continuing with the brush strokes, her waist-length golden hair pulled around over one shoulder. Finally she said, "Do I hear a 'but' there?"

"I guess so. I get the feeling he's hiding something, but then he and I haven't had much time to really talk. I tell him what to do, and he goes and does it. Always does a fine job too, especially with horses and people. See the way he gets around Manda? Now there's a strong-willed youngster if I ever saw one."

"You think they're related?"

"Why do you ask?"

"I don't know. I just get the feeling there's a lot of story there that we're not hearing." She rested the brush in her lap and turned to face him. "We could maybe help them if they'd trust us enough to tell us what's what."

"Why'd you ask?"

"Well, you know our Katy."

"Do I ever. Now, if I wasn't already married to the best wife in Dakota Territory, I might . . ."

She smacked him on the hip with her hairbrush. "Haakan Howard Bjorklund, how you talk."

He rolled closer and tweaked the end of the loose braid her fingers had made while they talked. "Ingeborg Bjorklund, always remember this. No matter that I *look* at other women sometimes. Men do that. But I will always come home with you and you only."

Ingeborg felt her eyes fill. "Oh, Haakan." She leaned back against him and snuggled close when he wrapped his arm around her waist.

It was some time later before they fell asleep, spoon fashion, with him curved around her back, keeping her safe.

Her last thought before drifting off with a smile on her face was *Perhaps a baby may come of this.*

They planned the house-raising for Metiz

for midweek. Instead of asking the entire community, they just invited the Baards and all the Bjorklunds. Still, they had six grown men, Petar, who thought he was full grown, and five youths. Goodie insisted on coming with Hjelmer and Ephraim, who came in from helping at the Valders'. Penny remained to run the store.

"I'm going to miss out," Penny moaned as she added two pies to the wagonload of supplies. The kegs of nails and glass for the windows had come in on the train the day before.

"You can come help with Lars and Kaaren's house on Saturday. Everyone is going to be there. That way you can close the store." Hjelmer checked to make sure he had all his hand tools.

"You want I should send Manda back to help you?"

Penny brightened. "What a wonderful idea. I like that little girl. She doesn't take any guff from anybody."

"Way I hear it, calling her 'girl' is what gets Thorliff and Baptiste in bad with her. She'd just as soon knock 'em down as spit."

"Spit!"

Hjelmer turned to her, the twinkle in his eyes making her smile. "Way Reverend Solberg told it, she won the spitting contest out behind the school by two feet or so."

Penny rolled her eyes. "Good for her. Teach those young pups a thing or two."

"Maybe you'd better set her to quilting or some such ladylike occupation."

"Hjelmer, get on with you. Goodie, get him out of here before I . . ."

"Before you what?" Hjelmer gave her a swat on the behind before mounting to the wagon seat.

Penny watched them leave until the jangling bell above the front door called her inside. She pushed aside the calico curtain that draped the door between home and store. "Why, Mrs. Magron, how are you? Seems like forever since I saw you last."

"This fall's been mighty busy, what with harvest and all." Mrs. Magron twittered just like the bird Penny so often thought her like.

"Hope your grain was heavy as the others'. This has been a good year so far." Penny took out a cloth and wiped the dust off the counter. "What can I find for you today?"

Mrs. Magron looked at her list, then handed it to Penny. "Seems I keep finding more things I'm out of. Did the needles come in? I broke my last one yesterday. I just don't think they make them as strong as they used to."

Penny led the way to the stack of cloth-covered bolts. By the time they'd settled on navy wool for a coat, black serge for a skirt, and various pieces for shirts, Penny had fabric draped all over everywhere.

"Miz Bjorklund?"

"Yes. Oh, Manda, you're just the person I want to see." She waved her hand at the mess they'd made. "You think you can roll these bolts of material back together and stack them over there?" She pointed to where the other bolts were stacked.

"A'course." Manda smiled at Mrs. Magron and went right to work.

Some time passed before they had a lull in customers. When the bell tinkled as the last person walked out the door, Penny breathed a sigh of relief. "Manda, you are one fine answer to prayer today. If you hadn't been putting things away, I'd have to close up to do so. You hungry?"

"Yes, ma'am." Manda leaned on the broom she'd found to sweep out the dirt clods carried in on boots. The street hadn't dried out all the way from the rain the day before, and Dakota soil stuck to boots like leeches on skin.

"So how are things out at the farm?" Penny asked a bit later as they sat down at the table.

"All right."

"I hear Deborah is getting stronger all the time."

"She is, thanks to the old Mrs. Bjorklund. She took us in with her just like we was long-lost family. Hamre and Zeb, they sleep out to the barn for now."

Penny smiled to herself. Manda had said more in these few minutes than all the times she'd seen her before. She'd turned the store sign to "closed" and then together they'd put the dinner out. While she'd cooked a big roast beef, no one had gotten off the train today for dinner, so it was just the two of them.

"Here, have some of these candied carrots." Penny passed the bowls of food across the table. "I heard tell you licked them boys in a spitting contest."

" 'Tweren't hard." Manda stared down at her plate. "Ol' Missus Valders came by and said young ladies shouldn't do such things." She looked up, her eyes dark. "I ain't no young lady, and I ain't never gonna be one."

"What do you want?" The question just slipped out.

"I want to go home."

"Where is home?" Penny had a feeling she was about to find out more than the others had.

"Southwest of here. On the other side of

the Missouri River. My folks got a home-stead there, and . . . and . . ." Manda took a bite of meat and chewed. After swallowing, she continued. "My ma died and Pa went for supplies, but there was a big snowstorm and he never came back. I figured maybe he got lost or something. Deborah took sick and I done the best I could takin' care of her. Then that old red cow up and drowned herself, and that's when I run into Zeb MacCallister. He come to our soddy lookin' for a place to get out of the storm. Pa said don't let no strangers in, but I already met him. Zeb, I mean. So he waren't no stranger — not really." She cut and chewed again. "You think I done right?"

Penny wanted to put her arms around the girl and hold her close. "Yes, I think you did the right thing. How long since your mother died?"

"Last winter, sometime after Christmas. The baby she was bornin' died too. My pa, he . . . he had a hard time of it." She glared across the table. "But he didn't run off and leave us. I know he didn't."

"Whatever made you think that?"

"One of the neighbors come by, and he said that. But I think he wanted our home-stead, and if'n we don't get back there, he just might get it. Zeb, he left a letter for my pa." Her voice dropped. "If he ever gets home."

At the desolate sound of the girl's voice and the sorrow in her eyes, Penny left her chair and knelt by Manda. "Oh, my dear, losing your ma and pa is about the hardest thing in this whole world. Mine were both killed in an accident when I was just a bit older than you. I still miss them all the time." She put her arms around the stiff body and smoothed the girl's hair. "Such a heavy burden you bear."

At that Manda collapsed against Penny's shoulder, her tears soaking the gingham dress and apron straps. "I want my ma and pa back."

"Me too. Oh, me too." Penny comforted and patted the girl until the storm of weeping passed. Finally she handed Manda a handkerchief from her apron pocket. "Here, blow your nose and mop your eyes. We got to think of a way to make sure you get to keep the homestead."

"You tell the sheriff, and he'll put Deborah and me in the orphanage."

"Over my dead body."

At that a smile tickled the sides of Manda's mouth. She sniffed and blew again. "Deborah woulda died too if MacCallister hadn't come along. She was right sick. She ain't so good yet, but the old Mrs. Bjorklund, she's taking good care of her. Them's good folks, the Bjorklunds." She smiled at Penny. "All of them."

"Thank you for the fine compliment, Manda, my dear. Now, as I see it . . ." Penny returned to her chair and propped her chin on her fists. "You can be right glad you still got your sister. I ain't seen mine since the day I moved in with my aunt and uncle Baard."

"Oh. That's bad. Deborah's the most special person in the world to me. I woulda died too, if'n she did."

"Well, as you can see, I didn't die, and now we got to figure out a way for you to keep the land. Where did you say it was?"

After Manda told her, Penny sipped her coffee and let her mind work on the problem. "You have any other relatives?"

"Not so I know."

"And MacCallister is no relative."

"Nope, none."

"You think he could find his way back there to your homestead?"

"I s'pose. Why?"

"I don't know. We'll have to find out the legal proceedings. I think we better talk all this over with Hjelmer and Haakan and Ingeborg. All together we'll find some way, I promise you that."

At the look that turned Manda's face to sunshine, Penny bit her lip. *Lord, please don't fail us now.* But as she well knew, sometimes the good Lord seemed to take an awful long time to answer the requests of His children. And sometimes the answer was no.

21

"It's all yours, Metiz. We should be able to finish the inside after the weather turns."

"Many windows." She looked up at Haakan, her eyes sparkling in the sunlight.

"Just like you wanted. And with it raised like that, if it floods, you won't get a house full of water."

"Just in under room."

"The cellar. Ja, can't do much about that. But now you won't have to go outside in the dead of winter to get things from the cellar."

"Never did."

"I know. This will be your first winter with us." Haakan looked from Metiz to the house. "Probably should've built it bigger."

"No want bigger. Too big now."

"I suppose, compared to your tepee, this house is a mansion."

"What mansion?"

"Huge, fancy house. Many, many rooms. Big like a hotel."

"Ah. Whole tribe live in mansion."

"Sure enough could. I hope that idea of

Lars's works — filling the walls with sawdust. But it works with an icehouse, so why not houses? And why didn't we think of it earlier?"

"Icehouse?"

"Big building to keep ice in for summer."

"Ice melt."

"Not if you pack enough sawdust around it. You'll see. Next summer we are going to have ice cream in July."

"Really, Pa?" Thorliff looked up from the butt he was splitting into shingles. He and Baptiste had already split the ones for Metiz' house and were now working for Lars and Kaaren's.

"You can't have ice cream in July." Manda split off another smooth shingle. After coming back from Penny's, she'd got the hang of it real quick, much to Thorliff's dismay.

"If'n my pa says it is so, it is so." Thorliff spoke so emphatically that his hair bounced. He brushed it back with one hand and reset his porkpie hat.

" 'Tain't."

" 'Tis."

"All right, you two, that's enough." Haakan raised his hands for silence.

" 'Tis," Thorliff muttered under his breath.

"Thorliff Bjorklund, what's got into

you?" Haakan looked down at his son seated on a chunk of wood and tapping the froe just right.

Thorliff split another shingle without looking up. His lower lip stuck out far enough to rest one of his shingles on.

Baptiste looked up at Haakan and grinned. "Fish are biting."

"They are, huh?" Lars stopped beside them. "Now wouldn't a mess of fish taste good for supper?" He looked at Haakan. "I think all these hard workers deserve some time off to go fishing, don't you?"

"Up to you. It's your roof they're splitting now."

"Then, fishing it is."

Baptiste leaped to his feet. "Come on." Thorliff, the Baard boys, and Hamre followed him.

"Me too." Andrew darted after the big boys.

Katy leaped and snagged him by the shirt-tail. "Hold up, short stuff."

Barefeet churning the dirt, he pulled against the restraint.

"Nei. No," his father told him, but Katy sent Haakan a pleading glance.

"Hey, Andrew, my boy, you can go when you get bigger." Haakan lifted the boy in the air and whooshed him down again, the breeze fluffing his near white curls. "Right now you can put all those chips in a basket, you and Ellie. Maybe Anji will help too."

Andrew stared longingly after the big boys. "I'm bigger now."

Haakan whirled him around and set him down with a tickle. "First one with a full basket gets a . . . a . . ." He closed his eyes to a squint. "A cookie?"

Andrew squinted back at him, hands on hips. "Two cookies."

Haakan nodded. "Two cookies."

"He's a horse trader already." Lars shook his head. "What a boy."

The tap of the mallet on the froe caught Haakan's attention. "Manda, did you want to go fishing too?"

She shook her head. "Not with them dumb boys."

The men swapped glances and raised their eyebrows.

"You don't like to fish?" Lars asked.

"Don't know. Never been. But if I did, I'd catch more than all of 'em put together." Tap, crack, and another shingle fell to the ground.

Zeb joined them just in time to hear Manda's growling. He raised his shoulders in the age-old shrug of men who have no idea why women or even young girls do what they do. The others matched it and, gathering their tools, headed for the place where Lars had dug out his cellar. If they hurried, they could get some of the cellar groundwork done before chores. With all the boys gone fishing, the men would have to do the milking too.

But Ingeborg had the female crew from Bridget to Ilsa in full steam and they took over the milking, even going to the Baards. By the time they returned, the strings of fish were already cleaned and ready for the frying pan. The batter-fried fish, fried potatoes, and green beans with bacon made a meal that left everyone patting their stomachs after second and even third helpings.

"I thought we were going to fry fish clear on till morning," Ingeborg said when the last filet had disappeared down someone's gullet.

"Ran out right time." Metiz handed Ingeborg a plateful of food. "Kept for you."

"Thank you." Ingeborg sat down in the rocker with a sigh and wiped her forehead with her apron. "This was just like feeding a threshing crew."

"They building crew. Same thing." Metiz picked a fish bone out of her teeth. "Good fish."

The next day Lars took some good-natured ribbing about pouring sawdust in his walls, but he laughed it off. "You'll be singing a different tune come winter. I bet you'll all be knocking on my door, asking for a warm place to sit."

"Makes sense to me," Haakan put in. "I'm thinking there must be a way to get the sawdust inside the walls of my house, too, and maybe even the barn. Hey, even the soddies can be warmer than these wood frame houses."

"Heaping manure and straw around the base will help. We did that in Ohio." Joseph Baard finished nailing off the length of flooring. "Then you spread it out on the garden come spring. Does double-duty that way. Horse manure works the best. Takes longer to rot."

"The things we learn when we get together," Haakan said, shaking his head.

As the walls went up, the men scurried over the building like ants at their nest. While to an outsider it might look haphazard, each one knew his best skill and did it.

"Sure do miss Anner on the measuring and cutting," Joseph commented.

"He's one who checks and double-checks so everything fits." Haakan threw down a board. "We got to be more careful."

Reverend Solberg looked up from sawing. "I went to see him yesterday. He's not doing good at all."

"The arm bad?"

"No, the arm seems to finally be healing, but . . ." Solberg shook his head. "I'm afraid for him, that I am."

Haakan let it go until the others were out of hearing range. "Is it the drinking?"

"How did you know?"

"Oh, I got ears and eyes."

"He's angry, Haakan, so terribly, terribly angry. And nothing anyone says makes a whit of difference." Solberg wiped his sweaty brow with the back of his shirt sleeve. "I'm afraid for him and for his wife. She looks twenty years older. She even walks like an old woman. How do we get him to understand that losing an arm isn't the end of his life? Or the end of the world?"

"God only knows."

"Wise words, my friend. Wise words."

"So what are we to do?"

"Pray for him."

"Anything else?"

"That isn't enough?" His smile said he was teasing.

"You know, it ain't easy being a two-handed farmer, let alone a one-handed one. Like the measuring here. It takes two

358

hands." Haakan demonstrated unfolding the wooden measuring stick, laying it out, holding it in place with one hand while marking the cut with the other. "See?" He refolded the tool and put it in his back pocket. "And have you ever tried milking with one hand?"

"It would take longer, but once the cow got used to it, would she give less milk?"

Haakan thought a moment. "I doubt it."

"And if he sold the land, surely there is something else he can do."

"Right now I can't think of anything, but I'll ask around. I just don't know what kind of things he is good at besides farming."

"And building. Measuring and cutting accurately especially."

By evening the house was framed, windows and doors set, sided on three sides, and the sheeting laid in close rows ready for the shingles.

"Pa, I bet I can shingle a roof now too." Thorliff stood as tall as he could beside his father.

"If you do that, then who will split the shingles? You're the best splitter we got." Lars ruffled the boy's hair, tipping off his hat in the process.

Thorliff leaned over and picked it up, dusting it against his leg before setting it back on his head. "Manda can take my place splitting. She's good at it." His tone said he offered this grudgingly.

"Well, we'll see." Haakan eyed the roof. "If you fell off there, your mother would nail my hide to the barn wall."

"I wouldn't fall." Thorliff wrinkled his nose and shook his head. "Nailing shingles is easier than lugging them, and I been doing that long as we been using shingles for the roofs."

The next day he lived up to his word. Slow at first, but when he gained the rhythm, he nearly kept up with the men.

"Son, you are right good with that hammer," Lars said when they quit for dinner. "Between the four of us, we'll have that house weatherproof in no time."

"I could miss school to help finish. Lots of the older boys stayed home through the harvest."

Haakan shook his head. "No, you missed today and that is enough. You can help again when you get home."

"But it gets dark so early these days. And we're going to have frost any night now."

"How do you know that?"

"Metiz said to watch the moon — it will tell you. And last night there was frost in the low places."

"Thorliff, you amaze me. You hear something one time, or read it one time, and you remember it from then on. What are we going to do with you?"

"Let me stay home and help finish the house." Thorliff gave his father a sly look out the side of his eye. "I'm so far ahead of the other kids, they'll never catch up." But when Haakan shook his head, the boy didn't argue any further.

That night when Haakan told Ingeborg about the conversation with Thorliff, she just shook her head. But the light in her eyes told of her pride in her elder son. "So . . . are you going to let him stay home?"

"You crazy? I like my hide too well."

"What?"

"Just men talk, dear. Come to bed."

Since Saturday had become market day and Penny couldn't leave the store, the women held their October quilting day on Friday at the church. The women gathered as soon as their older children left for school and the dinner had been set to cooking for those at home.

Kaaren started their time together with reading from Proverbs 31 about the ideal woman. " 'A good wife, who can find . . .' "

"Well, we do all that but the grape things.

I'd guess our gardens and fields can take that place," Agnes said when the reading was finished. "I sure could use a few more handmaidens and a slave or two. Or servant," she added at the gasp that went up.

"We're all slaves to the land, that's what," said someone else.

"But the labor is returning to us a hundredfold, wouldn't you say?" Kaaren looked around the group. "And we have one another for both help and encouragement."

"Speaking of help. I tried to do more for Hildegunn and Anner and she run me off." Goodie shook her head. "They let Ephraim work out in the fields, but that is all. She's trying to kill herself off, that's what."

"Or Anner is ordering her so." Ingeborg looked around the group. "We got to do something here, and I don't know what."

Bridget, Sarah, and Katy sat side by side, waiting until Kaaren translated for them. Then Bridget said, "Best thing to do is pray and let God tell us what to do."

"Ja, you are so right." Agnes, sitting next to Bridget, laid a hand on her arm. "One thing we can do right here is speak more Norwegian so these two can understand. I know we want all to learn English, but they ain't had time yet."

And so they all switched to Norwegian

and the conversation continued. Finally Kaaren raised her hand. "Let's pray now and then we can get on with our quilting."

"I have something to say first." Penny took the floor. "You know we talked about starting a bank here in Blessing, and I know Ingeborg sent out letters about that —"

"Got an answer too," Ingeborg raised an envelope. "Came yesterday."

"Good. But the other day I run into a problem concerning Manda and Deborah, who came to our community with Zeb Mac-Callister." As she said his name she glanced at Katy, who turned bright red. "Well, those two children are going to lose their inheritance if we don't do something about it. Their ma is dead, their pa disappeared, and now they aren't on the land either. Someone could come jump their claim, and all their parents' sacrifice would be gone for naught."

"Uff da," said one.

"Oh my," another murmured.

"We got to do something." Agnes said what they all were thinking.

"So MacCallister and the girls are not related?"

Penny shook her head. "He just saved their lives, is all."

The women looked at one another, then back at Penny.

"No relatives?"

"Not so they know."

"So what does the law say? Could one of us buy the land and hold it in inheritance for the girls? Or take over the farming until Manda marries or is old enough to go it alone?" Agnes shook her head. "Those poor children."

"I don't know the answers to any of those questions, but I know that all together we women can come up with something. And that brings up my next problem." Penny paused and again looked around the room, catching the gaze of each woman present. "Dakota Territory, be it one state or two, must let women have the vote. We have to help that happen."

"I don't see why," said one of the women. "What good is voting going to do us?"

"You think the men make all the right decisions?" Penny drew herself taller. "We need to be able to own land and have a say in our government. The constitution says 'for the people' not just for the men. Women are part of the people too."

"Whew, when you get on the soapbox, you do it good." Agnes wiped her brow as if she'd been thinking hard. Or working hard.

"We aren't chattel like the horses to be bought and sold, or dumb animals who slave from dawn to dusk."

"No, we work far beyond dusk and many before dawn." Ingeborg's sally drew a laugh from the rest but nods of agreement.

"Guess I've said enough." Penny leaned back in her chair.

"But how do we go about getting the vote?" Mrs. Magron asked. Without her friend Hildegunn, she hadn't said much.

"We read newspapers, ask questions, and I'm going to write to a group I heard of for help out here on the prairie." Penny leaned forward again. "But first, we got to save the land for those children."

"Let's pray and we can talk about all of this while we work," Kaaren said gently. When their heads were bowed, she began, "Heavenly Father, thou who knows all things, we thank thee for this day and this gathering here in the church thou hast given us. We thank thee that we can come before thee and that thou listens to our voices. Thank thee, Father, that thou dost love us and did send thy Son Jesus to die on the cross that we might be yours."

A sniff came from one of those present.

She asked for help in the problems they were experiencing and for wisdom to know what was right and what to do next. "And heavenly Father, we bring Anner and Hildegunn before thee now. I have not lost an arm, but we have all felt loss of something, so we have an idea how he feels, but, God, he is so angry and bitter. Please help him to see thy mercy and to know that life can be good again. Father, bring healing to each of us who have hurts in our hearts, and we give thee all the thanks and praise. To God be the glory and to Jesus His Son, amen."

At the "amens" from around the group, they raised their heads and many of them dabbed their eyes with their handkerchiefs.

"Ah, Kaaren, you pray so good. Would that I had words like that," Brynja said. "So often I only cry and plead, 'God help me.'" She looked up from staring at her hands. "Life is so hard at times."

The stark words lay on the table like a viper coiled to strike.

Ingeborg nodded. She too was one of those with hurt in her heart. She looked at Agnes and could see suffering mirrored in her eyes. *One of these days,* she promised herself, *I have to talk to Agnes and find out what's eating her.*

By the time they all headed home, they had heard Gould's letter, his offering assistance of any kind, including investment money to begin the bank. Someone had gone for the newspaper when the train went through, and Kaaren read aloud to them while they stitched and cut. They put Penny in charge of getting information on the homestead belonging to the two girls, and they set a date for the fall harvest celebration to be had in the Johnsons' newly finished barn.

"I think you ought to remind Haakan to speak with that young MacCallister," Agnes said to Ingeborg privately as they were getting into their wagons. "Reverend Solberg and Petar never made that girl shine like the mention of Zeb MacCallister. She was red as a beet every time I looked at her."

Ingeborg nodded. "You're right, of course. But getting information from him is like pulling a hen's teeth. I know. I've tried."

"Kinda makes one wonder, then, what's he hiding?" Agnes laid a hand on Ingeborg's knee. "And you and me, we got some talking to do too. You know it well as me." She turned and put a foot up on the wheel spoke, heaving herself up on the seat like it was a chore that took all her strength.

"You take care of yourself," Ingeborg called.

Agnes just waved and slapped the reins. "Hup now."

In the Bjorklund wagon, Bridget and

Katy helped settle the twins and toddlers in the back, along with themselves, and Kaaren joined Ingeborg on the wagon seat.

"You all settled back there?" Ingeborg asked over her shoulder. "Now, Andrew, you sit down by Deborah. My land, what a load we got."

"Giddup!" Andrew hollered, sitting down at the same moment.

Kaaren and Ingeborg shared glances and smiles. It had been a good day.

Haakan was having as much trouble prying anything out of Zeb MacCallister as Ingeborg had. Sure he talked about the daily farming, shared all the information he had about the homestead that Manda had left behind — but any mention of his home and life before the girls, and he clammed up tighter than a locked chest.

"If you aren't happy with my work, just tell me, and I'll move on," Zeb said. The shutters had fallen in his eyes only moments earlier.

"Now, you know that ain't the case." Haakan put down the harness he was mending. Zeb was working on another set. "Everything you put your hand to, you do well, and I've learned some things from you too."

"Thank you." Zeb pounded another rivet in place, making sure it was smooth on the underside so it wouldn't wear on the horse's hide. Rain pounded on the barn roof and ran off the eaves, making the barn a warm, dry haven.

Haakan waited, hoping the young man would volunteer something on his own. When it didn't happen, he sighed and picked up the harness again. Talk about a closed mouth — this man had it down to a habit. Finally Haakan asked gently, "Son, does your family know where you're at?"

Zeb shook his head and pounded in another rivet.

Haakan drove an empty wagon to the harvest celebration so he could swing by and pick up Anner and Hildegunn. He'd promised Ingeborg and Kaaren that he would bring them if he had to hog-tie Anner and throw him in the wagon.

It nearly took just that.

"Anner, you need to get out and be among us all again."

"I'm here, ain't I?"

With one sleeve folded to the inside on both his shirt and jacket, the man looked curiously unbalanced, as if the wind could blow him over with one puff. For all the weight he'd lost, that just could happen, especially in a winter blizzard.

Anner glowered at Haakan. "What makes you think you know what's best for everyone else?"

"Everyone voted, and I got elected to drag you here, not because I know what's best, but because we all miss you."

"Ha!"

Haakan looked over his shoulder at Hildegunn, who sat huddled in the back as if trying to disappear. "You missed the quilting meeting, Mrs. Valders. Ingeborg said it wasn't the same without you."

She didn't respond but huddled deeper in her black wool coat, a scarf tied over her head and knotted under her chin. Gone was the fine hat and the superior smile. Her eyes appeared dull, as though the light of her soul had gone out, leaving only a shell.

Haakan tried again to get Anner talking, but every sentence received only a grunt, if that.

Lord, help, I don't know what to do or say. He clucked the horses into a trot — anything to make the trip pass more quickly.

By the end of the day of festivities, Haakan knew one thing for certain. Anner was a mean drunk. And he wasn't the only one slipping outside and returning to the party in the barn rosier of nose and cheek and louder of voice. A growing number of women were hopping mad and about to do their men serious bodily harm for their despicable behavior.

The fiddle invited everyone to dance, the food pleaded for those present to lighten the groaning tables, and between the children playing upstairs in the haymow and the grown-ups down below, the barn was blessed in grand style.

Until one by one the women had spotted a returning spouse or son or brother who couldn't walk straight.

"I ain't putting up with this," Goodie whispered, her lips tightened into a line. "Olaf don't usually drink much, but today . . ."

"They think because this is a party, they can drink as much as they like." Penny felt like smacking Hjelmer with whatever she could pick up. He wasn't drunk by any means, but he *was* flirting with Katy.

Katy hadn't sat still for a moment. Every bachelor in the place had lined up to dance with her, as had many of the married men. But anyone could see that she had eyes only for Zeb MacCallister.

Petar staggered back in the door, and Agnes nearly bit her tongue off when she caught sight of him. Joseph was feeling no pain either, but he was an adult. Her nephew still had some ways to go to become one, and Agnes wasn't about to allow Petar that kind of freedom.

"Don't say anything here," Ingeborg whispered. "You'll only make it worse."

"If'n I could get hold of that stuff, I'd break every bottle in the country. Why don't we just march out there right now and pitch it all down the privy!"

Ingeborg giggled at the picture that leaped into her mind. "Now, wouldn't that be a sight?"

"May I have this dance?" Haakan took hold of his wife's elbow.

"Later," Ingeborg promised Agnes as she whirled away to a romping polka. "Haakan, can't you do something about the drinking?" she asked later as they sipped apple cider to help cool off.

He shook his head. "It's not against the law, you know."

A drunken man's voice yelled words that no woman or anyone else should have to hear. She followed on Haakan's heels as he parted the crowd, heading for the door. By the time they got outside, Anner had a knife in his good hand and was waving it wildly at another man.

The things he said made Ingeborg wish she'd stayed inside.

Spittle ran down his chin, and his long, unkempt hair now hung over his eyes since his hat lay on the ground. "You . . ." He weaved back and forth, the knife flashing in the late afternoon sun.

"Anner, you're using God's name —" Reverend Solberg pushed toward the fracas.

"There ain't no God," Valders shouted. Then lifting his face to the sky, roared, "If you *are* God, strike me dead right now!"

Others backed away, a safeguard in case the Almighty did just that and they got struck by accident.

Haakan and Lars looked at each other, nodded, and together came up behind Anner. One grabbed the hand with the knife and the other grabbed around the man's waist, hoisting him off his feet. With a quick twist, the knife fell to the ground. Anner let out a bellow that could be heard clear to Grafton.

"You better take him home," Reverend Solberg said.

"You folks go on and have a good time," Haakan called. "Lars and I will be back soon."

"You want me to find his wife?" Lars asked.

"No, let her stay and enjoy the visit."

"She hasn't talked with a soul," Ingeborg put in. "I tried to get her to talk with me, but nothing. She reminds me of poor Mrs. Booth when she just walked out into that terrible snowstorm and never returned." A shiver ran up her back. It didn't take much to bring on madness out here on the prairie, and Hildegunn had been through a lot. Just like the rest of them, only by a different means.

But when they got a now-blubbering Anner to the wagon, Hildegunn huddled in the back as if she'd never moved.

"What will become of them?" Ingeborg asked as the wagon drove away. "Whatever will become of them?"

22

"Those men sure did know how to kill a party," Agnes commented the next day after church.

Ingeborg looked around at the congregation, which that morning consisted mainly of women. "Many of our men seem to have come down with a nasty stomach and head ailment. And it struck so fast too."

"I'd strike something too if'n I could."

"I think we can." Penny joined the group. "I say every time we find a bottle of spirits of any kind, we break it."

Ingeborg thought a moment. "Wouldn't go that far, if it were me. Some is needed for medicinal purposes. Does a good job of cleaning out wounds and keeping one from feeling such terrible pain."

"I'd just as soon pour it over their heads."

"Sort of like the 'oil of blessing.' " Ingeborg grinned at her own joke.

"Don't you go takin' the Word of the Lord in a joke." Penny sounded so much like the Mrs. Valders of before the accident that the ladies chuckled behind their gloved hands.

Penny dropped her act. "That wasn't nice. I'm sorry. Near to broke my heart seeing Mrs. Valders that way yesterday. I'll take any and all bossing if she just gets back to being herself."

"I think she's scared half to death." Agnes lowered her voice so it wouldn't go beyond their small group.

"Scared? Why? Because her husband is sick?" Penny turned toward her aunt.

Agnes shook her head. "Just a feeling I have, but it ain't good."

"What can we do?" Kaaren carried Grace on her hip while Lars held Sophie.

"Break all the bottles and hide the ones for medicine." Penny's voice carried beyond the group.

Hjelmer looked her way and turned back to the group of men. "We're in for it, fellas. You just better be prepared."

"If all those idiots could only hold their liquor. No need to get drunk like that. Nothing wrong with a drink or two. Just don't go getting pie-eyed."

"Or mean."

"Or sick." Joseph had made it to church, but he still showed a bit of green around the edges. "My suspenders, but those cows wanted to be milked early. One bellered in my ear, and I thought my head was about to bust."

They cut off their snickering at the looks they received from the womenfolk.

"I say we declare war." Penny leaned into the circle. "Starting as soon as we get home. Agreed?"

"Agreed." The vote was unanimous. There would be no boozing in Blessing.

"You know," said Bridget, "people drink a lot in Norway, and no one seems to care."

"Really?" Penny raised an eyebrow. "Maybe they just don't get drunk there."

"Oh, they do."

"If it were your husband falling down drunk, wouldn't you care?"

"Ja, I guess. But Gustaf could hold his liquor, so it never bothered me." She thought a moment. "Much."

"So . . . what were you ladies discussing with all the secretive looks?" Haakan asked on the way home.

"Breaking bottles of booze."

"What?"

"You heard me. Our motto is 'No booze in Blessing.' "

"Oh, land, there'll be big trouble in Blessing. Mark my words. You know we don't have many heavy drinkers on a regular basis, only when the men get together in a group."

"What about Anner? Are you saying he's the only one?"

"No, I mean I don't know. That's not something we men talk about much."

"We women didn't either until things got out of hand. Someone could have been killed because of the drinking."

"No one wants to admit to things like that."

She shook her head. "Thank the good Lord above, it isn't a problem at our house."

"I got a letter from Solveig." Kaaren brandished the envelope as she came through the door. She shifted Trygve to the other hip and pointed the twins in the direction of the toy box Ingeborg kept just inside the parlor. "You two go on and play nice now." She set Trygve down on the rug where he immediately went on all fours and followed right after the girls, crawling almost as fast as they walked.

Bridget stopped stirring the boiler of diapers and pushed the coffeepot to the hotter part of the stove. "Be ready in a minute." She replaced the lid on the copper boiler and laid the worn stirring stick on top.

Then, using her apron as a potholder, she opened the oven and pulled out a pan of cinnamon rolls. "You got here at just the right time." With the ease born of long practice, she flipped the pan over on a clean dish towel, and the fragrance of cinnamon flavored the room.

"My, but that looks good." Kaaren sniffed and exhaled on a sigh.

"So, now, what does Solveig have to say?" Bridget pulled a corner roll off and slipped it onto a plate. "Perhaps this will give you the strength to read." Her smile brought an answering one from Kaaren.

She eyed the steaming roll in front of her but pulled the sheet of paper from the envelope first.

My dear family,

How I miss all of you, and thinking of you all together makes me green with jealousy. But we are busy here, and Mother Carlson lets me believe that I am in charge of the household while she manages things behind the scenes. I am just not used to having all these fine things to care for. I am not complaining, mind you.

I have good news. George and I will be parents in late spring, and our little one seems to want to make his mother sick. Being sick is not the good news. But that brings me to another point. Could you possibly spare Sarah to come visit for a time? Our maid, or cook, or whatever you want to call her, is planning on getting married next month, and if Sarah would like the job, it is hers. She would use this time to get used to the place.

Kaaren looked up from her reading. "Ingeborg, you could make a wagon trip with stuffs for the Bonanza farm, the last run for this season. And take Sarah with you." She waited for Ingeborg to answer.

"First of all, Sarah, do you want to go? And second, do we have enough produce to take to make it pay the way?"

The women gathered around the table as Bridget set a plate with a cinnamon roll at each place. After she poured the coffee, she took the last place at the table.

They all looked to Sarah for an answer.

Sarah studied the roll in front of her, then the design on the tablecloth, and shifted her fork to the right. When she finally looked up, she only shrugged. "If I got to leave, I guess I got to leave."

"But that's not true. You don't have to

go. It's just that this could be a good opportunity for you. They will pay you well, and wait until you see that house. Heaven should be so fine." Ingeborg leaned forward. "Sarah, it is solely up to you."

Sarah looked around at each of them. "I would miss you all so. Do they speak Norwegian there?"

"Well, Solveig does, that's for sure." Kaaren folded the letter and put it back in the envelope. "You don't have to make a decision today, you know."

"No, I think maybe it would be best if I go." Sarah clasped her hands in her lap. "If you think I could manage all that there would be to do."

"Between you and Solveig, George Carlson will think he's been doubly blessed. Besides, in the last letter Solveig said there was a real good-looking foreman on the farm there. Almost as handsome as George. Those were her exact words."

Sarah turned a becoming shade of pink. "Will you write, then?"

"No, we'll just go on up day after tomorrow." Ingeborg looked at Kaaren. "Will that give you enough time to get butter churned? We got plenty of eggs, and I have two wheels of cheese near ripe. We're going to have to build a bigger well house to cure cheese at the rate we are going. Penny can sell about all I give her too."

Two days later, in the frost of the near dawn, they loaded the wagon.

"If we had already butchered, we could've taken hams and such too," Ingeborg said as she covered the blanketed produce with straw.

"They don't have so big a crew right now either." Haakan slammed the wagon tailboard shut. "Now, you be sure to greet Mrs. Carlson for us. And give Solveig greetings. Perhaps she and George can come for Christmas."

"Strange to not have a list up to my elbow with things to pick up at the St. Andrew store." Ingeborg swung up onto the wagon seat. "Good thing I've been weaning Astrid or she would have had to come along. And it is downright chilly this morning for a little one."

They said their good-byes and left the yard as the first rays of the sun peeked over the horizon, tinting the whole world pink.

"Ah, look." Ingeborg pointed above the trees lining the banks of the Red River. "You'll warm up soon with that." The horses trotted up the road, harness jingling. A red-winged blackbird sang from a milkweed pod, greeting the sun with his notes. The maple and oak leaves blazed red and orange in the growing sunlight, while the birch trunks gleamed white against the riot of color.

"Even if it is so flat, this land has a beauty all its own." Sarah inhaled deeply of the nippy air. "But don't you miss the mountains of home?"

"Not so much anymore. But at first it was hard. The winters are bad. That north wind blows down through here like ten freight trains tied together. You are fortunate. The furnace in this house you are going to will keep you warm this winter."

Ingeborg didn't return until after dark, but the moon lit her way nearly as well as the sun. The trip home alone gave her time to think and plan for the months ahead, rejoicing in the gift of a cold breeze in her face, sweaty horses, and a sense of God's presence as if He were riding on the seat right beside her.

When she told Haakan of the sensation, he looked at her with a smile. "And He was, you know."

"I know." She crawled into bed and stretched from her toes to the crown of her head. "That is some fine house, that Carlson place."

"Ja, but he doesn't own his own house like we do. Wonder what will happen when the Bonanza farm breaks up. Some of the others down south are, you know."

"No, I didn't know that. How come?"

"With the drop in wheat prices, those money men aren't getting as much as they used to. So they are selling out. Guess they just don't realize that farming goes in cycles. Some years good, some not so good."

"But we've had such good years."

"Ja, but the grain prices keep falling, and the railroads are gouging the farmers left and right." He wrapped an arm around her middle and pulled her to him so she lay warm in the curve of his body. "I was about to ride out to find you."

"You weren't worried?" She turned her head to look at him in the darkness.

"Accidents do happen, you know."

"I know." Ingeborg turned on her side, comforted in the warmth surrounding her. *Didn't hurt him one bit to be the one worrying for a change.*

With the first heavy frost and deepening cold, hog butchering began, and again the neighbors worked together. They loaded the vats used for scalding the hogs onto the wagons and went from farm to farm. For weeks after, the smokehouses sent wisps of smoke into the blue sky. The women rendered the lard and, after seasoning the ground sausage, made some of it into patties and put them down in crocks, pouring hot lard over them to seal them and keep them from spoiling. They tanned the hides for boots and made headcheese out of the heads. As an old saying went, they used all the pig, right down to the squeal.

As soon as the hogs were butchered, soapmaking took over. The women saved the ashes from the cooking stoves and leached water through them to make lye. Lye mixed with leftover fat and some of the newly rendered lard became soap. Ingeborg added rose petals to some and lavender to others, but most of it was poured straight into wooden boxes and set to harden. Once hardened, they cut it into bars and let it cure.

"At least we don't need to make candles anymore," Ingeborg said one afternoon. "Kerosene lamps put out so much more light."

"One of these days we'll have the gas lamps like they do in Grand Forks." Haakan leaned back, dunked a cookie in his coffee, and alternated dunking and chewing.

"You think they will come out here?"

"Ja, eventually."

"Pa, can I dunk one?" Andrew leaned against his father's knee. Deborah stood right behind him. Haakan smiled at her and patted his knee.

"Come sit on my lap, and you can have some too."

Deborah didn't need a second invitation. She climbed up on his lap and snuggled against his chest as if she'd been waiting all her life for just this moment.

Andrew leaned closer. "My turn, Pa."

The children helped themselves to a cookie and made good use of the dwindling cup of coffee.

"You know, these cookies are good, but doughnuts . . . now that's something we haven't had for ages." Haakan looked at Andrew. "Right, son?"

Andrew nodded as he dunked the last of his cookie.

Bridget and Ingeborg looked at each other and shrugged. "Guess we'll have to make doughnuts, then," Ingeborg said. "Andrew, run out to the springhouse and get the buttermilk, will you? Think you can carry the little crock?"

Andrew gave her one of his "Oh, Mor!" looks and, motioning Deborah to follow, headed out the door.

"Put on a jacket. It's raining." But the

door slammed before she had all the words out her mouth.

"Guess I'll go get the schoolchildren in the wagon. That way they won't be soaked to the skin by the time they get home. You need anything from the store?" Haakan dusted the cookie crumbs from his shirt front into his hand.

"Why don't you send Zeb?"

Haakan shook his head. "Ain't you noticed? He never likes to go to town. Absolutely refuses to go to Grafton or Grand Forks. I sure wish I knew more about that young man. Besides, he's over to Lars's, helping him with the inside walls on the new house."

"Ja, so he can see Katy."

"Now, Inge, you wouldn't want to stand in the way of young love, would you?"

"There won't be any 'young love' with my daughter until we know more about him." Bridget plunked the heavy crockery bowl on the counter. "Much as I like him . . ." She frowned. "I don't take to hiding things. Bring 'em out in the open where we know what's going on."

"I feel the same."

"Here's the buttermilk, Mor." Andrew handed Ingeborg the half-full crock. "Can Deborah and me have some?"

Ingeborg poured two glasses and set them on the table.

"Cookies?" He donned his most winning smile.

Chuckling, Bridget set one in front of each of the children.

"I'm more hungry."

"Andrew Bjorklund, you could charm the wings off the angels." Bridget gave them each another, patting their heads as she walked by.

Haakan came back in from harnessing the horses. "Thought of anything you need?"

Andrew stopped before taking a last bite of cookie. "Peppermint sticks."

"Just the mail." Ingeborg glanced at Andrew. "And peppermint sticks."

"Oh boy! Doughnuts!" Thorliff led the raid on the platter of doughnuts on the table. "Thanks, Mor, Bestemor." He reached for the pitcher and poured himself a glass of milk.

"Hadn't you better serve your guests?" Ingeborg reminded him softly.

"We got company?" Thorliff looked around. "Where?"

"Baptiste, Manda, Ilse, Hamre."

"They're not company. They live here!" He looked at his mother as if she'd lost her mind. But at the look she returned him, he shook his head and poured four more glasses. "Help yourselves to the doughnuts. They're right good."

The platter had one remaining doughnut. Haakan snatched it up. "I sure hope you have more put away somewhere. This ain't fair. Doughnuts was my idea." He held out an envelope. "Here's another letter from Gould. I'll trade it for two, no three doughnuts."

Ingeborg smiled and retrieved three doughnuts from the crock. Glancing up as she took the envelope, she caught a frown snag his eyebrows and then vanish. *You don't want me to get letters from men you don't know?* Ingeborg almost chuckled. "Good, more things about starting the bank, I imagine. God surely is good to give us friends who can help us like He does." She tapped the envelope.

Slitting the envelope carefully, she saved the paper for Thorliff. Then drawing closer to the lamp on the table, she began reading. "Oh no." She laid a hand over her heart.

"What is it?" Bridget asked from the sink, where she was peeling potatoes.

"Mr. Gould's wife died in childbirth. Oh, that poor man. And his little children." Ingeborg tried to swallow the tears and failed. She wiped them away with a fingertip and continued reading. "He reminds us that he will be pleased to invest in our venture and wishes us all the best. 'Please advise me as to when and where you will be needing the funds. I remain your faithful servant and friend. David Jonathan Gould.'

"To think he sends us this when he is suffering so himself." Ingeborg sank down on the closest chair. She read the letter again, as if hoping she hadn't read the news that she had. Her heart felt squeezed with the weight of it. Even great wealth didn't keep people from losing ones they loved. A letter seemed such an insignificant way to say all she wished, but it would have to do. She knew too well the sorrow he must be feeling.

She glanced around her kitchen. Maybe they didn't have a mansion like the Goulds, but the love and laughter in this kitchen — why, she wouldn't trade it for all the gold in all the banks in the country. She looked up and sent Haakan a tear-washed smile.

"What is it?" he asked, bending over her chair.

"I am so grateful for you . . . and . . . and all this." She swept her hand out to include all within her domain. "Just thanks be to God for His great goodness to us."

"Amen to that." Haakan squeezed her

shoulder. "All right, all you doughnut eaters. It's chores time."

Agnes didn't come to the November quilting bee. While the women had mixed reports on what happened when the booze disappeared, nothing earthshaking had occurred. But Ingeborg reminded them that most of the drinking happened at the socials, and they had yet to have another. Penny hadn't heard yet on her letter to the land office in Morton County. Ingeborg read them the letter from Mr. Gould.

"So what do we do now?" Mrs. Magron asked. "And where will our bank be located?"

"Who is going to run it?" asked another.

"What are we going to call it?"

Ingeborg felt as if she was being peppered with buckshot. She raised both hands in the air. "I don't know the answers to any of these questions. We still don't know all the laws regarding banking, let alone how to set one up. I guess the next step is to go to Grand Forks and talk with Mr. Brockhurst."

"I think we should call it the First Bank of Blessing." Mrs. Magron twitched her red nose like the mouse she resembled.

Everyone looked at her, shock on all their faces.

"I . . . I . . . that was just a suggestion." She withdrew back into her stitching, gaze downcast as if afraid someone might accuse her of being uppity.

"I think that's a good idea," Penny said before anyone could talk against the name. "I been thinking we could add a room onto the store. It could be the bank and the post office combined. We'd buy a big safe, and Olaf could make a rack of little cubbyholes for the mail. One for each family."

"We probably should talk this over with the men," Ingeborg said. "But I don't see how they could find fault with these good ideas. Can't you just see it? FIRST BANK OF BLESSING on a big sign over the door."

"Or on the front window."

"In gold and black letters," Mrs. Magron added while she continued to stitch.

But when none of the Baards showed up in church on Sunday, Ingeborg resolved to go call on her friend the next day. Something surely was wrong.

That night she woke up sweating, her throat aching as though she'd been crying for hours.

"What is it, Inge? What's wrong?" Haakan wrapped his arm around her and pulled her close.

392

"The pit. That awful dead pit. I . . . I was teetering on the edge. Something pushed me, or grabbed me, or . . ." She put her hands over her eyes. "I can see it so clearly. Haakan, am I losing my mind again?"

"Oh, my dear one, you didn't lose your mind before, and you aren't going to now. I'm here. I won't let anything take you away." He stroked the tendrils of damp hair off her forehead with a gentle hand.

She turned and rested her head on his shoulder, tucked safely under his arm and next to his heart.

"Hush, now, and sleep. Always remember, if I'm not strong enough to keep the pit away, our heavenly Father is. Remember, He promises to walk beside us all the way."

Ingeborg let his soothing voice calm her. He was right. God would never let her go. But how to deal with the dreams — the terrifying dreams that so easily could become reality? *Had* been reality.

A verse floated into her thoughts like a down quilt spread over her on a winter night. "Have ye the mind then of Christ Jesus?" *So I put Jesus in my mind. Is that what the verse means? When the pit is there I see Jesus instead?* "But I must wake to do that," she murmured, sleep nearly overtaking her.

"Hush, my Inge, hush."

Even when she woke, she felt the dream hovering, as if she could spin around fast enough to catch sight of it before it hid. "No matter what, today I am going to see Agnes." She finished braiding her hair, put a clean apron on over her dress, and went downstairs to start breakfast. How good it was to be able to cook first thing in the morning, rather than go out and milk first.

By the time she finally got out the door, the sun had climbed halfway to noon. She clucked the horse into a trot, the wagon protesting the additional speed with every turn of the wheels. "Need some grease on these axles," she said. The horse twitched his ears back and forth. Driving alone like this gave Ingeborg some much needed thinking time. Ducks and geese flew the skies above on their trek south for the winter, their plaintive songs inviting her to follow.

"Follow no, but I sure wouldn't mind bagging a few, or more than a few. We could use the down for more feather beds. Uff da, all the people who will need covers this winter."

The horse snorted, as if answering.

"Even you agree, don't you?" She raised her face to the sun that nowadays reached noon before the real warmth could be felt.

Frost decorated the north sides of fence posts and rested on clumps of grass. Ingeborg breathed deeply of the brisk air and felt it tingle all the way to the bottom of her feet.

The heaviness of the previous night took wings and joined the flocks above, flying south and away.

After tying her horse up by the Baards' barn, Ingeborg hefted her basket from the wagon bed and crossed the yard to the house. If it hadn't been for the smoke rising from the chimney, she'd have thought no one was home, it was so quiet. She knocked once and the door swung open before she could tap it again.

"Agnes Baard, what has happened to you?" Ingeborg stopped as if struck.

"Just some kind of ailment that pukes up your guts and drains out your strength. I'm on the mend now." She covered her mouth to cough. "Don't know when I felt so bad."

"Are you sure you want company?"

Agnes leaned out the door and peered around. "I don't see no company, but I sure could use a good chat with my best friend."

Ingeborg thrust her basket into Agnes's hands. "Just some extra things I thought you might appreciate."

Agnes motioned her in and peeked under

the red-and-white gingham cloth covering. "Oh good, a chunk of your cheese. How good that sounds, and I tell you, nothing's sounded good for a week or more."

"Why didn't you send over and let someone come help you?" Ingeborg removed her coat and hung it on the coat tree by the door.

"And let them get sick too? No, it was enough with us here. Joseph had only a light spell, and Anji never caught it a'tall, so she's been the biggest help."

"And the boys?"

"They're about as much good in a kitchen as nothing. And Petar's the worst. You'da thought he was dying the way he carried on. Me and Rebecca and Gus got it the worst. Fact is, Rebecca's still sleeping off the effects." Agnes pulled the coffeepot to the hot front of the stove. "I don't have a cookie or cake to my name. Nothing to go with coffee."

"Check the basket."

As they made themselves comfortable at the table, Ingeborg studied her friend. Eyes sunken, hair straggling from the bun at the back of her head, skin hanging slack under the once strong jaw, now outlining the bones. "You need to get out in the sunshine."

"Ja, what little warmth we might have left before the snow flies." Agnes shivered. "I ain't looking forward to the dark days, let me tell you. Not at all." She sipped her coffee, dunked her cookie, and sucked on it. "And with no baby to care for this year . . ." Her voice trailed off.

"I'll loan you Astrid, and I know Kaaren would gladly send Trygve over."

"Ja, that would be good." Agnes stared out the window. "I wish . . . I wish . . . ah, the wishing does no good." She looked back at Ingeborg, her face creased in a mask of pain. "I can't get over that baby dying. What is wrong with me that I dwell on it so? And to not get pregnant again. Is God so angry with me? Is He not trusting me to care for His little ones?"

Ingeborg tried to blink back the tears she could feel brimming behind her eyes. She sniffed but it did no good. "At least you didn't kill yours."

The words fell like black coal tossed onto white snow.

"Oh, Ingeborg. No! You didn't kill that baby." Agnes reached for Ingeborg's suddenly cold hands. "O Lord in heaven, what burdens we bear. Why do we torture ourselves so?"

Ingeborg dug in her pocket for a handkerchief. Who was comforting whom here?

"Why can't we put these things behind us and go on like Paul says in the Scriptures. Why, O Lord, why?" A sob choked off the word.

"Maybe because Paul never had a baby?" Ingeborg tried to smile through her tears.

"Maybe." Agnes nodded and mopped her eyes and nose. "Things are different for men than women, that's for sure." She got up and refilled their coffee cups, taking the time to put wood in the stove before sitting back down. "Ingeborg, do you really think that — about killing the baby?"

Ingeborg shrugged. "Yes and no. When the pit yawns before me, I think falling in would be just punishment, but then I read my Bible and it says God forgets our sin, puts it as far away as the east is from the west." She took a sip of coffee. "Sometimes I have a hard time believing that. If only I had not gone out in the field, none of this would have happened."

"How do you know that? Besides, I thought a long time ago you and I agreed to not listen to the 'if only's.' " She reached a comforting hand to clasp Ingeborg's. "I think God brought you here today so we can cry together and talk all this out and let God's healing light come deep inside us where the hurts dwell."

"And burn them out?"

"Or love 'em out. I ain't sure which."

By the time Ingeborg left for home, the two had prayed together, cried some more, dug deep and laid bare all the heart hurts, prayed some more, searched the Scriptures for renewed promises, and finally laughed again.

Agnes looked ten years younger when Ingeborg went out the door, and Ingeborg felt ten pounds lighter. She turned and hugged her friend once more. "God surely did know what He was doing when He created friendship."

"Amen to that and to the power of the cross. You drive careful now going home."

"You send one of the boys over, if you need help?"

"I already got the help I need." Agnes blew her a kiss.

On the way home, Ingeborg let her mind wander. What other poor souls out there were suffering in silence when God gave them friends to share the burden? Hildegunn immediately leaped into her mind. "I've got to go see her one of these days, and it better be soon."

"Whoa." She tightened the reins at the same time, and the horse stopped. "Maybe I should go right now." She looked up at the sky. The sun had already slid beyond the midafternoon mark. To go or not to go. She looked toward the north to the Valders' then back to the town nearby. "Instead of that, maybe I'll give the children a ride home from school since I'm so close. Then I could get the mail too." She swung the horse around and headed for Blessing. Mrs. Valders would have to wait for another day.

23

"All right now, folks — er, class, come to attention." Reverend Solberg rapped his ruler on the desk.

The group kept on talking, a mixture of Norwegian and English that sounded like pure babble.

"The schoolchildren mind me much better than you do." He raised his voice and spoke in Norwegian.

The adults and children both exchanged sheepish looks and quieted down.

He smiled out at them. "There now, that is better." Turning to the blackboard he wrote four words in English and their Norwegian counterpart. "I have written both because some of you want to learn to speak Norwegian. Now let's say them together: Hello. Hallo. Good-bye. Adjø. Please. Vær så snill. Thank you. Mange takk."

They parroted what he said and smiled back at him.

"Very good."

"Very good," the echo came. They waited

for the Norwegian.

"No, wait." He raised his hands. "Please, you are trying too hard."

"Cannot say that," Bridget said in Norwegian. "You must slow down. You talk too fast."

Solberg switched to Norwegian. "Now, let me make myself clear."

As the pastor explained the rules of the classroom, Zeb glanced over at Katy sitting at the table across the aisle. Even in the dimness from the kerosene lamps on stands attached to the walls, her hair caught the light and made it seem brighter. *Spun gold,* he thought.

Her mouth quirked up and she slanted him a look out of the side of her eye.

She can tell I'm watching her. She can always tell, just like I can tell when she is watching me.

"Mr. MacCallister."

Zeb jerked his attention back to the front of the room. He could feel the warmth creep up his neck. Had anyone else noticed him watching her? "Yes, sir?"

"Do you speak any languages other than English?"

"Yes, sir. A bit of French."

"Shame it's not German. That would make Norwegian easier for you."

"Anyone else speak another language?"

Katy raised her hand. "Some German, a bit of French, and Swedish. We all learned Swedish in school."

Zeb wished he could understand everything she had said. *Let's get on with the Norwegian. We don't have all night. How do I say, "You are beautiful"?* But he kept his face straight and eyes forward. Was that her mama's eyes he could feel drilling into his back? Next time he would sit in the last row.

By the end of the class, he'd learned fifteen Norwegian words or phrases. Katy had learned fifteen English ones.

There had to be a way to speed up the solution to his problem. To have Ingeborg or Kaaren or even Haakan translate for him to ask Katy to go on a walk with him — just the two of them — would not do.

Bridget sat beside him on the wagon seat going home. Did she suspect? From the look on her face, he was sure of it. It seemed as though Katy's mother did not like him at all.

There was no one he could talk to.

With the first heavy snowfall, fieldwork ended for the year. Haakan and Lars parked their machinery in a three-sided shed they had built for that purpose and cranked up the steam engine for sawing lumber. People from up and down the river brought logs to be sawed into boards, leaving a fourth of the lumber in payment. As soon as the Red River froze over, folks from the Minnesota side would be skidding logs across the ice.

Lars and Zeb took the wheels off the wagons and replaced them with heavy wooden runners that curved up in front, with sheet metal nailed to the underside. After soaping and cleaning the harnesses and making sure there were no weak spots, they added bells to the collars. The horses seemed to enjoy the music as much as the people did.

"One of these years I'm going to buy a real sled for winter and a buggy for summer," Haakan said one afternoon as he sat in the parlor reading the Grand Forks newspaper.

"Wouldn't that be fine?" Ingeborg looked up from her knitting.

"We had a sled in Norway," Bridget said. "Gustaf built it and kept it painted black with red trim. So shiny it was. I wonder if Johann is keeping things up like his far would have liked."

"His last letter sounded like it." Katy looked up from mending her long black wool stockings. "Are you homesick, Mor?"

"Sometimes. Think, they are ice fishing

on the lake now. And there would be lutefisk and baked cod for dinner. Ja, the food is surely different here. But we will make lefse tomorrow, and that will be just enough of home to keep me happy." Her needles flashed in the lamp already lit, though darkness had not yet fallen.

All was silent but for the click of needles and the snap of wood in the parlor stove, the little ones being down for a nap. Haakan rattled the newspaper when he turned the pages.

"Why don't you read to us?" Ingeborg asked.

"But it is in English."

"True, but you could translate. Not word for word, just the ideas, you know."

So Haakan read, translated, and answered questions about the meaning of some of the issues and stories. Finally he laid the paper aside. "I've got some work out in the barn I better get at."

"You want some coffee first?" Ingeborg started to rise.

"No, no. You just sit still and keep on doing what you are doing." He fled out the back door like being chased by bees.

Ingeborg leaned over and picked up the paper. As she folded the pages, an article caught her eye. Suffragettes were on the march in Minneapolis. There had been speeches and a call for the women to unite that they might be given the vote. She read the quotes from the speeches aloud.

Bridget shook her head. "I think it's a big to-do about nothing. What good is the vote for women? You want to run for a public office someday?"

Ingeborg thought a minute, then answered quietly. "No, I don't want to, but generations from now, perhaps that will be important to some of the women. You never know." She thought again. "But I know how important it is for women to be able to own land in their own name, to own a business if they want, or go to college, just as the men do."

While Katy smiled at Ingeborg and gave a slight nod, Bridget looked at her, mouth in a perfect *O*. "Well, I never."

Weeks passed and somehow Ingeborg never made it over to the Valders'. Every Sunday when she saw they weren't in church, she thought this would be the week, but one thing after another seemed to come up, like Thorliff's eleventh birthday, and the weeks flew by. Birthday parties were a welcome break, even though they only invited their own family and the Baards. Then there was the disappointing meeting in Grand Forks with Mr. Brockhurst. Ingeborg still fumed at his refusal to be any more than the most basic of help. He declined Hjelmer's offer to work for free in exchange for training in banking ways and acted as if they were trying to steal his livelihood. It wasn't like he had no other customers than the farmers of Blessing, many of whom banked in Grafton anyway. She couldn't wait to remove their money from his establishment and begin their own.

Norwegian classes continued on Tuesday nights, and each week Zeb hoped Bridget would decide not to go that time. She often thwarted his attempts to sit next to Katy in church on Sunday too.

But when Reverend Solberg came calling at the Bjorklund farm, Mrs. Gustaf Bjorklund was all smiles and delight.

Zeb was finding it difficult to like the Reverend very much. Or was he having more trouble *not* liking the man? If only they weren't interested in the same comely young woman. If only John Solberg weren't so secure in his faith. Zeb had tried to forget his.

Through the months, Deborah's health improved until, as far as Ingeborg could tell, the little girl was back to normal. Andrew still missed seeing Ellie every day, but he took his responsibility of caring for Deborah very seriously. Ilse, however, only cheered up when she was playing with or caring for the twins. When Kaaren suggested that maybe the orphan girl would be happier living with them, Bridget agreed. One Saturday, Ilse moved her meager belongings to the other house and into a room of her own.

When Lars and Kaaren had moved into their new house, Zeb and Hamre had moved from the barn and taken over the other soddy, so now they had the women's soddy and the men's, besides the two frame homes where everyone ate, studied, did the winter handiwork, and enjoyed one another's company. Ingeborg looked around and smiled in contentment. This was life as she'd dreamed it . . . almost.

As the stack of lumber grew, they began making plans to help Penny and Hjelmer add another room onto the store, as Penny had suggested. And to build an icehouse. Building an icehouse out by the river was under discussion too. They needed to dig it out before the ground froze solid and finish it in time to cut ice before the spring melt.

"Who do you think will pay for ice in the summertime?" Ingeborg asked when all the adults, including Penny and Hjelmer, were gathered around the table after Sunday dinner.

"In the cities they do so all the time. Men go around with wagons, selling ice to all the housewives. They come by two or three times a week." Olaf tipped his chair back so it teetered on two legs.

"Where do they keep it? The ladies, I mean." Kaaren rocked Trygve, trying to get him to sleep. Another tooth about to break through made him unusually cranky.

"You can buy iceboxes from the Montgomery Ward Catalog."

"Really?" Kaaren patted the little one's back, whispering sweet words in his ear at the same time. "How do you get a catalog?"

"You write and ask for one." Penny swooped down and grabbed Astrid about the middle, bussing her cheeks and bringing forth the contagious chortle that made everyone smile. "I might have one in the cupboard where I keep the books I order from."

Ingeborg poured a round for everyone. She leaned over Goodie's shoulder and whispered in her ear, "You feelin' all right? You look a mite peaked."

Goodie shook her head. "I'm fine. We need to be thinking about adding on to the house too. For us it's a baby, but Olaf needs more space for his workshop."

Her whisper brought smiles to both Kaaren and Ingeborg.

"Where's Katy?" Bridget asked, returning from a trip to the outhouse. "I looked in the soddy and she isn't there either."

Ingeborg shrugged. "I have no idea. Maybe she is out in the barn with the bigger kids. They're talking about making an ice-skating circle out beyond the barn, you know, where that dip is in the pasture. I said if they wanted to haul water enough to do that, they were welcome to it."

"I haven't been ice-skating for so long," Kaaren said with a sigh. "Or skiing either."

"They could wait and skate on the river," Lars offered. "It'll be frozen clear across soon."

"But the river ice gets so rough. Besides, you never know where there might be a weak spot."

"Can't be too weak, the way they'll be skidding logs over."

Ingeborg and Kaaren exchanged glances as soon as Bridget went into the parlor to pick up her knitting. "I bet Katy's with Zeb," Kaaren whispered.

"I bet they're both out helping to make the skating pond."

"I bet they could use some more help

too." Haakan waved to Lars and Olaf. "Hjelmer, get your hunkers off that chair and let's see how much water we can haul. Ingeborg, you better get the cocoa hot and maybe think of making taffy for pulling later."

The men bundled into their coats, hats, and gloves and went out the door laughing, reminding one another of skating exploits when they were young.

It was cold enough that the water froze about as fast as they poured the buckets. That night after chores were done and supper over, they built a bonfire beside the sheet of ice and took turns with the four pairs of skates they had. Those without skates skidded on their boots, and others, like Andrew, ran and sat to slide.

"I can see I need to go into the skate business," Hjelmer said when he had to pass the skates on to someone else. "Hey, Zeb! You make the straps, and I'll fashion and sharpen the blades. How about that?"

"Sure enough. I just can't get the hang of this, though."

"Didn't you skate when you were a kid?"

Zeb shook his head. "Nothing froze this much back home." Just then Thorliff called him and off he went.

"Well, we know a little bit more," Lars

said in an undertone to Haakan.

"We already knew he came from the south somewhere by the way he talks."

"I know, but this confirms that." Lars turned to warm his backside at the fire. "That Katy might like Reverend Solberg as a friend and teacher, but she's got eyes only for our southern mystery man." He rubbed his mittened hands together. "You might want to have a talk with him."

"Me! Why me?" Haakan lowered his voice. "Let Bridget have a talk with him."

"She would, but what good would it do? She can't understand him, and he can't understand her."

"So what's so different? Ain't that almost always the case when men and women try to have a real talking?"

Lars cuffed him on the shoulder. "Now, what kind of an attitude is that? Kaaren and I talk just fine. I talk, she listens."

Haakan snorted and shook his head.

At the next quilting meeting, Ingeborg gave her report on their meeting with Mr. Brockhurst, owner of the bank in Grand Forks. While she tried to be fair and businesslike, she still got her back up, telling about the man's perfunctory refusal. They discussed the addition going up on the store and how this would be a good business thing for them all. But who would run the bank? The question was repeated over and over. Everyone was too busy as it was.

"I can put out the mail once a day," Penny said, "but with the new tables, sometimes I don't have time to see to the store. Cousin Ephraim does most of that for me. And now with Hjelmer building the new room . . . uff da, things are so busy." But the smile in her eyes told everyone she wasn't really complaining.

"In my mind, 'tis Hjelmer what should run the bank. He knows more about making money than all the rest of us put together." Dyrfinna Odell spoke with utter conviction.

"He's not doing so good with his black-smithing." Brynja surprised them all again with her comments made so freely and emphatically.

"Ja, but Anner, that's kind of his fault. He got so bitter about Hjelmer making money on the railroad land. I thought it rather brilliant myself." Agnes kept on stitching as she talked. "If he hadn't talked so bad about Hjelmer, then everyone would be trading at the store and getting machinery fixed at the smithy. I know Hjelmer has saved Joseph a lot of time and money."

After their dinner of soup and bread,

413

Ingeborg sat down by Agnes again. "I had hoped Hildegunn would be here today, but since she isn't, you and me are going to call on them tomorrow. I got a bad feeling something is terribly wrong."

"Me too." Agnes nodded. "Me too."

24

"You ain't comin' in and that's that!"

Agnes and Ingeborg looked at each other and shook their heads. Had Anner gone out of his mind? When a string of expletives followed his terse order, they backed away from the door.

Ingeborg gathered all her courage and called out, "We just came to see Hildegunn. Brought her some quilt pieces and such."

"She ain't to home."

Agnes caught a glimpse of a curtain falling into place. If he was at the door, then who was at the curtain? Ingeborg's look said she'd seen it too.

"Then we'll leave this basket here by the door and come back another day."

"Take yer basket with you and don't come back. We don't need the likes of you." At the profanity that followed, their ears burned on their way to the wagon.

"She's home," Agnes said.

"I know." Ingeborg gave Agnes a boost up the wheel spokes and went around the front of the horse to get in herself. While she stopped to check the bit, she glanced back at the house. Smoke from the chimney meandered into the still air. Cows stamped near the ice-cleared water trough by the barn, so at least they were taking care of the animals. Or someone was. Her foot slipped on the icy spoke.

"You okay?"

"Ja, just clumsy." She hauled herself up to the seat. "You think his voice sounded like he'd been drinking?"

"Yep. And plenty." They both turned and looked at the house again. This time they saw a curtain move in the upstairs window. A hand waved to them, then disappeared. "That's her saying thank you."

"I know. What is going on here?" Ingeborg clucked the horses forward and turned them in a circle toward home.

"I wish I knew. What can we do if he won't even let us in?"

"I think this is a job for Reverend Solberg. You s'pose he's been out here?"

"If he hasn't been, he soon will be."

While they switched to other things to talk about on the way home, Ingeborg couldn't forget the sight of that wave from the upstairs window. Was Hildegunn a prisoner in her own home?

"You want to go visit with Penny and Hjelmer?" she asked Bridget the next morning. Unable to get the Valders out of her mind all night, she resolved to see Reverend Solberg, whether she had to interrupt school or not. Taking cheese and smoked sausages in to sell to Penny was as good an excuse as any.

"Of course. Let me get my knitting."

"No hurry. I need to load up the wagon and get together a basket. Maybe we'll take time to talk with Goodie too. I'm in the mood for a good visit." She put the list of one hundred and one things she had to do out of her mind and began assembling a basket of good things for Reverend Solberg. She put in cheese, a few slices of ham, a jar of apple butter, a loaf of bread she'd taken out of the oven only minutes before, and a square of cake left from last night's supper.

She loaded the wagon with two wheels of cheese, a crock of soft cheese, butter that Kaaren had churned the day before, and several dozen eggs. Back in the smokehouse, she studied the supply there. Taking down a haunch of spekekjøt, she sawed off part of it and wrapped the dried mutton in a towel. Like many others with the new higher-roofed barns, she had hung the salted haunches up to dry in the barn during the hot days of summer. Penny would slice it paper thin and sell it by the ounce. She'd pleaded with Ingeborg to bring in more, as it sold quickly.

People riding the train had come to expect food at the general store, and while the train tanks were being filled with water, the passengers stocked up at Penny's. More than once they'd asked about a hotel or a boardinghouse. Who would like to begin an enterprise like that?

Her thoughts and hands kept pace as she harnessed the horses and hitched them to the wagon. She could have called one of the men to help, but they were busy in the barn or the machine shed or down at the sawmill. If winter was supposed to be a time of slowing down, someone had forgotten to tell the Bjorklund men and those who worked for them.

She dropped the children off at Kaaren's, much to Andrew's dismay.

"Want to see Tante Penny. And Ellie!"

"You just want a peppermint stick." Ingeborg leaned down and kissed his nose. "Is there anything you want from the store?" she asked Kaaren.

"Isn't it wonderful to be able to buy things so easily and not have to drive clear to

St. Andrew?" Kaaren took Astrid from Ingeborg's arms and kissed the little girl's fluffy curls. "This winter seems so much easier for that reason if none other."

"Bless you for reminding me. I'll bring any mail, for sure. Anything else?"

"I could use several yards of flannel for diapers. These are getting rather thin, even with the wool soakers Bridget's been knitting." The thick pull-on pants were to help prevent the babies from wetting on those who held them. "Katy said she'd hem them for me."

"All right. And if I see something else, I'll get it." Ingeborg blew Andrew a kiss, but he'd already taken over the building blocks Lars had made for the children and hardly paid her any attention.

"I've been thinking," Bridget said after they'd admired the beauty of the frosted countryside.

Ingeborg waited. Now what?

"Would you mind if I stayed in America?"

"Of course not. We love having you here."

"Well, some days I think I'll stay and other times I ache for Norway. But there are no grandchildren there, and I so love the babies. I can't bear the thought of leaving them."

Ingeborg nodded, letting the woman say her piece.

"What to do?" Bridget stared straight ahead. "And if I do stay, what will I do to support myself?"

"Why, you are welcome to everything we have. You're our children's bestemor. Is there something you need? Something you haven't told me?"

"No, but a man or woman needs to earn their own way."

"I will gladly pay you for all the work you do around our house. I just never thought you might want money of your own. I'm sorry. I just didn't think."

"Ingeborg, that is not the solution. We all work together because we are family, and no one gets paid for doing that. I am not asking for money, so don't you go misunderstanding me." Bridget turned on the seat, disturbing the elk lap robe that protected their legs from the cold. "I'm just telling you this so's I can think it through. Me'n Gustaf, this we did all the time. It takes two people to help one think good."

Ingeborg smiled. "All right, I know what you mean. So you want to earn some money of your own?"

"Ja." Bridget adjusted the lap robe over both of them.

"What about your knitting?"

"What about it?"

"Your sweaters are like a painting with all the bright colors you use and the thick wool."

"The wool is yours, from your own sheep."

"But you spun it and dyed it. It's your needles that turn out the hats and mittens and scarves. The soakers you knit for the babies are softer than any I've done. All those things could be sold through Penny's store."

"Ah. People make such things themselves."

"Not everyone. And not many as fine as you do. Let's mention it to Penny."

"If you think so, but . . ." Bridget shook her head. "We better come up with a better idea than that."

Ingeborg had to smile at the "we."

"Now if Penny and Hjelmer had a baby, I could take care of it while they work in the store and such."

"What, the ones at the farm aren't enough for you?"

"There can never be too many babies."

A pain shot through Ingeborg's heart. She believed that too, but God didn't seem to think the same way. At least not in her case.

Would there ever be another baby for her to rock in her arms, to nurse, to give as a gift of the heart to her husband?

After delivering the supplies to Penny for the store, Ingeborg left the horse and wagon at the barn by the blacksmith shop and walked on over to the school just in time for recess. Children ran and shouted everywhere.

"Hi, Mrs. Bjorklund," Gus Baard called just before someone tackled him and he went facedown in the snow. He tore after his attacker, threatening all sorts of retribution if he caught him.

Manda raced up to stop at her side. "Is Deborah all right?"

"Why, of course." Ingeborg laid a hand on the girl's shoulder. "I just came to talk with Reverend Solberg for a minute."

"Oh, good. You scared me." Manda turned and ran back to the fox-and-goose game.

Ingeborg looked after her. Never would that have entered her mind, but then she hadn't lost all her family except for one sister. Those two had certainly changed since they'd come to the Bjorklund house.

See, I've given you more children. It was like a voice right in her ear, so loud it boomed, yet so soft it could have been missed. She wanted to turn around and ask "Who said that?" but she knew.

"Mor, what are you doing here?" Thorliff came around the corner of the sod schoolhouse, cheeks red from the cold and eyes sparkling with delight at seeing her. He pointed to the basket. "You brought me more dinner?"

"Thorliff Bjorklund, I think you have two hollow legs, the way you eat." She wanted to grab him and clutch him to her. He was one of those given to her. Just because he was not of her loins, was he not her son?

Baptiste waved and Hamre nodded. Even Ilse almost managed a smile. So most of her children were half grown. Babies weren't the only sign of God's favor. She wanted to run in the fox-and-goose game, play "ante over" with the bigger children and fall down and make snow angels again with Andrew.

She waved to the children and knocked on the schoolhouse door. Just before she heard "Come in," she thought of Hildegunn and Anner. Could the lack of children in that home be part of the problem?

"Reverend Solberg?" She opened the door and stepped in.

"Ja, here." He stood from behind his desk. "Ah, Mrs. Bjorklund, what a nice surprise." He came forward, hand outstretched. "I thought it was one of my pupils with another question. Sometimes I wonder how they come up with such things, especially your Thorliff. My, that boy has a fine mind."

"Why, thank you." Ingeborg unwrapped the muffler from around her head and unbuttoned her coat. "I won't stay long. Here." She handed him the basket. "This is for you. Now I wish I would have brought cookies for all the children too."

He motioned her to a bench. "Sit down. How can I help you?"

"What I have to say is hard." She sucked in her bottom lip. "You know I don't hold with gossiping?"

He nodded and crossed his arms over his chest, perching one hip on the front of his desk. "I know that, so this must be very serious."

She looked up at him. "Agnes and I went out to call on the Valders' yesterday. They haven't been to church or anything else for so long, and I been knowing I should go see her." She looked down at her gloved hands. "But I been putting it off, God forgive me."

"He does." Solberg waited patiently.

"He, Anner, wouldn't let us in. He yelled for us to go away and my, the words he said." She shook her head. "Oh my. He was some mad. But we saw Hildegunn at the window as we left. She waved but that was all. You suppose he is keeping her locked up or something?"

"God above, I hope not. I've known for some time I should go out there too, but . . ." Solberg looked at Ingeborg. "If there is anyone guilty of neglect there, it is me. I've been praying for them, but leave it to you women to go beyond praying and do the doing."

"I don't want you feeling bad over this, I just think we need to help them, and I don't know how. Surely he would be polite to the pastor of his church."

"I wouldn't bet my Sunday dinner on it." Reverend Solberg straightened, nodding his head. "I will look into this, I promise you. And tell Mrs. Baard thank you from me too."

"For what?"

"For braving the lion in his den. This church and all churches would fall apart if you women didn't keep on doing all you do."

"I didn't want to be nosy." Ingeborg stood too. "You must want to call the children in. I will go now."

"There's a far difference between nosy and acting out God's love. Thank you for the prodding." He picked up a handbell from his desk. "Let's go call in the horde."

The children lined up at the door, from the smallest to the oldest, as soon as the bell rang. Ingeborg stepped out of the way so they could enter the building and hang their coats and scarves on the pegs along one wall. A shelf above held their lunch pails. Thorliff winked at her as he went by, and Baptiste nodded, his black eyes snapping with glee.

Ingeborg walked back to the store, thinking about what Reverend Solberg had said about the women. It *was* good to be appreciated, and they could do so much more if only there were more hours in the day. But she felt immeasurably lighter having left her burden for him to pick up. Maybe now things would be all right with the Valderses, and they could all go back to the way things used to be. She'd take a bossy Hildegunn over a hand fluttering from a window any day.

"Uff da. We never appreciate what we have until it is gone."

"Talking to yourself again, Inge?" Hjelmer asked. He'd just stepped out from the blacksmith shop, attached to the barn.

"Ja, and sometimes I answer myself too.

You never run out of a body to talk with that way."

"You know, I been meaning to ask you . . ." He paused and studied the snow at his feet.

Now what? thought Ingeborg. *He looks like a boy who got his hand caught in the cookie jar.* She waited.

"Ah . . . nothing. You staying for dinner?" At her nod, he continued, "Well, it'll be a while. Penny's got people lined up for the tables. Mor is helping her and Goodie too. They'd put Ellie to work if she was an inch bigger."

Ingeborg smiled up at him. Those Bjorklund blue eyes smiled right back, making her want to hug him. No matter what had gone on in the past between them, she had a special place in her heart for this younger brother of Roald's. He had grown up to be quite a man. *Roald and Carl must be looking from heaven with pride in him, for I sure am.*

"So you are hiding out in the shop?"

He nodded and whispered, "You caught me out." He glanced back in the shop. "But I really have to finish the cross I promised Reverend Solberg. He wants it for Christmas. That and the altar Olaf is building. Said I'd help with that too."

"How wonderful. That will surely make our little church more like a real house of worship. Hjelmer Bjorklund, your far must be telling all the angels about what a fine son he has still on this earth." She smiled up at him. "Why, I believe you are blushing." She patted his cheek like he was one of her children and headed for Penny's house.

Ingeborg entered through the back door, smiling and shaking her head. What a morning this had been. She heard the mixture of voices from the other room. So far, and from the sound of things, it wasn't over yet.

"Oh, Ingeborg, I'm so glad you are here." Penny met her with a bounce and a grin. "We're swamped. Could you start frying those steaks I just cut? I've run out of food, and there are more people waiting. Isn't this just awful?" But her laughing eyes belied her words. More customers spelled more money, and more money spelled more things to sell in the store. From the looks of things, they should turn that spare room into an eating establishment rather than a post office and bank. Ingeborg tied on an apron and set to work. After all, what did they know about starting a bank? But feeding people and making sure they got plenty to eat — now that they knew all about. Why was that man raising his voice in the other room? Had he been drinking, or was he just having a good time?

25

"I'm due the end of May or first part of June, near as I can figure," Kaaren announced.

Ingeborg felt a surge of jealousy that near to swamped her. It ate at her middle and up behind her eyes, making them burn and her heart race. "That . . . that's wonderful." Through superhuman strength she kept her tone even. *Why not me, Lord? I want a baby too.* She forced a smile to her quivering lips and turned to face Kaaren. "June is a perfect month for having a baby, before the heat makes you so miserable that you want to melt into a puddle and your feet swell up like boats and you wish to just sit on a cake of ice and let the world melt around you and . . ." Her voice trailed off. She'd been blabbering.

"You're not upset, are you?" Kaaren laid a hand on Ingeborg's shoulder. They stood in the kitchen of Ingeborg's house, which was silent for a change, except for the dropping of a chunk of wood in the stove.

"No, I am glad for you." *And crying for*

myself. She pointed to the table. "You sit down and we'll have a cup of coffee before the others come in and the babies wake up. Trygve might be coming down with something. He was that fussy."

"I know how bad you want another baby, Inge."

"Ja, well, that is as the good Lord provides." She brought the coffeepot to the table. "He knows both our needs and our desires, and if He thinks we don't need another baby, then . . ." She couldn't finish. "Ah, I am glad for you. And sad for myself. And Haakan." She locked her hands over the chair back and leaned on arms with stiff elbows. Staring at her whitening fingers, she whispered, "He never gives more than one can bear. He promised that."

" 'But with the temptation will provide a way of escape,' " Kaaren finished the verse.

Ingeborg tried to smile. She shook her head at the same time. "He must not have been thinking of Dakota winters when He said that. About escaping, I mean."

Kaaren stood and came to Ingeborg's side. "He's given you plenty of children, you know."

"I know. Just no more babies."

A whimper came from the bedroom where Trygve and Astrid lay sleeping.

Ingeborg looked toward the source of the noise. "And you for sure can't call those two babies any longer." She straightened, and this time the smile managed to curve her mouth and lighten her eyes. "What one can't think up the other will. We got our hands full in the years ahead, I can tell."

"Bless you, my sister." Kaaren stroked Ingeborg's arm.

They sipped their coffee in the silence that settled peacefully around their souls and shoulders like the lightest of shawls knit with love and big needles.

"You got the feeling that there's something going on that no one is telling us?" Ingeborg had her elbows propped on the table and the coffee cup nestled in her hands.

"Why sure, it's almost Christmas. That's the way it is supposed to be. You can't tell me you aren't hoarding a secret or two."

"No, it's different than that. Like everyone else knows but me." She glanced at Kaaren with a questioning eyebrow.

Kaaren shook her head. "I have no idea what you are talking about, so if you are trying to pump me, it won't work."

"Never hurts to try." Ingeborg cocked her head. "There's the sleigh bells. Now you watch, those kids are hiding something, and

Haakan is in on it."

The schoolchildren blew in on a snowy north wind breath, their laughter cutting off at the sight of Ingeborg and Kaaren at the table. Manda covered her mouth with her snowy mitten and giggled as she took off her muffler.

A glare from Thorliff only made it worse.

Ingeborg gave Kaaren a knowing look that said quite plainly, "See? What did I tell you?"

As soon as they'd devoured the milk and molasses cookies set out for them, they bundled up again.

"We got work to do out in the barn," Thorliff announced. He led the group out but peeked back in the door when they'd gone. "You're making something good for the program tomorrow night, aren't you?" The sound of his laughter floated through before the door slammed.

"Do you miss things like the program?" Ingeborg turned back to Kaaren.

"Yes and no. I loved teaching while I did it, and doing the *first* program made it even more special, but . . ." She paused. "I got so much to do with the three we have and another on the way that I don't have time to miss anything. Besides, I'm trying to find ways to help Grace be able to know what we are saying." She shook her head slowly, as if attached to a great weight. "That takes every teaching skill I have. She is learning to read lips, though. If she can see your mouth move, she is figuring out what things mean. Ah, Inge, she is so smart, that one. To be locked in a world of silence . . ."

Now it was Ingeborg's turn to shake her head. "I cannot bear to think it. Not to hear the song of a meadowlark in the spring, or the cry of a loon, or the beller of a cow. Or hear when a baby cries, or the dog barks to let us know someone is coming, or when something is boiling over on the stove. How will she even get along?"

"She will! God gave her to us for a special reason and us to her. Having Katy at our house all the time is such a help, and Ilse takes over the twins when she gets home from school. Oh, I am so blessed."

That evening after the children were in bed, the three adults brought out the gifts they were making for Christmas. Haakan took out his carving knife and continued fashioning feet and hands for the dolls Ingeborg was making for the three little girls. He had already carved the heads. Bridget knit away — sweaters for the boys and dresses for the girls. Ingeborg stuffed sawdust into the cloth doll bodies she had sewn. A dress, pinafore, and pantaloons were already finished and tucked out of sight in a box, along with other treasures she'd been working on.

"I think yarn will make the best hair," Bridget said after looking again at one of the carved heads. "I was thinking to use wool, you know, before it is carded."

"That would work." Haakan held up a small hand. "Only one to go. Are you sure you can't find someone else who needs a doll too?"

His question made Ingeborg smile. The one they'd made for Deborah, along with a cradle and quilt, was hidden on the top of a shelf and behind a blanket. She couldn't wait to see the little girl's eyes light up. She loved the rag doll Ingeborg had made earlier and carted it with her everywhere.

"You finished Trygve's train yet?"

Haakan shook his head. "Got to smooth it out and put on the wheels. I got Andrew helping me with that. He's learning to use the deer horn to smooth wood. He's pretty strong for his age, you know."

"And stubborn."

"Ja." Haakan grinned, a look of pride creasing his face. "He's a Bjorklund, ain't he?"

"You got ants in your pants or something?" Ingeborg laid a hand on Thorliff's shoulder and held him in place.

"But we're going to be late."

"No, your pa will leave with you children in a few minutes, and the rest of us will come with Lars."

"I want you to get a front seat."

"We will come soon, then." She tousled his hair. "You better go comb your hair, son."

He wrinkled his nose at her. "My hat will mess it anyway." He nibbled on his lower lip.

"What is it?"

"N-nothing." He shook his head and bounded off, ricocheting off the kitchen counter as he went out the door. "Ouch!"

"That boy. He's growing so fast he's lost track of his body. Why, he's knocked more things over or banged into them in the last weeks than in his whole life."

"It will get worse before it gets better." Bridget turned from putting the last of the fattigmann and sour cream cookies in the basket.

"Wait, do you hear that?" Bridget paused.

"It's a wolf howling." Ingeborg finished banking the stove. A tap at the door and

Metiz entered, kicking snow off her boots before stepping on the braided rag rug.

"Wolf back."

Ingeborg clasped her hands to her breast. "Oh, Metiz, how wonderful. I hated to ask, afraid that maybe he'd gone away to die or something got him."

"Me think so too. But he back."

"Wolf?"

"Metiz saved a wolf puppy from a trap once, and he's sort of stayed around. He saved our sheep one winter from marauding wolves, and he's the one that brought Andrew back when he got lost in the tall grass. Remember, I wrote you about that?"

Bridget cocked an eyebrow.

"And then again, maybe I thought to and didn't." Ingeborg felt a flash of guilt. The prick of it made her wince. "There were many things I wanted to write and tell you, but there were never enough hours in the day, no matter how early I began it or how late I fell into bed. But the thoughts were there."

"You think I didn't know that?" Bridget tipped her head to one side. "Our prayers went up for you all the time. Now that I am here and see what life is like in this Dakota Territory, I do not know how you did all that you did." She shook her head. "Nor

Gustaf either. He so often said, 'How will Ingeborg and Kaaren make it, the two of them alone like that after losing their husbands?' You had his highest admiration."

The jingle of sleigh bells and a halloo from out front sent them scurrying for their coats. "Come on, Andrew, Deborah. Bring Astrid with you. We're ready to go." Once they were all bundled into their coats, along with hats, scarves, and mittens, Lars carried Astrid out to the sleigh and tucked them all under the elk lap robes and quilts.

Ingeborg brought rocks she'd heated in the oven and tucked them at everyone's feet, then climbed in herself, snuggling under the robe with the children. Metiz chose to ride in front with Lars.

"Wolf back," she said when he hupped the horses.

"So you are saying, 'Don't shoot' if I see him?"

She chuckled. "That right."

As they entered the church, giggles and shushes came from behind the curtain stretched from one side of the church room to the other, but there were no schoolchildren to be seen. Haakan waved them to the places he'd saved in the front row, and they all took their seats, removing their coats for Lars to carry back to the cloakroom.

"Where's Thorliff?" asked Andrew.

"Back behind the curtain with the other children." Astrid bounced on her mother's lap. "Uff da, you are much too big to do that." Ingeborg looked over to Haakan, who reached for his daughter.

"Here you come, missy. You can bounce all you please."

A hush fell as Reverend Solberg strode to the front of the church. "Welcome to our Christmas program for 1886. We gather in the name of the Father and the Son and the Holy Ghost." He made the sign of the cross and smiled out at his audience. "I have a special announcement to make tonight, one that the children have kept secret with a great deal of effort. And some of you have made that even harder for them by asking questions."

A few titters rippled through the packed room. Latecomers lined the walls as the center aisle had to be kept clear for some reason.

"And now for the revealing of that secret. Our program this year was written by our own budding writer, Thorliff Bjorklund."

Ingeborg could feel her jaw drop. She looked to Haakan, who wore a look that she knew matched her own. "Thorliff wrote the program?"

"That's what he said."

"What program? What did Thorliff write?" Andrew's *whisper* could be heard clear out on the snowdrifts.

"Shhh, listen." Ingeborg pointed to the front of the room, where Thorliff now stood before the audience, a sheaf of papers in his hand.

" 'Once upon a time, long ago in a small land, there lived a band of shepherds who took care of the sheep for the people in the village.' " He cleared his throat and continued reading.

The story told of a small boy who helped the shepherds, but who never felt he was a part of a family or the shepherds or belonged anywhere.

At the end of the program, after the story was told, the songs all sung, and the gathering had oohed and aahed over the production, Reverend Solberg returned to the front of the church. He started to talk, then had to clear his throat. Not once, but twice.

Ingeborg wiped the tears from her eyes. Her son wrote that play. She could hear others sniffing and a man hawk the lump out of his throat. She felt as if she'd been at that manger when a little boy saw the Christ child and knew the Savior had indeed come. She felt in her bones that if they all trooped outside right now, they too would hear the angels sing, "Glory to God in the highest and peace to men on earth."

Ah, that they might all know that peace this evening. A picture of a hand waving at them from the upstairs window of the Valders' home flew through Ingeborg's mind. There was no peace in that home for sure. *You have to go back and try to see her again!* It was her own voice ordering her, but she knew where the idea came from.

"That was a magnificent play," Kaaren whispered. "And to think our Thorliff wrote it. I knew he wrote well, and he talks of being a writer. Face it, Ingeborg, he *is* one."

As soon as he could, Thorliff came to stand in front of Ingeborg and Haakan. "Did you like it?" His voice trembled.

Ingeborg wanted to fold him in her arms, but she knew that would embarrass him, so she just took his hands. "Thorliff Bjorklund, I have never been so proud in all my life. You wrote a fine play and you narrated the story wonderfully."

"I'm so proud of you I could bust." Haakan laid a hand on the boy's shoulder.

"And that goes for all the rest of us." Kaaren took the liberty of being an aunt and kissed him on the cheek.

"I like doing it." He looked into

Ingeborg's eyes. "Do you think it made people think more about how it felt to find Jesus?"

"Yes, my son, I think all of us feel closer to Him tonight because of your story. It made more than one person get tears in their eyes. Couldn't you hear the sniffles?"

"Ja, but I thought maybe some of them had colds or something."

"Ah, Thorliff, God gave you something special, and now it is up to you to grow the gift wisely." Kaaren patted his cheek and turned to answer one of the children who'd been her student.

Each one of the children received an orange and a tiny bag of candy for a gift, and the parents accepted the cutout stars their children had made for them.

Metiz stopped beside Thorliff. She looked up and into his eyes. "Great Spirit say things through you. Don't forget." She swept an arm to indicate the evening and all that had happened. "I got news. Wolf come home."

"Merry Christmas, Metiz." Thorliff smiled back at her. "That's your present."

"Good gift from Great Spirit." The old woman nodded. "Best gift is baby in manger." She melted through the crowd until Thorliff couldn't see her. He turned to find his mother staring with her mouth open.

"She knows." Ingeborg clasped a hand to her throat. "Metiz knows and believes the real story of Christmas." Surely the angels were singing this night.

"I wish the Valderses were here." Kaaren handed Trygve to his father and picked up Grace. While she cuddled the little girl close, she shared a look with Ingeborg.

"I know. I plan to go see her as soon after Christmas as the weather permits."

The Christmas service several days later was almost anticlimactic after the children's program. Folks were still talking about the play after church and during the visiting that went on from house to house. With all the Bjorklunds at Ingeborg's, the house was busting at the roof ridges. After they'd eaten and the presents had been opened, all who could headed for the skating pond. Thanks to Zeb and Hjelmer, everybody had skates.

"Look at Bestemor!" Thorliff tugged on Ingeborg's coat to get her attention.

Bridget swooped and circled and skated backward, cutting long curves in the ice with her sharp skates. She waved to Hjelmer and he joined her, the two of them skating as if the finest waltz were playing. When they finished, everyone cheered and clapped.

"Bestemor, teach us!" Thorliff skated out to her.

Bridget took Manda by the hand. "Come with me, child. You will learn this in no time." Then with hands crossed in front of them, she led all those who wanted help back onto the ice.

"Look, I'm skating backward," Manda shrieked, her face split by a broader smile than any had yet seen from her. When she started to slip and flail her arms, Hjelmer skated in front of her.

"Put your hands on my arms," he said. And so she did. The setting sun painted the white snow in reds, then pinks, firing sparkles like diamonds, and none were brighter than those in Manda's eyes.

"Bless you." Ingeborg took Hjelmer's hands when he asked if she would skate with him.

"Did you see her face?"

"Ja, and she has never looked so beautiful. Mange takk, my friend, mange takk."

The day Ingeborg chose to go calling on the Valderses dawned bright and clear. With the temperature up near the thirties, water dripped from icicles on the house and barn, causing a song of their own. The chores were caught up. The baking done. All were healthy. Ingeborg had no excuse.

"You planned it this way, didn't you?" She looked heavenward as she drove the horse out of the yard. A basket full of julekake, fattigmann, cheese, and a loaf of fresh bread sat close beside her. Other neighbors had tried to visit the Valderses but always reported no answer to their knocks on the door. "But I'm sure you have another plan, don't you?"

The horse flicked his ears back and forth, hearing her voice above the jingling of the harness bells. The sleigh runner hissed through the snow. Because of the frozen snow crust, Ingeborg cut across the fields, not confined to the roads as usual. She kept up the conversation with her Father in heaven, bringing to Him all the hurts and needs of those around her, but she kept coming back to the Valderses.

Each time she thought of the snarl in Anner's voice the last time she went to their door, she got a cramping in her belly. Would the man yell at her again? What would she do if he did?

And each time she had to go back to thanking God that He had a plan.

" 'Fear not,' you have said. That is so easy to say but right now my stomach is full of fear. My head knows this is your idea, but my belly sure is arguing."

Was that a heavenly chuckle she heard or just the hiss of the runners? She took in a deep breath, grateful that the cold didn't hurt clear to her middle. Maybe the air would calm her insides.

Smoke rose from the chimney of the Valders' house, straight up in the still air. Someone was home.

Ingeborg slowed the horse so the jingling wouldn't be so loud. "I should have left the bells off." She slowed the horse even more, and finally came to a stop.

The crunch of her boots as she approached the home sounded like rifle shots in the stillness. The horse stamped his foot and snorted.

She jumped.

At the bottom of the steps, she took in another deep breath, settled the basket on her arm, and put her foot on the bottom step.

The door opened a crack. "Wait there." Hildegunn waved a hand and withdrew. A moment later she stepped out the door, wrapping a scarf around her head and neck as she came, but not quickly enough to keep Ingeborg from seeing the black bruises on her neck and one side of her face. She limped across the porch.

"Hildegunn, what happened to you?" Ingeborg whispered, but the shock made her voice sound loud.

"Ah, n-nothing. I fell down on the ice." Her hand went to hide the bruises.

"On the side of your face like that?" Ingeborg wanted to reach out and wrap her arms around the woman, who shivered in front of her. Hildegunn looked as though she'd aged twenty-five years into an old woman. Her eyes, what Ingeborg could see of them, seemed as devoid of life as the windswept prairie.

"No matter. I am just so glad to see you." Hildegunn reached out a hand.

Ingeborg took it. Shudders came from the shrunken woman before her.

"I brought you some things," Ingeborg said. "I wasn't sure if you had time to bake, and I know Anner likes the cheese I make."

"I will tell him you left the basket on the porch. Others have done so. Oh, Ingeborg, I . . ." She stopped herself. After a glance over her shoulder that shouted of fear, she turned back. "I better go back in before he wakes up. Thank you for coming."

She scurried back into the house like a mouse being chased by a very big cat.

Ingeborg stood a moment, staring at the closed door. "Dear God, this is so bad. He

447

has been beating her, has he not?"

While God didn't answer, Ingeborg had no doubt that was the case. But what to do about it?

26

"Katy, would you take Grace for me?" Kaaren asked.

"Of course." Katy took the little girl off the dresser where Kaaren changed her diapers. Sophie had by now learned to use the potty chair, but Grace had no great inclination to imitate her sister in this way. Katy swung the pink-cheeked child up in the air, loudly smooched her on both cheeks, and set her on the floor. Grace lifted her arms to be picked up again.

"Me too!" Sophie ran over and pulled at Katy's skirt. "Me up too."

"How about if I come down there?" Katy crossed her legs and sank down to the floor, her skirts flaring about her and settling down around her like swirling leaves. She settled Grace on one leg and let Sophie climb onto the other. "Now then, Grace, Sophie, let's play the naming game." Touching one of her own eyes she asked, "What is this?"

"Eye," Sophie said loudly, and both she and Grace touched their own eye.

"We have two?" Katy asked.

"Eyes." Sophie covered both eyes. Grace watched her sister and immediately copied what she did.

"Eyes, nose, and so it goes." Katy hugged both wriggling little bodies. "You girls are so smart." She squeezed and rocked them back and forth, her slender body swaying like a sapling in the wind.

"You are so good with them," Kaaren said, settling into the rocking chair with Trygve so he could nurse. "You will make a wonderful mother."

"I hope so. Since I was the youngest, I didn't have babies to care for like the older ones did. Oh, I cared for other people's children, like Hamre, cousins, and such, but you know that's different somehow. Maybe because you can go home and leave them behind."

Katy nuzzled the soft hair of the girls perched on her legs. "How could anyone go away and leave precious little ones like this behind?"

Grace reached up and patted her cheek, the smile that she bestowed clenching Katy right in the heart.

"So you want babies of your own?"

"Of course."

"And who do you have in mind for a

father? Or rather husband first, then father."

Katy could feel the heat start in her neck and burn its way up to her hairline. "Whew, it got warm in here all of a sudden." She clutched the two little ones in a big hug before they wriggled off her lap to go play. "Is it so obvious?"

"Ja, to me it is. Zebulun MacCallister is handsome enough to steal any young woman's heart."

"And he is as fine a man as he is good-looking." Katy's tone turned to dreamy. "He is gentle and laughs at the right things. Look at the way he took Manda and Deborah under his wing. A lesser man would have ridden off and left them to starve."

"Or taken over their homestead."

"That too. And even though we take a long time to say much since my English isn't good yet . . ." She glanced up from looking at her hands while she talked. "He's even learning Norwegian. That surely says something for him."

"Ja, it says he is interested in one Katy Bjorklund. But what does your mor say?"

"You know what she says. The same thing Lars and Haakan and everyone else says." She parroted their words. " 'He is a man with a secret or has committed a grave sin.' " Her eyes flashed fire. "But isn't that what forgiveness is for? The Bible says no sin is worse than another, that sin is sin."

"True, and I believe that if he has asked for forgiveness for any sin, God has done just that. But there is a consequence in this world if the sin is also a crime, a legal issue. Then it becomes a matter of the law."

"I know. But if he asked me to ride off with him, I would do so." She glanced up to see the horror on Kaaren's face. "Of course we would have to stop by Reverend Solberg's on the way out for the marriage ceremony."

"I certainly am glad to hear that. And I'm sure your mor will be too."

"You won't tell her about our talk?" Katy tried to appear unconcerned, but the look she cast Kaaren's way was colored in worry.

"No, but . . ."

"But what?"

"But promise me you won't ride off without telling me." Kaaren sat Trygve up in her lap and patted his back for a burp. At the gargantuan belch, the two women laughed.

They stood and made their way into the kitchen, where the two-year-old twins quickly ran to the cradle Lars had made for their rag dolls.

"Well, Katy? Are you going to promise me?"

"Would you like a cup of coffee? That sounds good to me."

"Katy!"

"Oh, all right. I won't leave in the middle of the night or anything. Besides, he hasn't asked me."

"Reverend Solberg asked your mother if he could call on you."

"I know, but he's just a friend, besides being our pastor. Can you see me as a minister's wife?" She poured two cups of coffee and set them in their saucers on the table. "Sophie, Grace, you want bread and jam and a cup of milk?"

Sophie immediately scrambled to her feet and, grabbing Grace's hand, dragged her to the table. The two climbed up on their chairs and onto the burlap-covered blocks of wood Kaaren had set on the chairs to make it easier for them to reach the table.

"Gracie might not hear, but she sure doesn't let that slow her down any." Katy tied a bib around each little neck and pushed their chairs in. "Now, you be careful with the milk, Sophie. You're not in any hurry."

"That child is always in a hurry." Holding Trygve, Kaaren handed him a bread crust to chew on and sat down at the end of the table.

"You want bread and jam too?" Katy asked Kaaren. After fixing it for both of them, she glanced out the window on her way back to the table. A team pulling a siedge caught her attention. She would recognize that jaunty wave anywhere. She tossed the bread on the table, ran to the door and leaned out to wave, calling "God dag, ah, hello" at the same time.

When Katy got back to the table, a self-conscious smile tickling her cheeks, Kaaren just shook her head. "Ja, girls, she has it bad. Our Katy is caught hook, line, and sinker."

Sophie shook her head, just like her mother. "Bad."

Reverend Solberg stopped by the Bjorklunds' and asked if Lars and Haakan could come to his house to meet with several others the next evening.

"Of course," Haakan said. "Is there a problem?"

Solberg turned his head to reveal a blackening eye. "Ja, I guess you would say so. I tried to talk with Anner Valders." He raised a hand to his cheek. "This is what it got me."

"Uff da." Ingeborg shook her head. "Did you put a snowpack on it?"

Solberg shook his head. "Never thought of it."

"Would keep the swelling down. Good thing there was no school today. The children would have teased you for the shiner."

"What all happened?" Haakan pulled out a chair and turned it so that straddling the seat he could rest his crossed arms on the back.

Reverend Solberg shrugged. "I went up to the door, knocked, and when he peered through the barely cracked opening, I asked if I might come in." He fingered the swelling on his face. "Next thing I knew, his fist connected with my eye. If it hadn't been for the post on the porch, I mighta fallen down to the ground. A'course the snowbank woulda saved me. Mrs. Valders screamed and I guess that shocked him enough that he slammed the door and ordered me not to come back." He wiped the hair off his forehead with one hand. "I don't know what to do. It was obvious he'd been drinking. I could hardly understand a word he said, he slurred so."

"I didn't know he was this bad. Ephraim goes out there to help with the farm work, and he's not said anything like this."

"Maybe I just got him on a bad day. Nevertheless, we got to help that man whether he wants help or not. I know his wife does. She called out 'I'm so sorry' after he hit me."

"We'll be there at the meeting," Haakan said. "Anything you want us to bring?"

"Not sure at this point. I'll put the coffee on."

Word got around church the next morning, and Anner Valders became the center of attention whether he wanted to be or not. Reverend Solberg's eye was still swollen halfway shut and colored red with black underneath.

He preached on Jesus admonishing His disciples to turn the other cheek if struck on one.

"Looks like Reverend Solberg didn't get a chance to do that," Haakan whispered to Ingeborg.

"Shhh." Ingeborg tried to look reproving and failed.

But at the meeting that night, levity soon faltered behind the sobering weight Reverend Solberg was laying on them.

"I believe God is calling us to help our brother. Anner Valders is not listening to God calling him, so we must be God's hands and feet. We must be His ear that listens to an angry man. We must be the means to draw this man back, because the way he is going, he will not last a long time."

Haakan thought of adding, *I wouldn't want to be God's cheek in this situation,* but he knew that was uncalled-for. "So what are we to do?"

"I don't know. Do you have any suggestions? I have been praying that together we will come up with some ideas."

"Well, we already got his fieldwork taken care of for fall, and Ephraim is doing the barn chores. We could go over there and go over his machinery, I guess."

Haakan blinked. *Was that the still small voice of God he heard?* No, couldn't be. But he repeated what he'd sensed anyway. "Does anyone know if Anner paid his debts this fall? I know Olaf paid him for the wheat, but did it get to the bank? I'm sure he has borrowed against his harvest. We all have."

No one knew the answer to that.

"I can see that having our own bank will be a good thing."

"You really think that will happen?" Mr. Johnson asked.

"If our wives have anything to say about it, we'll sure enough have a bank." Joseph Baard kept a straight face, but chuckles went around the room.

"Well, we can be sure Anner isn't going to tell us anything so private. If we can get him to talk with us at all."

"I'll move my small forge out there so we can repair whatever needs it. I'm sure his wheel rims need refitting," Hjelmer said.

"You would do that?" Mr. Johnson looked at Hjelmer in surprise. "After what he's done to you?"

Hjelmer held out his hands. "I still have two good arms."

Haakan nodded, pride softening his gaze. His young cousin was indeed growing into a man, or had already grown into one, as the case may be.

Joseph added, "He ain't brought his cows over to the bull this fall either. I shoulda thought of that. I'll ask Ephraim to let me know when they come in heat, then I can walk Bruno over there."

As the discussion wore down, Reverend Solberg said quietly, "I have one more favor to ask of you."

The men all stopped what they were saying and looked at him.

"We must undergird this mission of ours in prayer. That means each of us must covenant to pray for Anner every day, to pray for him every time God brings him to our minds." A silence stretched, several of the men squirming in their chairs. "Now, your womenfolk pray regular. I think this is God calling us men to do the same. I'm not saying you don't pray already — please don't get me wrong — but this is separate and . . . private."

He looked each man in the eyes. "Now, are you in? There is no shame in refusing if you do not believe you can make this commitment. All you got to do is come tell me that you've reconsidered."

Joseph cleared his throat. "Two things. Can we ask our wives to pray too, without going into all the ins and outs? And will the rest of you pray for me? This is a hard thing we are agreeing to do, and I want to be faithful." His voice cracked on the word "faithful."

"Indeed." Again Reverend Solberg looked around the room. When all the men nodded, he nodded again. "Let's bow our heads in prayer. Gracious heavenly Father, we come before thee now with a heavy burden. Thou hast called us to help our struggling brother, Anner, and we have to depend on thy wisdom, for this is a touchy subject. Thou alone can bring a stop to his drinking, for man is without power over some things. Father, give us a love for this man, that he truly sees thee shining through us. And give each one of us the will and the faithfulness to pray daily, both for Anner and for one another, that we may be faithful in our calling. In Jesus' name, amen."

Lars and Haakan didn't have a whole lot to say on the way home. They rode side by side, but each spent the ride thinking of the meeting and the days ahead. Would God indeed bring about a miracle? For that was what they knew it would take. If Anner would strike a man of God, what would he do to the rest of them?

"Where's he getting his liquor?" Lars finally asked.

"Must go to Grafton."

"Funny, no one can remember seeing him out of his house since he come back from the hospital. You think he goes at night?"

"Whyever would he do that?"

"I don't know, but if he were makin' it himself like he used to, Ephraim would know. Think I'll ask him."

"Mighty interesting way to bring in January, ja? See you tomorrow," Haakan said when they reached his yard. He rode on out to the barn and, after opening the big door, led the horse inside. The warmth of the cows and horses flowed around him as he lit the lantern and unsaddled his horse. *Nothing smells as good as a barn,* he thought,

460

dumping a small measure of oats in the grain box. *Unless, of course, it's the resin smell of a newly felled tree.* He stopped for a moment, stroking the horse's neck. Did he miss the north woods of Minnesota and the lumbering there?

"Not with the wife I've got waiting for me up to the house." He slapped the horse on the rump and strode out the door. Overhead and to the north, the northern lights flickered and danced on the horizon. Stars seemed close enough to touch, at least if he stood on the roof of the barn. His breath froze to the scarf around his neck.

"God, you surely have given us a big order. I admit this ain't my first idea of a wonderful thing to do with my time. How can I show your love to that man when right now I don't even like him? Anner Valders never has been one of my favorite people. You know that." He watched the stars as if waiting for God to move one of them aside and talk directly to him.

Ingeborg would say God already spoke to him once tonight. Did he want to be selfish?

He broke into a trot. The cold air burned down into his lungs. What was he doing standing out here in the cold when he had a warm house and a warm wife waiting for him?

461

"What in the —" A string of profanity followed. Anner stood on his porch, screeching at the men who drove up to his barn with wagons, unloaded tools and a forge, and went inside the big doors. He spun around and disappeared into the house.

"What do you think he'll do?" Lars asked.

"Probably get his gun and shoot us," Haakan returned. "Here, help me carry this box, will you?"

"We could hole up in the barn." Lars kicked open the door with his foot.

"I was fooling."

"I ain't. I don't trust him any farther than I can throw that big team of his." They set the box of tools down and looked around. There was no sign of a liquor still. Of course it could be set up in the old sod barn.

A jingle of harness and a "whoa" told them Hjelmer had arrived. The three of them carried the forge just inside the door so the smoke would go outside and no sparks would burn down the barn. When Joseph Baard and David Johnson got there, they looked over the plows, the harrow, and the rake.

"I'll take the harnesses," Joseph said. "They need some work for certain." He held up a broken trace. "This surely ain't like Anner."

Noon came. The only sign of life in the house was the smoke rising from the chimney.

"Bet his curiosity is near to killin' him," Joseph said before taking a bite of his beef sandwich. "I sure could use a hot cup of coffee."

"I s'pose you want me to go up and ask," Reverend Solberg said with a grin.

"Nei. We'll live. But something else I just thought of. Splitting wood one-handed wouldn't be no easy thing either. I could go see." Mr. Johnson looked about as eager as a ten-year-old boy ordered to the wash-basin.

"Difficult but not impossible," Haakan said, remembering the pull of the muscles when hefting his ax. It used to be almost a part of him, but no longer. "Besides, they might be burning coal — getting it in Grafton."

"You want I should check?" Clearly he hoped someone, anyone, would say no.

"I think not." Reverend Solberg sucked in a deep breath. "If anyone needs to go up there, it should be me."

Hjelmer got to his feet. "I better get the forge hot again. That plowshare looks like it's been plowing rocks. Ephraim might work pretty good in the store, but he's no great hand at sharpening the plowshare."

They were all back to work, talking and laughing when the barn door swung open. Anner stopped in the doorway, the right arm of his black wool coat tucked in.

"Why are you all here messing up my barn?" he roared, catching their attention. He leaned against the jamb as if holding up the coat he wore took all his strength.

"Good afternoon, Anner. How good to see you." Haakan walked forward, hand outstretched. Realizing he'd extended his right hand as usual, he quickly shifted to his left.

Anner ignored the peace offering. He glared at Haakan, spun on his heel, and marched back to the house.

What was it he'd seen in the man's eyes. Rage for certain. Hurt? Or was it relief?

27

Anner broke on the third day.

"Why? Why are you here?" He looked as though he hadn't slept for the last three nights. Standing there in the barn, swaying from either an excess of liquor or a lack of sleep, he looked as if death hung right over his shoulder. The skin that stretched tautly over jaw and cheek needed sunlight to warm the blood back into it. Newly gray hair straggled from under the tromped-on fedora.

"Because we care," Reverend Solberg said simply.

"But you can't care. I don't." Anner leaned against the post. "I want to die."

The words lay on the floor with no will to rise.

"Well, Anner, I guess God isn't ready for you yet." Joseph Baard rose from the bench where he'd been mending harness and rebraiding tie ropes. "And we need you here."

Anner looked down at his empty sleeve. "I

ain't good for nothin' anymore. If God didn't want me yet, why'd He take my arm?"

"No one knows the answer to that part, but as for the other part of you, He still has a place for you here. Something for you to do."

"What a pile of —" He stopped himself.

"Anner Valders, stop beating yourself to death." Reverend Solberg's voice sounded like God himself. It rang in the barn, setting the hens to flight in the haymow. And both words and tone rang in the men's hearts, clear deep into their souls.

"We come to help you, to bring you back to us. We have missed you." Joseph reached with his left hand, took Anner's limp hand and shook it. He covered their two hands with his other. "I don't know what God has in mind for you, but He has something."

"But why would all of you keep coming back when I . . . I even struck one of you and tried to scare off others? Even your women-folk."

"Anner, listen to me. We are a family, the family of God, and the Good Book says when one hurts, we all hurt. You've been hurting, so we have felt the pain. Now you can begin to get well. Then we will all be well again."

"But my arm."

"Yes, it is gone."

Anner stared at Joseph, as if willing him to take back his words. He looked around at each of them, perhaps really seeing them for the first time. "You would do all of this for me?"

"And more if need be."

"Well, I never." Anner sank down on the bench Joseph had vacated. "Farming with one arm ain't easy."

"Farming with two arms ain't easy. There ain't nothing easy about farming," Haakan said, giving everyone a much needed chuckle. "So you hire someone to help you, or you sell the farm and do something else."

"What else can I do? All I know is to farm."

Hjelmer cleared his throat. "I been thinking. Maybe you could work in my wife's store. Now that the post office is in place, and with her serving dinners and all, she needs more help."

"Really?"

"But you know the women — they don't tolerate no boozing."

Anner studied Hjelmer. "Did she offer?"

"No, but she'll think this a grand idea. She's been right worried about you . . . and your missus."

At that Anner's face crumpled. He covered his eyes with his remaining hand. "Yes, and she was right to be. But I cannot do this, don't you see?" He stood and made his way to the door, listing to the right side as if carrying something heavy. But the right arm was no longer there and dragged all the heavier because of its absence.

For the next three weeks, each of the men took turns spending the day with Anner, and sometimes the nights. Ten days into the vigil, Haakan showed up right after supper.

"How you be?" He removed his hat and coat as he talked.

"I don't need you here anymore," Anner said. "You go on home and spend the time with your family."

Haakan peered across the table to Anner. The man wouldn't look him in the eye. *Dear Lord, now what?* He sniffed. Was that whiskey he smelled?

He looked over at Hildegunn, who kept stirring something in a bowl on the counter. She refused to look at him either. And whatever she was mixing was indeed being beat to death. All the while he stood there, Haakan sent prayers heavenward.

"Surely you have a cup of coffee to offer a man who rode clear over here on such a frigid night. Why, that north wind like to froze my bones." A sense of utter rightness brought him a feeling of peace. He was where he was supposed to be. "You hear it howling? You wouldn't send me out in that, would you?"

Anner sighed and flopped back in his chair. "No, I guess not. Hildegunn, pour the man some coffee, why don't you?"

Haakan looked over just in time to see her shoulders shake. She used the corner of her apron to wipe her eyes and turned with a smile, trembling at first but growing more confident as she moved to the cookstove.

The hand she laid on Haakan's shoulder as she set the coffee cup in front of him gripped with the strength of the distraught. "Thank you for coming in spite of the weather." Gratitude shone in her eyes, eyes that had come to life again in the last weeks.

"You want to tell me about it?" asked Haakan some time later.

Hildegunn had gone up to bed, and the two men had moved their pegs halfway around the cribbage board.

Anner looked up from studying his cards. "I was going to get roaring drunk tonight."

Haakan waited. *Please, Lord, let all the men be praying. I don't know what to say or do. Help me.*

The ticktock of the clock on the mantel marked the seconds like an anvil pounding in the stillness. The north wind wept around the eaves, crying the desolation of the damned.

"I . . . I thought to . . ." Anner waited. A sniff, a hawk of his throat. With shaking hands, he drew a red handkerchief from his back pocket and blew his nose. Then he spit into the fabric and used a corner to wipe his eyes. "I thought to walk out that door after Hildegunn went to bed and just keep on walking. They say freezing to death is painless. You just go to sleep."

God in heaven . . . Even Haakan's thoughts froze. "And . . . and n-now?"

Anner's attempted smile went back into hiding. "Now I'm beating you at cribbage, and I don't hear that wind calling my name any longer. Or maybe it wasn't the wind after all. Maybe it was the devil himself."

"Maybe."

"And maybe God not only brought you here tonight but kept you here?" Anner gave Haakan a questioning stare.

"There's no 'maybe' about that, Anner."

Silence again. The clock ticked away steadily and the wind fell still. The cat got up from its place on the rug in front of the stove and wound around Anner's ankles, mewing for attention.

Anner leaned down and picked up the

animal, settling it on his lap, from where the purring now filled the silence. The coals in the stove settled with a whoosh.

"Would you pray with me?" Anner stroked the cat and slowly raised his gaze to meet Haakan's.

"Ja, I would be glad to." At a feeling of insistence, Haakan got to his feet and walked around behind Anner. He set his hands on the man's shoulders and closed his eyes. "Father God, we come before thee with thankful hearts. Thank you that Anner is not lying in some snowbank but is here and seeking thy face. Thank you that I didn't stay home tonight when it would have been so easy. We see thy hand at work and we praise thee." He stopped. And waited.

"I give up," Anner whispered. "Whatever you want is fine with me. You take the whiskey. I don't ever want any again. Only you, heavenly Father. Only you."

Haakan waited again, only this time there was no tension in the room or in his hands or in Anner. "Amen."

The day Hildegunn came back to quilting, the women crowded around her, patting her shoulders, grasping her hands, wiping their eyes with handkerchiefs gone soggy.

"And to think Easter is nearly on us,"

Agnes said. "This winter has fairly flown."

"Ja, that is because it is early this year. Hard to get the spring housecleaning done when there are still blizzards in the works." Ingeborg wiped her eyes again.

"I didn't think to see another Easter," Hildegunn confided. "But thanks be to God, we will."

On Palm Sunday a plain hammered-iron cross hung above the new altar, which was fashioned from a slab of maple burl that Olaf salvaged from the sawmill. The gleam of the burnished natural wood looked nothing like the intricately carved altars they were used to in Norway, but as Petar said, "It suits us." A cross was carved through each of the three-inch-thick sides that supported the altar, and Olaf had curved the fronts and backs of the legs.

"Now ain't that beautiful?" breathed Agnes.

"We dedicate this altar to the glory of God, with thanks to Olaf Wold and Hjelmer Bjorklund, who so willingly have used their gifts to fashion such beauty for us." Reverend Solberg looked from the altar to the congregation. "How blessed we are. And now let us sing." The music rose triumphant as they celebrated Jesus' ride in majesty into Jerusalem.

"I think this Easter means more to me than any other," Ingeborg said.

"Why is that?" Katy asked.

"One of our own has come back from looking into the grave, and we can truly rejoice. Thanks be to God. That was a close one."

"I heard that Anner isn't the only one to have seen the pit," Agnes said with a barely perceptible wink.

"No, and probably not the last. So thank God for Easter every day."

With the coming of warmer days, Zeb took over the training of the young horses, breaking them for both riding and harnessing. He'd already done much of it over the winter, but now he had two teams of young oxen and six horses.

"They've still some to grow, but they look to be settling in," he told Haakan one afternoon. He had one of the young oxen yoked with an older, and the same with the horses, older teaching younger.

"You have a good hand with them. You ever think of going into the horse-raising business?"

"Costs too much."

"But have you thought about it? If you

had a place, what would you do?" They both leaned against the corral, their backs to the sun.

"If I had a place, I'd go west and round up some of the broomtails I been hearing about. I'd bring back mares and young stock, then buy a heavy stallion back east somewhere and begin breeding and training. I heard you can sell horses to the army too. Back home . . ." He stopped. "Ah well, it is all just a dream, anyway."

"Anything else?"

Zeb gave him an appraising look. "I'd ask Katy to marry me and make her the happiest woman this side of heaven." He looked down and scuffed a ridge in the dirt. "Fine dream, but dreamin's for fools and simpletons." He looked back at Haakan. "You got a dream?"

"I'm living my dream, only when I came here, I didn't know this was what I wanted. But God gave me a good shake and said, 'Open your eyes, son. I have this home and woman for you and two strong sons.' So I turned my back on the north woods, opened my eyes, and here I am."

Zeb nodded. "Wish to God all lives could be like that, but sometimes . . ." He heaved a sigh. "Sometimes things just happen."

Come on, tell me. Haakan waited.

"Well, I better get back to work. That young filly won't learn to pull on her own." He turned away, then back. "Thanks for listening. And asking."

"Anytime." *Ask him.* Haakan willed his tongue to say the words, but nothing came of it. A man's business was his own, and until Zeb either volunteered or asked for help, he wasn't one to intrude.

"Zeb, I . . ."

"Yes, sir?"

"Ah . . ." He couldn't do it. "You're doing a fine job with those animals. I appreciate it."

"Thank you."

Haakan strode off to the house, calling himself all kinds of names on the way. What if that had indeed been the prompting of God and he hadn't followed through? *What kind of a spineless, lily-livered so-and-so are you, Bjorklund?*

"Whatever is wrong?" Ingeborg asked after one look at his face.

"Ja, do I wear my feelings on my sleeve or my face too?" The tone of his voice brought Andrew on the run.

"Pa, are you mad?" His eyes rounded and his lower lip quivered.

"Only at myself, Andrew, son." Haakan picked the boy up and held him high to touch the ceiling.

"Again, Pa," Andrew shrieked in glee. "I can touch the ceiling."

Haakan held him up so he could touch the ceiling. Looking down, he saw Deborah in the doorway. "You want to touch the ceiling too?"

She shook her head but her eyes pleaded for him to pick her up.

Haakan set Andrew down on the floor, swatted his rear to make him giggle, and knelt down. He held his arms out and Deborah shuffled over to him, as though afraid if she ran like Andrew he would disappear. "You ready?"

She nodded.

Slowly, clasping her close to his chest, he stood. "Reach up high now."

As he raised her with his hands clasped firmly about her waist, she clutched his neck, then his hair. Slowly, her grin as wobbly as her hands, she reached up and touched the ceiling. He lowered her a bit, then raised her up again. Her eyes rounded. Her face split in a smile wide as the sun.

"I touched the ceiling." She laughed down at Haakan. "Again."

Haakan swallowed around the lump the little girl so often brought to his throat. Life had been mighty hard for her out on the prairie, up to now anyway. He looked over to Ingeborg to see her eyes glistening.

Andrew wrapped his arms around his father's leg and sat down on his boot. "Ride me?"

"As soon as Deborah gets set." He put the little girl down and she copied Andrew, sitting herself on his boot toe. "Ready?"

"Yeah." They hung on to his knees and he walked across the room.

"You two are heavy."

"More, more."

"What is all the noise?" Bridget called from the parlor, where she sat at the spinning wheel, her foot pumping the treadle while she fed the wool into the spinning wheel to turn it into yarn.

Haakan waddled into the other room, the two children giggling and urging him on.

"Looks like you got heavy feet."

"Ja, think I better sit down before I fall down." Haakan sank into the rocking chair. He patted each of the towheads. "You two go play again. Oh, I know, the woodbox needs filling if we want mor to make supper."

The two little ones dashed for the door, grabbing their coats as they ran by.

"Zeb talked with you about his feelings for Katy?" Haakan asked Bridget after the children had left.

"No, and he better not bother. No drifter is marrying my daughter."

"I'd talk with him if'n I were you. I think we can help that young man out. You know Katy's daft about him."

"Daft never hurt no one. Marrying a man with secrets does. When he comes clean with what happened in his life, then we can talk."

"Lots of people put the past behind them and begin a new life going west. He wouldn't be the first one and certainly not the last. Just a suggestion, mind you."

With the arrival of spring, the Red River kept on rising until it overflowed the banks and filled every basement with silt and stink. Being only a mild flood, it receded within ten days and left behind enough mess to keep everyone busy.

"Good thing we built the house up high," Ingeborg said for about the fiftieth time as they scrubbed out the basement. They'd already cleaned the springhouse and the smokehouse. Haakan had the boys out scrubbing the barn walls and trying to catch the chickens who'd taken refuge in the haymow.

"How is Metiz?" Katy asked.

"She says tepees are easier. When the

floods come, you just pack up and move."

"She's right." Bridget brushed a lock of gray hair out of her eyes with the back of her hand. "Spring cleaning will never seem hard again compared to this."

"It doesn't happen every year. All depends on how warm it gets in Winnipeg. With the river flowing north, the head melts faster than the mouth. Can cause all kinds of problems."

"This dirt grows good food, but it sticks worse'n anything I ever saw." Bridget picked a gob of gumbo off the doorjamb. With the cellar doors swinging upward, they'd had to scrape the wood before they could open the doors. They emptied the cellar, bucket by bucket, until only the ooze remained on the floor. They would let that dry by itself.

"Good thing the floodwaters didn't get as far as the town. Cleaning the church and school would have been bad."

"What about the store?" Katy shook her head. "Penny would have lost a lot of her supplies."

"What with Hjelmer staying in Grafton for his training at the bank, she would have really been in a mess."

Bridget put her hands on her hips. "I still can't think of my son as a banker. Hjelmer is a fine blacksmith. Banking ain't for him."

"How do you know, Mor?" Katy asked. "He's never tried. He was always good with numbers, and like Ingeborg said, he made good money off selling land to the railroad. I think he'll make a fine banker."

"So who's going to run his blacksmith shop then?"

Ingeborg dumped her bucket of dirty water over the rose bushes, where the new sprouts were already three inches long. "Anyone else need clean water?"

"Ja, me." They both handed her their buckets.

Ingeborg stopped at the well and kneaded her aching back with her fists. She always got soft over the winter and paid the price in the spring. She lifted her face to the sun, rejoicing in the warmth. How wonderful to have heat and light again. But this winter hadn't been so bad. As Haakan had promised, many windows indeed made a difference.

The geese sang their song overhead. The meadowlarks couldn't quit singing. Ah, to go for a walk and look for the first violet down in the shady places. She shaded her eyes to look across the prairie. The grass had already been coming up before the flood, and now it lay like a haze of green upon the land. She knew if she watched closely enough, she could see it grow.

The lambs gamboled beside their mothers, and two new calves bellered out in the barn. The sow was due to have her piglets any day. With all the babies already born or about to be, Ingeborg couldn't help but think of herself. All this time and no quickening in her womb. There would be no new baby in this Bjorklund household.

Kaaren was a different matter, however. She was due in June.

"I wouldn't care when it was," Ingeborg muttered as she drew the water and filled the buckets. "God, are you listening? I really want to give Haakan a son of his own. Is that such a terrible thing to ask?"

As usual, there was no answer. But then, she really hadn't expected one.

"This meeting will now come to order." Haakan clapped his hands. When no one paid any attention, he raised his voice. "That's it, folks. Let's get going on this." He waited as the shuffling and twittering died down. "Good. Welcome to our first meeting to organize a community bank here in Blessing."

A spattering of applause was cut off when Haakan glanced toward the altar, reminding them they were in church. No other building was large enough, and tonight the church was packed from wall to wall.

"Now, you've all received letters telling you about the process of beginning a bank and defining the terms so we can all be talking the same language."

A harrumph from the back let loose a spate of twittering again.

"I know this is new for all of us. I never dreamed starting a bank could be so difficult. In my mind it should be like any other business, but far as I can tell, it isn't. Now, I'm going to read to you — you have copies to follow along — the articles of incorporation, since we are going into this as a co-op. That means we all have a say in the matters, and there will be monthly meetings to make decisions."

"I just want to know who is going to be taking care of my money," one of the men announced.

"We all are. That's what this meeting is about. We will elect a board of directors, but that won't happen tonight. Tonight we are just trying to make sense out of this and make sure that all your questions get answered."

"I don't know enough to ask a decent

question," someone muttered.

Haakan could feel sweat trickle down his spine. He wiped his forehead and sent a pleading look in the direction of Reverend Solberg, who shook his head.

"Right now, I'd like to introduce to you Mr. Jason Kent from the First Bank of Grafton. He will explain anything we don't understand." He nodded to the man sitting in the front row aisle seat.

Dressed in a black frock coat with gray pants, Mr. Kent straightened his tie and stood. "Thank you, Mr. Bjorklund. Now, ladies and gentlemen, let us begin."

By the end of the hour and a half of questions, answers, and discussion, his tie was askew, and he'd swept his hands back over his head enough times to make his dark hair fly every which way. But with a unanimous agreement, Hjelmer would be running the bank, and the papers would be drawn up by a lawyer in Grafton. Another meeting would be held in three weeks.

"I can't believe it all went so smooth," Ingeborg said as they left the building.

"That's because we laid the groundwork first." Haakan sucked in a deep breath of crisp air. "You can smell spring coming."

"Ja, but we can have more winter too. Just you wait and see."

28

May 1887

"I still ain't happy about this." Bridget shook her head as she adjusted the skirt on Katy's dress one more time.

"But, Mor, you gave us your blessing." Katy turned to her mother. "Don't you like Zeb?"

"Ja, I like the boy."

"Man."

"Ja, well, be that as it may, if he would only tell us about his other life. There's something that isn't right." She stepped back to get a better view. "And why do you have to be in such a terrible hurry?"

"He's not married."

"How do you know?"

"I asked him if he'd ever been married, and he said no, he never wanted to until now." The smile that had gone into hiding burst forth again.

"And you think he is telling you the truth?" Bridget crossed her arms over her chest.

Katy nodded. "I do. Zeb MacCallister does not lie."

"Harrumph."

"Have you ever known him to lie?"

Bridget had the grace to shake her head. "No, never. But there is something he's not telling us."

"Mor, we've been over and over this. Haakan has talked to me, so have Kaaren and Lars, even Penny. Everybody likes Zeb, so can't we just let the other — whatever it is — go and start from this moment?"

"You could have married Reverend Solberg."

"I know, and you could marry that railroad man. He comes to eat at Penny's, and he can't take his eyes off you."

"I'm too old to be starting all over again. Besides, we ain't talking about me. We're talking about you."

Katy smoothed the front of her watered-silk dress. "Such a beautiful gown. Kaaren knows just what to do to make something that's already lovely even lovelier." She twirled so the skirt would bell out. "I wish Far were here. Hjelmer said he is happy to give me away, but . . ." A tear glistened and ran over. "You still miss him?"

"Every day of my life."

Katy turned and wrapped her arms around her mother. "I always said I wanted to marry a man as good and strong as my far. And if I can be even half the wife that you are, I'll be happy."

"You about ready?" Ingeborg entered to find both women with tears streaming down their faces.

"Ja, we are ready."

The ceremony right after church that Sunday morning led to more than one teary eye in the gathering.

"Why are you crying?" Andrew asked over and over until Thorliff told him to hush.

Katy and Zeb both spoke their vows out strong and proud. Katy had practiced enough that she never stumbled once on the English words. Reverend Solberg had given them the choice of using English or Norwegian, and Katy, after a loving glance at Zeb, chose the new language.

"I, Zebulun MacCallister, take thee, Katja Bjorklund, to be my wedded wife."

Hearing love in his deep voice as he said her Norwegian name, she about broke down right there. And if hearts could talk, his did through his eyes. Those beautiful hazel eyes. She felt she could drown in the golden flecks.

"I, Katja Bjorklund, take thee, Zebulun MacCallister, to be my wedded husband."

He swallowed hard, his jaw working.

"I now pronounce you man and wife.

What God has joined together, let no man rend asunder." Reverend Solberg made the sign of the cross. "The blessing of Almighty God be with you now and forevermore." He looked them both right in the eye, then turned just a mite to Zeb. "You better take good care of her," he whispered.

He lifted his gaze to the congregation. "Go in peace."

The newlyweds turned and led the way out of the church.

The next day they finished loading their saddlebags, along with a pack horse, to head west for Montana. They planned to follow Zeb's dream and round up wild horses to bring home to Dakota Territory as a start for a breeding herd.

"See you get back in time for harvest," Haakan said, handing up a pouch that jingled. "For you, in case you need this." He stepped back.

"Thank you, Haakan. There is no way this side of heaven that I can repay you for all you've done for me."

"Just pass it on. Your turn will come." Haakan locked his thumbs in his suspenders. "If you get as far as the mountains, take extra looks at them for us. I hear they're mighty proud."

Ingeborg gave Katy a small packet of soft

leather. "Here's the simples I told you about. I labeled each one. Just hope you don't need them. When you get near a post office or telegraph, write."

"Wish we was going." Thorliff glanced at Baptiste. "We could catch every broomtail in the entire state, huh?"

Baptiste nodded. "But keep only the best ones."

Dawn was just bright enough to light their backs as the two rode off.

"God be with you," Ingeborg called, then whispered, "God be with you."

Haakan put his arm around her shoulders. "He is and He will be."

The entire town and half the surrounding countryside turned out for the grand opening of the First Bank of Blessing. Hjelmer showed off the safe the Bjorklunds had brought in clear from Chicago, guaranteed to be theft proof, or so the flier read.

"I never did a safe blessing before." Reverend Solberg stood on the wooden sidewalk in front of the store-*cum*-restaurant-*cum*-post office-*cum*-bank. "But here goes." The crowd clapped, then quieted.

"In the name of the Father, the Son, and the Holy Ghost. We are called to be a blessing, and now we dedicate this safe to the benefit of the people and to the glory of God. May it be used wisely and with total honesty according with His holy purposes." He grinned at the children gathered at his feet. "And now what do I say? I now pronounce you men and safe?"

Everyone chuckled and when one person began clapping, others followed.

"The women of the church have dinner ready for us." He waved to the accordion player. "Heinrich, strike up the band."

With that, they all paraded over to the church, led by one man playing the accordion and Uncle Olaf on the fiddle.

Hjelmer gave a speech after dinner, promising to do his best as the bank manager. He reminded them that he was the manager, but they were the owners.

"That young man's gotten right smart since he came to America, wouldn't you say?"

"I agree, and if he does again like he did with the land deals, there'll be more money for all of us."

Ingeborg overheard the conversation and saved it to tell Hjelmer later.

"I found the mistakes." Anner handed Penny her two accounts books. "Now everything matches up."

"You are a miracle worker, Mr. Valders. I hunted three days for them."

"Ja, well, I find I like numbers. It's like cutting lumber. If you are accurate, it all comes right in the end."

Penny looked at him, slightly nodding with eyes narrowed. "How about if you take over the bookkeeping for both the store and the post office? Columns of figures aren't my specialty, that's for sure. I'd be willing to bet that you could help Hjelmer in the bank too."

"I guess I could do that." He cocked his head, like a robin watching for a worm. "You know, I like the numbers part better than the waiting on customers. I have a suggestion to make, if'n you don't mind."

"Mind? Heavenly days, of course not. Anything to make my store operate better."

"I been noticing that people buy more things when you wait on them, because you always say, 'Did you see this' or 'I just got thus and so in.' And for the meals, same thing. Why don't you have the elder Mrs. Bjorklund do the cooking, you do the taking of orders and serving, and you tend the counter in the store? I can do the book work, stock the shelves, that kind of thing. Now that your cousin is taking care of my farm for me, and Petar is helping Hjelmer with the blacksmithing, Hildegunn and I could get a house built in town and I'd be close enough to help out even more."

Penny caught her bottom lip between her teeth. "You are willing to do that? Move into town?"

"I 'spect it's the best idea. I heard the elder Mrs. Bjorklund talking about starting a boardinghouse. We need such a thing here, and it won't hurt none if Blessing grows. Now that we got a bank and a post office, next thing will be a telegraph office." He gave her a slanted grin. "Unless of course someone starts a saloon first."

"There'll be no such thing in —" Penny dismounted from her high horse as soon as she caught on that he was teasing her. "Well, if that don't beat all."

"What?"

"You were making a joke, Anner. You realize how long it's been since I heard such a thing as a joke come out of your mouth? Welcome back, Anner Valders. You been gone a long time."

He extended his left hand and shook hers. "And much of it is thanks to you and to Hjelmer for giving me this chance. You, him, and the men of Blessing. I thank our God for all of you and will every day of the rest of my life." His voice broke on the last couple of words.

"Did I hear someone call my name?" Hjelmer, his vest unbuttoned and tie hanging loose, strolled out of the banking room and into the store.

"No, but your ears must have been burning." Penny smiled up at her handsome husband. "Anner has a proposition for you. Why don't the two of you go back and pour yourselves a cup of coffee and talk this out? I'll yell if anyone needs the banker."

She hummed as she straightened shelves and dusted around the spice tins. Standing on the step stool, she had just reached for the stack of buckets when she thought she saw something out of the corner of her eye. But when she looked again, nothing was there. She dusted on but kept one eye out for something that moved.

There it was again. Couldn't be a mouse or rat because she saw a flash of red. Climbing down from the stool, she tiptoed over to the main counter and peeked over the top. Two strange children huddled against the counter, stuffing crackers in their mouths as fast as they could chew. Their clothes looked like moths had held a convention in them, a dirt convention at that. Dirt and holes held together by a few threads.

Who are they and how did they get in here without the bell tinkling? How long have they been here?

"You know, if you'd told me you were hungry, I'd have gotten you some real food."

One dashed one way, one the other, around the counter and making for the door. She grabbed for the one on her right and got hold of his coat. Or was it her? Impossible to tell. She had no time for thought because the child slipped out of the sleeves, leaving her with a handful of coat. She leaped and hit the door just before they did, throwing her weight against it so they were trapped. They darted down one aisle, heading for the back door.

"Hjelmer! Anner!" Penny's screeching could be heard clear outside.

The two men came running. The children collided with the men's legs. They caught themselves and darted around the men. Or rather tried to. One made the mistake of going to Anner's good side. The other stumbled. One man per child. Caught.

Kicking and screaming, the children struggled for freedom. Hjelmer held his captive up by the back of his coat.

"And what do we have here?" Flailing the air with his fists, the boy called Hjelmer every name he could think of, none of them complimentary.

Anner, however, had the smaller child clutched to his chest with his one arm and suffered myriad kicks to his thighs and shins. "Be still, you little thief, or I'll —"

"You leave my brother alone!" the older one yelled.

Penny watched the proceedings, her mouth going from an *O* of astonishment to a widening in laughter. It started with a single giggle, but as the other battle continued, she lost hers. She laughed until her sides ached. Soon all four male creatures were staring at her as if she'd lost whatever mind she'd started with.

When she tried to stop, the look on Hjelmer's face set her off again.

"Do you care to share with the rest of us what is so funny?" Hjelmer quirked an eyebrow.

"Y-y-you." She held her hands up in surrender.

With the boys still, the men got a better grip on them and plunked them both on the counter.

"Now, stay still." Anner glared at his charge.

Hjelmer fixed them with a stern look. "Who are you, where are you coming from,

494

and where are you supposed to be?"

Both boys crossed their arms over their chests and stared at their knees. The younger one was the first to look up. He cleared his throat.

"Don't you say nothin'!" the older one hissed.

The little one dropped his gaze again.

All Penny could see was two well-ventilated stocking hats. Blond hair stuck out of the holes of one, slightly darker out the other. "How long have you boys been on the road?"

"Ain't been on the road."

"I told you to shut up!" the older boy scolded.

"Been on the train."

"Oh, I see." Penny nodded as though refugees arriving from the train was an everyday occurrence.

"Can't you never shut up?"

Hjelmer and Anner, while keeping a close watch on their captives, let Penny do the talking.

"So where were you going?"

Shrugs of both sets of thin shoulders.

"Guess we better take them to the sheriff," she said after a long silence. "Maybe he can get them to talk."

"The sher—" Anner bit off his word. He

nodded to Penny, his eyes crinkling around the edges. But when he looked back to the boys, his face wore the stern mask she'd known for so long.

"Don't want no sheriff."

"Then you better talk to me." Penny walked around the counter and, taking the dome off the cheese wheel, cut two small wedges. "Here, this might go well with those crackers."

The older boy clenched his hands under his armpits.

The younger stared at the cheese, glanced at his brother, and snatched the food. It disappeared into his face as fast as he could stuff it.

"Now you did it." The older one cuffed the younger.

"Yeow!" He rubbed his shoulder. "You din't need to do that."

"All right, that's enough. Now let's get some answers. Where is your ma?" Penny made her voice tough as hog hide.

"Runned off." Spoken to the one remaining button on his too-small coat.

"Your pa?"

"Dead."

The one-word arrow stabbed her heart.

The older boy slammed his hand on the counter. "Now ya did it. I was trying to keep us out of the orphanage, and you tossed us right in."

Penny turned to him. "Why do you say that?"

"Everywhere we go, folks try to take one of us, not both, or they talk about the orphanage."

"We don't have an orphanage in Blessing. But I know we got some families that would take both of you in without any kind of argument. Where you from?"

The younger boy peeped out of the corner of his eye to his brother.

The boy sighed. "Way east. We hopped trains whenever we could. There's no one to write to that cares beans about us. We're on our own, and we're gonna make it. You just watch." Both tone and face grew fierce.

"I'll be glad to, but first we'll find you a place to stay where there's some clothes that will fit and plenty to eat." She leaned closer to the little boy. "What's your name?"

"Toby."

"Toby what?"

"White and him's Gerald. We call him Jerry."

"Toby and Gerald White, huh?" She turned to Hjelmer and Anner, who stood ready in case the boys bolted. "So, what do you think? The Baards, or Olaf and Goodie, or —"

"Why can't they come to our house?" Anner asked. "We got room, and when we build the new house, they can have a room all to themselves."

"We can collect some clothes for them."

Anner shook his head. "No, we can buy some, and my wife will make the rest." He looked at Penny, then Hjelmer. "Unless, of course, you . . ."

Hjelmer leaned forward just a hair. "I think you've already made the best suggestion possible. The gift of two boys is something mighty special for one afternoon."

Penny started to say something, then stopped. This reminded her far too much of her own situation years earlier. Only then it had been relatives splitting up the children, never again to all be together. There could have been room at their house for these two. She loved them already. But Anner and Hildegunn needed these boys as bad as the boys needed them.

"Well, Mr. Valders, I get to help with something. Come on, you two. The boots are right over here, and from the looks of your feet, you need some right bad."

"Why don't you go on home and talk this over with your wife," Hjelmer said in a low voice. "We'll bring the boys later."

"No need. She'll be scrubbing them clean and fixing clothes all night. I can't give her anything better. Don't you see?"

"I do see. And even more, I see that you have come a long way, Anner, and I'm proud to call you my friend."

Anner hawked, almost spit, then remembered where he was and drew out his handkerchief. "Thanks to the good Lord above and all you men who kept coming to care for me even when I spit in your faces. I can never repay what I owe."

"Ain't that the truth for all of us?"

The bell over the door tinkled.

Anner turned to the newly arrived customers and asked, "Can I help you?"

As Hjelmer headed back toward his office, he heard Penny and the two boys laughing over in the boot section. Maybe he should have claimed the boys for their own. But surely God was going to bless them with children soon as He deemed the time was right, wasn't He?

29

August 1887

"They're here! They're here!" Andrew and Deborah shrieked together.

"Who's here?" Ingeborg wiped her hands on her apron.

"Katy's home! With horses. Lots'a horses." Andrew fairly danced in place at his news.

"Glory be to God, they're safe." She followed the children out the door and shaded her eyes with one hand. It sure enough did look like *lots'a* horses. "Come on, Andrew, Deborah. Let's go open the corral gate." She grabbed the children's hands and ran with them across the yard to the corral by the old sod barn. She flipped the rope loop off the gate post and pulled it open wide. Latching it to a rail, she took the children to stand in the door of the sod barn.

"Pretty horses," said Deborah, her mouth and eyes matching *O*'s.

"I get to ride?" Andrew tugged on her skirts. "Mor, can I ride now?"

"No, son. Those horses aren't tame

enough to ride yet. Zeb has lots of work to do with them first."

"Oh." He leaned against his mother's side, letting her pat his curls with an absent-minded gesture.

With a whoop and a swirl of dust, the horses streamed through the open gate, following the lead mare that Zeb had snubbed to his old faithful mount. Katy brought up the rear, swinging a rope and hollering at the stragglers. In a broad-brimmed hat and men's britches, she reminded Ingeborg so much of herself that she laughed out loud. No wonder people were scandalized at her men's clothing.

With the last horse in, Katy swung the gate shut and latched it. "There now, you broomtails, you're trapped for sure." Then turning to Ingeborg, she said, "We did just that, Inge. We trapped them. Zeb figured it out. We drove them into a box canyon that we'd fenced off. Worked so perfect we could choose which to keep and which to let loose. The stallion was the only one left out, and he tried to get his mares back a couple of times. You should have seen him." She swung to the ground as if she'd been riding all her life. "He was happy when we let the ones we didn't want loose again. He rounded them up and hightailed it out of there as if to say 'so there!' "

"You look like range life agrees with you." Ingeborg could feel her smile nearly touch her ear lobes.

"Oh, it does. We saw the mountains, and all I could think of was Norway. They were so rugged and majestic, they made my heart ache."

"Who has a heartache?" Zeb led his mount out of the gate, making sure none of the wild horses were following.

"No one, silly." Katy tossed her long braid back over her shoulder.

The three of them crossed their arms on the top rail of the corral. Andrew and Deborah scrambled up to sit beside them, bare feet hooked around the lower rail.

"You sure got pretty horses." Andrew patted Zeb's shoulder.

"Glad you like them, young sprout." Zeb looked around at Ingeborg. "I think he grew three feet while we were gone."

Andrew looked down at his feet, shaking his head. "No, I only still got two." He stared from one adult to the other, bewilderment written all over his face, but started to laugh just because they did.

"Andrew, my boy, I sure did miss you." Katy tousled his hair, knocking his hat into the horse pen. When Andrew started to climb down to get it, she grabbed his arm. "Oh no, you don't."

At the same moment Zeb bent over and reached inside for the hat, straightening and plunking it back on Andrew's head. "You stay out of there. Those horses would stomp you right into the dirt."

Andrew looked at him as if he'd taken up telling tall tales.

"All horses aren't gentle like ours." Ingeborg turned from watching a particularly fine filly. "But give Zeb time with them and they will be. You just remember to do as he says."

"Yes, Mor." Andrew laid his arm across her shoulders. "You going to ride?"

"One day."

"So what all has gone on while we've been gone?"

"The usual."

"We got new calves. Belle had a baby. Paws is a pa."

"There are new chicks." Deborah held out her hand to show a scabbed spot. "That hen near to tore my hand off."

Katy and Zeb both looked to Ingeborg, who shrugged and grinned at the same time. "A lot of love and she's healthy again. She can talk your arm and both legs off."

"But, Mor —" Andrew started but

Ingeborg cut him off.

"I know, you got two legs and so does Zeb. You and Deborah go crank up a bucket of water. I'm sure a cold drink would taste mighty good to these travelers."

The two leaped to the ground and ran off yelling, "Race you!"

The look the newlyweds shared brought a lump to Ingeborg's throat.

"Shall we ask her? Tell her? What?" Katy locked her arm through her husband's.

"What now?" Ingeborg raised an eyebrow.

"Well, we want the girls to come live with us. Since they started out with Zeb —"

"I guess I think they should be mine — er, ours," Zeb finished.

Ingeborg dropped her chin on her hands. Both Manda and Deborah had become like daughters to her. "G-guess we'll have to talk about this later." The wrench of losing them already knotted her stomach. "Manda should probably have the say in it."

"We wanted to ask you first," Katy whispered.

One of the horses snorted. Another one got nipped on the rump and squealed. Ingeborg kept her gaze on the horses. She couldn't bear yet to look the two young people in the eye.

After a bit Zeb broke the silence. "Have Anner and Hildegunn moved to town yet?"

"Just last week, in fact. They have two boys now." Gratitude for his changing the subject flowed through her.

"They were surely busy while we were gone."

"Zebulun MacCallister!"

Smiling at the shocked look on Katy's face, Ingeborg turned to Zeb. "Penny caught two boys stealing crackers in her store. Come to find out, they came in hiding on a train car. Anner volunteered to keep them, and now they're one happy family."

"Well, I'll be." Zeb tipped his hat brim back with one finger. "I s'pose you'll be tellin' me old Anner is the manager of the bank by now too."

"Close. He's taken over the bookkeeping. For both the bank and the store."

"So what other news have we missed out on?"

"Bridget is planning on building a boardinghouse this fall. And let's see . . ." She tapped her cheek with one finger. "Kaaren had a baby boy June fifth. They named him Samuel. Sam fits him perfectly."

"That's wonderful." Katy sneaked a peek at her husband. "Shall we tell her?" At his nod, she turned to Ingeborg. "We're in the family way too. Or at least I'm pretty sure."

"Wait until your mor hears that. She'll be over the moon with joy." The three linked arms and meandered up to the house. They waved at Metiz coming across the field and gratefully sank down on benches in the shade of the house.

"Fields look like it will be a good harvest," Zeb said, stretching his hands over his head. "We got back just in time."

"Ja, Haakan and Lars plan on starting here next week. Joseph already began cutting."

"And here I was hoping to go get us a heavy stallion before harvest begins."

"You should be able to do that. A couple days each way on the train. Joseph has a cousin near Cincinnati, Ohio, who raises draft horses. He's got everything all laid out for you, just waiting to make sure that's what you still wanted to do."

"What he'd really like to do is go homestead some of that Montana country." Katy leaned close to Ingeborg. "We saw valleys that were break-your-heart beautiful. Maybe someday we will do that."

Ingeborg wanted to ask if Zeb had ever confided his secret to his wife, but she refrained. That smacked of being downright nosy.

★ ★ ★

That next night after the children were in bed, the Bjorklund families, the Mac-Callisters, and the Wolds gathered around the table at Ingeborg's house. After Zeb and Katy regaled them with tales of rounding up wild horses, silence fell for a moment.

Zeb cleared his throat. "Well, I talked with Anner, and we are set to buy his place. He's agreed to let me get a team trained and sold to make the down payment. Then he'll take a portion of every harvest to pay it off."

"That sounds real fair," Lars said.

Murmurs of agreement came from the others.

"Also I talked with Joseph, and I'll be leaving to get the stallion soon as I can get things moved over to the other place and settled."

"I can take care of everything else once we get the horses moved," Katy said.

"You need a bigger corral. They'll go right through a barbed wire fence, don't you think?" Hjelmer asked.

"You're probably right." Zeb sucked in a deep breath.

"We can get that corral enlarged in a day or so." Olaf looked to Lars, and he nodded.

"Got the poles all cut. Was going to make

a new one at my house, but it can wait."

"I'll replace 'em for you." Zeb nodded and ticked off another finger. "Looks like I can leave on Saturday, if all goes well."

Again nods of agreement circled the room.

"That brings us to the girls."

Ingeborg clamped her teeth together and shut her eyes. She'd hoped he'd — they'd changed their minds. Andrew would be heartbroken again. First Ellie and now Deborah.

"I wish we could get that thing about their homestead straightened out. Sure hate to see them lose that." Kaaren continued rocking Trygve, who would rather sit and watch than go to sleep as he was supposed to.

"I thought about going back and raising horses there, but —"

"But I didn't want to leave all of you if we didn't have to." Katy spoke up, her voice as soft and gentle as the looks she sent her husband.

"If we could get a clear title to the place, then you could sell it and bank the money for the girls' future," Hjelmer said.

"So speaks our resident banker." Olaf's smile took any sting from his words.

"Ja, that is a good idea," Haakan agreed.

"But we don't seem to get answers to the letters Penny has sent."

"Maybe that is a job for the banker." Hjelmer rolled his eyes.

"Get on with you." Bridget nudged him with her elbow, but the look she gave him spoke of her pride, even though she still thought he made a better blacksmith than banker.

Haakan nodded. "Maybe so, but it will have to wait until after harvest."

Again sounds and nods of agreement.

"I can write another letter, though. Maybe they'll pay attention this time. I'll warn them that we are thinking of turning the matter over to a lawyer," Penny added.

"A lawyer!" Bridget's tone shouted horror.

When the chuckles quieted, Zeb leaned forward. "So we all agree that Manda and Deborah will come to live with me and Katy?"

"If they want to." Ingeborg held out a last bit of hope, even though she knew it was futile.

"Yes. If they want to."

The next day Zeb brought the subject up to Manda.

"You mean we'd live with you and Katy forever?" Manda turned a suspicious eye on

Zeb. "You won't be going off to Canada?"

Zeb nodded. "We are buying the Valders' place."

Manda looked from Ingeborg to Katy to Zebulun and back to Ingeborg. "You want us to stay here?"

"Yes, if that is what you want. You will always have a home here with us."

Manda scratched her chin. She shifted from one foot to the other. "What I want most is to go home to see if my pa came back." She watched Zeb shake his head. "I knowed you'd say that. Sure them folks said he'd left for home, but nobody ever saw his body or nothing. Maybe he got hit on the head and forgot where he was going."

Ingeborg shut her eyes. *Heavenly Father, how well I know how she feels. Help this girl to accept that her pa is gone just as I had to accept that Roald would never return. Give me the words to help take her hurt away.*

But no words came to her mind, so she kept silent. Another time perhaps.

"I got one condition," Manda said.

Zeb rolled his eyes. "Dear Lord preserve us." His mutter brought a smile to those around.

"Now don't you go takin' the Lord's name in vain, or I ain't goin'."

"Manda Norton, I wasn't takin' the

Lord's name in vain. I need every bit of strength He's got to send."

She studied him, checking to see if he was teasing. When she seemed assured that he was serious, she cleared her throat. "We will come live with you if . . ." She paused. Cleared her throat again. "If when my pa comes, we can go with him."

"Oh, land, of course you would go with him." Katy reached out and gathered the girl into her arms. "But in the meantime, we can pretend you and Deborah belong to us, all right?"

Manda nodded and finally relaxed her shoulders.

With four men and the boys digging postholes and erecting the corral fence, they finished in one day. While the men did that, the women scrubbed the already clean house from roof to cellar. They laid pallets in the upstairs bedroom for the two girls and hung their clothes on wall pegs.

Someone gave the new family a table, and Olaf promised to help build chairs when he had time. Meanwhile, Haakan nailed together two benches. That was the extent of their furniture. Finally, Katy brought in her trunk that had carried her things from Norway.

"Thank God they left the cookstove here." Katy gave the cast-iron range a last polish with the blacking rag.

"Let's go see how the corral is coming." Ingeborg stepped out onto the front porch. Andrew and Deborah sat together on the top step.

"Now, you got to show that biddy who's boss," Andrew was saying. "I ain't here to do it for you."

"You could come on the horse."

"No, you got to do it."

"I will. But I don't like being pecked."

"Then ask Katy to help you, but —" He turned to look up at his mother. "You tell her, Mor."

"You have to move fast, Deborah. Just go right up to the nest and grab her and throw her off. Unless you want her to set, you know. Then you'll get chicks if she has eggs under her. We brought a rooster too."

"And he'll chase me." The little girl propped her elbows on her knees. "I wish we didn't have no chickens."

"Maybe Manda will help you." Ingeborg sat down by the children and, reaching over, brought them close to her side with a loving arm.

"All Manda wants to do is work with the horses." Deborah leaned closer. "Maybe I

512

could go back and stay with you." She looked up at Ingeborg, hazel eyes trusting.

"Then who will stay with Katy if Manda is so busy?"

"Oh." Deborah thought a moment. "She could come to your house too."

Katy laughed and sat down on the other side of Andrew. "Moving is hard, I know, and you two been through a lot together. But I heard Olaf say that a lady on the other side of town has a little dog that needs a home. Maybe you and me could ride over and see about it. What do you think?"

"We had a dog at our real house. But it run off after we left."

"Manda said it stayed at a farm where you rested for a few days."

Deborah nodded. "I forget some stuff."

"That's 'cause you were real sick."

"Yup." Deborah leaned some more against Ingeborg. "Just me and you get the dog?"

"Yup."

"Guess I better stay, then."

The next day they brought the horses over.

"Keeping them fed and watered is your job," Zeb told Manda. "When I get back we'll see about getting a cow."

Manda looked at the twenty-some head of

horses that nearly filled the corral. "That's a lot of hay and water."

"I know." Zeb leaned on the corral rail. "I fixed the leak in the water trough so you don't have to go in the pen. They might look peaceful right now, but they're still wild horses."

"I know." Her lower lip stuck out and a wrinkle appeared between her eyebrows.

"Just reminding you." He let the silence stretch. "I'm glad you chose to come live with us."

She brushed a strand of hair back from her cheek. "You better pick out a good stud if'n you want heavy workhorses." She glanced up at him from the corner of her eye. "My pa always wanted a good team."

"Dinner's ready!"

The two of them walked up to the house together. Manda matched her steps to his.

Zeb arrived in Cincinnati on the morning of the third day. He had almost arrived later, since he'd given in to a desire to see his sister and had telegraphed her from Fargo to meet him at the Cincinnati station. He'd barely made his train in Fargo because of it.

With the ease born of long practice, he scanned the crowd on the platform, looking to see if there was a familiar face. His gaze stopped for a moment at a woman who had turned the other way. Did he know her? More importantly, did she know him?

He nearly knocked a child over in his haste to get to her side. By the time he'd righted the youngster, apologized, and looked up, the woman was gone. Then suddenly he heard a familiar voice.

"Zeb! Zebulun MacCallister, I'm over here!"

He looked toward the voice and saw Mary Martha standing on a bench by the wall, waving her handkerchief and ignoring the stares she'd earned. He quickly strode on over to his sister. "What's the matter with you? You want everyone in the world to know I'm here?"

"Poo, you don't have to worry anymore." She flung herself into his arms. "The Galloway brothers are dead and gone. I'd have written to you if I knew where you were. Your telegram was a real answer to prayer." She hugged him close. "Ah, Zeb, we have missed you so. We weren't even sure you were still alive."

"Wait a minute. Back up." He looked down into her merry face. "You've lost me, so let's go back to the beginning."

She locked her arm in his and led him

into the station. "We can sit down for a few minutes here."

"Or we could find a place to eat. I'm starving."

She looked him up and down. "Don't look like you've gained any weight since you left home. Mama would want to put some meat on your bones first thing."

"Mary Martha MacCallister." The threat in his voice stopped her chatter.

"Oh, all right. There's a cafe right around the corner. Come on."

Once seated, she propped her elbows on the table and her chin on her hands. "Now, ask away."

"Did the Galloways ever inform the law that I'd shot their father?"

She shook her head. "Nope. They wanted to get you themselves. Leastways that's what I heard. They didn't try to keep us apprised of their actions."

He glared at her teasing. "Thank God for that." He let out a breath he'd been holding for three years. "So . . . when did they die? What happened to them?"

"They got in a fight. One got killed out-right, and the other died some time later. I never did get straight who was who."

"Who is left in the family?"

"Their sister, Lubelle, but she's loony

and has been for years. Besides, she moved away last year when the missus died. They say the mother died of a broken heart. A'course I never thought any of them had any heart anyway, but . . ." She quit at the look he gave her.

Mary Martha leaned forward, reaching for his hands. "Don't you understand? You can come home now."

"No, you don't understand. I have a farm and a family now and a whole herd of horses to train."

"Oh." Her eyes flitted from sad to bright again. "But that doesn't mean you can never come home. You can bring your family, and . . ." She stopped. "Family. How many children do you have?"

"Two girls. One thirteen and one five. Another on the way." He kept a straight face with difficulty.

"I can tell we're going to be here a long time for me to hear *this* story."

The waitress came to take their order.

Zeb watched his sister as she debated over what to have. She'd grown from pretty to lovely, her cinnamon curls bound by a ribbon at the back of her head. The sparkle in her eyes looked to be a permanent fixture, but then that had always been the case. The forest green of her dress reminded him of summer in the mountains, and her laugh resembled a stream trickling down the rocks of the hillside. How he had missed her and was never so much aware of that ache as right now.

When she looked back at him, he smiled and took her hand. "Now, what about you? Who did you marry, and how many young'uns are making our ma happy as a duck in a pond?"

He watched her eyes dim and her mouth crumble. Her chin quivered. "None. He died before the wedding. Cholera took many, oh, about a year and a half ago."

"I'm sorry." He stroked the back of her hands with his thumbs.

They spent the next two hours catching up on their lives before Zeb paid the bill and they left.

"Now where are you going?" Mary Martha asked.

"I'm going out to buy my stallion. You're getting on the next train home."

"So this is all the time I have with you?"

His heart turned over at the look on her face. "I'm truly sorry, but I got to get that horse and head for home. Harvest is already started, and I got to be there soon as I can."

"I could come with you to get the horse."

He shook his head. "Where would you

stay? What would you ride? I got enough money for one horse and that's that."

"We could double."

Again he shook his head. "How about I send you money for a ticket to Dakota Territory come fall? I'll have money again after harvest."

She clamped her jaw in a way he'd come to know meant she was digging in her heels. "Zebulun MacCallister, you mean you got me clear up here just to visit for an hour or two? You know what that ticket cost?"

"I know. But I had to let you know I was alive and find out what was happening with the Galloways."

"I could have written you a letter." She wore her stern mother face. "Mama too."

"Are you sorry you came?"

Her face crumpled. "N-no. Just disappointed the time is so short."

"When does the next train south leave?"

"At six."

"And you'll be on it?"

"If you say so."

"Good." He walked her back to the train station and took her in his arms for a goodbye hug. "There she is again."

"Who?"

"A woman who looks so familiar."

Mary Martha turned and looked around.

"I don't see anyone. Must be your imagination playing tricks." She reached up and kissed him on the cheek. "We will look forward to hearing from you. And it best be soon. Mama's not getting any younger, you know. And Uncle Jed — well, your leaving kinda took the starch out of him, it did." She sighed. "You could bring your family and come home where you belong."

"I'm not sure where I belong anymore." He hugged her once again and gave her a push toward the doors. "Get on with you. I promise I'll write."

He was back in town, returning his horse to the livery by midmorning the next day.

"That's a fine horse you got there." The livery owner eyed the bay stallion as he took the reins of his own horse.

"He'll do." Zeb held the lead line under the halter and stroked the horse's sweaty neck.

"You planning to raise horses?"

Zeb nodded, not taking his attention away from his new animal. "Got me some mares just a'waitin' for him." He dug in his pocket. "How much do I owe you?" He paid what was asked and started to lead his horse back out of the yard.

"Oh, there was a woman lookin' fer ya. I near to forgot."

"What'd you tell her?"

"That you'd be back today sometime."

"She leave a name?" *If that sister of mine — why would she stay on? Something gone wrong?* Questions raced through his mind like hounds after a rabbit.

"Nope. Y'all have a good trip now."

Zeb led the stallion out of the yard and down the street. The freight yard where he'd board a boxcar for the trip west was only a couple blocks away. Even so, sweat made rivulets down his spine by the time they walked there.

He loaded the horse into the boxcar assigned to him and made sure there was feed and water enough for the trip. He tested the two-by-sixes that fenced off one end of the boxcar and, satisfied that all was secure, headed back to the office. "Can someone keep an eye on him while I go get some food to take with me?"

"Sure enough." The man checked his pocket watch. "Should be ready to pull out in about two hours. Make sure you're back by then, or we leave without you."

"Oh, I'll be right back."

Zeb strode out to the street and turned the corner, heading for the general store he'd seen up the block.

"Zebulun MacCallister?"

He stopped at hearing his name called. People flowed around him on the board sidewalk as he looked to see who called him.

"Zebulun MacCallister!" A woman dressed all in black beckoned from the door of a hotel.

It wasn't Mary Martha, that was for certain. But who else knew him here in Cincinnati? He tipped his hat. "Yes, ma'am? Do I know you?"

She lifted her chin, the veil covering her face rippling in the movement. Her whispered words were lost in the noise of the street around them.

He leaned closer. "Sorry, I didn't catch that."

She took a step forward. "An old friend of yours has a message for you."

"Pardon me. What old friend?" *If you'd just talk up, lady, I could answer you and be on my way.* He tried to still the impatience welling up within him. If he wasn't his mother's son, he would have kept on walking. But a man didn't ignore a woman or be rude.

She took a step closer. "This one." With a motion faster than a striking rattler, she raised her reticule and fired.

"What the — ?" He could feel something tear through his side, the force of it reeling him backward. "You shot me!"

"That's for my father and my brothers." He reached for her arm, but she jerked away. The taunting voice continued. "We Galloways pay our debts. May your soul rot in hell." A laugh that made his hair stand on end followed her words.

"Mister, yer bleedin'," a boy said from behind him. Then he shouted, "Someone help! This feller's been shot!"

Zeb clapped his hand to his side. He looked down to see warm blood oozing between his fingers.

In that instant, the woman disappeared.

30

Contrary to what Zeb's sister thought, Lubelle Galloway was *not* in the loony bin.

Zeb had plenty of time to dwell on that fact as the train rocked westward. During the days, the air coming between the slats of the cattle car felt like a blast furnace. He wished they could travel only at night.

His fingers wandered again to the bandages wrapped around his chest, just like a tongue will do when there is a toothache. His side burned. No, "burned" wasn't a strong enough word. It hurt like nothing he'd ever known before. He sat with his back against the slatted wall.

The stallion leaned his head over the fencing and nosed Zeb's good shoulder.

"You're a fine horse, Blaze, you know that?" Zeb reached up and scratched the white strip down the stallion's face that earned him the name. The horse hung his head lower, making it as easy as possible for the man to keep scratching.

Zeb finally dozed off, waking to see dawn

pearling the horizon through the slats of the cattle car. He jerked awake — surprised that he had slept through an entire night. He heard the shriek of train wheels being shunted off the main track. Another screech of metal on metal, a jerk, and he could hear the engine disappearing down the track.

He stood, blinking his eyes once and yet again. No, the blur was in himself. He leaned against the wall as a wave of dizziness crashed over him and receded, sucking out his strength as the ocean sucks at the sand.

"Where are we?"

Blaze snorted and stamped a big front hoof.

Zeb dipped water out of the half-full barrel and splashed it over his head. He felt like crawling in the barrel and letting the cool water bathe his fiery side.

His strength spent by the exertion, he slumped to the floor again and dozed fitfully. Visions of Lubelle Galloway following him across the plains brought him sweating out of his sleep during the hottest part of the day. Even with the doors open, there was no breeze.

"Whyever did we get shunted out here like this?"

But the crow flying over them had no answer either.

Another sunset and the welcome relief of evening coolness settled about him. He waited for the train to move again. Why were they stopped for so long?

Sometime in the night he heard a pounding on the door.

"Mr. MacCallister? Mr. MacCallister!"

Zeb shook his head and blinked. "I'm here." He got to his feet and crossed to the big door, sliding it open.

"Are you all right? I can't believe they left you out here like this. Please accept my apologies." The man, wearing a railroad uniform, swung a lantern at his side.

"Can we get goin' now?" Zeb cleared his throat.

"Right away. Can I get you anything? Water? Food?"

"Something to eat would be right neighborly. Where in tarnation are we?"

"We'll be in Minneapolis in an hour or two."

Zeb groaned. Another day on the train to reach Dakota Territory. What if Lubelle really was coming to see if she could finish the job? What if she followed him clear to Blessing? He had to keep Katy and the girls safe. He steadied himself at the clashing of metal and then a lurch.

"Here you go, sir. Again, I'm sorry." The

man handed Zeb a packet and blew a whistle.

With some more jockeying to get the cars in order, the train finally got a full head of steam and settled into the rocking that put Zeb back into that no-man's land of half sleep and half wakefulness — the land where Galloway women and men banded together to search out one Zebulun MacCallister.

"God, where is the justice?" he ground out between teeth clenched against the burning in his side. Far as he could tell, the pain was getting worse.

"I sure do hope you're taking better care of Katy and the girls, Lord, than you are of me."

Guilt made his heart burn. He was alive, wasn't he? And fed? And watered? Watered was right; water was dripping in between the slats. When had the rain begun?

When the painful journey finally ended and he led the stallion off the train at Blessing, all he could think of was to get home.

"Man, he's a beaut," Manda breathed.
"Stay out of his way!"
"What's got into you?"
"Nothing."

"Nothing? You got a burr under yer saddle or some 'at?" She planted her hands on her hips, ready to take on the world. "You don't look so hot."

"Just get out of the way." Zeb spoke from between clenched teeth.

Manda backed up, then followed a few paces behind as Zeb led the stallion into a box stall. "I put in hay and water. You want me to get oats?"

No answer.

She raised her voice. "I put —"

"I . . . heard . . . you!" Each word made a separate statement.

"Katy and Deborah are over to Bjorklunds. We din't expect you back so soon."

A grunt was his only response.

"A man came lookin' to buy a team." She waited. Nothing. "I told him to come back in ten years."

Still nothing.

She stepped closer and looked over the door to the box stall. Zeb slumped with his forehead resting on the arched neck of the bay stallion.

Manda tiptoed out of the barn. "Somethin's really wrong," she whispered to the sandy-haired dog who whimpered at her side. "I sure wish I knew what it was."

She sank down in the shade of the barn and hugged the dog to her.

"Manda?"

"Here." She left off petting the dog and stood.

"How about going after Katy?"

"She'll be back before dark."

"Well, you could go over there and tell her I'm home."

"I s'pose."

"Take your horse."

"A'course." She looked at him carefully. "You look sick."

"Just do as I ask, please."

"All right, but Katy's gonna be right disappointed you don't come too."

Keeping himself upright with every bit of strength he could muster, he walked off to the house. In a few minutes he heard Manda's horse loping out of the yard.

Hurry! While his mind gave the right orders, his body refused to function at any more than a step at a time. He gathered food, his rifle, a change of clothes, and rolled them in his quilt. *Get out of here before Lubelle comes.* Like an army drummer leading the troops, his brain ticked away. *Get out. Get out.*

Need shells. He groaned when he took down the tin that held his ammunition.

He laid the letter he'd written the night before on the table as his last act of blessing.

Saddling his horse brought the sweat already beading his forehead into running rivulets, like spring freshets in the mountains. His tongue felt too big for his mouth, and only if he squinted could he narrow his vision to one horse, not two.

He finally led Buster to a bench, and with one arm clenched to keep his side from erupting, he struggled into the saddle. He put his horse at a dead run to put as much distance as possible between him and home before Katy returned. He headed due north, not west as he'd said in the letter.

"Maybe he rode over to talk with Haakan." Manda sneaked a peek at the hooks where Zeb had hung his rifle. The wall looked naked without the gun in place.

Katy followed Manda's gaze. "Now what would he want with his rifle?"

"Maybe he went hunting. We need some meat."

"Let's just go about our chores. We'll give him what for when he gets back, you can count on that." Katy set to bustling around the kitchen, frying bacon and plopping eggs in the snapping grease.

"Ow!" She drew back and wiped the spatter off on her apron. Tears came to her eyes and she dashed them away.

Manda knew the tears weren't for the burn on her hand. Right about now she could cheerfully whup Mister Zebulun MacCallister with his own leather reins. What had got into that man? She wandered into Katy and Zeb's bedroom. The envelope propped against the pillow caught her attention immediately. She snatched it up and ran back into the kitchen.

"Katy, read this!"

"Now what?" Katy turned from her cooking. "Oh, Lord in heaven, what has that man gone and done now?" She pushed the frying pan to the cool side of the stove and, taking the letter, sank onto one of the benches. Fingers trembling, she opened the envelope and unfolded the single sheet of paper.

Dear Katy, Manda, and Deborah,

First of all, know that I love you all with a love that only God can give, and that is why I have to leave. Many times I have wanted to tell you what sent me from home to the west. I shot a neighbor. No matter that it was self-defense, we figured the only way out was for me to leave home. I did, and finally found another home with you, and this one is far harder to leave.

But the family of the man I shot is still after me. I met up with one of them in Cincinnati, and she shot me. It is only a flesh wound, but I cannot have them coming for you, so I am heading farther west. May our God keep you safe in His loving arms. Maybe someday I can come home again, but do not wait for me. Go on with your life with my blessing. I love you far too much to keep you from whatever happiness is in store for you.

Your loving husband and father,
Zebulun MacCallister

"So that's why he looked so peaked," Manda said, rubbing the inside of her cheek with the tip of her tongue. "He looked right bad."

"Why didn't you tell me that?" Katy grabbed her arm. "Manda!"

" 'Cause he said to get on over there and get you and so I did. Never thought he'd leave." Manda choked on the last word. "I'm sorry, Katy." She struggled against the tears, her body rigid with the effort.

Katy put an arm around Manda's waist

and drew her close. "Manda dear, this isn't your fault. You can't take care of the whole world."

"But, but if'n I —" The tears came in earnest. She buried her face in Katy's shoulder.

"If'n nothing. Zeb made this choice, and now we have to deal with that." Katy bit back her own tears. Right now there was no place she would rather be than held by *her* mor as she was holding Manda.

Guess this means you're all grown up, my girl. While she still struggled with speaking English, all her thoughts played out in Norwegian. "Uff da!" One minute she wanted to strangle the man and the next her heart broke for want of him. *He must be sore afraid. But he's afraid for me and the girls too. Letter said so. What kind of people are there who . . .* But she knew what kind. Norwegians could seek a vendetta too. Like the Book said, the sins of the fathers are visited unto the third and fourth generation.

Father God, help! I don't even know how to pray. Help us. Please help us. The "please" continued as she hugged Manda again and got to her feet. "Come, saddle our horses. We have some serious riding to do."

"What? What are we gonna do?" Manda snagged both of their hats off the pegs by the door.

"We're going after him, that's what. If he's as sick as you thought, he won't get far."

"How will you track him? You know how to do that?"

"No, but Metiz and Baptiste do." She slammed the door behind them.

They rode into the yard at Ingeborg's at a dead gallop.

As soon as she told the story, Ingeborg sent Thorliff to saddle horses and sent Baptiste for his grandmere. "The men are all at Baards' harvesting."

"That's okay. We don't need them. Manda, you stay here and watch out for Deborah." She hugged the smaller girl to her. "We'll be home soon as we can, so you stay here with Andrew, as you did today." She ticked things off on her fingers. "You'll need to go home, though, and care for the livestock. Ingeborg, can I take some things from your medicinals? He said he'd been shot, so I'll need bandages and whatever else you think."

"Of course." Ingeborg gathered up what she knew to be necessary, including a small kettle, and filled a canvas pouch with them. Another bag she filled with meat, cheese, and bread. "Andrew, get a jug of water from the well." She looked up.

Metiz trotted up the steps and into the house. "Me ready."

"Metiz, you have a flint along?"

The old woman nodded. "And simples."

"Inge, will you tell my mor what is happening when she comes back from Penny's?"

"Ja, I will." Ingeborg took a woolen blanket off the bed and wrapped everything in it. She handed it to Katy. "Go with God."

"He always go with us." Metiz slung her bags over her shoulder.

"The horses are ready," Baptiste called from outside.

Within seconds the three were mounted and loping down the road. When they reached the horse farm, they circled, looking for tracks.

"Trail easy to see." Metiz pointed to hoofprints spaced far apart, with dirt thrown up at the road. "He riding hard. North, not west like he say."

They crossed the ford on the Park River, near its confluence with the Red River, and continued north along the banks of the Red River. With the sun sinking beyond the horizon and setting the world and clouds on fire, Katy continued her prayers. *Help us! Help us!* kept time with the pounding hooves and with her heartbeat.

Was he still alive? They hadn't come across a body yet. If he was going to Canada, due north was the easiest track. And while she could no longer see hoofprints in the growing darkness, Metiz seemed positive they were on the right track.

Stars sprinkled the heavens when they heard a horse whinny. Katy's horse answered.

"That's Zeb's horse. These two became fast friends." Katy pulled her mount to a halt.

"Zeb! Where are you?"

Only the wind rustling the cottonwood leaves along the bank of the Red River answered.

Katy called again. This time a horse answered. They followed the sound.

Even in the dark, the horse looked darker, standing under the arms of a huge oak. Buster nickered, the sound friendly in the night. He bent his head and nosed the body lying at his feet.

Katy hit the ground before her horse stopped. *God, don't let him be dead. Please.* She knelt at his side and took his hand. Still warm. Touched the side of his neck and felt a pulse.

"He's alive."

Metiz knelt beside her. "Not his fault."

Baptiste tethered the horses and joined them. "How bad is he?"

"Some bad." Metiz listened to Zeb's chest and felt his head. "Hot." She turned to her grandson. "Dig hole for fire." To Katy. "Make him drink." Getting to her feet, she brought the canteen from the horse, along with her bags. Handing the water to Katy, she muttered, "I get wood. More water."

She returned quickly and poured water from a deerskin pouch, soaking Zeb's shirt and pants. "Cool him."

Katy brushed the mosquitoes away and put an arm under Zeb's neck. "Come on, Zebulun MacCallister, you got to drink. And don't you go dying on me, you hear?" When he moaned in response, she put the canteen to his mouth and trickled a bit of water over his lips. When he licked it away, she did the same again. "If you'd open your mouth, you stubborn thing, you could drink better. Metiz says you got to drink a whole lot."

He did as told without opening his eyes.

In a few minutes Metiz and Baptiste had a small fire crackling in a shallow hole. Baptiste used a branch to clear the brush and dried grass away from the fire pit. At the same time he fed small sticks to the growing flame.

In the flickering light, Metiz knelt beside Zeb again. She slit his shirt with the tip of her knife and peeled it back. The blood-crusted bandage stunk. Gently she cut the bandage in half and let Katy peel that back. "Bring lighted stick."

Baptiste pulled a burning brand from the fire and held it for them to see better.

"Bad."

"What will you do?"

"Burn with knife."

"Oh." Katy swallowed hard. She leaned back to get a breath of clean air. "Will that be enough?"

"Great Spirit knows." Metiz set the end of the knife in the hottest part of the fire. Baptiste already had water near to boiling in the kettle. "You wash him."

Katy took the hard lump of soap and a rag from the pouch, dipped them in the hot water, and worked up a lather. She sponged gently at the edges of the wound until she realized Zeb was still unconscious. Then she scrubbed harder, keeping herself from gagging at the smell only by superhuman will.

"Hold him." Metiz beckoned to both Katy and Baptiste. The boy took one arm and, crossing it over the man's chest, clung to them both. Katy sat on his feet.

Metiz looked skyward, murmured something unintelligible, and applied the flat side of the knife to the wound. The flesh sizzled. Zeb shrieked and bucked against the pain.

Baptiste lay across his belly. Katy picked herself up from the pummeled grass and took hold of his boots again. Her arm pounded where he had kicked her.

Metiz held the knife back in the fire.

Crickets sang their song of summer. Mosquitoes swarmed, their whine loud in Kathy's ears. "Again?" She knew the answer before she asked.

This time both she and Baptiste were better prepared. But this time Zeb screamed in agony. Tears streamed down her face, dropping on his pants leg.

Metiz sniffed the wound before answering.

When the old woman shook her, Katy collapsed across Zeb's lower body but only for a moment. "What do you need me to do?" She pushed herself to her knees.

"Mash this." Metiz handed her a mixture of herbs and roots. "Mix with hot water. Put paste on, then bind up."

Katy did as she was told, using the handle of the knife to mash the mixture in the tin cup she'd brought. She added a few drops of water and ground them again, adding more water until a paste formed.

She shuddered when she looked at the charred wound but smeared the paste in place. Then taking the rolled strips of cloth, she bound them over the poultice and around his chest. As she tied the final knot, she heard him mumble something. Leaning close to his mouth, she heard "water."

Metiz handed her the canteen. She dribbled the precious clean liquid into his open mouth, just enough for him to swallow and then again.

He sighed, "Good."

"Now, we don't know what kind of condition that boy is in, so we just ask that all of you pray for him. And pray for Katy and Metiz, that they find him before he dies, if he is that bad wounded." Agnes sat down again.

Everyone in church bowed their heads while Reverend Solberg led them in prayer. "Lord God, we bring Zeb MacCallister before thee. We don't know what all has gone on, but thou dost. Keep him in thy tender care. Protect him from whatever and whoever might try to harm him. We ask that thy Holy Spirit intercede on his behalf before thy throne of grace." At his "Amen," all those present joined in.

At the end of the final hymn, Deborah looked up at Ingeborg. "I asked God to bring my new pa back to me. Manda says it don't do no good to ask God, but my ma said God answers the prayers of his children, and I'm one of his children, right?"

"Right." Ingeborg glanced over at Manda who sat with her arms clamped across her skinny chest and her chin squared so you could feel her snarl.

"Manda is too, huh?"

"Ja, she is."

"Even though she's mad at God?"

"Even then."

Deborah sighed. "That's good."

"Ah, child, yes, that is good. We are all His children."

"Grown-ups too?"

"Grown-ups too."

Deborah settled against Ingeborg's side, reaching over to tickle Astrid under the chin. Astrid giggled and tried to tickle Deborah back until Ingeborg hushed them both.

After the service, Anner and Hildegunn stopped beside Ingeborg. "I want you to know we are praying for them," Anner told her. "Sorry his secret caught up to him, but if he makes it through this . . ." Anner choked up and cleared his throat. "Well, he's a fine young man, and I wish him and Katy the very best." He turned a bit to look at Hildegunn. "We know the power of prayer, don't we? Especially of those around here. I'm living proof of how God answers prayer."

"You and all the rest of us." Ingeborg shook his left hand. "Thank you, Anner. Come children, Bridget, Haakan is waiting with the wagon."

When they were all aboard and driving down the road, Haakan turned to Ingeborg. "Think I'll take the wagon and head north. I get the feeling that's what I'm supposed to do."

"Then that is what you should do. Let's pad it with hay and quilts in case he is too sick to ride his horse. We can pack food and things while you get it ready."

"Pa, can I go?" Thorliff asked.

Haakan shook his head. "Someone needs to be home to do chores. With Hamre over to Zeb's, and Baptiste off with Katy . . ." He left it for Thorliff to figure out for himself.

Thorliff sighed and sat back down. "All right."

"Maybe you and Manda could go fishing

this afternoon. A mess of perch would taste mighty good for supper." Ingeborg turned to look over her shoulder.

"You better catch a lot," Bridget added. "They just might all be back in time for supper."

"What is that you are making?" Katy looked at the willow branches lashed between two long poles.

"A travois." Baptiste looked up from his lashing. "We will tie these ends to your saddle and lay Zeb here." He indicated the web of willow. "Much easier on him than trying to ride."

"You think he is ready to be moved?"

"Better now while he sleeping. It will hurt much." Metiz poured water from the kettle on the dying fire. "Be good to get home."

Zeb groaned but still didn't waken more than enough to drink when Katy dribbled liquid into his mouth. She and Metiz had taken turns all night changing the water-soaked cloths to try to cool the raging fever. Willow-bark tea didn't help much either.

They lifted him with the blanket and laid him in the travois. While he groaned and thrashed some, he didn't wake even with that. Metiz mounted her horse.

"I ride behind. Baptiste go ahead."

With the sticks bouncing in every rut, Katy searched out the flattest and shadiest way, guiding her horse carefully. When she heard Zeb shouting, she stopped and looked back at him.

Metiz waved her on. "He not know what he say."

He's delirious, and here I am dragging him halfway across Dakota Territory on one of the hottest days of the year. Father God, only you can save him. Please cushion him and bring healing to his body. Father, I love him so, and I know you love him more.

They met Haakan just north of the ford on the Park River.

"Ah, thank you. I didn't know how we were going to get him across." Katy dismounted and laid a hand on Zeb's forehead. Just like laying her hand on a hot stove. She bent down to listen to his mumblings, but they made no sense whatsoever.

"How long's he been like this?"

"Since we found him last night. He'd gotten off his horse and not made it back on."

"Leastways he didn't fall off. Could have broken some bones that way." Haakan nodded toward Baptiste. "Let's get him in the wagon. He should be more comfortable there."

When they started out again, Katy sat in

the wagon pillowing Zeb's head in her lap and changing the cloths as they dried. She tried to block out Zeb's ramblings, but when he shouted, "No, I'm not going!" she wondered what evils tormented him. Several times she ducked when he flailed an arm around, but weak as he was, even that wouldn't bruise her too badly.

Darkness had firmly settled over the land when they drove into the Bjorklund yard. But Haakan kept right on going.

"Let's take him to the icehouse," Haakan said. "Between that and Metiz' medicinals, we'll just see if we can't keep this boy alive. And when we done all we can, we know God can finish the job."

Once there, Haakan hung the lantern on a peg and shoveled sawdust back off the blocks of ice. Then laying down hay first, blankets second, they carried Zeb to the new bed and laid him on it. Kneeling beside him, Katy could feel the coolness through the padding and her skirt.

Haakan chipped some ice off and brought her the slivers. "Put these on his tongue, a little bit at a time so he don't choke." He touched her shoulder. "And, Katy girl, know that everyone around here is praying for him. And you."

They changed the poultice some time

later when Ingeborg brought the supplies, and already Katy could feel that Zeb's temperature was dropping. He lay quiet now, his breathing barely stirring his shirt front.

"Is he dying?" Katy finally found the courage to ask Metiz.

"No. Resting. You sleep; I watch."

"No, I'll be all right." Katy sat beside the pallet, feeling the cold up through her clothes. She took Zeb's hand in hers and stroked the dark hair covering the back of it. Such a fine hand he had, long fingers that calmed a horse and stroked her hair, both with gentleness and filled with love.

She laid her cheek against the back of his hand. Oh, to feel it move over her skin again. *Father, please.*

She jerked awake. What had she heard? The rooster crowing?

"Katy?"

"Zeb, you're awake." She swallowed the tears that clogged her throat and burned her eyes. "Glory be to God, you're awake."

"Are you trying to freeze me to death, or did you think I was already dead and you were keeping the body from stinking?"

She could only hear him by bending close. "Zebulun MacCallister, if that don't beat all." She kissed him full on the mouth. "Are you hungry?"

He nodded. "Thought I was hearing the Grim Reaper's song during the night, but then I felt sure I heard the angels sing. Strange." The words came slow but they came.

They both fell silent. A meadowlark greeted the dawn, its liquid notes praising the Creator.

Metiz glided in the open door. "Ha. He better."

Zeb shivered. "Maybe we can get me off the ice now?"

The old woman nodded. "He get well now. Here, drink this." She handed him a cup of steaming liquid.

He sniffed it. "That smells terrible." But when Katy crossed her arms over her chest, he drank it anyway.

"Good, now we'll move you."

"Can we sit outside? Or maybe I'll lie down, but I want to see the sunrise. I feared never to see one again."

He bit back a groan when they helped him stand, and with his arm draped over Katy's shoulders and both women holding him up, they staggered outside. Once they were settled against the icehouse wall, he let out a long, slow breath. "Now, ain't that the grandest sight?"

Katy blinked her eyes to stem the tears. "All

the colors. Can you imagine such colors?"

She looked up at her husband, who was staring down at her. "After we dragged you clear out here, you weren't even watching the sunrise, were you?"

"No, ma'am. I was watching the greatest gift God ever gave a man this side of heaven." He leaned his head against hers. "And I plan to keep on thanking Him for you and everything else that He'll bring my way for the rest of my life." He paused. "Even if it means going back home and dealing with the law and the Galloways."

"I'll be waiting."

"I know. Just like I knew you'd come for me. Fool that I am, I knew that." Silence fell for a time.

Katy thought he'd gone to sleep when he said, "You know what my name means?"

"No, what?"

" 'From the dwelling place.' I been far from mine, but now I've come home."

And Katy knew he meant more than just to her.

"How long till she gits here?" Manda shifted from one foot to the other.

"Soon." Katy peered around Zeb and up the track. No sign of the train yet.

"My dress itches."

"You'll live." Zeb grinned down at her.

"Well, I don't see you wearin' no itchy dress." Manda poked him with her elbow.

"You be nice to our pa," Deborah hissed.

Manda rolled her eyes. And scratched.

"Manda." Katy laid a hand on her shoulder. Off in the distance they could hear the mournful whistle of the afternoon train. Harvest had come and gone and now Zeb's sister was coming to visit. The train chugged and let off steam, its iron wheels shrieking against the brakes.

"Zeb!" A hand waved from the open doorway before the conductor could even put his stool down.

Zeb caught her before she could leap off the bottom step and swung her to the ground.

"My land, she's pretty," Manda whispered.

Zeb introduced Mary Martha to them all and hustled them over to the wagon. "We got friends waiting at the church," he said as he threw her bags in the wagon bed. "The train was late, so they're probably all starvin' to death, waitin' on the guest of honor and all."

"Don't pay him no nevermind," Manda said. "He carries on like this all the time."

Zeb let out a hoot of laughter. "Come on, horses. Let's be going."

That night after the party broke up, the MacCallisters sat around the table in their own farmhouse.

"So you recovered from where Lubelle shot you all right?" Mary Martha asked.

"Almost joined the angel choir, but my Katy here brought me back." Zeb took her hand in his. "I thought to go on back home with you and stand trial or whatever I have to do."

"Whyever for? Lubelle is now a permanent resident of the asylum over to Lamblin. They say she sings to herself and points her finger like she has a gun every once in a while. I can't believe she got so close to shoot you."

"I can't believe she missed, not at such close range." Zeb took in a deep breath and let it all out. "You mean I'm really a free man?"

"That you are."

"I been watchin' over my shoulder so long now, it's become second nature. Guess it'll take some learnin' to get over that." He smiled at Katy. "But I got me a good woman to help."

"Better'n you deserve, that's for sure, after runnin' off like you did."

Katy patted her hand over a big yawn.

"Think I'll take your son and his mother off to bed now." She stood, her belly showing round under her dress. She laid a hand on her middle. "Welcome to Dakota Territory, Mary Martha, and watch out for Petar. By the look on his face, I think he got poleaxed when he saw you." Her laughter drifted off behind her as she left the room.

"Well, if that don't beat all." Zeb looked at his sister. "Mary Martha MacCallister, you're blushing."

LAURAINE SNELLING is an award-winning author of over twenty-five books, fiction and nonfiction for adults and young adults. Besides writing both books and articles, she teaches at writers' conferences across the country. She and husband, Wayne, have two grown sons, four grand dogs, and make their home in California.